FROZEN OUT

The discovery of a corpse washed up on a beach in an Icelandic backwater sparks a series of events that propels the village of Hvalvík's police sergeant, Gunnhildur Gísladóttir, into deep waters. Although under pressure to deal with the matter quickly, she is suspicious that the man's death was no accident; and once she has identified the body, she sets about investigating his final hours. The case takes her away from her village and into a cosmopolitan world of shady deals, government corruption, and violence. Gunna finds herself alone and less than welcome in this hostile environment as she tries to find out who it was that made sure the young man drowned on a dark night, one hundred kilometres from where he should have been — and why.

SPECIAL MESSAGE TO READERS

THE ULVERSCROFT FOUNDATION
(registered UK charity number 264873)
was established in 1972 to provide funds for research, diagnosis and treatment of eye diseases. Examples of major projects funded by the Ulverscroft Foundation are:-

- The Children's Eye Unit at Moorfields Eye Hospital, London
- The Ulverscroft Children's Eye Unit at Great Ormond Street Hospital for Sick Children
- Funding research into eye diseases and treatment at the Department of Ophthalmology, University of Leicester
- The Ulverscroft Vision Research Group, Institute of Child Health
- Twin operating theatres at the Western Ophthalmic Hospital, London
- The Chair of Ophthalmology at the Royal Australian College of Ophthalmologists

You can help further the work of the Foundation by making a donation or leaving a legacy. Every contribution is gratefully received. If you would like to help support the Foundation or require further information, please contact:

THE ULVERSCROFT FOUNDATION
The Green, Bradgate Road, Anstey
Leicester LE7 7FU, England
Tel: (0116) 236 4325

website: www.foundation.ulverscroft.com

FROZEN OUT

QUENTIN BATES

First published in Great Britain 2011
by
Robinson
an imprint of Constable & Robinson Ltd.

First Isis Edition
published 2017
by arrangement with
Constable
An imprint of Little, Brown Book Group

The moral right of the author has been asserted

A catalogue record for this book is available from the British Library.

ISBN 978–1–78541–339–1 (hb)
ISBN 978–1–78541–345–2 (pb)

Published by
F. A. Thorpe (Publishing)
Anstey, Leicestershire

Set by Words & Graphics Ltd.
Anstey, Leicestershire
Printed and bound in Great Britain by
T. J. International Ltd., Padstow, Cornwall

This book is printed on acid-free paper

Author's Note

The village of Hvalvík is fictional, but not entirely imaginary.

My imagination has placed it on the south-west coast of Iceland, a dozen or so kilometres east of the fishing port of Grindavík, which Hvalvík resembles up to a point. Hvalvík is real enough in that it is a combination of the features of many of the quiet villages dotted around the coast of Iceland, where most people make their living from the land or the sea in one way or another. The place is fictional to avoid giving offence to a real police officer, mayor, taxi driver or petrol pump attendant by choosing a real location. Other locations are genuine, although a few liberties have been taken with place names.

With thanks to everyone who provided help and encouragement — you know who you are. Particular thanks are due to Bylgja for her patience in answering even the most obvious questions.

CHAPTER ONE

Tuesday, 26 August

Water gurgled between the piles of the dock and the car's tyres juddered over the heavy timbers. Somewhere a generator puttered on board one of the longliners tied up at the quay.

The driver turned off the engine and killed the lights before stepping out of the car and taking a deep breath of fragrant summer air, still and laden with the tang of seaweed. He looked about him carefully and walked along the quay, watching the boats for any sign of activity.

Satisfied, he opened the passenger door. He lifted the passenger's legs out and then stooped to drape an arm over his shoulders. Grunting with exertion, he hauled the passenger to his feet.

"Waas goin' on?" the passenger slurred as the driver steadied himself, planting his feet wide. He half supported, half dragged the passenger the few metres towards the gangplank of the nearest boat.

"Come on. Almost there."

The passenger staggered against the driver. "W-w-where's this?"

"Nearly there," the driver muttered to himself as much as to his passenger.

He braced one booted foot on the heavy timber parapet running the length of the quay, and quickly straightened his back as he tipped the passenger headlong into the blackness below. The splash competed for a second with the muttering generator on board a nearby boat and the driver stood still, listening intently. Hearing nothing from below, he nodded to himself and padded back to the car.

A moment later the engine whispered into life and the car vanished into the night.

The phone buzzed angrily. Gunna fumbled for the handset in the dark and barked into it.

"Gunnhildur."

"Good morning. Sorry to wake you up. I did wake you up, didn't I?" asked a familiar voice as she cast about for the face that went with it.

"You did," she yawned. "Who is this?"

"Albert Jónasson."

Gunna stretched a hand to the curtain and twitched it aside to let in a glare of early morning sunlight.

"And what can I do for you at this ungodly hour?" she asked, knowing that Albert Jónasson was not a man to trouble a police officer without good reason, especially one who had arrested him only a few weeks before.

"Thought you'd be the best person to talk to. There's a bloke down by the quay."

"You woke me up to tell me there's a stranger by the dock?" Gunna growled.

"Yeah. A stranger who's dead."

She snapped awake and swung her feet on to the cold floor. "Where?"

"On the beach by the pontoons. Saw something in the waves and went to have a look."

"Right. Stay where you are. I'll be right there."

Gunna drove past the half-dozen longline boats tied up at the quay and slowed down as the car rumbled on to the black gravel that made up the track leading to the small boat dock. She could make out a solitary figure standing next to the only boat there, a bearded bear of a man in orange oilskin trousers pacing the pontoon dock next to a spotless fishing boat that puttered with its engine idling.

She parked at the top of the dock among the fishermen's pickup trucks and Albert Jónasson strode to meet her, pointing at a bundle lying among the waves lapping on the black sand of the beach a few metres away.

"Down there," he said grimly, following behind as Gunna trod gingerly, wary of disturbing anything.

"Have you been down here, Albert?" she called over her shoulder.

"No fear. Leave well alone, I thought."

"You haven't had a look? How did you know it was a body?"

"I got here a bit late. All the others were away before daybreak. I was just starting up and saw something floating, so I had a look with the binoculars and saw what it was. So I thought I'd better give you a call."

Gunna ripped a pair of surgical gloves from the pouch on her tool belt and snapped them on before she squatted by the bundle and gently smoothed matted red hair back from a face that looked peaceful but lost. She pressed the button on her Tetra communicator and spoke into the tiny microphone on her collar.

"Nine eight four one, nine five five zero. Are you there, Haddi?"

She retreated and pulled her phone from her pocket.

"Albert, are you going to sea today?" she asked as the dialling tone buzzed.

"I was going to."

"All right. Ah, Haddi, that took a while," she said, switching her attention to the phone. "Look, shelve everything, we have an unidentified body floating in the small boat dock. You'd better get the cavalry out."

Albert watched Gunna nodding as she paced back and forth, admiring her solid frame inside the uniform that didn't do it justice.

"No," she continued. "Ambulance and the technical division, discreetly if that's at all possible. Get Bjössi over from CID in Keflavík if he's not too busy with the Baltic mafia. OK?"

She ended the call and looked over to where Albert was waiting patiently for her.

"Am I all right to go to sea today, then?"

"When will you be back?"

"Three. Four, maybe."

"Go on then. But I'll need you to make a statement when you've finished landing your fish."

"No problem," Albert said gratefully, already making his way along the pontoon and throwing off the boat's mooring ropes in the process. "See you later, Gunna," he called out as the boat surged from the quay.

And I'll stay here and wait for the professionals to turn up, Gunna thought, opening the squad car's boot to get out a roll of tape to cordon off the area. She wondered if the tape had ever been used before in Hvalvík, a village where a speeding ticket or an uncooperative drunk were the most serious crimes she or Haddi normally had to deal with.

26-08-2008, 0944

Skandalblogger writes:

You can't keep a good blog down!

So, we're back and once again the Icelandic scandal blog has a brand-new home! We've been tarred and feathered and run out of town on a rail one more time, so this time we're back stronger than ever in a delightful part of the world where they respect the power of Mr Visa to overrule the pathetic attempts of those-who-run-things to silence free speech. Hurrah for the Tiger economies! Free speech is there for those willing to pay for it!

Making friends and influencing people!

But anyway, folks, and we mean that most sincerely, our favourites are still up to their old tricks. Gunni Benedikts at the trade ministry, no doubt after a looong lunch with his old chum Óli at agriculture, has just decided to block imports of New Zealand lamb to our fair country. Now, some of you may find this a bit hard to stomach, what with all the claptrap these guys have been spouting over the years about free market economics, going for the most competitive bid, and all that shit. But let's remember which party holds trade? And agriculture? Of course, it's our old friends the Progressives, and we can't go upsetting the farmers, or at least the half-dozen who are still in business and who vote for them, just by letting them be undercut by cheap foreign imports. That wouldn't be fair, would it?

(Private) Power to (a few of) the People!

As for everyone's favourite minister . . . Bjarni Jón, now just who are your new friends? And we don't mean the guys at InterAlu, it's their friends from further east we're interested in this time. From what a little bird whispers in our ear, these are oil people. Energy people. Money people. Powerful people. Watch your back, BJB, and when you've shaken hands with them, you'd better count your fingers, just to make sure.

We've heard the rumours circulating around environment and trade, and the PM's office, and we're not going to believe it, as we know what a great guy you really are. We're absolutely certain that you'd never sideline the National Power Authority by inviting a foreign company to build and run a private power station to sell electricity to InterAlu. So, please, BJB, tell us it ain't true?

Watch this space, there'll be more tomorrow!

Bæjó!

Haddi firmly believed that a whirlwind of unwarranted attention had descended on Hvalvík and its tiny police station. By mid-morning the station's older, but junior, police officer would have preferred to be making his accustomed tour of the village in the station's better Volvo, taking in coffee, gossip and a doughnut or three with the lads at the net loft or maybe with one of his cousins in the saltfish plant's canteen. Instead he found himself fending off a flood of questions through the phone and from the huddle of newspaper and television people outside.

Outside on the grass verge a serious young woman in a thick parka over a smart city suit presented take after take with the little harbour and Hvalvík's pastel-painted houses in the background, as if to make sure that Reykjavík viewers understood this was a report from outside their city limits.

Teams from *Morgunbladid, DV, Fréttabladid*, state TV and radio, Channel 2, Channel 3, and a few more that Haddi had never heard of had all demanded information, been told there was no statement yet and they'd just have to wait. Haddi was putting the phone down from telling the local paper the same thing when a young man with a mess of gelled fair hair that appeared to defy both gravity and the breeze outside pushed his way through the door into the station's reception area.

"Yes?" Haddi asked brusquely, arms folded on the counter.

"Er. Hi. I'm Skúli Snædal from *Dagurinn*."

Haddi rolled his eyes ceilingwards. "Look, son, I've told all of you that there'll be a statement this afternoon. Yes, we have found an unidentified person. No, I can't tell you where. No, I can't tell you any more than that."

"But I'm —"

"Sorry. That's all I can say right now."

"But that's not what I'm here for. I've come to see Gunnhildur. I'm shadowing her for a while. For *Dagurinn*," he added.

Haddi took a deep breath "So you're not here because of the body?"

"No. What body?"

"Never you mind. The chief's not here right now, and I don't suppose she'll be back for an hour or two."

"Couldn't you call her up? I'm expected."

Haddi pulled his glasses down from among his curls and peered over them.

"If it was something important, then I could call her up," he agreed. "But on a day like today, then it would have to be something more than usually important."

Skúli tried again. "It's all arranged. I can call the press representative at police headquarters and confirm with them again."

"Sorry. Not now. Look, we have a very serious incident to deal with, so I'd appreciate it if you'd call Reykjavík and sort it out with them. We're a bit busy right now. Hm?"

Haddi's frown and raised eyebrows made it plain that this was not a matter for discussion and the young man appeared to concede defeat.

"All right then. But do you know when she's going to be back?"

"Normally, about now. Today . . ." Haddi shrugged his shoulders.

The young man nodded glumly and made for the door. The look of disappointment on his face aroused a sudden pang in Haddi's heart and he called across as the young man had the door half open.

"Not from round here, are you?"

"No. Reykjavík."

"D'you know Hafnarkaffi?"

"What's that?"

"It's the shop down by the dock. It's getting on for lunchtime and odds are that's where the chief'll be. But you didn't hear that from me, all right?"

The young man grinned in delight. "Thanks. That would be great. How do I recognize her?"

"Gunna? Can't miss her. She's a big fat lass with a face that frightens the horses."

Hafnarkaffi stands between the fishmeal plant and Jói Ben's engineering shop. Originally a shed used for storing tarred longlines through the summer, Hafnarkaffi has grown gradually since it was turned into a drive-in kiosk thirty years ago, then expanded into a shop and had an extension built to add a small café for harbour workers and fishermen. The final addition was the petrol pumps outside, but by now hardly anything of the original corrugated iron shed is to be seen and the place has become an enduring nightmare for council planners who have visions of it spreading across the road.

Skúli looked through the steamed-up glass panels of the door and made out figures sitting at tables. Pushing it open, he ventured in, thought for a moment and decided that he really was hungry anyway.

At the end of the long counter he collected a tray and pushed it in front of him, picking up bottled water on the way and stopping before the row of steaming steel bins.

"Fish or meat?" a grey-faced woman behind the counter asked.

"Er — what do you have?"

"Fish or meat."

"What sort are they?"

"It's Tuesday. Salted fish or salted meat."

Skúli's heart sank and he began to wish he hadn't bothered with a tray.

"Saltfish, please," he decided, knowing that he would regret it.

The woman ladled fish and potatoes on to a plate. "Fat?"

"Sorry? What?"

"D'you want fat on it?"

"Oh, er, no. Thanks."

She dropped the spoon back into the dish of liquefied fat and pointed to a pot. "Soup?"

"Oh, no thanks."

"It's included."

"No, thanks anyway."

"Up to you. It's there if you change your mind. Coffee's included as well. That's eight hundred. Receipt?"

Skúli handed over a note and received change and receipt. He scanned the room and quickly located a bulky figure in uniform at the far side, hunched over a table. At a distance it wasn't easy to see if the figure was man or a woman, but Skúli hoped he had found the right person. He edged between tables, forcing a row of blue-overalled workmen to haul in their bellies and chairs for him to pass, before planting his tray on the table.

"May I sit here?"

The figure looked up and Skúli saw that, in spite of the broad shoulders, the solid woman with the short fair hair was not the bruiser Haddi had given him to expect. Although she would never be a beauty, she had an angular, handsome face that radiated authority. He wondered briefly if this was natural, or the product of a police career.

"Help yourself," she said, between spoonfuls of colourless soup.

"You must be Gunnhildur?"

She nodded, scraping the bottom of the soup plate. "Known to every man and his dog as Gunna the Cop," she corrected. "And you must be the lad from *Dagurinn*. I suppose Haddi told you I'd be here, did he?"

Skúli picked at the saltfish on the plate in front of him. This kind of traditional food had never been on the menu at home and he wasn't ready for the overpowering salt flavour of the first forkful.

"So. Now that you're here, what is it you're after?"

"Nothing special, really. The idea is a series of feature articles in the Saturday magazine about the work of rural police. I'm not looking for anything out of the ordinary — just the opposite, actually."

"Not because of what's been going on this morning?"

"No . . ." Skúli said slowly.

"So you don't know," she said with slow satisfaction and a broad smile that lit up her face. "Well, you must be the only reporter in Iceland who hasn't heard that an unidentified corpse was found just round the corner this morning. You must be the only one, because practically every other hack in the country has either turned up here or else phoned the station to demand a statement. Poor old Haddi's been going spare."

"Oh. I see."

Skúli dropped his cutlery and dived into his coat pocket to bring out a mobile phone. He switched it on and within seconds it was buzzing angrily with a series of voice and text messages.

"Shit. I forgot to switch it on when I left this morning, and I didn't even have the radio on in the car," he admitted. "Sorry, I didn't know anything."

"Anyway, now that you're here, I suppose you'd better have a story to take back with you."

"That would be . . . great."

"You mean it would save your sorry arse from being fried?"

"Er, yes, probably."

"There'll be a statement this afternoon, so you can have it half an hour before it comes out officially. I don't suppose that'll do any harm."

"Thank you. That's brilliant."

"Right. But you'll owe me a favour there straight away. How old are you?"

"Twenty-five."

"What are you on this paper, then, a junior reporter, or what?"

"No. I'm the crime editor."

"What? There's a whopping story here and you didn't even know about it, Mr Crime Editor?" Gunna asked with a second sly smile.

Skúli shuffled fish about on his plate. "Actually I've only been the crime editor for a week. And that was because someone put the by-line as a joke on something I wrote about a woman who had been caught shoplifting from the shopping centre at Kringlan. It stayed in by mistake, so I'm the new crime editor."

"How long have you been working for *Dagurinn*?"

Skúli was starting to resent Gunna's quickfire questions, reminding himself that he should be the one asking. "A couple of months. *Dagurinn* only started up in January."

"What were you doing before that?"

"I finished my master's last year and then I was at *Jyllands Posten* as an intern for a few months until I came home."

"Denmark. Where?"

"In Århus. How long have you been in the police?" he asked, trying to wrench the conversation around so that he could ask the questions.

"Far too long. And who are your people?"

"The Snædal family."

"Oh. Top people, I see."

"My uncle was in the government years ago."

"I know. I might even have voted for him."

"That's nice to know. I'll tell him."

"I'm not quite that old," Gunna replied coldly. "Now, get that down you and we'll make a start. I have masses of things to do and if you're going to tag along you'll have to keep up and preferably keep quiet. All right?"

"That's fine," Skúli replied, laying down his knife and fork with a premonition of failure. He realized that, for a reporter, he had asked no questions and found out almost nothing about the person he was supposed to be profiling, while she had found out practically everything about him. "We can go, if you want. I don't really like saltfish," he admitted.

"Then you won't grow up to have curly hair. Come on then," she said with a grin, rising to her feet and pulling a phone from her jacket pocket as it began to chirrup.

"Hi, sweetheart, just a moment," she answered it in a gentle tone.

"You'd better take your tray back to the counter, and you can take mine while you're at it. I'll see you outside in a minute," she instructed Skúli, marching towards the door with the phone at her ear. Skúli wondered who she could be addressing as sweetheart.

"So, what does a crime editor actually do?"

The second-best Volvo bumped off the tarmac and rumbled on to the track leading to the pontoon dock. Skúli sat in the passenger seat, laptop on his knees, getting down as much of the story as Gunna was prepared to give him.

"Mostly I just check the police websites every morning. Unidentified, you say? A man or a woman?"

"Male."

"Age?"

"Too early to say."

"What else can you tell me?"

"That's all for now," Gunna replied, bringing the car to a halt with a crunch of gravel behind a white van. Skúli followed her as she picked her way easily between rocks to the foreshore, while he found his feet slipping from under him.

Two people in white overalls crouched on the sand where the falling tide had left the man's body, while a tall uniformed officer stood and watched as a photographer systematically took pictures of the area. Gunna lifted the Do Not Cross tape and ducked under it.

"Hi, Snorri, what's new?" Gunna asked the man in uniform.

"Nothing yet. They've not long been here."

"And Bjössi?"

"Been and gone for a snoop around. Said he'd see you at the station in a while."

"Fair enough. Oh, by the way, that's Snorri," she announced, looking at Skúli and jerking a thumb at the uniformed officer. She used the same thumb to point at Skúli. "This is Skúli. He's my shadow. From the newspapers, so be careful what you tell him."

Skúli saw her smile again while Snorri looked doubtful.

"Camera?" she asked Skúli.

"What?"

"Do you have a camera?"

"No — well, only the one in my phone."

"All right. Take any pictures and I'll lock you up."

Gunna moved closer to the white-overalled pair crouched around the body and hunched down next to them. Skúli caught a glimpse of a young face, lifeless eyes half-open, and he felt himself engulfed in a sudden deep sadness at the sight.

"Gunnhildur," Gunna introduced herself brusquely.

"Sigmar. That's Selma," the man replied absently, while the woman did not look up.

"Anything useful?"

"Not really. He's not been here long, I'd say. Nothing to indicate any injuries. More than likely a case of falling in the water followed by hypothermia or drowning."

"Any identification?"

"Nothing so far. Nothing in his pockets. No rings, no jewellery. We'll know more when we've had a proper look at him on the slab. If he's Icelandic, then we'll probably have an identity in a day or two, sooner if he has a record of any kind. If he's a foreigner . . ."

He shrugged, scratched at the stubble on his chin and yawned.

"Makes a change to get out into the country once in a while," he observed with a thin smile.

"Taking him away, are you?"

"Yup. Almost finished, actually. We'll probably be off in an hour and we should have a report for you in a day or two. There's no sign of any violence, so how urgent do you want this to be?"

"Sooner the better, as far as I'm concerned. This kind of thing doesn't happen every day round here."

"All right. We'll do what we can," Sigmar said, pulling a mask back up over his mouth and nose.

"Are you all right, lad?" Gunna asked Skúli kindly. "Not seen a dead person before?"

Skúli's face had gone from pale to white. He shook his head.

"It's all right. You'll get used to it. But if you're going to puke up, please don't do it over anything that might be used as evidence."

The young man had departed in an ambulance to the National Hospital's mortuary in Reykjavík before the inshore boats began to appear in the afternoon and the pontoon dock became a hive of activity. Gunna could see plenty of curious faces and knew that Albert Jónasson must have been chatting over the VHF while he steamed out that morning.

"Nothing to see, people," she muttered to herself as she and Skúli were the last to drive away, leaving the beach to be reclaimed by the rising tide.

"I'd best be getting back to town," Skúli said as Gunna parked in the mayor's space outside the police station.

"All right. I hope today was useful, but it's quite unusual to have a body. In fact, it hasn't happened for years. So that's a bit of excitement for you."

"Do you know who it is?"

"No idea. Might be a seaman, could be a foreigner. But whoever he was, my guess is he had a bit too much to drink and fell into the water trying to get on board a boat."

"When do you think you'll know?"

Gunna shrugged. "Anybody's guess, I'm afraid. Now, you're not going to write any of this, are you? There'll be a statement this afternoon with everything in it that we can say before he's been identified. Things get a bit delicate with relatives and whatnot. You understand?"

"No, of course not. I mean, yes. I'll be back later in the week if that's all right."

"Fine by me. It won't be so interesting, though. Most of what we do here is traffic. There's bugger all happens in Hvalvík, so I really don't know why they wanted to send you here."

Gunna opened the car door and swung her legs out. "Give me a call when you want to come over. Shouldn't be a problem."

"Haddi!"

"In here."

Gunna put her head round her own office door to see Haddi in one chair and the morose figure of Bjössi from CID sitting behind her desk with his feet perched on the window sill.

"Ah, Bjössi. So that's where you've got to. Make yourself comfortable, will you?"

Bjössi languidly put his hands behind his head. "Will do, Gunna. Two sugars for me, if you don't mind, and a few doughnuts wouldn't do any harm."

"Bugger off. I don't want your clogged-up arteries on my conscience. But I'm sure Haddi has some coffee on the go somewhere?"

"All right," Haddi grumbled, standing up. Gunna waved Bjössi to Haddi's vacated seat and planted herself behind her desk.

"Right then. What have we got?"

Bjössi sighed. "Dead bloke. Late twenties to mid-thirties by the look of him. Been in the water a few hours, but not long. Not a thing in his pockets. No rings, no watch, nothing round his neck, no piercings that we could see. No visible injuries."

He took a deep breath and carried on. "Clean-shaven probably yesterday, I'd say. Ginger hair, nails clipped, no shoes, black jeans and a black shirt with long sleeves. That's it, in a nutshell. He's probably on the slab at the morgue right now being looked at carefully. With any luck we might get something more tomorrow."

"He's not a local, but he must have gone into the water here. The tide wouldn't have washed him into the harbour from anywhere else, surely?"

"Nope. Hasn't been in the drink long enough for that. If he'd been rolling around in the water for long enough to drift along the coast, he wouldn't be in such good condition."

Haddi returned with a thermos and mugs.

"I suppose you want milk, Björssi?" he grumbled.

"Black's fine with me."

"That's just as well, because we don't have any milk anyway. Need me, do you?"

"No, you'd best knock off now, Haddi," Gunna replied. "I'll see you in the morning."

Haddi waved as he let the door swing shut behind him and Gunna heard him greet the woman reading the morning's paper at the post office counter next door as he left the building.

"Björssi, how much help with this can I get from CID?"

"Not a lot, I'm afraid. Looks pretty clear to me. Once he's identified, inform the relatives and get on with the rest of it. There'll have to be an inquiry, but I'd be surprised if it came up with anything other than death by misadventure, either drowning or hypothermia."

"Seems reasonable enough to me," Gunna agreed. "No sign of foul play, not yet at any rate. I'll check the missing persons list before I finish today and get on to pathology in the morning and see what they can tell us."

She yawned.

"Been a long day?" Björssi asked.

"It has. And I'd better be off in a minute. How's Dóra, anyway?"

"Ach, she's fine. Moaning, but nothing unusual about that. How about your kids?"

"Laufey should be back from school soon, so I'd better be there when she gets home. Gísli's at sea, been on *Snæfugl* since January and says he likes it, or he likes the money anyway."

"He's got his head screwed on, your boy has." Bjössi grinned. "Don't know where he gets that from."

"From his mother, of course," Gunna said stoutly. "There's no bloody sense in his father's family."

"Ah, I wouldn't know about that. But I reckon if things keep going the way they are, fishing's about the best place your lad could be. Interest rates and prices going up all the time. You know, it doesn't seem right." The furrows across Bjössi's brow deepened.

"Yup, it stinks. But fishermen and coppers will be fine, just you see," Gunna assured him.

Bjössi refilled his mug from the thermos. He wedged a hard lump of sugar between his teeth and sipped his fresh coffee through it.

"I hope somebody's going to be fine," Bjössi mumbled with the sugar lump still between his teeth. "The exchange rate's up and down. I don't care what the government tries to tell us, I can see prices of everything going up and Dóra says it's dearer just to live now. Half of the Poles and whatnot have already left, except the ones running lucrative dope businesses."

"You're probably right, but what's going to change? Nothing. Anyway, what's keeping you so busy over at Keflavík that you can't help an old colleague out for a few hours?"

"Dope, dope and more dope." Bjössi sighed. "It's just never-ending and I'm sick of it. It's dealing with these bloody low-lifes that I'm fed up with, day in, day out."

"Well, you shouldn't have joined the police in that case."

"Probably right," Bjössi said, standing up. "But I reckon we're both stuck with it now, Gunna. Come and find me if you're in Keflavík tomorrow. By the way, who's the toyboy?"

"What?"

"Your young man."

"Oh, him. He's a journalist on *Dagurinn*, says he's here to write a profile of a country police station."

"Fun for you." Bjössi sniggered while Gunna glowered.

"It was wished on me," she said. "Shit, that reminds me."

"Of what?"

"I've just remembered I had a meeting with Vilhjálmur Traustason this morning."

"Don't worry about it, sweetheart. I told our glorious leader that you were a bit busy today."

CHAPTER TWO

Wednesday, 27 August

Gunna's flat soles slapped on the polished floor of the hospital corridor. Sigmar's office was at the far end of the passage, marked only with a handwritten sign that indicated the occupant's name and not his position.

Hearing voices within, she knocked and pushed the door open without waiting for a response. Sigmar swivelled round, the phone at his ear.

"I'll have to call you back. Sorry, I have a visitor. Yes, an hour at least."

He dropped the phone on to its handset and smiled. "Good morning, sergeant. You've come to my rescue."

"Morning. In what way?"

"One of the administrators," he said with distaste, glaring at the phone. "More cash-saving incentives needed, although obviously that wouldn't extend to bureaucrats. But hopefully in an hour when the lady calls back, I'll be on my way home for lunch," he added with satisfaction.

"A result, then?"

"Indeed. Now, our young man." He shuffled through papers and came up with a handwritten sheet. "Of course you'd have the full report tomorrow, but I understand that you'll need to know as much as possible straight away."

"It helps."

Sigmar consulted the sheet. "Actually I can't tell you much more than I did yesterday at the scene, except to confirm he hadn't been in the water for more than a few hours. Six, at most."

"The body was located at six thirty."

"Around midnight, not before. He was also extremely drunk, almost double the drink-driving limit. At any rate it's not surprising that he may have missed his footing. He'd certainly have had trouble walking in a straight line at that level of intoxication. The cause of death was drowning."

Gunna scribbled notes in a pad as Sigmar spoke. "So he was alive when he hit the water?"

"Oh, yes. But apart from that, there's not much to tell. He was in good health, didn't smoke, or at least not often, wasn't overweight. He clearly didn't do any kind of manual work as his hands are as soft as a baby's bottom."

"Any distinguishing marks?" Gunna asked.

"Ah, yes. We have a tattoo. On the left upper arm."

Sigmar tapped at his computer keyboard and swivelled the monitor round so they could both see it.

"There you are. Wonderful things, computers," he said appreciatively as Gunna looked at the magnified image of the young man's pale skin and the stylized motif of a book with E^3 on one open page and V^2 on the page opposite.

"Will you email me these pictures? E-three?"

"E cubed, EEE. Someone's initials, maybe?" Sigmar mused. "Who knows? It could be anything. But that's your job, sergeant."

"Of course." She made a note and moved on. "Any DNA evidence?"

Sigmar frowned. "This isn't CSI, you know. If he has a criminal record, we'll know in a couple of days. But if he's an honest man, then the answer's no."

"We'll see, then."

"A little conundrum for you, sergeant?" Sigmar smiled. "Now, I'll give you my mobile number in case you have any more questions. But if you don't mind, I'd really like to not be here when the financial controller calls back."

27-08-2008, 1339

Skandalblogger writes:

Keeping our end up!

We're still here, ladies and gentlemen, and we know how much you all appreciate the Skandalblogger's efforts to keep you up to date with the great and the good.

The latest is that our last gem of gossip, brought to us by word of mouth from someone who knows, has resulted in the abject fury of a certain recently re-elected former jailbird, who has been going apeshit over our revelation that he's had a hair transplant.

Strangely, he didn't seem to mind too much about being called a disgraced convicted criminal. Well, you can't argue with the truth . . . But, no, it's the rug thing that's really got his goat. That's putting his priorities in the right place.

Bæjó!

An hour later Gunna was at the police station in Keflavík. Like Sigmar at the hospital, Chief Inspector Vilhjálmur Traustason had a surprisingly small office and, at more than two metres in height, he seemed to fill most of it. No lightweight herself, Gunna felt that the room could burst if a third person were to try and squeeze in. She sipped weak coffee and placed the cup awkwardly on the corner of his desk.

"Sorry about yesterday. It was something of a busy day," she apologized without a shred of remorse in her voice.

"Understood. Investigation has to take precedence," he said stiffly. "Now, resources."

"Indeed. How much is there in the kitty for me to spend?"

"Less than ever," he replied with a tiny sigh, finally looking up from the screen of the laptop on the desk.

"I need —"

"I know what you need."

"How do you know?"

"Because you tell me at every available opportunity exactly what you need, as does every other station officer in the county. And I have to keep telling you that there are fewer financial resources available. But . . ." Vilhjálmur Traustason tailed off, attention on his screen.

"But what?"

Throughout her career, she had been mildly irritated by Vilhjálmur Traustason, as well as occasionally tempted to punch his prominent nose. Promotion had sought him out in the same way that it had steadfastly avoided Gunna. She was fully aware that only an unusual set of circumstances had made her a sergeant in a rural area instead of still being a constable in the city force, and that further promotion was less than likely. The chief inspector's steady rise put them at odds when it came to the increasingly frequent issue of funding.

"I know how you love figures, Vilhjálmur. So I've prepared some for you," she said, passing a sheet of paper across the desk to him.

He looked doubtful and scrutinized the list of requirements.

"You don't really need all this, do you?" he asked, aghast.

"Probably not. But I'm sure we can strike a happy medium somewhere."

"But — all this? Why? How can you justify it?"

"Since the smelter construction started on the far side of the harbour we simply have so much more to do. Traffic through Hvalvík has increased by around four hundred per cent and virtually all of that is heavy goods. Basically, trucks going to and from that new aluminium plant. The place is awash with heavy traffic and Polish labourers."

"But you're coping well."

"For the moment, Vilhjálmur, for the moment. There's only me and Haddi, and Haddi doesn't speak enough English or anything else to deal with these people."

"You can call for additional manpower when you need it."

"I can call and it's not going to come half the time. That's why I'm putting in for two additional officers for the Hvalvík station."

"Two?" Vilhjálmur squeaked. "There's a request for an additional car here as well. You have two cars already and normally a station like yours has only one vehicle."

"It's a big area we have to cover. The Volvos are getting old and we could do with a jeep for the winter."

Vilhjálmur consulted his laptop again, scratched his head and sucked his teeth while Gunna watched him carefully while pretending to make notes on the pad resting on her knee.

Eventually he sighed heavily. "Gunnhildur. What do you really need? What are your priorities?"

"Manpower. Then an additional vehicle. Then all the other bits and pieces."

"Well, you're in luck, actually, as I have a very experienced officer who has asked for a transfer and I'm sure he'd suit you."

"Not Viggó Björgvins?"

"How did you know?" he snapped.

"Because the man's being transferred all the bloody time. No. I want someone a lot younger than that idiot."

Sour-faced, Vilhjálmur consulted his laptop. "You can have one officer on permanent secondment."

"Who?"

"You can have Snorri Hilmarsson or Bára Gunnólfsdóttir. They've both been seconded to you occasionally, I believe."

Gunna thought quickly. She knew and liked both officers. Bára was small, fair and quick-witted with an ability to get straight to the heart of things, while Snorri was the beefy, likeable young man with an endless reserve of good humour who was normally the one sent to help out at Hvalvík. Gunna knew him as tenacious but without Bára's spark of fierce intelligence. She had seen plenty of both of them and paused over a less than easy choice.

"Snorri," she decided.

"Why?"

"He's a plodder. Methodical, gets on with it. Country copper material. Bára has a great future in CID, as long as you can keep her on the force."

Vilhjálmur winced at the reference to the police force's retention rate.

"All right. I'll interview Snorri when he comes on duty and we'll see if he's prepared for a transfer to Hvalvík."

"Oh, he is. He lives in Hvalvík anyway, so he's happy with it."

"How do you know?"

"I've already asked him."

"Gunnhildur, you know you shouldn't bypass procedure," Vilhjálmur admonished grimly. "Now, vehicles."

"Yes."

"It's August now. How long are these vehicles you have going to last?"

"Search me. I'm not a mechanic."

"I don't have a vehicle for you. I can't justify it."

"Come on. That old Volvo's going to fall apart soon."

He tapped his teeth with the pencil. "Make it last the summer. I'll allocate you a jeep, but not until October."

Gunna wanted to spit on her palm and shake his hand, but was still suspicious. It seemed to have all been too easy.

"Done. Can I have Snorri from next week?"

Gunna used the CID room. She could have gone back to Hvalvík as soon as Vilhjálmur had agreed to let her have both Snorri and a jeep, but she felt the need of the buzz of colleagues around her rather than Haddi's dry chuckle from the next room.

"Hvalvík police," she heard Haddi answer gruffly after a dozen rings.

"Hi, it's me. Are you all right without me for a few hours?"

"Yeah. I reckon I can maintain law and order for a while. Are you busy with that bloke?"

"Pretty much. CID have better things to do, so this is down to us."

"That's all right. Tomorrow's going to be busy, though."

"Why's that?" Gunna asked.

"They're bringing some low-loaders through to the smelter site so we'll have to close a couple of streets and escort them through."

"Shouldn't be a problem. D'you want the good news?"

"No news is normally good news."

"We have Snorri from Monday and get a jeep in October."

Gunna heard Haddi snort, which she recognized as a laugh of sorts. "And what did you have to do to persuade Vilhjálmur? Did you beat him round the head or just threaten the old fool?"

"Didn't have to do either. Just set out the case and explained how busy we are. But he did try and palm me off with Viggó Björgvins."

"But you got Snorri instead?"

"So he says. But I'll wait and see if it's Viggó who turns up on Monday morning."

"If he does, I'll be asking for a transfer," Haddi growled.

"Me too," Gunna agreed. "Anyway, I'll see you later."

Rather than use Bjössi's desk, she sat herself opposite his empty place in the chair that would belong to the station's second CID officer — when recruitment and financial constraints might allow the post to be filled.

It took more than an hour on the computer to plough through the national register that lists the full name, date of birth and legal residence of every Icelandic citizen and foreign resident. She emerged from the E section with ten candidates for men with the initials EEE, of whom six could not be ruled out by their age. Encouraged, she plunged into the V section of the register, but found that VV was a very common set of initials and decided to concentrate on E3.

Referring to the list of names and dates of birth on the pad next to her, she clicked the mouse on the telephone directory and began with the first of the names. She added the phone numbers given to the list on her pad, pulled Bjössi's phone across the desk towards her and dialled the first number.

"Hello?" a woman's voice answered.

"Good morning. This is Gunnhildur Gísladóttir at Hvalvík police. Could I speak to Eiríkur Emil Eiríksson?"

"He's not here," the voice answered sharply.

"Could you tell me where I could find him?"

"You're not his . . ." There was a pause. "You're not his bit on the side, are you?" the voice continued with suppressed fury. "Because if you are —"

"I'm an investigating officer with Hvalvík police and I assure you I've never met the man, but I'm trying to eliminate certain people from an inquiry. Can you tell me where I can find him? This is a serious matter."

The voice on the line sighed. "He's at sea as far as I know. But sometimes he doesn't bother to come home when they're ashore."

"And you're his wife?"

"I don't know about that. I'm his kids' mum at any rate."

"I see. I apologize, but I have to eliminate a series of people from an incident. Could you describe him for me? Height and hair colour?"

Gunna could hear the click of a lighter and a long exhalation.

"Eiríkur's about two metres, a bit over. Dark hair, going a bit bald at the back, big nose."

"In that case I don't think I'll have to trouble you any more as that doesn't fit the description of the person we're looking for. But can I have your name, please? It's just in case I need to follow this up later."

"Aldís Gunnarsdóttir."

"And is that an Akureyri phone number?"

"Dalvík."

"OK. Thank you for your help. I don't expect we'll need to trouble you any further."

"What's he done?" Aldís asked sharply.

"Excuse me?"

"What's he done, the bloke you're looking for? Eiríkur gets up to all sorts."

"Nothing as far as I know. It's a missing person inquiry."

"Oh. Shame." The woman's disappointment was palpable.

Gunna ended the call with relief, carefully noting names, numbers and the time of the call. She looked back at the list and dialled again.

"Good morning. This is Gunnhildur Gísladóttir at Hvalvík police. Could I speak to Elmar Einar Ervík, please?"

It was long past midday when Gunna realized that she would have to be quick getting back to Hvalvík before the station closed its doors at six. But she consoled herself with a job well done that left only one name unaccounted for on the list she had started with. One person had not answered his home phone or the mobile number that the telephone company's website listed. She reflected that this was nothing out of the ordinary, as the person could be out of the country, at sea, a meeting or simply asleep. Out of curiosity, she opened a search engine on the computer, typed in Einar Eyjólfur Einarsson and clicked the search box.

The personnel page of a company website was at the top of the list that appeared within seconds. Gunna followed the link to the site and scrolled down the list of staff to the name she was looking for. Some entries had a picture alongside the staff listing, but there was no picture of Einar Eyjólfur Einarsson, just the name and the mobile phone number she had already called unsuccessfully twice.

She scrolled back through the list until she found the company's personnel manager. Gunna pulled the phone over and dialled again.

"Good afternoon. Spearpoint," a soft voice purred.

"Good afternoon. This is Gunnhildur Gísladóttir at Hvalvík police. I'm trying to contact Einar Eyjólfur Einarsson."

27-08-2008, 2114

Skandalblogger writes:

So what's going on here with the health service? We hear whispers from the inside that times are hard at the coalface of government and plans are being floated to open "areas of health provision" to the "private sector" as we've been told.

Excuse us? Isn't this Iceland, not some tinpot banana republic run as the President's personal bank account? Or is it? We're supposed to be the pinnacle of well-being and happiness. So what's gone wrong? Why is government floating these proposals in secret and coming over coy when anyone asks about it?

It seems uncomfortable to contemplate, but all the signs are there that the parts of the health service that actually produce a few quid for the state coffers are likely to be flogged off cheap to friends of the party, while the taxpayer continues to prop up the bits of it that aren't profitable.

So let's cast our minds back a year or two to when the guys at the top sold off our state-run telephone system to their golfing buddies. Now, wasn't the rationale at the time that the proceeds would be used to give us, the Icelandic taxpayers, a second-to-none health service? In which case, did the fat guys in suits simply trouser the cash they got for the phone company, considering health is now in such a poor financial state that the only option is to privatize?

Flummoxed . . .

Bæjó!

CHAPTER THREE

Thursday, 28 August

Gunna drove into Reykjavík late in the morning when the roads should have been fairly quiet, but still found herself caught up in a straggle of traffic crawling along main roads. In spite of the falling housing market and the jittery business environment that dominated the news, things seemed busy enough as the second-best Volvo swung on to Miklabraut and down towards the city centre. New buildings and cranes dotted the skyline.

Passing Lækjartorg, she reflected that while much had changed, there were undoubtedly more changes to come. The city had altered out of all recognition. What had been a quiet town centre when she moved south and joined the Reykjavík force all those years ago had become a buzzing sprawl of boutiques and bars. Stopped at the lights, she checked what had once been the quiet restaurant with dark wooden tables and solid food where she and Raggi had celebrated their secret wedding. The place had gone entirely, replaced with three storeys of steel-framed opaque glass.

The lights changed and Gunna pulled away along Sæbraut, passing the Ministry buildings at the corner of

Skúlagata now dwarfed by the rows of new offices and apartment blocks facing the sea and the shell of the huge Opera House rising where the fish auction had stood. She wondered which of the glass-fronted giants housed the offices she was looking for.

The top of the building wasn't quite as smart as the ground-floor entrance had indicated, and the back of it, overlooking building sites and car parks, wasn't as exclusive as the front with its view over Faxa Bay and the brooding presence of Mount Esja in the distance.

Gunna found the office suite and was about to push open the door emblazoned with a Spearpoint sign, its curved logo ending in a sharp point, when a raised voice inside made her pause. She stood still and listened carefully. It was clearly a woman's voice, in a state of fury she would normally have expected to hear outside a nightclub in the early hours.

The voice ranted with hardly a break, occasionally pausing, possibly for breath, before continuing with its tirade. No answering voice could be heard. Although few distinct words could be made out, Gunna was caught between concern and admiration for a woman who could rant at quite such length and volume.

Eventually, tired of waiting for the tirade to come to an end, she shoved at the door and heard a buzz inside as it swung open. The voice came to an abrupt halt and Gunna found herself in front of a high reception desk where a young woman with a pinched face looked up in surprise to see a police officer in uniform.

"Morning. I'm looking for Sigurjóna Huldudóttir. I believe I'm expected."

"She's here. A moment," she replied in a dazed voice. As Gunna stowed her cap under her arm, she wondered if the receptionist had been on the receiving end of that magnificent rant.

The girl stood up and went to a door behind her, knocked and opened it gingerly, before putting her head inside and muttering a few words of which "police" was the only one Gunna could make out as she stood with her back to the desk and admired the building site next door. A tower crane stood almost level with the office window and Gunna could see the figure of the operator in his tiny cage at the top, concentrating as he deftly lifted and swung steel bars into place in the framework of a new building.

More bloody offices. As if there aren't enough already, Gunna thought.

". . . the hell do these bastards get away with this . . . ?" a strident voice barked suddenly, cut off in mid-sentence as the office door hissed shut.

The receptionist smiled wanly as Gunna looked around inquiringly.

"She'll see you in a few minutes. Could you wait a moment for her to finish her meeting?" the receptionist asked sweetly. "Take a seat if you like."

Gunna sat on a hard leather couch and flipped through a gossip magazine, wondering why she didn't recognize the faces of all the country's top people plastered across the pages.

"Out of touch," she muttered to herself.

"Excuse me?" the receptionist asked, and Gunna realized that she had spoken out loud. "Nothing. Just thinking out loud," she apologized.

"She'll see you now," the girl said, as the door behind her opened and a beefy young man in a suit, his face burning, made his way out, giving every impression of being on the point of breaking into a run and leaping through a window.

Gunna stopped for a second in the doorway and took in a large corner office, thickly carpeted and with a desk topped in smoked glass dominating the far end, facing away from a window that filled one entire wall. Although the view was better from here, Gunna was pleased to note that the jib of the tower crane still protruded across it.

"Good morning. Come in, please."

The voice was warm, and apart from a slight heave of prominently displayed bosom there was no trace of the fury of a few minutes before from the statuesque woman with an unmistakable air of decision about her sharp features. Gunna took in a smartly tailored suit and dark blonde hair cut simply.

She extended a hand which was quickly taken and firmly shaken.

"Gunnhildur Gísladóttir, Hvalvík police."

"Hvalvík? OK. Well, I'm Sigurjóna. My PA told me that you had called. Is this something to do with the site?"

"Which site do you mean?"

"The Hvalvík smelter project, of course."

"Are you involved with that?"

"Our subsidiary company is playing a prominent part in the project development," Sigurjóna said smoothly.

"No, nothing to do with the site. Actually this is an inquiry about one of your former employees and I spoke to one of your people yesterday afternoon. Ósk Líndal?"

"Ósk handles human resources and stands in for me when I'm away."

Gunna looked down and flipped through the sheaf of papers, going past the picture of the dead man taken at the morgue by a police photographer and moving on to the driving licence photo from the national archive.

"Do you recognize this man?" she asked, handing the picture across.

Sigurjóna took it and looked carefully. Gunna watched for a reaction, but there was none to be seen.

"Einar," Sigurjóna said finally. "Einar Eyjólfur Einarsson. He works here, although we haven't seen him since last week and he hasn't called in, so I can't say I'm delighted with him right now."

"No explanation?"

"No, not a word."

"Did you make any inquiries?"

"Of course. He's a highly valued member of the team here and we can certainly use his skills. He's one of our best account managers — it's very difficult to explain to his clients that he just isn't here. I'll be very pleased when he comes back, not that I'd tell him so."

Gunna nodded and scribbled on the notes, more to give herself a second to think than to write anything down "And who have you contacted to find Einar?"

"Well, it's not easy because I don't believe he has much in the way of family and he's from somewhere in the east originally. I'm not sure that his parents are still alive, even. I recall that he mentioned once that he had been an afterthought, the child of elderly parents."

"No brothers or sisters? No friends? Girlfriend?"

"Well, Dísa, the girl on reception, moved in with him for a while, but I believe that didn't last for long and you'd have to ask her about it. But, no. I assume he has a circle of friends, but not people that I'm aware of." Sigurjóna was starting to sound irritated. "Look, inspector, just where is this going? What's he done, if you can tell me?"

"It's sergeant, actually. I have reason to believe he's dead."

"Oh my God!" Sigurjóna gasped, hands flying to her mouth in a gesture that Gunna found a touch too theatrical to be fully convincing. "Hvalvík? You mean he's the dead man they found there? On the news the other night?" Her voice shook slightly, and one finger tapped furiously on the polished surface of the desk.

Gunna nodded, and looked down at the papers in her lap. She wondered what the reaction would be to the morgue photograph, but decided against showing it.

"The identification is only preliminary at the moment, as we'll need someone to identify him formally. But as he had his initials tattooed on his arm, identification wasn't difficult. I need to know a little more about him and what his work was, what he was working on. Can you tell me when he came in to work last?"

Sigurjóna opened a slim laptop on the desk in front of her and tapped with swift fingers.

"He was here last week," she said slowly, circling a finger on the mouse pad. "Here. Last Friday. I know he had a meeting on Monday this week but I'd have to ask Ósk about that. He was due to meet the same client in Copenhagen on Wednesday, and never showed up. The client called us and we had to reschedule. Luckily it wasn't anything delicate, only a preliminary meeting with a new prospect, so no harm done."

"So, if you can tell me which airline he was travelling with, we can find out easily enough if he really did travel or not."

"Dísa can tell you that. She books flights for our people, but it was probably the Express airline."

"Cheaper?"

Sigurjóna nodded. "And more flexible."

"How had he been getting on here until last week?"

"Fine. Like I said, he was a very competent and successful account manager."

"No tensions? Arguments?"

Sigurjóna flushed noticeably. "No. Not at all."

"Did Einar have any disagreements with you or his manager?"

"Spearpoint is growing very fast," Sigurjóna said proudly. "But this is a small company and everyone reports to me. No, we did not have any disagreements.

We got on very well. He was entertaining some Danish clients for a few days and was due to meet them again in Copenhagen on Wednesday, but didn't show up. My assumption was that he had gone over there, found himself a nice little Danish lady and decided to stay. It's hard to say. He could be impulsive."

Gunna scribbled in the file. Noticing that this was making Sigurjóna uneasy, she also took the time to note down on the side of the page that she needed to buy butter, milk, bread and some fruit and vegetables in Hagkaup before driving back to Hvalvík.

"Do you know if Einar had any enemies? Anyone who might wish to harm him? Anyone with a grudge?"

"No idea. In personal terms, the others here had a closer relationship with him than I did. You might want to speak to them. Dísa probably knew him best and he often worked with Jón Oddur, so he might know something about his movements."

"I will need to, but at present I'm mostly trying to build up a picture of his movements so that we can establish a time of death and who the last people he saw were. Can you tell me what your movements were on and after the weekend?"

Sigurjóna's eyes opened wide. "Surely you don't suspect me of anything."

"Of course not," Gunna said smoothly, noting down that she would also have to stock up on toilet paper, so much cheaper in town than at the Co-op in Hvalvík. "Purely routine. We have to ask and I assure you I'll want to know the movements of all your staff at the same time if that's possible."

"I was with my husband in Akureyri. A business trip."

"Anyone other than your husband who will confirm that?"

"Oh, yes."

"Just routine, you understand. Anyway, thank you for your time. But if you recall anything that could help the investigation, I'd appreciate it if you could give me a call. Now, it would be useful if I could talk to Jón Oddur and Dísa."

She stood up and Sigurjóna did the same, coming around the desk to accompany her to the door. Gunna felt a whiff of something powerful on her breath as Sigurjóna held the door open for her and called out to the girl at reception.

"Dísa, would you call Jón Oddur? This lady would like to speak to him," she instructed and closed the office door behind her.

At the reception desk, Gunna looked down at where Dísa sat at the switchboard, speaking quietly into the microphone of a headset. She pressed a button to finish the call and looked up with eyes that Gunna could see were full of concern.

"Are you here about Einar?" she asked immediately, with a backward glance to make sure the door was shut.

"Yes. You knew him pretty well, Sigurjóna tells me."

"I did. Where is he?"

"He's dead, I'm afraid."

Dísa dropped her head and looked down at the desk in front of her. Then she buried her face in both hands for a moment before sweeping them up and through her hair, looking up bright-eyed. "Do you know who killed him?"

"Why do you ask? Is there anything you want to tell me about?"

"I don't know. Maybe," she said dully as the young man with the red face Gunna had seen earlier escaping from Sigurjóna's office appeared.

"What does the old witch want now?" His harsh tone did nothing to hide the trepidation behind it. The expression on his face was briefly of panic when he saw Gunna standing by the desk.

"It's not the boss. This lady wants a word with you," Dísa said quietly.

"That's a relief. You'd better come to my office."

Jón Oddur sat with his back to the window and fiddled with a laptop on his desk as he spoke.

"Is it Einar Eyjólfur you're here about?" he asked nervously.

"What makes you think that?"

"We haven't seen him for a few days and I can't get through to his mobile."

"As it happens, we have every reason to believe that he drowned in Hvalvík harbour in the early hours of Tuesday morning."

"So it was him," Jón Oddur said with a sigh. "Dísa was right."

"When did you see him last?"

"Monday," he replied promptly. "He didn't come in, but we met in the evening with some clients from

Denmark he was supposed to meet again on Wednesday."

"In Copenhagen? So he was due to fly out there on Tuesday?"

"That's right, Tuesday afternoon. He didn't show up, so I'm going there next week to pick things up."

"What business is that?"

Jón Oddur smiled sourly for the first time. "It's a Danish sweet company that manufactures chewing gum. They want to see if Iceland's a market for them, so we're doing market research, putting them in touch with retailers, that sort of thing."

"Sounds interesting."

"Yeah. Right," Jón Oddur said bitterly.

"Not an exciting prospect?" Gunna probed gently.

"Einar Eyjólfur didn't think so, and neither do I now that it's been dumped on me."

"What was he doing before that?"

"The Hvalvík smelter was his project. He'd been on that since it started. He wasn't very pleased when he was taken off it and put on this chewing gum thing instead. What happened to him?"

"Drowned," Gunna repeated. "In Hvalvík harbour."

"God. What the hell was he doing in that dump?"

"That's what we'd like to know. What do you know of his movements?"

"We took the chewing gum guys to dinner at that Chinese place on Hverfisgata and then we went to a few bars after that."

Gunna sat in silence, waiting for him to continue.

"The Danes bowed out about eleven and went back to their hotel. We went for a few beers."

"A few?"

"Yeah. Einar Eyjólfur liked a drink, but he didn't have much of a head for it."

"Where did you go?"

"Gaukur á Stöng. Then that really loud place with all the lights on Laugarvegur and then the Emperor."

"Quite a night, then. So when and where did you part company?"

"At the Emperor. About one. I told him he needed to get some sleep if he was going to catch his flight in the morning, but he said it was an afternoon flight so he didn't need to be up early."

"Did anything happen that was unusual?"

"No. We had a few beers and I left him in the Emperor. That's it."

"Will anyone else corroborate that?"

"Hell, I don't know," Jón Oddur said wearily. "The barmaid might recognize us, I suppose. But it was a busy night. I got talking to a group of tourists and there was some really drunk bloke who bumped into Einar Eyjólfur and wanted to start a fight, but nothing out of the ordinary."

Jón Oddur transferred his attention from the keyboard to a rubber band that he wrapped repeatedly around his fingers.

"You seem nervous," Gunna said as the rubber band flew off his hand and hit the wall.

"You would be if one of your best mates had just drowned," he snapped back. "What the fuck was he doing in Hvalvík, anyway?"

"Like I said, that's what I'm trying to find out and the more you can tell me, the more likely it is I'll be able to get to the bottom of it all."

"Sorry," Jón Oddur apologized with a sigh. "That's it. That's all I can tell you."

"Thank you. Now I'd better have a word with Dísa. She was his girlfriend, right?"

"Sort of. They kind of split up when he moved out, but they were still sort of together."

Sort of, thought Gunna as she stood up to leave Jón Oddur to his fidgeting.

"If you recall anything else that might be useful, then I'd appreciate a call," she said, placing a card on the desk.

Jón Oddur nodded vaguely, his attention split between her and the laptop in front of him.

"Yeah. I'll let you know," he said half-heartedly, his attention back on his computer screen. "Dísa's at reception. She normally leaves at four, so you'd better be quick."

Dísa sat behind the reception desk and Gunna could see that she was watching her approach.

"What did Jón Oddur say?" she asked before Gunna could speak.

"That you knew him better than almost anyone. Is that right?"

"What's happened to him?"

Gunna could see the anxiety and waited to see tears well up in those wide eyes.

"Do you know who killed him?" Dísa whispered.

"Why do you say that? There's no indication of foul play."

"How did it happen?"

"He drowned, in the harbour at Hvalvík."

"What was he doing there? He'd been taken off the smelter project," Dísa said angrily.

"That's just what I think I need to find out," Gunna replied grimly. "Have you finished for today?"

Dísa nodded, eyes awash with tears.

"In that case, do you need a lift home?"

28-08-2008, 2041

Skandalblogger writes:

It's our birthday! Two years down the line and we're still here. It's been two whole anonymous years of providing the nation with completely reliable, totally unsubstantiated and extremely libellous gossip about the great and the good of Icelandic entertainment, business and politics. So happy birthday to us! We'd like to ask all our readers — and there are plenty of them! — to raise a glass to the Skandalblogger tonight and wish us plenty more years of risking our necks bringing you malicious libel for your delectation. We know you love us and you'd hate to see us go . . .

Just to keep in the spirit of things, we'd like to know who says gentlemen prefer the real thing?

Here are Skandalblogger's top five falsies. Here we are, for your delectation, in reverse order, the top five society ladies who have gone under the knife in the noble cause of chest enhancement.

5. A certain notorious fitness expert who went from 32A to 34C overnight. She must have been getting a discount for bulk, so to speak, as she had her schnoz done at the same time.

4. The lady who looks after the extramarital needs of a particularly needy businessman who owns a newspaper, a record store, a chain of grocery shops and a transport company. Judging by his girlfriend's impressively upholstered new frontage, he can't be quite so needy any more.

3. A well-known PR guru had hers done in the States. There's nothing like mixing business with pleasure, is there, Sugarplum?

2. Pop stars have to look a million dollars, but our guess is that, this warbling national treasure's boob job was a cut-price deal, as it looks like her arse has simply been sliced off and stuck to her chest. We like it, though.

And number 1 . . . is, tan-tan-tara. Sorry, but it has to be our favourite newsreader. They looked better before, darling. And we decided to put you at number one for outright daring. Who do you think you're fooling?

See you soon!

Bæjó

Dísa's flat was in the basement of a large house in Vogar, twenty minutes' drive out of the city on the road to Keflavík, among the black lava crags of the peninsula that ends with the airport and was until recently the NATO air base.

Much of the main room was filled by an ornately framed double bed stacked with neatly folded clean laundry and piles of magazines. In the corner a light winked on a computer with a darkened screen.

"Let's sit in the kitchen," Dísa said, dropping her bag on the kitchen table and draping her jacket over the back of a chair.

Gunna sat down and scanned the room. There were film posters on the walls, but she had the impression that the kitchen didn't get used often.

"No problems at work?"

Dísa shook her head. She pulled on and huddled inside a thick checked shirt several sizes too large that Gunna guessed had once belonged to Einar Eyjólfur.

"No. Not at all. Sigurjóna's fine."

"How about the others? It's quite a small company and you must have all worked closely together."

"Sigurjóna's not happy. Everyone knew that Einar Eyjólfur wasn't about. Fjóla the accountant is really shocked as well. She's quite old, almost forty, and Einar said she was a bit like his mum except younger."

Gunna wondered if Dísa even had any coffee in the flat.

"Well, forty's not that old, you know," she said softly.

Dísa sniffed. "Sorry. I didn't mean to be rude, but everyone at Spearpoint is young except for Fjóla."

"That's OK. No offence taken."

"How old are you, if you don't mind my asking?"

"Me? Thirty-six."

Dísa nodded dumbly and Gunna took a deep breath. "We identified Einar Eyjólfur from the national register.

The E-three tattoo we figured out stood for EEE, and there aren't that many people with those initials. You'd recognize that tattoo?"

"Yeah. I've got one the same," she said, shrugging a shoulder out of the thick shirt to reveal the book and letters just below the nape of her neck.

"And V-two?"

"That's me. VV. Dísa is short for Vigdís. Vigdís Veigarsdóttir."

"That explains it."

Dísa huddled back inside the shirt.

"So. What can you tell me?" Gunna asked.

"I don't really know."

"How about starting at the beginning? What's your background?"

"I was brought up here."

"In Vogar?"

"In this street. This is my uncle's house. Dad and my uncle built their houses at the same time. This flat is here because they expected my grandmother to come and live here one day when she was too old to live on her own. But then she died and the place stayed empty. When I started going out with Einar Eyjólfur and we decided to live together, my uncle said we could live down here."

"And your parents live close to here as well?"

"Just Mum. Dad left ages ago. He's got another wife and small children now. They live in Reykjavík."

"How long had you known Einar when you moved in together?"

"Not long. Five or six weeks."

"And how long did you live together?"

"Almost a year."

"Did you meet at work?"

"Yes," Dísa said hollowly. "Jón Oddur bet him he wouldn't ask me out, and he did. So he told me about the bet and it was like a private joke between us that we'd have a couple of dates and then split the winnings."

"And what then?"

"Well, we just liked each other, I suppose."

"Can you tell me anything about him, what sort of a character he was?"

Dísa puffed her cheeks out and thought for a moment. "He was one of those people who is lovable and infuriating at the same time. You know what I mean?"

"Precisely."

"He would do the stupidest things. Like, completely idiotic. He'd put potatoes and ice cream in the same dish, things like that. But at the same time he was really clever and could do all kinds of things. He could speak English and Danish and bits of other languages as well, and he could do anything with the computer and electronic stuff."

"Was he a bit of a nerd, if you don't mind me using that word?"

"He was a nerd and he was proud of it. Sometimes he could be totally thoughtless and at other times he could be so considerate as well."

"And what happened? Why did you split up?"

"Mum didn't like him much, and he didn't like her either, so that didn't help. He really missed his friends being out here in Vogar and it's a pain getting into town, because he said he didn't want to own a car."

"Why's that?"

"He said that the combustion engine is destroying the earth and he didn't want to contribute to it. But all that meant was that I drove us everywhere instead."

"A man of principle?"

"When it suited him."

"But you were still close at the time he disappeared?"

"We were."

"And when did you last see him?" Gunna asked.

"The day before he was found. He stayed here all weekend and had to meet some people on the Monday, so he went to town with me on Monday morning and went to his place and I went to work as usual. I thought I'd see him the next day, but he didn't come in to work. Then you called on Wednesday to talk to Ósk."

"And you answered the phone?"

"Yeah. And I knew right away something was wrong."

"Did he say anything about the people he was meeting?"

"Not really. But he didn't get off on drinking and always complained about having to take clients around the nightlife."

Gunna nodded. "Was there anything you noticed in the time up to his disappearance that was different? Changes in his behaviour or habits? Sigurjóna says that there was nothing she noticed in his work that was any different."

Dísa shook her head. "Sigurjóna's a strange woman. Some things just completely pass her by and other things she watches like a hawk. If he hadn't been doing his work, she would have noticed straight away."

"But there was nothing you noticed?"

"There was something and I didn't want to say anything about it at the office. Y'know, there wasn't time and, it's, like, work."

"Go on."

"This is what I thought you ought to know about. It was in the spring. There was this friend of Einar Eyjólfur's who was killed in a road accident. I'd never met the guy, but it really shook him up."

"Do you remember the man's name? Or where the accident occurred?"

"No. Sorry. I keep saying sorry, don't I? I think he was a teacher or something, and the accident happened right outside his house, so he said, up in Grafarvogur."

"And you never met this man?"

"No. Just heard them talking a lot through the computer. On Skype."

Gunna made a few notes on her pad, angling it on the edge of the table so that it couldn't be seen. She wrote "Computer — talk? How? Ask Snorri."

"If this man's death upset him so much, do you know if they were related, or old friends, or anything like that?"

"No, nothing like that. They talked mostly about all this ecological stuff, dams and power and electricity, that kind of thing. I think they were working on some sort of website together, something to do with Clean Iceland."

"The environmental group?"

"Sigurjóna doesn't like them."

"And if Sigurjóna had known that Einar Eyjólfur had something to do with Clean Iceland, would that have caused a problem at work?"

"Shit, yeah."

Gunna looked at Dísa in silence, hoping that the silence would prompt her to continue.

"Actually he was more than upset. He was scared, I thought, but he didn't say anything about it. I saw him watching the street outside in the evenings and checking to see if we were being followed if we were out somewhere, and I told him not to be silly."

"And he never mentioned what he might be anxious about?"

"No, he'd just change the subject if I asked him, but I could see he was uncomfortable with it."

"Do you think this was anything to do with his friend's accident?"

Dísa nodded in silence and looked down at her hands.

"And do you believe that there might be some connection to his work?"

She nodded again.

"Do you believe that you are in any danger?"

"No, I don't think so," she replied in a small voice.

"All right. Thank you for all your help, and I assure you it is a help," Gunna said, rising to her feet. "But I expect I will want to come and ask you a few more questions later. By the way, I know it's not pleasant, but it seems Einar Eyjólfur had no next of kin. Would you be prepared to identify him formally?"

Dísa gulped and turned pale. "I've never seen a dead person before."

"He'll look as if he's asleep."

"OK. I'll do it."

"Tomorrow?"

Dísa looked doubtful. "I will if you'll come with me," she finally said in a small voice.

"Of course," Gunna said, trying to sound reassuring. "I'll pick you up as well if you like."

"Please. I'll take the day off. Sigurjóna won't mind if she knows why."

"Fine. I'll go over to the hospital with you. You're going to be all right tonight, aren't you?" she asked, the front door open in front of her.

The sun was low in the sky and it was still warm after a hot day, but a stiff breeze was blowing uphill from the sea, whipping dust from the street to fill the air with grit.

"Dísa, you're not on your own here, are you?"

"It's all right. My uncle's family is upstairs and Mum is down the street."

Gunna pulled her cap lower and prepared to trot over the road to her car.

"The guy's name, I remember it now."

"And?"

"Egill. Egill Grímsson."

* * *

The phone buzzed on the kitchen worktop and Gunna debated with herself whether or not to answer the "unknown number" call. After all, she was off duty. Laufey looked up from the homework she had decided to spread across the kitchen table.

"Phone, Mum."

"I know, sweetheart." Gunna picked it up. "Gunnhildur."

Vilhjálmur Traustason's voice was an octave above its usual pitch, and for once he didn't even bother to introduce himself.

"Why on earth were you in Reykjavík?" he demanded.

"You keep telling me what a wonderful city it is and how you can't understand me living in a backwater like Hvalvík."

"Don't play games, Gunnhildur. I've had a complaint from a very senior level that you have been harassing a prominent figure in the business community. *Very* prominent."

"And who is that supposed to be?"

Vilhjálmur's voice rose slightly further and Gunna toyed with the idea that if it were to go up any more, then only dogs and dolphins would be able to hear the chief inspector's tantrums.

"You know perfectly well and I'm instructing you to be careful. This is a very influential lady and I can't see how she could be connected in any way to anything suspicious."

"Look, our dead guy worked for her. This was a perfectly ordinary interview, nothing heavy, simply to try and find out what his movements had been before we found him dead a hundred kilometres from Reykjavík. Is that OK?"

She could hear the chief inspector taking deep breaths to calm his nerves. She knew he found it difficult to haul her over the coals, just as she found it hard to take his rapid rise through the ranks seriously.

"Well, in that case —"

"And just so that you know, your prominent figure had just finished screaming blue murder at some unlucky dogsbody as I got there, and she reeks of vodka at two in the afternoon."

"In that case —"

"In that case, I should have informed traffic, just in case the bloody woman decided to drive herself home."

"Gunnhildur, listen, I don't want any trouble arising from this, you understand? We don't need a repeat of, you know, what happened before."

"Just following procedure, Vilhjálmur, going by the rule book."

Well, mind you do. Do you understand? We can't have that sort of person causing a fuss because a regional officer oversteps the mark."

He stressed "regional", and Gunna found herself resisting the temptation to snap back. She jammed her phone against one shoulder while opening the fridge and peering inside.

"What do you mean by overstepping the mark?" she asked angrily. "Since when has trying to find out why someone died in suspicious circumstances been overstepping the mark?"

"Progress briefing tomorrow. Don't forget." The phone went dead in her hand.

"You can just go to hell, chief inspector," she muttered, tossing the phone back on to the worktop where it spun in circles before coming to rest behind the toaster. Laufey looked at her mother with wide eyes.

"All right, Mum?"

"Yes. It's just something you need to learn as you go through life, my love."

"What's that?"

"That most of the people in charge are idiots."

"You have to find these — these — these *bastards*!"

Sigurjóna Huldudóttir's composure had disappeared entirely. Her shoulders shook and her voice trembled in fury.

"There's nothing more I can do, Sigurjóna," Bjarni Jón Bjarnason said in a voice he hoped sounded soothing, while bracing himself for the storm. "The computer crime squad have been investigating this for weeks without getting anywhere and I've badgered the Minister of Foreign Affairs to put pressure on countries that host these websites, but it's not as if Iceland has so much weight that we can bully other governments," he added bitterly.

"But it's just disgusting," she spat. "Absolutely revolting. How do they find these things out? Have you seen this?"

"No, I haven't," he lied.

"Just look at it. Go on, read it. Look what this scumbag is saying." She wrenched the laptop around on the table.

"Who?"

"Just read the bloody thing!"

Bjarni Jón read. He recognized every one of the blogger's targets easily enough, and anyone with more than a passing acquaintance with any of the gossip magazines would be able to do the same.

Sigurjóna stood up and paced the living room from end to end, smoking furiously, and spun back so that the parquet floor squealed under her heel.

"Have you read it? Well, have you?"

"Yes, I have now."

"And?"

"And what?"

She gathered her breath. "And what the hell are you going to do about it?" she shrieked, while Bjarni Jón quailed at the onslaught.

"Look, Jóna. We've had this bloody site closed down already a couple of times, and it just pops up somewhere else. The blog's hosted in some former Soviet state where all that counts is money and they don't reply to official communications if they don't feel like it."

Sigurjóna threw herself into a chair, looked around briefly for an ashtray and ground out her cigarette clumsily on a saucer that still had a cup in it, spilling cup and cold coffee on to the table. Anger was something she did well and she knew it.

"How does this bastard know all these things?" she hissed.

"Like what things?" Bjarni Jón asked.

"Like how Inga Katrín had a nose job at the same time as she had her boobs fixed?"

"How should I know?"

"And how does this shitbag know about . . . Sugarplum?"

Bjarni Jón winced. This one was painful.

"Well, how do they know?" she yelled, bringing her fury to the whirling climax that Bjarni Jón had known was coming. "That's our name! Nobody else's! Unless you've been whispering something in your secretary's ear!"

"Jóna, please. Calm down."

"Why the hell should I?"

Bjarni Jón summoned his scattered courage and tried to keep his head high. "Look, Jóna, I wouldn't touch Birna even if it was on offer. She's as cold as a dead fish."

"And how do you know? Tried it on, have you?"

In spite of herself, Sigurjóna was starting to enjoy herself. Occasionally she revelled in letting her temper and tongue have free rein and, however much Bjarni Jón was tempted to yell back, his self-control was never allowed to slip that far.

"Listen. Birna is completely frigid. I have it on good authority. She's not been involved with a man since she left university. She gets off on her career, nothing else."

"All right, then."

Bjarni Jón stifled a sigh of relief as Sigurjóna's temper suddenly cooled, but he knew at the same time that his wife's icy side could be just as unpleasant.

"Are you going to do something about this Skandalblogging arsehole?" she demanded quietly.

"Jóna, my love, I've already done everything I can."

Sigurjóna sniffed and tapped another cigarette from its packet. "If you don't, I will."

"What?"

"You heard me."

"How?"

"Maybe I'll ask Mr Hardy to keep his eyes open for me."

Bjarni Jón caught his breath. "Jóna, I'm warning you. These aren't nice people and they aren't the sort you want to owe too many favours."

"I don't care. I have to stop this. I can't stand it any more. And if you don't do something, I'll find someone who will."

CHAPTER FOUR

Friday, 29 August

Haddi and Snorri were already at the station when Gunna arrived, out of breath, irritable and late.

"Afternoon," Haddi said.

"Hell. Sorry, Haddi. Laufey desperately needed a lift to the stables this morning and she didn't bother to tell me until two minutes before I was ready to leave. Children, nothing but trouble from day one," she grumbled.

"Never had a moment's trouble with mine," Haddi said with the satisfied look of a proud parent on his face.

"Haddi, my dear friend. That's entirely due to the fact that you had the sense to stay at sea until your lads had grown up a bit."

"Well, there is that," he agreed and bustled to the spitting percolator. "Not putting you off, are we, Snorri?"

Haddi put three steaming mugs on the table and sat back down again. "So, what's on the agenda for Hvalvík's guardians of law and order, chief?"

Gunna came back to the front office from her own room holding a batch of papers which she slapped on the table.

"Simple. Haddi, I need you to mind the shop. Snorri, you can take the smart Volvo and go up to the InterAlu compound. Introduce yourself to the manager there. He's called Sveinn, nice enough bloke, but don't make any promises. Most of what we have to deal with here at the moment is traffic to and from the InterAlu site, which is the smelter they're building on the far side of the harbour. There are dozens of trucks every day and every now and again there are low-loaders with the heavy equipment."

"They go right through the town?"

"Not now. The back road was built up in the spring, so most of it can bypass the town itself, and sometime in the autumn they're due to start dredging the harbour to deepen it, after which they'll start bringing in the very heavy stuff by sea. All right?"

"Yup. I'll go and see Sveinn. What's happening with the other construction — the hydroelectric one?"

Gunna sighed. "That's going to be a nightmare when it really gets into gear. There's going to be a huge volume of traffic going both ways when they start clearing the site. Haven't you been up there?"

"Not since the project started," Snorri said.

"It's a bloody awful road up there past Stjáni at Læk's place. But it's their problem, so they can sort it out when the time comes. All right? You'd better be back from the InterAlu place before eleven so Haddi can do his usual tour of the docks."

Haddi smiled to himself.

"Don't get the car dirty, or Haddi'll be furious."

"And what might you be up to today, Gunna?" Haddi asked.

"I have a meeting with Vilhjálmur Traustason to brief him on our dead guy's case in half an hour. And considering it's a good forty minutes' drive to Keflavík from here, I reckon I'm going to find the old fool in a bad mood when I get there."

She planted her cap squarely on her head and made for the door.

"So I'll see you boys later. Look after the place for me."

Gunna didn't break any speed limits getting to Keflavík, although by the time the Hvalvík station's second-best Volvo pulled up outside the Keflavík police station she was running almost an hour late.

"What brings you over here, darling?"

Bjössi's question was her first greeting inside the door, where Bjössi was standing with a mug in one hand and a pack of filterless Camels in the other on his way to the back door for a quiet smoke in the bright morning sunshine.

"Can't keep away. Nothing like a visit to the big city to remind a girl of what she's missing out in the country."

"That's what I keep telling you," Bjössi agreed, pushing backwards through the doors with his hands full. "See you in a minute . . ."

"Ah, Gunnhildur, I'm terribly sorry to have to keep you waiting," a breathless Vilhjálmur Traustason apologized, bustling past in the opposite direction. "A meeting with the Sheriff took a little longer than anticipated," he explained as if to a wayward child, while Gunna strode along in his wake.

In his small office Vilhjálmur waved Gunna to a chair and carefully placed his cap on the top of his filing cabinet on his way to his own chair. He leaned on his desk and placed his palms together in a steeple in front of his face.

"Now," he said, as if preparing himself for action. "The drowned man, Einar Eyjólfur Einarsson."

"You have my interim report already, so you know everything I do for the moment."

"I want to know what you think."

"I think he was murdered."

"Really?" There was a brief note of fright in his voice. "Why? The man had a very high blood alcohol content and Sigmar at pathology says drowning was the cause of death."

"That's right. But we don't understand how a man on a night out in Reykjavík managed to drown in an obscure backwater a hundred kilometres away."

"You think it's suspicious, not just an unfortunate accident?"

"Of course I do! His blood alcohol content was so high that the man could probably hardly walk, let alone get from a bar on Laugarvegur to Hvalvík without some help. I understand that Einar Eyjólfur wasn't a habitual drinker at all — quite the opposite."

"Of course this matter warrants further investigation, but it isn't a murder inquiry until there's evidence of foul play. There'll be an inquest, but unless there's evidence to the contrary, the verdict will certainly be death by misadventure."

"It stinks. There's just so much that needs to be explained."

"Well, I suppose you'd better do your best. But I'm concerned that this could be a waste of your time. Find out what you can in the next week or so, and then we'll see. Hm?"

Gunna knew that Vilhjálmur was a man who played everything by the book and would sooner cut off a hand than break a rule. She desperately wanted to ask why he was so unconcerned about Einar Eyjólfur's death, but restrained herself.

"I could do with some help on this one. CID are too busy with narcotics as it is. Can I have an officer for a week to help me out with the leg work?"

Vilhjálmur lifted his steepled hands to bring the fingertips in line with his prominent nose.

"We are overstretched as it is and I don't have a single spare officer at my disposal, at least not now that Snorri Hilmarsson has been transferred to the Hvalvík station," he said pointedly. "However, I had in fact anticipated your request and have already discussed this. The city force will be working with you on this case and Sævaldur Bogason will be assisting you."

Gunna groaned inwardly. "Bloody hell. The man's like a bull in a china shop."

"Sævaldur is an experienced and effective officer who gets results," Vilhjálmur said coldly.

"Fair enough," Gunna sighed. "I'll get over there and talk to him."

"That would be advisable," Vilhjálmur said, picking up the old-fashioned fountain pen from his desk, his attention already on the top report in a pile, indicating that the meeting was at an end.

"Do you mind if I ask some background questions?" Skúli asked timidly.

"Fire away, young man. If there's anything I don't want to tell you, you'll find out."

Skúli sipped his Coke. They were sitting at one of the few small tables at a truckstop at the top of the heath halfway between Hvalvík and the handful of small communities to the east. Rain from a sudden shower pelted down outside from clouds as black as inky fingerprints on the western sky and formed rivers that flowed down the truckstop's windows.

"How does the station at Hvalvík run?"

"It's not a main police station, so it's staffed during the day. Normally there're three of us: me, Haddi the old guy and Snorri the new boy. We belong to Keflavík, so out of hours any police services have to come from there — in theory. In reality the three of us are in and around Hvalvík most of the time. Then we have the rural areas we have to visit on occasions, like today."

"So you do a nine-to-five day?"

"It doesn't work like that, I'm afraid. We run watches outside station hours so one of us is always on call all the time, so you can be at work even if you're asleep at home. I like to keep work and personal life separate as far as is possible in a little place like this, but a lot of the time it's just impossible."

"How do you mean?" Skúli asked.

"Well, in Reykjavík or even Akureyri, you can change out of uniform and not be a copper any more. You can't do that here. Everyone knows you're the police, whether you're in uniform or mowing your lawn."

"So it really is a full-time job?"

"Absolutely. And that's something that people can fail to grasp. Yesterday evening some kids were out playing behind the school and they found a mobile phone somebody had lost. They could have taken it home and given it to their parents to hand in at the station, or tried to find the owner, or just kept it, I suppose. But no, they knocked on my door and gave it to me, because they all know where Gunna the Cop lives and it didn't occur to them that I might be off duty."

"Is this a problem for you?"

"Not at all. It's just part of being on the force in a rural area. It's part of the package. But it's the same in town to some extent. Your neighbours are always going to know you're in the force and they might treat you slightly differently, or they might not."

Skúli wrote hasty notes on his pad.

"So. Young man. Tell me, why Hvalvík?"

"Don't know really. It was partly my idea, I suppose, and Reynir Óli said it might make a good feature."

"Who's Reynir Óli?"

"My editor. It was all set up through the police PR department. I asked the lady there for somewhere rural to go to, but not too far from the city, so she called back the next day and suggested Hvalvík or somewhere up in Snæfellsnes."

"So you chose Hvalvík."

"Yup. Closer to town," Skúli said, delicately wiping the detritus of hot dog from his chin. "And it sounded a bit more interesting as well," he added sheepishly.

"Why?"

"Well, one of my colleagues said it might be a better feature because there are so few women in the police."

"You what?"

"He reckoned it might make a good story because there aren't many female police officers of your experience."

"You mean all the policewomen you see are these young ones who've been in the job for five minutes and you might get something more out of an old bag like me?"

"Um. Yes."

Gunna grinned. "Good answer. When being questioned by the law, just tell the truth. And who told you this?"

"Jonni Kristinns, the political editor."

"I know Jonni well enough from when I was in the city force. He's a friend of the bloke who was my partner at the time."

"Your husband?"

Gunna looked sourly across the table at Skúli. "No. My police partner when I was on the city force. You work together a lot of the time and I suppose in many ways your partner is someone you get to know better than a husband or a wife."

"Is this guy still in the police?"

"Bjössi? Yeah. But he moved out of the city as well, and out of uniform. He's in CID in Keflavík now."

"What's his name?"

"Björn Valsson, known as Bjössi. I haven't seen Jonni in years. He was on TV as well, wasn't he?"

"I think so, a while ago. He's one of those old guys who can't keep away from paper."

Skúli was acutely aware that he had asked few of the questions he had lined up, but had again ended up doing most of the talking while Gunna asked the questions.

"How long have you been in the police?" he asked finally.

"Sixteen years, with a break in the middle."

"What for?"

"You know, children, all that stuff."

"So you're married?"

"Not any more."

"Is it long since you split up?"

Gunna gave Skúli a sharp look. "Is this really necessary? The last thing I want to see is my private life splashed across *Dagurinn* on a Saturday morning."

"No, it's not for print. It's just, you know, for me to build up a picture of you," Skúli gabbled. "I don't want to put in too much personal stuff, but people like to see it."

"All right," Gunna said unwillingly. "I have a son from a relationship when I was in my teens. Gísli's nineteen now. I have a thirteen-year-old daughter with my husband, who died eight years ago in an accident that I don't want to discuss. Is that enough for you?"

"Plenty, thank you," Skúli said gratefully. He had noticed the broad gold ring on Gunna's finger and wondered why she had never mentioned a husband. "How did you wind up in a place like this?"

"You mean, what's a girl like you doing in a nice place like this?"

"Yeah. I mean, no," Skúli stumbled. "Sorry. That's not what I meant. Are you from around here originally?"

Gunna smothered a grin. Making the lad gabble with embarrassment was becoming a source of light relief during an otherwise dull day.

"No. I'm not from round here. I'm from Vestureyri."

"What? Right up there in the western fjords? Wow. So, why Hvalvík?"

"All right, here we go. I was brought up in Vestureyri, worked in the fish when I was twelve, all that stuff. When I was nineteen one of my uncles suggested I could be a copper for the summer. I thought — why not? My mum was happy to babysit for me. I gave it a try as a probational constable for a few months and got a kick out of it. Less money than working in the fish, but a lot more interesting."

"So you stayed with it?"

"Yup. Applied to the police college and was accepted straight away. There weren't many women going into the force then, so they were glad to get applications, although my family weren't too pleased when I moved south for the winter so I could go to college."

Skúli decided to try Gunna's tactic and sat in silence for her to continue.

"So, we moved back west in the summer and I was on the force in Vestureyri for a few years. Then I met Raggi and moved south to live with him, and transferred to the city force."

Skúli sat in expectant silence, already chastened once, while Gunna's face hardened.

"After my husband died I was on compassionate leave and then sick leave for the best part of a year. The posting at Hvalvík came up and I applied and got it, which was something of a surprise. And I've been here ever since," Gunna concluded with a deep breath.

"What, er — what happened?"

Gunna glanced at him sharply and Skúli felt he had been slapped. "Are you listening or not?"

"Listening."

"Like I said, it was an accident. I don't want to talk about it. You can look it up in the cuttings, February 2000. That's the end of the potted biography, and I don't expect to see any of that in print. Understood?" Gunna instructed with a chill in her voice.

"Understood."

"The rain's stopped," Gunna observed, looking out at the sun bursting through the ragged clouds. "If you've finished eating, we can be on our way."

CHAPTER FIVE

Saturday, 30 August

"He got pissed and passed out, fell in the water. Drowned while unconscious," said the barrel-chested man squeezed into the passenger seat.

"Sævaldur, we know that," Gunna told him sharply. "How the hell did he get from a bar in Reykjavík to Hvalvík harbour? He didn't drive and he was already so drunk he could hardly walk. So who helped him?"

Sævaldur Bogason yawned and tried to stretch. Gunna frowned, drumming on the wheel with the fingers of one hand. She wondered whether or not to call home and find out if Laufey was out of bed. She stifled the idea straight away, telling herself that there was practically no chance that her daughter would be awake at this early hour of a Saturday morning without a particularly good reason.

Gunna forced her thoughts back to Einar Eyjólfur. She was concerned that her interviews at Spearpoint had yielded nothing concrete beyond a picture of a young man who kept very much to himself and did his job well. Unusually, he had no immediate family and only a small circle of friends made up mostly of past and present colleagues from work, with the exception Dísa had mentioned of Egill Grímsson.

Dísa's comments that Einar Eyjólfur had been worried during his last few months of life stuck in Gunna's mind, especially as Sigurjóna claimed to have been unaware of anything out of the ordinary. She made a mental note to search for Egill Grímsson's name among filed reports.

"So, where are we now?" Sævaldur asked. "I vote we just sit here until it stops raining."

"This is Reykjavík. It's not going to stop raining."

Gunna scanned the notes she had been keeping as they tracked Einar Eyjólfur's last night. He had been with Jón Oddur and the Danish chewing gum manufacturers on Monday evening. After a meal at a Chinese restaurant on Laugarvegur, the group had moved on to a faux-Irish bar called McCuddy's. Around eleven, the Danes politely bowed out, pleading an early flight home the next day, while Einar and Jón Oddur had carried on to several bars, of which the Emperor was the last, a bar where trouble could generally be easily found.

Gunna looked up through the rain-streaked windscreen at the Emperor's windows across the street. The place looked no more inviting than had McCuddy's half an hour ago. A narrow face peered out at the street through the glass panels of the door and vanished.

"Come on then," Gunna instructed, swinging open the car door.

It was dark inside the deserted bar. Chairs were still stacked on tables and the floor was littered with last night's debris.

"Hey! Anybody about?" Sævaldur called out.

The lights flickered on and the face Gunna had seen at the window scowled around a door.

"What do you want?"

"A word with the manager," Gunna replied, stepping forward. At the sight of the uniform, the man scowled again. "Monday evening. Who was here then?"

"That was days ago. How should I know?"

"You mean you don't keep staff records?"

"Well, yeah. Of course I do."

"Then you'd better look it up."

In the bar's cramped back office the man flipped through a diary while trying to stop himself yawning.

"OK," he announced at length. "Me, Adda, Noi and Gugga on the bar, Geiri and Gústi on the door."

"Full names? And is that all of them?"

The man groaned.

"Look," Sævaldur broke in. "We're not looking for dodgy work permits and I couldn't give a shit about who's working on the black. Just tell us who these people are, all right?"

The manager nodded his understanding, tore a page from the back of the diary and wrote a series of names on it, adding phone numbers from the mobile hanging on a cord around his neck.

"Thank you," Gunna said smoothly as he handed over the sheet of paper. "Now, you wouldn't recall this face, would you?"

She held up Einar Eyjólfur's photograph.

"Dunno, sweetheart. Get all sorts in here. Ask the guys on the doors. They'd remember if there was any trouble."

Satisfied, Gunna put the photo back in her folder.

"Geiri and Gústi. Where do these guys live?"

"I don't know," the man groaned again.

"Surely you have a record of all your staff's legal addresses?" Gunna said, handing back the sheet of names.

"Shit. All right."

He scribbled on the page and Gunna noticed that there was no need to look anything up.

"Thanks. Now, I'm sure there won't be any need for you to call these guys and warn them that we're on the way, will there? Any more than there'll be any need for us to pass anything on to the tax office?"

She raised an eyebrow. Boxed into a corner, the man shook his head.

30-08-2008, 1205

Skandalblogger writes:

It's who you know . . .

Just how does Scaramanga stay open? Mundi Grétars still has the enviable reputation of running Iceland's last-remaining house of ill repute. Of course, we all know that the place is supposed to be a club like all the others. But unlike Odal and Bohem, where what you see is pretty much all you're going to get, Mundi has a different set of rules. He knows that not discouraging the dancers from having their out-of-hours freelance activities doesn't do the bar takings any harm at all.

So just how much public money goes across Mundi Grétars' bar, and how much of it makes its way back again? Skandalblogger hears that there's a surprising number of our elders and betters who find their way to Scaramanga now and again, and some of these fine gentlemen are so concerned about the young ladies' well-being that they send after-hours taxis to drive them home . . .

A little bird whispers to Skandalblogger that several of our respected public servants, including a gentlemen's club of highly placed law enforcement officials, have repeatedly torpedoed civic plans to withdraw Scaramanga's licence. One of these guys, so we're told, has formed a frequent and meaningful relationship with a young lady who dances. We're sure his missus would be delighted if she knew . . .

We're the soul of discretion . . .

Bæjó!

"You know either of these guys, Geiri and Gústi?" Gunna asked as she parked the car outside the block of flats in Breidholt among everything from wheelless wrecks perched on blocks to shiny SUVs.

"Gústi's an old favourite. Goes back a long way, assault, dope, the usual." Sævaldur grinned. "It'll be interesting to catch up with him again. Ágúst Ásgeirsson, his name is. Didn't you come across him when you were on the city force?"

"You mean Gústi the Gob? Remember him well, a right creep he used to be. Wonder if he's mellowed since we last met?"

The outside door was wedged open and Sævaldur stepped inside to peer at the mailboxes. He wrinkled his nose at the sour smell in the block's lobby.

"You've forgotten what fun it is going to places like this, eh, Gunna?" he said grimly as they ascended the bare concrete stairs.

"Not having to deal with slobs like these is one of the perks of being a country copper. Maybe you should try for a transfer to Skagaströnd?"

"Bloody hell, no. I don't know how you manage with all those yokels. Right, this should be it," he said, hammering on the door.

There was silence. Sævaldur hammered again.

"Gústi! Open the bloody door, will you? It's the law!"

An eye appeared at the peephole and after a moment the door inched open to reveal a stubbled face, puffy with sleep.

"What do the coppers want with me?" he growled.

"So you do remember us? How nice. Open up, we need to talk."

"Got a warrant?"

"Don't talk crap. I said talk, not search."

The little two-room flat was bare. A full-barrelled snore could be heard from the flat's one bedroom. Sævaldur and Gunna took kitchen chairs while Gústi sat back on the sofa, flexing generous biceps and letting the towel he was wearing slip open, and leering at Gunna.

"Who's the bird, Sævaldur?" he demanded. "I like big strong girls."

Gunna ignored the question and held up Einar Eyjólfur's picture. "Seen this guy?"

"Dunno," Gústi replied without looking.

"He's dead."

"Poor bloke," Gústi said flatly.

"He was in the Emperor on Monday evening, probably around or shortly after midnight."

"Shit, that was days ago. How should I know?"

Gunna pretended to consult her notes, looking down at the paperwork in front of her as Gústi spread his knees a little wider.

"Ágúst Ásgeirsson," she muttered as if speaking to herself, and looked up sharply. "This could well be a murder investigation, and you're one of the last people to see this person alive. I can see you've had convictions for assault in the past, according to your record. I'd like to be able to rule you out as a suspect, but with this in front of me, I could have doubts."

Gunna was amused to see a brief look of fury in the man's eyes, quickly replaced with irritation and finally with concern at the realization that not cooperating would do him little good.

"Yeah, I seen him."

"When? On that night?"

"Dunno. A few nights ago. Got into a ruck with some bloke in the bog. Must have trod on his toe or something."

"And what happened? Who was he arguing with?"

"Don't know. Don't care," the surly mountain of a man replied, clearly not used to being overawed by the police. Gunna eyed him frostily, and scribbled notes in silence for long enough for Gústi to start fidgeting with the errant towel.

"Tell me more."

To Gunna's relief, Gústi closed his knees and sat up as his confidence ebbed away.

"I heard a racket from the Gents and went to check it out. Happens all the time, two drunks having an argument, and one of them was him," he said, suddenly cooperative and pointing at the dead man's photo. "That's all. Told 'em to pack it in or get out. End of story," he added lamely.

"And the other man?"

"Dunno. Big bloke. Foreign. That's all."

"Time?"

"Dunno. Early. One-ish."

"And what happened?"

"Dunno. Wasn't any more trouble, so they must have packed it in or fucked off out."

"As for this foreign bloke. Description?"

"Tall. My height. Hell, it was dark, y'know?"

"Thank you," Gunna said smoothly, rising to her feet as Sævaldur hauled himself upright. "You've been a great help."

"That's all right. Always happy to help police ladies," he replied with a grin, before shooting a scowl towards Sævaldur.

"Don't push it, Gústi. We can always do you for indecent exposure, just like last time. Remember?" Gunna asked sweetly.

"How do you know? That was years ago . . ." he protested as Gunna stepped out of the flat without waiting for Sævaldur to follow.

CHAPTER SIX

Monday, 1 September

Gunna took advantage of Snorri and Haddi being out of the station to shove open the long lower panel of the office window and light a furtive Prince, in defiance of state policy on smoking throughout government buildings. Without feeling even slightly guilty, she leaned back in her chair and read through her interim report on Einar Eyjólfur Einarsson's miserable death.

Nobody appeared to have seen Einar Eyjólfur, 178cm tall, short fair hair, dressed in a pair of jeans and a black shirt, leaving the Emperor sometime in the early hours of 26 August.

With no more evidence to work on and nothing to indicate violence, the case would probably be shelved indefinitely, an unsolved case to haunt her on sleepless nights. Gústi the Gob was not a realistic suspect and the news that Sævaldur had brought him in for questioning was disturbing. She hoped it was for no good reason other than for Sævaldur to vent his spleen on someone.

"But why Hvalvík?" Gunna muttered to herself.

"Chief?"

A door banged and Gunna dropped the butt of her cigarette out of the window before closing it. "In here, Haddi."

She decided to end her interim report and hit Save before standing up. There were other matters that needed to be attended to as well as Einar Eyjólfur Einarsson's case.

"All right?" Haddi asked, sniffing the air accusingly.

"Yup. Fine. I'm going to lunch if you'll be so good as to man the barricades."

Outside Hafnarkaffi, Gunna debated whether to have lunch there or go home for a sandwich. She weighed the idea of a hot meal, heavy on the potatoes and swimming in thick sauce in a noisy cafeteria, against tuna and tomato sandwiches washed down with fruit juice while skimming yesterday's papers.

Hot and noisy won. Inside, she picked up a tray and filled it with a dish of cauliflower soup and a plate of fried fish and boiled potatoes. Looking around for a seat, she noticed an arm waving to her.

"Gunna. Here."

"Hey. Stefán, when did you get in?"

"Just now. The missus is at work, so I thought I'd drop in here and catch up on the news."

A cousin of Gunna's husband, Stefán Jónsson had gone out of his way to take her son Gísli under his wing after Raggi's death. There had long been an unspoken bond between her and Stefán built on deep respect, but which had never become an outright friendship. Gísli had followed Stefán to sea on one of the trawlers owned by the village's only large fishing company after

Stefán had gone out of his way to put a word in on his behalf.

"Good trip?" Gunna asked, starting with the soup, contrary to local custom.

"Not bad. A hundred and twenty tonnes. Blowing a bastard all the way home, though."

"Where were you?"

"Deep off the west."

"So, will my Gísli be going there this year as well?"

"No. It's the Barents Sea for them. We took their quota as well as ours last year. This year they can have ours. I'm getting too old for these long trips."

"Get away, Stefán. There're years left in a young man like you."

Stefán impatiently drummed his fingers on the table.

"What's on your mind?" Gunna asked, recognizing the symptoms, in particular the heavy grey eyebrows swooping down over a frown as he tried to understand something he hadn't fully got to grips with.

"I was coming to see you later today anyway. About this chap."

"Which chap?"

"The one you found out there down at the dock."

Gunna looked up from her meal. "And? What about him?"

"I'm damned sure I saw him, or his car, or something."

"Tell me more," she said softly, knowing that there would be little need to ask many questions.

"It was the night we sailed, Monday – Tuesday. I was up very early and went up the valley to have a look at my stables and had a drive round the dock too. You know, like you do."

"I know."

"The boys look after the horses for me. But it's in the blood. We were sailing at five that morning and I don't like to go without seeing them off."

Gunna nodded, lunch forgotten in front of her.

"Well, it was still dark, of course. Anyway, someone was there on the quay, which is a bit odd, but I thought nothing of it at the time. Who was the dead man, anyway?"

"A kind of yuppie type who worked for a PR company in Reykjavík."

Stefán sniffed. "Then what the bloody hell's someone like that doing out here in the middle of the night?"

Gunna thought carefully while Stefán looked expectantly at her. It was unfortunate that the only potential eyewitness to what had happened up there had spent the last week at sea, but if this unidentified vehicle had anything to do with Einar Eyjólfur's disappearance, then it pinpointed the time and date of the crime.

"Anything else, Stefán? Make, model, number, anything like that?"

"Big jeep sort of thing, not a Land Rover. Dark colour, black, blue, maybe? Couldn't guess what kind, though. I only saw it for a moment as it went past. It looked pretty new to me, but what do I know? But I can tell you there was a JA in the number. That's all."

"JA?"

"That's right. JA, Jóhanna Arnarsdóttir. It's the missus's initials, otherwise I wouldn't have noticed."

"Thank you, Stefán. That's a big help," Gunna said finally. "Now, if you'll come up to the station with me for half an hour, I'd like to ask you to give me a statement. And then I have a report to rewrite, and some questions to ask," she added grimly.

CHAPTER SEVEN

Tuesday, 2 September

"Gunnhildur?"

Vilhjálmur Traustason's hair was not so much carefully brushed as painstakingly sculpted. Youthful dark waves had long since given way to a thick distinguished grey that swept back from a parting as straight as a line ruled on a page. Admittedly the grey made him look older than his years. But all the same, it suited a senior officer, it suited his spare frame that had once been athletic, and he felt it suited the gravitas he wanted to project.

"Yes, Vilhjálmur, what can I do for you?"

Gunna turned to face the chief inspector. She had hoped to make one of her regular visits to the Keflavík station without running into Vilhjálmur Traustason, but there was no such luck on this occasion.

"I wanted to speak to you about, er . . ." he mumbled. "I wanted to speak to you. We had better go to my office," he decided.

Vilhjálmur shut the door and waved Gunna to a seat, where she watched him as he scanned his desk.

"Sævaldur has charged this man, Ágúst Ásgeirsson, with the murder of Einar Eyjólfur Einarsson."

"What? Gústi the Gob? He's a nasty piece of work, but he's not up to murder," Gunna said angrily. "That bloody Sævaldur, always taking the shortest cut he can."

Vilhjálmur looked pained. "Sævaldur is a very competent officer and he —"

"Gets results, as you keep telling me," Gunna finished for him. "And how often do they get released as soon as it comes to court? How many times have Sævaldur's victims sued the police for wrongful arrest or whatever?"

Vilhjálmur Traustason was certain that he had a winning smile that he could treat his staff to when they needed his support. But in reality the sight of a slab of pearly dentistry without a shred of warmth to go with it was chilling rather than encouraging.

"Well. Your record of arrests is actually rather impressive," he smiled. "Very good work with the arson case and with that fisherman landing over his quota."

"The arsonists were a bunch of fourteen-year-olds who didn't need a lot of tracking down and you know perfectly well that Albert Jónasson's case was all down to the Fisheries Office and not me."

"Still, you were the arresting officer and that's what counts. Results," Vilhjálmur said with an imperious lifting of his angular nose. Gunna suddenly realized that he reminded her of nobody more than a Roman emperor. A toga would suit him.

"It's a crying shame we have to arrest people like Albert for just catching a few bloody fish. The man's a perfectly law-abiding character and —"

She stopped short, seeing Vilhjálmur's eyes glazing over.

"We'd best leave the politics to the politicians, shall we?" he said, unable to conceal his lack of interest. "What I wanted to discuss with you is the review procedure."

"Review procedure?"

"I've already had the files emailed to you, so you can assess your team's performance against a set of criteria and we can collate statistics on effectiveness, initiative, et cetera, all of which can be cross-referenced against age, experience and a whole range of other factors. You'd be amazed at what a useful tool this can be in assessing which staff are best placed in which spheres of activity. Which areas our training needs to be focused on. That kind of thing. Spreadsheets are marvellous things."

"More paperwork?" Gunna asked, trying unsuccessfully not to sound sarcastic.

"The thing is, Gunnhildur," he continued, as if she had not said a word, "we have been working on identifying officers who might be suitable for new roles, and you are one of those we have identified."

Gunna stared, waiting for the next revelation.

"You see," he went on smoothly, "in some divisions we have isolated personnel resource shortfalls that we are looking at rectifying."

"Which means you're short of staff here and there, and you want to shuffle people about to plug the gaps?"

"Erm. Those weren't my words, but in essence, well, yes."

"And?"

"As you are aware, there are difficulties with personnel and although recruitment is improving we have a problem with retention. So we have a need to deploy people to meet their optimum potential."

"Which means?"

Vilhjálmur grimaced. He was getting a familiar sinking feeling that he was no longer running this meeting. Leaning forward, he looked down his nose at Gunna sitting in front of his desk.

"Which means," he continued in what he hoped was a tone of voice that would spin the conversation around, "that as a skilled investigator, if you were to put in an application for a vacancy in detection, there is every possibility that you would be successful."

Gunna sat in amazed silence for a moment.

"Does this take you by surprise?"

"It does," she was forced to admit.

"It would mean stepping up a grade, as the post carries an inspector's rank."

"And what's the catch?"

Vilhjálmur looked pained. "Catch? What do you mean?"

"I'm sorry. I've never believed in free lunches. So, being an experienced investigator, I'm naturally always looking for what's underneath. Force of habit."

He cleared his throat, looked upwards and Gunna thought again of how a laurel wreath would suit him, nestling around those grey waves.

"New grade effective from the first of October, you'd take over your new post on the first of December and you would have two months' leave after stepping down at Hvalvík to relocate."

"Aha. Where to?"

"There would be a reasonable relocation grant. The post is with the Egilstadir force, based in Seydisfjördur."

"So there is a catch," Gunna said with satisfaction.

"It depends how you wish to look at it. Some officers would see it as an opportunity. A small force, fairly quiet, a chance to make an impression with the switch to plain clothes. You aren't tempted?"

She thought quickly. The east coast, deep fjords and high mountains, virtually as far away from Hvalvík and Vilhjálmur Traustason as could physically be possible without leaving the country. A pay grade up in salary wouldn't be unwelcome, though.

"I'm wondering what I've done, or haven't done, to deserve this. To be honest, it's rather unexpected. Have I upset someone, or what?"

"Not at all," he purred. "There's a changing demographic in the east, a large immigrant population, and a major narcotics problem with smuggling that urgently needs to be addressed, so the Egilstadir Sheriff's Office has put together an action plan with funding for additional officers to bolster their efforts on narcotics in particular."

"How long do I have to think about it?"

"Not long. There are other candidates in the running."

"All right. I'll think it over. Anyway, is that all?"

* * *

The man's face was grey with fatigue, even under the orange cast of the lights in the interview room at Reykjavík's Hverfisgata police station. All the pride had disappeared from Gústi the Gob as he leaned forward on the table, stubbled head in his hands.

"Look. I've told you. I saw him that night in the bogs, told him and that other bloke to shut it or fuck off out. That's it. End of story."

Sævaldur sat back in his chair as Gunna stood uncomfortably by the door.

"Come on, Gústi," Sævaldur said in a patient voice. "You've got plenty of form. You and your mates turned the guy over and dumped him out of town when it went wrong. Come on, come clean."

"No. No. No."

"Gústi, we've been here all day yesterday and all day today and we've got all night and all day tomorrow. And all day the next day."

"It wasn't me." A hint of desperation crept into his voice as this time he smacked the table between them with the flat of one vast hand. "I'm telling you, it was nothing to do with me."

Sævaldur's voice hardened. "So where did the cash come from?"

"Savings," Gústi mumbled. "I saved it all up."

"You mean you had a spending spree on Einar Eyjólfur's credit card? Come on, Gústi. We found the receipts in your flat. We know it was you."

"'No. It wasn't me did him in. I want a lawyer, now."

Sævaldur tried to outstare him but failed.

"All right," he admitted. "All right. We'll get your legal eagle in. But it doesn't look good for you, Gústi. You could get ten years for this. You did five years before, so you know what it's like."

"It wasn't me. I found the wallet in the bogs after we closed. All right, the old woman bought a few things with the bloke's card, but that's all."

"OK, so that's your story."

Sævaldur stood up, reached for the tape recorder and switched it off.

"Now I'm going outside for a smoke and you're staying here," he sneered, shoving his chair back. "D'you want to take over?"

Gunna shook her head. "I'd like a word outside. Can Viggó sit in for ten minutes?"

Sævaldur knocked on the door and it whispered open.

"Viggó, would you?" Gunna asked the thickset officer outside as he waddled into the room and sat down with the air of a man ready for the long haul.

"Well, Gústi. Haven't seen you for a while. How's tricks, then?" he asked as Gunna and Sævaldur left the room.

At the back of the building, Sævaldur and Gunna lit up. Although she had been inside the bowels of the building since the middle of the day, she was still surprised to see that night had fallen. It had started to rain and fat drops pattered around them.

"I don't like it," Gunna said. "It stinks."

"Come on. We have a crim with form and a link to the dead guy."

"Did you search his place yesterday?"

"Yup. Found your guy's credit card under the bathroom sink, receipts in the kitchen bin. It fits."

"It doesn't fit. Einar Eyjólfur disappeared around midnight. We know that Gústi was on the door until after four in the morning."

"We can work around that. Gústi has mates."

"The barmaids confirmed Gústi was there until they locked up. Even that Thai girl who doesn't speak Icelandic."

Sævaldur ground out his cigarette against the wall. "What's the matter with you? Don't you want to get a result on this? Is this PMS week, or what?"

"Oh, for crying out loud . . ."

"No, come on, tell me."

"Inside. It's bloody cold out here."

In the empty cafeteria they sat face to face over a table and Gunna wondered if Sævaldur felt he was back in the interview room. In the far corner of the room a TV set showed a topical news programme with a Member of Parliament being interviewed. Gunna turned the sound down to a murmur.

"So, what's the problem?" Sævaldur asked pugnaciously. "Crim. Link. Dead man. It adds up."

"It doesn't add up. You won't get a conviction without more evidence and I don't think you'll find any."

"We can make it fit. I can get a confession and a result on this," Sævaldur argued and Gunna noticed how "we" had been replaced with "I".

"And whoever did this gets away while a brainless minor crim with a record of nothing but petty crime is banged up. That leaves someone very dangerous out there."

"Upstairs wants this sorted out quickly."

"Quickly doesn't mean hanging a murder on an innocent man."

"Gústi the Gob isn't innocent."

"He is of this, whatever else he may have on his conscience."

"He's done plenty. Gústi doesn't have a conscience."

"If you think you can get a confession out of him, good luck to you. There's no evidence on Einar Eyjólfur's body, no marks, no bruises, nothing to show any rough handling. I think you're wasting your time."

Sævaldur drained his mug and rattled his chair back as he stood up. "Well, I'm going to batter it out of him whether he likes it or not."

"Sit down, will you? There's something I want to know about," Gunna said sharply and the tone of her voice prompted Sævaldur to do as he was asked.

"What?"

"Egill Grímsson. Tell me about him."

"Who?"

"He was run over and killed in Grafarvogur in March."

"What the hell's that got to do with anything?" Sævaldur demanded, refilling his own mug but forgetting to offer Gunna a refill.

"They were close friends, Egill Grímsson and Einar Eyjólfur. I'd like to know if there's a link."

"Christ, what are you playing at? It's staring us in the face. All we have to do is haul it out of Gústi the Gob without having to drag all kinds of other stuff into it," Sævaldur fumed.

"Fair enough. Have you found the car or the driver responsible for Egill Grímsson's death yet?"

"Well, no. But whoever it was will show up soon enough."

"Have you ruled out a link between them?"

"Between a schoolteacher in his forties and a nerd in his twenties? Come on, Gunna, talk sense, will you?"

"There are links and we need to look into them. There's more here than meets the eye, Sævaldur."

He shifted back in his chair and swung his feet outwards to cross his ankles, throwing his head back in mock despair. "All right. If you want to follow trails that go nowhere, that's up to you. As far as I'm concerned, we have our culprit right here and he just needs to be cracked."

Gunna sighed. "OK. There's enough to charge him with theft or fraud for the credit cards. That gives you plenty of time to try and get a confession out of him, but I don't reckon you will."

"Why not?" Sævaldur demanded with a sneer in his voice.

"Because Gústi didn't do it. Even if you charge him, you won't get a conviction."

"You're wrong. Gústi's our man." Sævaldur levered himself to his feet. "What's the matter with you, Gunna? Don't you want a result on this? That's what upstairs wants to see, and that's what they're going to get. Come and watch the master at work, you'll see," he said and swaggered from the room, leaving his mug on the table for Gunna to pick up.

She rose to her feet as the door banged behind him and, seething with suppressed anger, rinsed out her own mug and placed it carefully by the sink, ignoring Sævaldur's.

CHAPTER EIGHT

Wednesday, 3 September

03-09-2008, 2315

I'll be your back door man . . .

Maybe the government's hippest young gunslinger should be paying more attention to his über-fashionable old lady, as rumour has it that she's already signed up for a week's conference in Miami next month at the International Federation of Arse-Lickers and Bullshitmongers (known otherwise as the PR Practitioners' Guild). But is she going alone? Of course not . . . And why should she when there's a whole stableful of eager young hunks manning her office for her to pick from for a little companionship, just in case she needs a little manning herself?

So, in case you've popped by to read the latest — and we know that you have, guys — this is just to let the lucky stud know that he needs to stock up on some lube at the airport, as we hear the lady has some unusual preferences. Hmmm, tasteful . . .

Check back soon . . .

Bæjó!

CHAPTER NINE

Thursday, 4 September

A burst of sunshine broke through the bank of tattered clouds rolling in from the west and glinted first on the wavelets lapping at the harbour walls, and then on the blackened concrete of the crumbling quayside at the tiny village of Sandeyri.

Gunna leaned on the breakwater and puffed a Camel as two young officers watched a crane taking up position on the dockside. To her satisfaction, Sævaldur had still failed to extract a confession from Gústi but had charged him with an array of offences relating to Einar Eyjólfur's credit cards. Added to a morning's drive out to Sandeyri, this made the day a good one and she basked in the warmth of the autumn sunshine.

She was grateful for a brief respite in the routine at Hvalvík, where managing heavy traffic and relations with InterAlu were increasingly occupying her working hours even with the addition of Snorri to the station. Construction work continued at the new smelter at the far side of Hvalvík harbour and the long trucks taking earth movers and heavy gear had begun the trek up the

Sléttudalur road to the new site that would become the Hvalvík Lagoon power station.

She looked down at the shimmering water, and what at first appeared to be the slick head of a seal among the miniature waves lifted itself from the water and hauled a mask up its face. The diver hung on to a rusting ladder and called up to one of the officers on the quay.

"Going to be long?"

"Two minutes."

The diver nodded and waited patiently while the crane was jacked up on to its lifting plates and the jib lowered out over the water. As heavy canvas slings dropped to the surface, the diver pulled his mask back down and slipped below the surface with hardly a ripple. A minute later he reappeared, dropping his mouthpiece to shout.

"Away you go!"

Gunna stood up straight, stamped on the cigarette butt and walked smartly to the quayside. The diver sculled gently away from where the crane's wire disappeared into the water.

The engine roared. Black smoke belched from the crane's exhaust and drifted lazily down the quay in the still air. Wire spun on to the drum and scattered shining droplets where it left the water until the slings appeared and finally the roof of a car broke the surface. Clear water sparkled and streamed from its open windows as it was raised high into the air, turning in slow circles.

The car swung over the dock, was gently lowered on to its wheels and crouched there, a small jeep with paintwork covered in a thin layer of green growth. One of the officers detached the slings that the diver had passed through the car's windows so it could be lifted by its roof. The diver clambered up the ladder and sat on a bollard to remove some of his equipment. Gunna helped him unhitch the tank from his back and put it down carefully.

"See anything else down there?"

The diver pulled his hood off to reveal a shock of grey hair and an older face than Gunna had expected to see, adorned with the kind of walrus moustache that had gone out of fashion with bowler hats.

"Not much to be seen down there. The bottom's all sand — if there was anything big, it would probably show up well enough. The tide's pretty strong around here, so anything small tends to get swept out anyway. You're Raggi Sæm's wife, aren't you?"

"Was. And you are?" Gunna responded in surprise.

"Unnsteinn Gestsson. Your Raggi and I sat for our tickets together, bloody years ago it seems now."

"Unnsteinn? I don't recall him mentioning you."

"Steini the diver?"

"Of course. You were on *Ægir* as well for a while, weren't you?"

"A good few years, actually. I think Raggi must have been second mate about the time I joined the ship, and then he transferred to *Tyr* and . . . Bloody shame."

Gunna looked down at the cracked concrete at her feet. Raggi was in her thoughts every day, often at the most uncomfortable moments. For the first time in many months she felt the familiar stab of grief behind her breastbone and ruthlessly blocked back tears that threatened to bully their way down her cheeks. "So. You left the service, then?"

"Yup. Retired a couple of years ago with twenty-five years' undetected rule-breaking and skiving behind me. Now I just do a bit of work for the harbour authorities. That's how we found this old heap. After the earthquake in the spring the town surveyor asked me to have a look at the pilings under all the quays to see if it's all solid. I've only just got round to Sandeyri. Down I went and there it was, sitting on the bottom minding its own business. On its wheels, windows wide open, just as if it had been shoved off the edge and into the water. Very neat."

"Thank you. That all helps."

"You're welcome," he replied, hauling himself to his feet. "If there's anything else, give me a call," he added in a tone that indicated a call would be welcome.

Gunna left him to pull himself out of the old-fashioned wetsuit, sitting in the back of a van that had seen better days. She turned to the forlorn jeep squatting on its wheels on the quayside.

"Good man. That would have been me otherwise," she called to the young officer who opened the car's passenger door to release a flood of water that engulfed his feet. She ran a finger along the bonnet to expose a streak of blue paint under the green algae. As the policeman who had opened the door stood to one side in embarrassment, she peered at the sodden interior, looking carefully at the ignition with the key still in it.

"Right, then. Plain clothes will be here any minute to have a look over this and I've already asked for forensics to see what they can find," she told the uniformed man.

Gunna ran practised eyes over the sodden interior of the car. There was nothing to be seen apart from drifts of fine sand in every corner.

"We'll get the tyres checked and see if there's anything there that might link it to something useful," Gunna muttered to herself. "Right then, young man. What can you tell me?"

"I've already checked the number through the computer. It belongs to Rögnvaldur Jónsson, address in Akranes."

"How did you do that so quickly?

"The diver already gave me the registration number, so I checked it."

"Good lad."

"And I've spoken to the owner. He says he left it at the airport while he went to Tenerife for three weeks in March."

"March?"

"Yeah. When he came back, it wasn't there any more."

"Which is when he reported it stolen?"

"Yup. The guy's a plumber and he was more upset about losing the tools in the back than the car itself, so he was quite cheerful when he found out he might get his spanners and stuff back."

"If it's still there. I don't want to mess about too much until CID have had a look. I don't suppose I'll need to trouble our plumber again if you've already got a statement from him," Gunna said with her eyes narrowed. She crouched on to her haunches, reached inside the open driver's door and ran a hand under the seat.

"A plumber who spends three weeks off his face on sangria doesn't strike me as the bird-watching type," she said, lifting out a compact pair of binoculars, light glinting from the lenses. "So, what do you suppose these were used for?"

"I'm not buying it. Sorry," Gunna said forcefully.

"What else do you have then?" Sævaldur demanded. "Come on, who else could have bumped Einar Eyjólfur off?"

"That's just what we're not going to find out if you refuse to investigate anything other than the first thing that pops up in front of your eyes."

"Rubbish," Sævaldur sneered. "Gústi is as guilty as hell. No doubt."

"No doubt in your mind, that is. Look, I've a witness who saw a car on the dock late that night, quite likely around the time that Einar Eyjólfur landed in the water."

"So what? Some bloke driving around who might or might not have seen something?"

"It needs to be followed up."

Sævaldur looked unconvinced and Vilhjálmur Traustason sighed.

"If you are certain, Sævaldur, that this man is the perpetrator, then I think we should proceed and charge him formally. You don't agree, Gunnhildur?" he asked as if calling on deep reserves of patience.

"You know I don't," Gunna snapped. "Gústi's a scumbag but he's not a killer. He's a minor villain who'll grab an opportunity if it presents itself. He doesn't kill and he certainly doesn't plan anything to the extent of driving a hundred kilometres to dispose of a body."

"Gústi's done plenty of nasty stuff. It's common knowledge. A murder like that's just a step up to the next level for his sort," Sævaldur said. "He did five years of an eight-year stretch for GBH. Come on, Gunna. You've seen the bastard's file."

Gunna's eyes narrowed and Vilhjálmur's widened as he listened to the two of them sparring.

"For your information Gústi confessed and did those five years for one of Mundi Grétarsson's hoodlums. Gústi didn't commit the crime, but he did get a very generous payoff for doing the time. I thought you'd know that. It's common knowledge," she snapped.

Vilhjálmur looked horrified. "Is this true?" he demanded, looking hard at Sævaldur.

"Who the hell knows? The man confessed and he didn't have an alibi anyway."

"Not that anyone looked too hard for one," Gunna added. "And from what I hear, he's not the only one to sit out someone else's time."

Vilhjálmur frowned. "Gunnhildur, are you sure that this man is not connected with the death of Einar Eyjólfur Einarsson?"

"He may be, but only indirectly as one of the last people to see him alive. I'm completely confident he's not the killer."

"Sævaldur, you have this man in custody?"

"Of course. We've charged him with theft and fraud already for the credit cards."

"In that case, keep hold of him as long as you're able. Gunnhildur, you have until Monday to give me a convincing reason why Sævaldur's suspect shouldn't be charged with the murder."

CHAPTER TEN

Friday, 5 September

Gunna immersed herself in the national vehicle records and quickly came up with dozens of cars with JA in the number. She was able to eliminate the majority immediately, taking out all of the smaller cars that could not possibly be mistaken for a jeep, even on a dark night.

She worked through the remainder of the list. When Haddi appeared at her door with an expectant look on his face, he found her among a pile of paperwork with a pencil behind one ear and the phone firmly at the other.

He waited expectantly for her to finish speaking.

"OK. No, not a problem. Thanks for your help," she said before putting a finger out to end the call, keeping the receiver in her hand.

"Any joy?"

"Not much," Gunna admitted. "A few possibles. Plenty eliminated."

She replaced the receiver, leaned back and held up the long list in front of her.

"There are more than two hundred cars with JA in the number. Around ninety of them are jeeps of some kind and I've eliminated all but a dozen or so. There's a Toyota in Stokkseyri, haven't reached the owner yet, four of Swiftcar's rentals which are all BMWs, a few Toyotas and Fords in Reykjavík, even a couple of Hummers. That's it so far."

"Still, it keeps you occupied."

"Just a bit. It's not as if we don't have enough to keep us out of trouble," she grumbled. "Anyway, what time is it?"

"Gone five."

"Hell. I'd better be on my way. Laufey'll be back from school in a minute and I ought to clean the place up and buy some food before she gets home."

Haddi nodded sagely. "Y'know," he observed, "that's the kind of thing I'd have expected Laufey to say if you'd been away, not the other way around."

"Come on, Haddi. I'm never going to win any perfect housewife prizes, am I?"

Haddi spluttered with what Gunna's long experience told her was laughter. "God, no. Which reminds me, there was a bloke here this morning looking for you while you were over at Keflavík hobnobbing with the chiefs."

Gunna straightened her stack of papers and placed them in the middle of her desk.

"Who was that?" she asked.

"Haven't a clue. Old bloke. Moustache. Said it was just a personal call and he'd drop in again later."

"Can't have been important, then," Gunna said, squaring her cap. "Are you on duty tomorrow, or is it Snorri?"

"Me tomorrow. Snorri's off until Monday."

Haddi waved and retreated as the phone began to ring, while Gunna debated whether or not to answer it, well knowing that she would.

"Gunnhildur."

"Hi, sweetheart."

At the sound of the familiar voice, she pushed the chair back and lifted her feet on to the upturned waste paper bin that had taken on a new role as a footrest. "Get stuffed, Bjössi."

"Come on, what kind of language is that?"

"Bjössi, my dear friend, it's the only language that you understand. Don't forget that I'm a tough country girl from the westfjords and I've sorted out bigger and nastier men than you."

Bjössi sighed.

"You say the nicest things, Gunna."

"All part of the Hvalvík force's service. Being rude to outsiders is what we do best. Now. What do you want?"

"That blue jeep from the harbour at Sandeyri. Just as you thought, it's the one that was reported missing."

"I knew that already, so what do you have that's new?"

Bjössi continued, oblivious of Gunna's interruption. "Owner, Rögnvaldur Jónsson, aged thirty-four, Eggertsgata eighty-seven, Akranes. Left it parked at the airport while he went to get pissed in Tenerife. Got off the plane with his straw donkey, and there it was, gone."

"Are you going to stop telling me stuff I already know?"

"Probably not. Forensics have given it a going-over. There are a few dents that the owner couldn't be sure about, says they might have been there before. Apart from that, no fingerprints. Nothing out of the ordinary apart from those binoculars you found. Good quality ones, the sort that serious bird-watchers use."

"Do you really think some twitcher stole a jeep to go bird-watching and then rolled it off the quay at Sandeyri?"

"Haven't a clue. We're up to our ears in it here and I'm going to have to leave it with you. I'll email you the report. All right?"

"All right. What are you so busy with over there, if you've got better things to do than give us a hand?"

Bjössi groaned. "Don't ask."

"Go on. What is it?"

"The usual, trying to interrogate dodgy Eastern Europeans who don't speak Icelandic and pretend they don't speak English either."

"Fair enough. Rather you than me."

"You said it. See you tomorrow morning if you're here for the briefing."

"Briefing? On a Saturday? Nobody's told me."

"Vilhjálmur Traustason's new efficiency review procedures. You're better off out of it, believe me," Bjössi told her. "Bye, sweetheart."

Gunna sat back again with her hands behind her head as she thought. She looked at the clock, saw that she had time in hand and prodded the computer into life. Ten minutes later she locked up behind her, nodded to the woman in the post office next door and walked up the hill towards home with a thick printout under one arm.

05-09-2008, 0216

Skandalblogger writes:

Don't say we didn't tell you.

It seems it's all starting to unravel at last, and don't forget we warned you all a long time ago that these guys weren't to be trusted.

We know that the Ministry of Environmental Affairs set up a small think-tank a few years ago, under the innocuous name of Energy Supply Consultation, otherwise known as ES Consult, or just plain old ESC. But has anyone noticed that ESC is now a limited company listed on the stock exchange?

Have a look, click here* for the stock exchange website and dig a little further to find out who the main shareholders are. It's enlightening reading.

But the really interesting reading would be the internal report commissioned a month or two ago by the major lender set to bankroll ESC, which it now seems is too explosive for anyone but a couple of the top dogs to see. Come on, guys, what did the economists from London have to say about you? And why don't you want your shareholders to know about it?

Well, enough of the corruption in high places, as we can hear you baying for us to get back to the usual filth. So here it is, in an easily digested format.

Which owner of a fashionable downtown tanning parlour has been laying off some of her staff, replacing them with fit young things from further east? It seems that some of the local staff weren't too happy about the "executive happy finish" service that the place likes to offer its exclusive (for "exclusive", read "rich") customers, and walked out. Luckily, Eastern Europe is awash with leggy beauties who can't afford scruples. So business as usual, even with the krona taking a dive!

And which presenter of a primetime popular slot on national TV was this week observed making his way along Laugarvegur in odd socks and bumping into walls, people, parked cars, etc? There's nothing unusual about this extremely thirsty motormouth, well known for a flamboyant lifestyle, becoming . . . what shall we say, overwrought after extensive hospitality, but at 10.30 on a Tuesday morning? Incidentally, it seems that the odd socks were particularly visible, as our presenter friend was clearly wearing someone else's trousers and the someone else must be a good bit shorter than our flamboyant friend.

It'll all come out in the wash . . .

Bæjó!

"Can I go out, Mum?"

"No, my love. It's late."

"But the others are out."

"I know, but it's gone ten."

"Aw."

Laufey Ragnarsdóttir frequently found it difficult to be a police officer's daughter. Other parents could let their children stay outside until after dark. But Gunna knew that there would be whisperings and complaints if she were to do the same and she wondered how long her authority would remain unchallenged.

"Half an hour, Mum? There's no school tomorrow."

"Laufey, I said no. All right? Come on, you'd better be off to bed soon. Aren't you going riding with Sigrún tomorrow? Get your stuff ready now and you can have the TV on for a while," Gunna added as gently as she could.

Laufey shrugged and began slowly picking up schoolbooks scattered across the living room.

"Make sure you've got clean clothes for the morning," Gunna instructed.

"I'm not thick, Mum."

Gunna bit back a sharp reply. She left Laufey to get on with it and went to the kitchen to read the report on Egill Grímsson which she had printed out from the police records and which had been waiting for her all evening on the table.

She scanned the first page of the printout, frowning as she saw that the investigating officer was Helgi Skaftason. They had been recruits together at training college where Helgi had been a latecomer to the force and the oldest man in that year's intake. He was now a painstaking but unimaginative officer.

Egill Grímsson had been run down and killed, crossing the road outside his own house, by an unknown vehicle, possibly blue according to some neighbours who had racked their brains to remember seeing any unfamiliar cars in an otherwise quiet neighbourhood of Grafarvogur.

There had been no witnesses and death was judged to have been instantaneous, although Egill Grímsson could have been lying in the road for as long as an hour before he had been found by the neighbour who called for an ambulance.

Routine questioning of people living in the street revealed nothing beyond the fact that the man had been a clean-living, rather private person, a middle-aged schoolteacher at a comprehensive college. An odd person for a character in his twenties such as Einar Eyjólfur to be associating with, Gunna thought, until a burst of sound from Laufey's room had her jumping to her feet.

"Turn it down, will you?" she demanded, banging on the door before opening it. Inside, the music stopped abruptly as Laufey turned the stereo down to a whisper.

"Sorry, Mum."

Back in the kitchen, Gunna returned to Egill Grímsson. The man had been out all day on Sunday, 9 March and it appeared he had just parked his own car on the other side of the road when the accident had occurred at between seven thirty and eight that evening. There had been no other traffic along the dead-end street and the man's glasses, some notebooks, maps and a camera had been found scattered near his body. All of these had been identified by the distraught widow as being the dead man's property.

According to Helgi Skaftason's report, there had been no progress in finding out who had been responsible for what was regarded as a tragic accident.

Nobody had seen anything and the assumption was that this was a hit-and-run accident in which the perpetrator had panicked and fled. The only unusual aspect of the case was that the driver of the car had not been found. The description of a possibly blue car, according to a bored petrol station clerk on the main road a kilometre away, was far too broad for any kind of search. Although the case was still open, it was clear from the text that little was being done to take it any further as there was no indication of any kind of foul play.

Gunna sighed out loud. She decided against calling Helgi Skaftason, knowing that he would resent what she was sure he would see as interference. She stood up, leaving the report on the kitchen table, and went to the bathroom to brush her teeth, noticing as she did so that Laufey had gradually increased the volume of the music in her room so that it could again be heard throughout the house.

Toothbrush in hand, she tapped on Laufey's door.

"Come on, sweetheart. Turn it off. Time to go to sleep."

CHAPTER ELEVEN

Sunday, 7 September

The car park's manager would dearly have liked to go home, but with Gunna and Snorri in his office he had little choice but to stay while they went through the surveillance tapes. Snorri sat in the manager's chair and watched the computer screen, fingers idly tapping the mouse, while Gunna peered over his shoulder and the manager tried not to look at his watch.

"So, how far back do the tapes go, and how long do you keep them?" Gunna asked.

"It's not tape any more. It's all digital files and now we keep it all for ever."

"So how far back do these go?"

"Since the system was installed last year."

"Good. Should be long enough, then."

"See, that's the jeep there," Snorri said, pointing at the grainy monochrome as the jeep entered the car park. "That was the eighth of March at 13.25, so that ties in with Rögnvaldur Jónsson's statement."

"Yes," said Gunna. "Now we're just going to have to sit here and watch until it's driven out again, which hopefully won't be too long."

A pained look crossed the manager's face as Gunna turned to him.

"Do you know exactly where this vehicle was parked while it was here?"

"Er, no."

"But you must have more than one set of cameras covering the car park, don't you? I thought they were everywhere?"

"They are. But one or two of them are dummies."

"That's just brilliant. Right, you'd better tell me which ones are which."

She slapped the statement Bjössi had sent that morning on to the man's desk, turned it over to the blank side and handed him a pen.

"There you are. Draw me a plan."

Leaning over the wrong side of his own desk, the man sketched an outline of the car park, marking crosses where cameras covered the lanes of dormant cars. He was squinting with concentration when Snorri yelped.

"There it is!"

"Where?"

Snorri clicked the mouse and scrolled back, stopping the blurry picture with the jeep parked in a bay off centre and squashed by the camera's perspective. Gunna fumbled with her glasses and jammed them on her nose. "Well?"

"Well, like you said, now we just have to sit and wait until it moves."

Gunna turned to the manager. "What other information do you have? There must have been a payment of some kind?" She reeled off the jeep's registration number.

"I'll see when I can get to my computer," he replied morosely.

Gunna turned back to peer over Snorri's shoulder as he fast-forwarded through the footage. A few cars moved in stop-go motion and occasional people could be seen walking at high speed across the car park, even those weighed down by heavy suitcases.

"Five o'clock and nothing yet," Snorri pointed out, a finger on the time indicator at the bottom of the screen.

"Keep going."

When the clock reached 17.03, Snorri slowed the replay as a tall man with no luggage approached the jeep. "Chief. Look."

"OK. Play it slowly. Can you get the picture any better than that?"

"This is as clear as it's going to get, I reckon."

The man went straight to the jeep's driver's door and within a few seconds it was open. A moment later it surged forward, out of the bay and out of shot. Snorri paused the replay and summoned the manager.

"I need to switch viewpoint to here," he explained, finger on the makeshift diagram.

The manager clicked and a new window opened on screen. "Do you have a time?"

"Yeah. 17.03."

"Right." The manager tapped at the keyboard and a view of the gates appeared with 17.03 on the clock.

"Scroll there," he said, needlessly as Snorri was already fast-forwarding until the jeep appeared at the bottom of the screen and bumped towards the gates. At the barrier, the jeep stopped, and the window rolled down. An arm emerged, put a ticket in the machine, and was gone. The barrier swung jerkily upwards and the jeep rolled forward and again out of shot.

"Is there another camera on the gate?" Snorri demanded.

The manager pointed and Snorri clicked. An image of the driver's window appeared and moved jerkily until the man's short hair, square face and dark coat could be seen, with clear eyes looking impassively at the camera.

"At least we have a face and a time now. 17.07 on the eighth of March. The engine must have still been warm. The cheeky bastard."

Gunna turned to the car park manager "Judging from that, is there any way we can find more footage of this?"

The man sighed and mentally wrote off his afternoon's golf for good. "No, that's it."

"All right, any payment details?"

"Do you mind? Can I get to my desk and I'll see what I can find for you?"

He tapped at the keyboard, opened new documents and studied them carefully.

"Like you saw, it came in at 13.25 on the eighth of March, and left at 17.07 the same day. Paid by credit card. I'd have to go to head office for the card details. We don't have that information here."

Snorri scrolled back to the point where the man stood by the car door and was preparing to get inside.

"Now, can we see the man there any more clearly?"

The man's blocky image filled the screen.

"That's about the best I can manage. The system's only really designed to record number plates," the manager apologized.

"All right. We'll just have to live with what you've got, if that's all there is. Was there anyone on duty that night?"

"The whole thing's automatic. If something goes wrong at night, then it sends a message to one of our phones so we can get down here and sort it out. But that never happens unless the computer crashes, and even then it switches to a backup first."

Gunna wished the man would stop sounding so apologetic. It was making her want to snap at him.

"Snorri, do we need to confiscate this computer?"

A look of abject horror appeared on the manager's face.

"Or can you copy the files you need?" Gunna asked, taking pity on the man.

"I'm doing it already, or the screen grabs anyway," he said, reaching under the desk to remove a flash stick from the computer. "But I'll come back in the morning with a laptop and download all the surveillance files for those dates."

"In that case, we can leave you to it. Thanks for your help."

Gunna was already outside and getting into the car as Snorri loped down the steps and joined her.

"What was that all about, chief?"

"You mean your suspicious mind hasn't figured anything out?"

"I don't have a suspicious mind."

Gunna started the engine and the Volvo spat gravel from beneath its wheels as it left the car park.

"Remember months ago there was an alert about a blue car that might have been involved in a fatal hit and run incident?"

"Vaguely," Snorri admitted.

"The victim was a man called Egill Grímsson. Helgi Skaftason investigated and came up with absolutely nothing beyond the idea that a blue jeep might have been involved. Hence the alert back in March."

"I get it. Now you find a blue car?"

"That's it. A blue car that was stolen very professionally the day before the hit and run, and which looks as if it had been carefully hidden. If it hadn't been for the earthquake, the dock at Sandeyri might not have been checked for years and that car could have stayed there quietly for, well, anybody's guess how long before it was found."

"Very suspicious."

"It's beyond suspicious," Gunna said grimly. "This deserves some looking into, whatever Vilhjálmur Traustason thinks."

"I see. You're not going to pass this on to CID?"

"No. Not for the moment. Bjössi doesn't have any spare time to do anything on top of what he's already doing and I can't see Helgi Skaftason welcoming us telling him to dig the case notes out again."

"Which means?"

"That we're going to do a little discreet investigation of our own until there's more to work on, especially if I tell you that Egill Grímsson was a close friend of Einar Eyjólfur Einarsson."

Snorri's eyebrows knitted together in a frown of concentration. "Sounds very suspicious."

"Doesn't it just?"

Snorri admired the scenery as Gunna slowed to take the turnoff for Hvalvík.

"I thought that chap was going to have a heart attack when you said something about confiscating his computer," he said with admiration.

"So? You've just done your first aid refresher, haven't you? Now, you're in tomorrow. Haddi's off so I'd like you to maintain law and order for an hour or two in the morning while I have another little jaunt to the airport."

CHAPTER TWELVE

Monday, 8 September

What their editor liked to think of as the key elements of *Dagurinn*'s editorial team crowded, yawning, around Jonni Kristinsson's laptop as he scrolled through Skandalblogger's latest page, reading out the choicest nuggets of gossip.

Dagurinn's third full-time reporter, a diminutive, rotund and permanently cheerful young woman called Dagga, stretched to look over Jonni's shoulder while Skúli crouched down to see past the other.

"The host of which television quiz show has a predilection for dirty baby-talk in the sack?" Jonni asked, reading off the screen in a mock-serious news anchor voice.

"No idea. Does it say which show?" Dagga asked.

"Nope. That would be taking it a bit far."

"That looks interesting there." Skúli pointed, reading out loud. "A political gunslinger and former 'non-paying guest' at Kvíabryggja prison has just come home from a three-week stay in California. Friends say that he has come home with a west coast accent, a deep belief in the power of crystal energy, a tan and a suspiciously fuller head of hair than he left with."

"Only one person that can be!" Dagga whooped.

"Hell, yeah. Everyone's favourite."

"He'll be furious."

"He'll be on the warpath over this one. His lawyers would already be choosing themselves second homes in the Canaries on this one if they knew who to sue," Jonni guffawed, reading further as he scrolled down. "Friends are concerned and speculation in the Parliamentary canteen is rife. Has he gone for a transplant, or has he just bought a succession of wigs so that he can wear a short one after having a 'haircut', then a slightly longer one, then a full-length hairpiece so he can comment loudly that it's about time for a trim? Bets are being taken on the transplant theory. Click here for the before and after pics. Skandalblogger welcomes inside info — anonymity guaranteed!"

Jonni clicked the page shut, sensing the approach of the editor without having to look behind him, a skill that Skúli and Dagga had been trying unsuccessfully to cultivate.

"Five minutes!" Reynir Óli Vilhjálmsson snapped as he swept past and into a vacant meeting room, papers under one arm and a sleek laptop under the other.

The three looked from one to the other. Jonni raised an eyebrow.

"He looks smart today. Anything special happening?"

"He doesn't look happy, though, does he?" Dagga said.

"We'll see . . ."

* * *

"Good morning. Margrét?" Gunna asked. "I spoke to you this morning."

"Yes." The fresh-faced woman behind the desk wore a hoodie sweater and looked as if she would be more at home in a stable than manning a car rental desk at an international airport.

"I'd like a word, if that's OK," Gunna said in a voice that indicated anything else would not be acceptable.

In the small back office Margrét spread out the rental agreements that Gunna had already asked for. "Right, here they are. It was one of our BMW X3s I think you're asking about. You said the ones you want to know about have JA in the registration and the date was the twenty-fifth of August. Right?"

"That's it."

"We have four vehicles that fit the description, they all came together so the numbers are consecutive, but only two of them were in use on that date."

"Can you account for the other two?"

"Yup," she said with confidence, opening a desk diary and pointing out entries. "One was returned the previous day and was still being valeted. The other one was being serviced."

"Right. Carry on."

Margrét slid the rental agreements across. "This one was rented by an Ian Donegan, arrived on the twenty-fifth of August on an Icelandair flight from Manchester and he returned it on the thirtieth. All the details are there, passport number, credit card number, driving licence, et cetera."

"And the other one?"

"Rented on the twenty-fourth, returned on the fourth of September, name of Gunnar Ström, arrived from Stockholm with Iceland Express."

"How do you know that?"

"The flight number's there on the request. We always ask for that so we can match the vehicles to the flights people are arriving on."

"Of course. OK," Gunna said, looking at the photocopied passport page and into the face of the man she had seen on the car park's CCTV system at the wheel of the blue jeep.

"Well, the same information's there, name, address, passport and all that stuff. I've photocopied it all for you," Margrét continued.

Gunna shook herself back to reality. "Thanks. Do you recall either of these people?"

"Maybe. It's hard to say. We see so many faces, but I might recognize a person if I saw them again."

"Would you recognize either of them?" Gunna asked, holding up one of the passport photocopies with its blurry photograph of the holder.

"Yes," Margrét responded instantly. "The face rings a bell. Good-looking guy," she added appreciatively.

"Which one is it?"

"Ah, not sure." Margrét looked through the rental notes. "He's the Swedish guy. The Englishman's too old. Look, he's fifty-five," she said, finger on the date of birth on the photocopy of the man's driving licence. "The Swede returned the vehicle very clean, it hardly needed valeting. But the English guy we had to bill extra because he'd been smoking a pipe in the car. It stank and there was ash everywhere."

"Fine. We have a clean Swede and a smoking Englishman. Anything at all you remember about Donegan or Ström? Anything at all? Any details about the rentals? Did either of them mention where they'd be going?"

Margrét shook her head. "I can't recall anything about him at all. He must have been polite. You tend to remember the rude idiots because we don't get many of them. Most of our rentals are businessmen who all look the same, sound the same. You know what I mean?"

"Didn't you see them when the cars were returned?"

"Not that I recall. Normally we just ask people to leave the car in the lot outside and post the keys through the box if there's nobody here."

"Do you have a record of the mileages?"

"Yup. Donegan was just over six hundred kilometres, fairly low for a six-day rental. Ström did twenty-two hundred kilometres over eleven days, which is average."

"Good. Then that's everything, thank you. My colleague will get a statement from you later. Now, I only need the paperwork for both of them."

"Take those. I've already copied them for you."

"Thank you. If I ever need to rent a car, I'll come straight to you."

"Ideas, please?"

Reynir Óli had a pad open next to his laptop. Jonni lounged back in his seat, while Dagga and Skúli sat upright and attentive.

"Now," Reynir Óli said sharply. "Jonni. Politics?"

"Power's still the big issue that everyone's trying not to mention by hiding behind the City Council and the opera house rumpus. Maybe we should just short-circuit the whole thing and go for the power issue?"

Jonni sat back. Reynir Óli rubbed the almost invisible strand of blond fuzz that straggled down his chin. "Risky. Is that all?"

Jonni sighed and pretended to make some notes. Skúli glanced down to see Jonni had written, "Look at his chin. Told you so," on his pad.

"Bjarni Jón Scumbagson has called a press conference this afternoon. No real idea what it's about yet, possibly something to do with that Hvalvík smelter project, or it might be about endangered spotted eider ducks for all I know. Could be something for tomorrow," Jonni drawled.

"OK. You'd better be there. Do four hundred words for the website straight away and a piece for tomorrow's edition if it's any good."

"I was going to take the lad as well," Jonni said, jerking a thumb at Skúli. "He hasn't had the pleasure of a ministerial press call yet."

"Whatever. What do we know about this Skandalblogger?" Reynir Óli demanded. "He's upsetting a lot of people. Is this guy a story?"

"Or girl," Dagga said. "He or she would be a story if we could find him."

"Or her. Or them," Jonni added.

"It's incredibly popular, but it's dangerous. There's so much there that's libellous. Even if it is true," Dagga continued, ignoring him.

"I know that's not what they teach you at university, but truth and journalism are pretty dangerous bedfellows," Jonni sighed as Dagga and Skúli looked pained. "No need to let the truth get in the way of a good story."

"But this blogger," Reynir Óli butted in. "Like Dagga says, everyone reads the blog and nobody has a clue who writes it. It's a massive story if we find out who it is."

"There are plenty of scores waiting to be settled and there are a good few people who would be very pleased if we could track Skandalblogger down. That Spearpoint woman is going completely apeshit over what he's being saying about her."

"That's the obnoxious PR bimbo married to the environment slimeball, right?" Jonni asked.

"Right," Reynir Óli said, ignoring Jonni. "So where do we go from here? Skúli, you've been trying to dig something out on this, haven't you? How far have you got in tracing who's behind it?"

"Nowhere. Now it's hosted by a service provider in some obscure former Soviet republic where they take the cash and don't ask questions, or bother answering them."

Jonni coughed and scratched his head. "Maybe this is the wrong way round. Whoever the Skandalblogger is, and speaking personally I say good luck to them, they're getting some top-quality information, not just what days the Minister of Health's secretary wears a pink thong, but real stuff, like all that about Bjarni Jón and the Russian connections. Good stuff, right on the nail."

Reynir Óli raised both eyebrows. "Meaning?"

"This is a person, or people, on the inside, with access to real government and financial information, not just recycled salacious gossip."

"So what are we looking for?"

"Not sure," Jonni admitted. "My guess would be a Parliamentary secretary, a researcher, someone with access to government but not necessarily right at the top. Maybe a party official?"

"Or how about a top political journalist?" Dagga asked sweetly.

"Don't talk such rubbish, girl," Jonni growled. "It'd have to be someone at board level who goes to the right parties, not a grunt like us."

Reynir Óli sensed the switch in mood and brusquely changed the subject.

"This week? What do we have? Jonni, you're working on the finance bill issue, aren't you? I need that today and I'd like you to do the editorial comments this week as well."

Jonni's eyes rolled up to the heavens, but he kept quiet and Reynir Óli continued.

"Dagga, fashion pages, for the Saturday supplement. Commission freelancers to do some if there are gaps left to fill. The same with the travel pages. Gossip?"

"Get it from Hot Chat and rehash it if that's OK? The usual agency stuff from London? The Beckhams? Paris Hilton? Madonna?"

"Whatever. Fine by me. The others use it, so we'll have to do the same. Skúli, crime reports for the Tuesday and Thursday editions, and something a bit meatier for Saturday? How are you getting on with your redneck cop profile?"

"Fine. It'll be a good series. I'd like it to run over a couple of weeks if that's OK with you?"

"If it fills up the inches, it can't be bad," Jonni grinned.

"That'll be fine, Skúli," Reynir Óli said primly. "I'd like you to keep tabs on this blogger and dig up what you can. Get on to the Ministry of Justice, someone like that. Can you do that? Get an angle on how they're managing to keep him on the run all the time."

All three of them pretended to take notes for the week ahead. Jonni was drawing a series of boxes across the page of his notebook, while Dagga typed straight into her laptop.

"Er, Reynir? A question?"

"Yes, Skúli."

"I just wondered — if we track down the blogger, then what do we do?"

"Why do you need to ask?" Reynir Óli asked in astonishment. "We'd splash it across the weekend edition."

"Well, it's just that without the Skandalblogger there, we'd struggle a bit for stories. I mean, he's such a great source of material."

* * *

Gunna dispatched a relieved Snorri to the InterAlu compound to discuss a wide load that the construction contractor wanted to bring in. Snorri was only too pleased to escape the confines of the station and Gunna reflected that maybe she was asking him to do too much.

She shrugged and decided that as long as Snorri wasn't complaining, she wasn't going to feel sorry for him, knowing that he was relishing the responsibility. With the office to herself, she spread the two rental agreements out on the desk and read carefully through all of the details for both of the men.

Gunna frowned, pulled the phone across and dialled Stefán Jónsson's number from memory, peering at the photocopied passport photos as she listened to it ring.

"Hi, Siggi? It's Gunna the Cop. Is your grandad home?"

"He's asleep on the sofa," the thirteen-year-old replied guardedly.

"Now, young man, I need you to do something for me. All right?"

"Yeah . . . ?"

"I want you to go on the internet and find pictures of BMW X3s. Got that? It's a big jeep."

"Duh. I know what an X3 looks like," the boy replied with disdain.

"So much the better. I'd like you to find a couple of pictures and show them to your grandad. Then tell him that Gunna wants to know if this is the model of car he saw that night. OK?"

"Yeah. What's it for?"

"Can't tell you. But it's important. Don't tell anybody else, but I really need you to call me back as soon as you can and tell me what your grandad says. OK?"

"Is it, like, a criminal car?" There was a new note of excitement in the boy's voice.

"I'm not sure. It could be. Can you do that for me?"

"Yeah."

"Oh, Siggi. Ask your grandad as well if he remembers what colour it was. All right?"

Gunna smiled as the line went dead, imagining Siggi racing up the stairs to his computer. She sat back and waited for the phone to ring while she looked at the rough photocopy of Gunnar Ström's passport picture and the blocky image taken from the airport parking lot's surveillance camera of the blue jeep's driver. The two looked similar, but the images were not clear enough for her to be certain.

Siggi worked faster than Gunna had expected. The phone buzzed after only ten minutes.

"Gunnhildur."

"Hi. It's me. Grandad says yes. He's certain it's the same kind of jeep."

"Absolutely certain, or just fairly sure?"

"Grandad says ninety per cent certain and he isn't sure what colour it was, but it was dark — dark blue or grey, or maybe black."

"That's excellent, Siggi. There might be a future for you with the police one day," she said. "Give your grandad my regards and tell him I'll pop in and see him in the week."

She sat back and looked at the rental forms again, even though there was no need to check the colours of Swiftcar's jeeps. She knew that they were all black.

CHAPTER THIRTEEN

Tuesday, 9 September

Fat Matti stuck a thumb under the waistband of his trousers and snapped the elastic. Switching from jeans to tracksuit bottoms had made his life so much easier that he couldn't understand why he had put it off for so long.

He reached forward to turn on the engine. The taxi had been still for so long that it was starting to cool and he needed to burn a little diesel to warm up. This wasn't just for his own sake. Customers like a warm cab as well.

He peered over his shades into the mirror, hoping to see a customer hurrying towards him. At this time on a Tuesday morning a few revellers were still making their way home. Weekday mornings were good with business people hurrying to meetings, but evenings were best when the nightclubs, parties in people's houses and revellers with a deep need to score could keep a man busy well into the small hours.

Matti peered into the mirror and examined his eyebrows. He took out a comb and swept back his thick black hair before giving each eyebrow a tweak and then clenching his buttocks to lift himself in the seat and bring his moustache into view. This too needed a minor readjustment. In fact, the long-out-of-fashion Zapata tache was Matti's only remaining gesture towards elegance. A porn star moustache, one very refreshed customer had called it, before being dropped miles from his destination and outrageously overcharged.

For a man who habitually wore jogging bottoms and hadn't seen his feet for years, Matti was a keen follower of fashion. He thoroughly approved of the new fashions for young women to wear ever tighter clothes and delighted particularly in the warm spring weather that brought the short tops and miniskirts out as sure as the geese started flying north. Not that this applied on the night shift, when all year round skimpy skirts could give him a flash of knicker — or better — as the young things jumped into the big Mercedes to be ferried between bars, nightclubs and parties.

Matti was deep in reverie when a phone rang. He patted his pockets until he found which one was buzzing.

"Yeah?"

He listened briefly, grinned and ended the call. Matti put the big taxi into gear and pulled out of the taxi rank, switching off the For Hire sign as he did so. Private jobs, paid for in notes, were always worth having.

Gunna spread the newspaper out on her desk and waited for Skúli to turn up. He had spent anything from a day to an hour or two shadowing her doing routine work. She admitted to herself that it was quite enjoyable having someone so young tagging along behind her asking questions — frequently questions so simple that she wondered how someone with a university education could know so little.

She was about to give up trying to work out the newspaper's recipe for a beef casserole when she heard Skúli greeting Haddi at the front desk.

"Madame's in the executive suite," Haddi grunted when Skúli asked where she was.

"He means I'm in here, Skúli," Gunna called and Skúli's windblown face appeared in the doorway, with a young woman half a head taller at his shoulder.

"Hi," he said awkwardly. "Er, this is Lára. She's come to take some pictures today if that's OK."

Lára extended a hand and Gunna crunched it in hers.

"Fine by me. But preferably nothing embarrassing."

"Have you heard about the march?" Skúli asked excitedly.

"What march?"

"So you haven't. Clean Iceland Campaign are organizing a march to protest against the aluminium industry. You must have heard about it. It was on the news this morning."

Gunna stared. "In case you hadn't noticed, this a TV-free zone. The only news here is yesterday's *Dagurinn*. So you should at least be pleased that we're reading your newspaper. When's this march supposed to happen?"

"It's next weekend, but it starts tomorrow morning."

"Skúli, make sense, will you? It's Wednesday tomorrow, so how can it be happening at the weekend?

"What he means," Lára broke in, "is that the march starts outside Parliament tomorrow morning and they plan to be here on Saturday afternoon."

"Here?" Gunna demanded.

"That's right," Skúli went on breathlessly. "They plan to march from Reykjavík to here. It's a hundred kilometres, so if they cover thirty or so in a day they'll be here for Saturday and they're planning a public meeting outside the InterAlu compound on Saturday afternoon."

"Bloody hell."

"They reckon on a thousand people at least taking part," Skúli added.

Gunna's desk phone rang and she picked it up with the frown still on her face. "Gunnhildur."

"Good morning, Gunnhildur. Vilhjálmur here. I was just wondering if you were aware of the events that are being proposed for next weekend?"

She could feel the distaste in the chief inspector's voice.

"Ah, you mean the Clean Iceland Campaign march?" she asked smoothly, grinning at Skúli. "As it happens, yes. But if you want to tell me more, then go ahead."

Matti only had to drive a few hundred metres and as he pulled up at the lights to wait for the turning on to Sæbraut, the door swung open and his passenger appeared silently in the seat.

"Where to today, Mr Hardy?"

"Out of town this time. Borgarnes."

It was a bright day with unbroken sunshine in an azure sky as Matti gunned the taxi up the main road out of town, leaving trucks and old ladies in Skodas standing. Hardy sat and looked as if he were enjoying the scenery as they passed the sprawling grey concrete suburbs of Grafarvogur and Mosfellsbær until they found themselves bowling through open country at the feet of Esja, the hulking mountain that dominates Reykjavík from across the bay.

Matti effortlessly hauled the taxi past tractors and coaches, carefully keeping not too far over the speed limit. Hardy enjoyed the unaccustomed ride through the dusty green countryside, so much harsher than the wooded landscape he was used to.

"Aren't there any trees here, Matti?" he asked lazily.

"No. No trees here. The Vikings cut them all down for firewood and they never grew back."

Matti cut his speed as they approached the tunnel at Hvalfjördur and was careful to keep under the limit until they emerged, blinking in the bright lights after the dim tunnel, past the toll booths at the far side.

He forced himself not to be curious. Matti knew that any discussion of Hardy's work was strictly off limits unless his opinion was invited, which it seldom was.

The road became a switchback of turns and hillocks through the lush farmland north of the tunnel. Hardy wound down the passenger window to let in the breeze that brought with it the rich aroma of cut grass. With every farm along the route making the most of the dry weather for haymaking, Matti kept a cautious eye out for tractors pulling vast trailers of hay along the highway.

Hardy's phone didn't ring. It just buzzed discreetly in his top pocket. Matti pretended to hear nothing as Hardy, sitting casually in the passenger seat, took the call.

"Of course. I'll call you right back. I'm not alone right now but I'll return your call when we can speak confidentially," Matti heard him say smoothly into the slimline phone. "Of course. Yes, a few minutes," Hardy continued before snapping the phone shut. He looked over at Matti, who was trying not to catch his eye.

"Can we stop somewhere? Somewhere there's a landline phone?"

"Yeah. I reckon so. We'll be in Borgarnes soon and you can make a call from the gas station, I guess," Matti hazarded, inclined to ask why a mobile wasn't good enough, but then thinking better of it.

Matti pumped fuel while Hardy went inside to find a payphone. He filled the tank and ambled inside to pay, deciding on the way that this would be as good a time as any to eat. He paid in cash at the desk and looked around for Hardy but failed to see him.

"Excuse me, darling. Is there a phone here?" he asked.

"Over there," the cashier replied, jerking a thumb behind her towards the toilets.

He made his way over and shoved open the door of the Gents. On the way out, relieved, he spotted Hardy leaning against a wall, handset to his ear. Matti went over to him and made an eating gesture, raising hands to his mouth. Hardy frowned and looked away. Matti shrugged his shoulders and went towards the cafeteria where Hardy found him ten minutes later.

"I thought you might be hungry," he said through a mouthful of burger, simultaneously skewering half a dozen chips on his fork and dipping them in a tub of bright pink cocktail sauce.

"I might be," Hardy admitted. "But I don't eat shit like this."

"You should have said."

"I was busy."

"And I was hungry."

"Big man, sometimes I think that you are a little too hungry for your own good," Hardy said with a hint of acid in his voice that passed Matti by.

"Yup. Always been hungry, me. We was hard up when I was a kid and there wasn't never enough to go around. Scars you for life, that does."

Hardy nodded sagely and stood up. Matti was almost finished when Hardy returned with a bottle of water and a sandwich for himself, and mugs of black coffee for each of them. He carefully used Matti's discarded knife to scrape more than half of the mayonnaise from his prawn sandwich on to the empty plate before taking a bite.

"So, who are we going to visit this afternoon?" Matti asked through yet another mouthful of food. Hardy was disgusted by Matti's table manners, but enforced confinement had taught him not to comment on other people's behaviour without good reason.

"The man I have to speak to is a consultant who advises a lot of companies on various things. It's not important for you to be present. The man speaks English perfectly and I don't expect I'll need you to translate."

"Going to be long?"

"I doubt it. Twenty minutes, maybe. Then I have to be back in Reykjavík in good time after that."

"Another job?"

"You could say that. I have to go to Spearpoint, so you can leave me there."

"Suits me. Right, I'm going outside for a puff before we go and find this guy. You got an appointment with him?"

"In a way."

"What do you mean — in a way?"

"He doesn't know about it yet."

Matti pulled up outside what looked like a dilapidated farmhouse. The building needed a coat of whitewash and the windows on the seaward side were caked with grime and salt.

"This is the place?" he asked Hardy doubtfully.

"It should be. Wait here for me, will you?"

Matti switched off the engine and opened the door. There was almost perfect quiet outside. Only a few songbirds and the distant chatter of a brook broke the silence.

Matti levered himself out of the car and perched his backside on the bonnet, listening to the faint tick of cooling metal under the bonnet as he lit a cigarette. He watched Hardy walk purposefully up the path and open a garden gate that needed both oil in its hinges and a coat of paint.

He was halfway to the front door when it opened and a man appeared with spectacles perched among sparse hair that nevertheless curled about his shoulders.

"Can I help you?" he asked vaguely. "I heard your car pull up outside."

"I'm looking for Arngrímur Örn Arnarson," Hardy replied, hurrying to reach the man before he came too far from the house's front door. "I've been told you can help me out with some information."

"I don't know about that," the man said doubtfully.

"Ah, but I'm sure you can. Einar Eyjólfur said you would be able to give me some answers."

"I'm sure I don't know who that is," the man said quickly.

"But you are Arngrímur Örn Arnarson?" Hardy asked softly, hoping his voice would not carry as far as where Matti was basking in the sunshine. "Can we sit down and talk for ten minutes? I know you're a busy man and I won't take much of your time."

The man cast about as if unsure and gestured towards an iron table flanked by a barbecue and a pair of garden seats near the door of the house. Matti looked lazily across at the two men sitting face to face outside the house and wondered what could be so important that it was worth driving all this way when a phone call could have done the trick. He hauled himself forward and sauntered around the back of the car to get a cloth. He busied himself polishing dead flies from the car's windows while he caught snatches of the conversation that carried in the still air. In spite of himself, he couldn't help straining to hear more.

"You're telling me you're unaware of this?" Hardy asked.

"It's not something I'm involved with," Matti heard the man say.

"But how easy would it be to set something similar up? It would have to be secure and in an environment where interference is not easy," Hardy asked casually.

"It can be done easily enough. Full access and any questions are ignored as long as suitable payments are made in the right places."

Matti willed himself not to be nosy and straightened up from polishing the windscreen. As he did so, the two men at the table also stood up and came forward a few paces. He saw Hardy stretch out a hand and the man uncertainly put forward his own hand to shake it, while Matti hastily dropped the cloth and the cleaning fluid back in the boot to be ready to move off.

As he closed the boot, he heard a howl that set his teeth on edge. Looking up, he could see the two men with their hands locked, but by now Hardy was on his feet over the man who cowered on his knees, his right arm extended and twisted unnaturally into Hardy's grip.

Hardy whispered something that the man clearly missed as Matti stood transfixed.

"This is a message to your friend the Skandalblogger that it has to end and it has to end now," Hardy repeated. "Do you understand?"

The man nodded furiously.

"This is just to make sure the message is taken seriously," Hardy added, leaning forward sharply as he put his weight behind his grip on the man's arm. Although no stranger to a little persuasion himself, Matti shuddered at the sharp crack of the man's wrist snapping and the thin screech that followed it.

Hardy stood up and dusted himself down with a smile.

"I hope that's all in order," he said to the whimpering man on his knees, one shattered arm cradled in the other. "I wouldn't like to come back and do the same to the other one. Ready, Matti?" he asked with a smile.

CHAPTER FOURTEEN

Thursday, 11 September

The percolator spat and hissed while Gunna spread slices of bread with butter and then layers of ham. Forcing her thoughts elsewhere, she wondered how long Sævaldur would be able to hold Gústi the Gob with no real evidence to back up his suspicions.

With Laufey away from home for the week, Gunna found that she hated being in an empty flat and wondered when Gísli would be back. Although Gunna worried about him working at sea, she reflected that the trawler was a fine ship with an unbroken safety record and that crossing a busy street was probably more hazardous than working on deck among an experienced crew. She debated whether or not to call Laufey, but decided that the girl would probably see it as interference.

With nobody else in the house, cooking was too much trouble. She toyed with the idea of a takeaway, but felt slightly revolted by the idea of the stodgy pizza that was all Hvalvík could offer.

She placed four sandwiches on a plate and opened the fridge to search for mustard. Right at the back, a half-full bottle stared at her. It called suddenly, sweetly, insistently, telling her that one glass would be fine, that she could handle a small one.

Gunna quickly picked up the mustard jar and shoved the door closed, but the image of the cognac bottle remained with her as she ate at the table while the TV news reported four people escaping from a house fire in Akureyri.

She ignored the whisper from the fridge when the next item appeared. This time the chairman of a union commented that housing conditions for overseas workers employed to build a power plant in the east of Iceland were far below standards required and the work camp would have to be shut down if things did not improve. The camera swung and she recognized the young man she had interviewed at Spearpoint's offices, now sporting a goatee and almost invisible frameless glasses. She turned the sound up quickly as the banner at the bottom of the screen read "Jón Oddur Finnbogason, Spearpoint".

". . . really can't comment on these allegations," blustered the pale young man with the fringe of ginger beard.

"But surely you must have checked the accommodation that these people were going to be living in before they arrived?" a reporter asked.

"Of course. Everything was vetted at the project's preparation stage. We carried out extensive checks."

"And did you do this personally?"

"We have representatives on the ground who do this kind of work on the company's behalf and this was entrusted to them. As far as I'm aware, this was all done satisfactorily."

"But your company didn't send anyone personally?"

There was silence for a moment. "No. As I have already said, we have representatives who —"

"Jón Oddur Finnbogason of Spearpoint." The reporter had cut the young man off in mid-sentence as the camera tracked to a huddle of sorry-looking sheds crowded between the half-built steel skeleton of a hangar and a gaggle of trucks. A second later the picture flashed back to the studio.

"And now, a light aircraft made an emergency landing this afternoon at Bíldudalur. There were no injuries, but the aircraft has been badly damaged. Investigators are already on the scene and the airstrip at Bíldudalur is closed until flights hopefully resume tomorrow . . ."

She quickly muted the sound as the phone rang beside her. "Gunnhildur."

"Ah, good evening. Gunna?" a gruff voice asked.

"That's me."

"Er. Hi. It's Steini."

"Steini? Sorry . . ."

"Steini the diver."

"Ah, right. Hi. Anything else about that car in the dock at Sandeyri?"

She heard him muffle a cough. "Well, no. Actually . . . No, nothing new there. I was, er, wondering if you'd like to meet up for a drink or even a meal or something?"

Gunna sat in surprised silence for a moment. "That's good of you to ask, Steini, but . . ."

She thought for a moment. Steini and Raggi had been good friends and she was suddenly terrified of reopening old wounds.

"What did you have in mind?" she asked finally.

"If you're not busy this evening, there's a place in Grindavík called the Salt House that does a fine seafood buffet on a Thursday evening."

Gunna felt an unaccustomed fluttering in her stomach, chuckled and quickly stopped herself.

"Old ladies like me don't get that many invitations," she said. "See you there in an hour?"

She snapped off the TV and marched to the kitchen with her plate and mug. She placed the crockery in the sink with the rest of it. Alone in the flat, she hadn't bothered loading the dishwasher all week. The cognac bottle in the fridge whispered its sweet promises through the door, but now she dismissed them sternly. Gunna breathed deep, and made for the shower.

CHAPTER FIFTEEN

Saturday, 13 September

It was already a hot day and the marchers had gradually discarded more and more clothing as the sun rose higher in the summer sky. With bare arms, midriffs and legs displayed everywhere, Skúli felt uncomfortably overdressed in heavy jeans and an anorak.

Anticipation had been building up for days as the march drifted slowly out of Reykjavík and gathered way, straggling past the last of the houses and shops and on to the open road. Under a glaring sun in an azure sky, the marchers sang and chanted while around them the bilberry-covered tundra gradually gave way to black rock and lingering pools of still water.

By the time it reached the top of the first pass on the way to Hvalvík, the march had doubled in size as brightly dressed people joined in handfuls and carloads, swelling the procession to a respectable band. As it approached the outskirts of Hvalvík, TV news stations began estimating the size of the march in thousands and also reported that several groups of activists arriving from Britain, Germany and Scandinavia had been detained at Keflavík airport.

Certain that this would be tomorrow's lead story, Skúli felt nervous about covering something so visible and volatile, made up of such a large number of people he felt an uncomfortable empathy with.

He wondered where Dagga was. This was a story big enough to warrant two of them covering it, as well as the freelance photographer Reynir Óli had been forced to agree to hire for the day.

Behind them somewhere was a support car that Skúli hoped would not be too far away. Ahead of him was Lára with a heavy camera over one shoulder and another at her eye as she took pictures of a tall young man in an oversized green bowler hat who juggled red, white and blue balls, winking suggestively at her as he loped along ahead of the Clean Iceland banner at the head of the march.

"Any luck?" an out-of-breath Dagga asked as she caught up with Skúli.

"Not a lot."

Dagga pulled a sheet of paper from her shoulder bag and tried to read it without slowing her trot. The sun was high in a perfect blue sky and a miasma of dust kicked up by many feet hung in the still air.

"There's a woman called Ásta who's supposed to be the media contact, but her phone is dead or out of range and I can't reach her. Then there's this Kolbeinn who's supposed to be in charge of the schedule, but it doesn't look like there's a schedule anyway, so maybe he's not here either."

"I suppose we can get a few quotes from some of the marchers and then take police quotes from the TV reports."

"How about your policewoman friend? Isn't she likely to be round here somewhere?" Dagga asked.

"Gunna? I expect so."

Skúli looked up to where a helicopter swung into view and swooped low as the procession waved at the cameras levelled at them.

"Police or TV?" he wondered.

"Channel Three, I think. Must be nice working in TV, just a quick jaunt in a helicopter and back home to do a ninety-second report."

The procession picked up pace as it approached the sprawl of Hvalvík. At the Please Drive Carefully sign a hundred metres outside the village's furthest house, a small group of police officers stood resolutely in the middle of the road.

The marchers whooped as the procession drew to a halt and the group at the front went ahead to confer. Lára stepped forward and was rewarded with a scowl from the senior police officer and a grin from the juggler as she raised her camera.

"We're just going straight through the town and out the other side. Anything wrong with that?" the juggler demanded.

"I'd like to know where you're planning to go after that. I'm warning you right now that I will have no alternative but to make arrests if there is any trespassing on private land."

Skúli had his recorder in his hand and tried to edge closer. Apart from the calm senior officer, the five police officers appeared ill at ease. Lára shot half a dozen frames of the juggler and the senior policeman facing each other, and this was enough for one of the younger policemen, who detached himself from the group.

"Who are you?" he demanded.

"Press," Lára retorted. "You know that, Gummi."

"Press cards?"

Lára pulled out a wallet, flipped it open in front of his face and quickly closed it again. With a touch of pride, Skúli showed his very new press card.

"Identification?" the policeman snapped at a tall man who appeared to have come from nowhere.

"Very sorry. I don't speak your language," the man replied smoothly in English.

"Papers, please. Do you have a press card?" the policeman asked more politely this time and the man delved into an inside pocket to draw out a laminated card.

"From Germany?"

The man nodded.

"Newspaper?"

"News magazine."

"OK."

Satisfied that he had done his duty, the policeman rejoined the group where the senior officer and the juggler were still sparring.

"Are you able to assure me that there will be no attempts to enter private land?"

"This is an entirely peaceful protest. I can assure you that Clean Iceland has no intention of carrying out any illegal acts."

"I'm pleased to hear it. But before I can allow you to carry on with this gathering, I have to be sure that there is no intention to provoke a confrontation. If I have reasonable suspicion, then I will prevent you from continuing."

"You mean you're prepared to stop a peaceful gathering making its way along a public road? I'm sure that will look good on the news, and there's more than just a few local hacks here today," the juggler pointed out.

Skúli felt a close presence and glanced sideways at the tall man with German press credentials.

"Can you tell me what they are saying?" the man murmured.

"Well, it's just a game really," Skúli replied. "They want to go up to the construction site and the police can't really stop them."

"Why not?"

"Like the guy in the hat said, it's a peaceful demo and unless they have a really good reason to believe there's something illegal likely to happen, then they can't stop them from using the road."

"Is that enough?"

"Yes, probably," Skúli said slowly. "It's hard to say how the police will handle this and it's not easy to see exactly who's in this group. I think there are a lot of people here who aren't part of Clean Iceland."

"Who, then?"

"There are people here from Asia and South America, places where InterAlu already does business. And there seem to be some kind of professional activists, people who were at that big camp at Heathrow airport in England last year."

"Do you know which ones they are? They might be worth talking to."

"They're everywhere. Most of the foreigners are experienced campaigners. Hey, which magazine did you say you were working for?" Skúli asked, turning to find that the man had silently disappeared.

The march drifted cheerfully past Hvalvík and along the gravel road to the smelter site on the industrial area. A bevy of police cars preceded the marchers and a small convoy of cars followed, with an ambulance bringing up the rear. The music died away and the mood darkened as the village dropped out of sight and they approached the chain link fence where Gunna and Haddi were waiting for them with a group of men in high-viz jackets behind the fence. Skúli was suddenly glad of his anorak as a cloud bank blotted out the sun.

The colourful crowd gathered at the fence around the site where they joined hands and chanted slogans. There was little for the police to do other than watch and stop a group from lighting a fire to grill hot dogs.

A low podium of crates and planks was erected and a small sound system rigged up so that representatives of Clean Iceland could speak to the whole gathering. A Green Party MP spent too long at the microphone and by the time he had finished, the crowd were becoming restless. Then the juggler stood up to take the microphone, speaking in clear but accented English.

"We're here today to protest against an environmental crime that is taking place in our country and against our will. Unfortunately the members of the government who have allowed this to happen by giving away the birthright of the people they were elected to serve are not here today," he declaimed in a ringing voice. "We invited them. We invited the Minister for Environmental Affairs, Bjarni Jón Bjarnason, to meet us here. We had hoped these people would be here to answer our questions, but it seems they have better things to do. Other business to attend to. More national assets to sell off to big business. More dirty deals to be done."

He paused. The crowd roared. The juggler's voice rose in fury.

"These men and women are guilty! These people are criminals! They'll sell our birthright and line their own pockets with a lot more than thirty shitty pieces of silver and expect us to keep quiet and accept this! I'm warning you here and now," he said as his voice dropped.

"Warning you here and now," Skúli muttered, scribbling down the juggler's words in his notebook, even though his recorder was running. Lára stood behind him shooting frame after frame, trying to capture the depth of the juggler's passion. The man's eyes bulged in anger and the veins along the side of his neck stood out like wires.

"We do not accept this. You will be made to answer for these crimes and there will be much to answer for.

Mark my words, Bjarni Jón Bjarnason and your cronies, one day you will be called to account for this."

He swept an arm behind him towards the silent bulldozers and the arc of broken ground inside the fence where the vast steel-framed building was taking shape. He stepped down, drained, as the crowd whooped and cheered.

A grey woman in a traditional sweater took the stage and spoke sensibly about how successful the march had been, before asking people to start returning to Hvalvík and the buses that had been ordered to take them back to town. With evening upon them, the crowd moved willingly and Gunna let herself relax. She raised a hand to the site manager, who had spent the day standing with his posse of booted heavyweights inside the wire, and got into the station's better Volvo with Haddi at the wheel.

"Job done, no problems, eh, Haddi?"

"Pleasant enough day out, I suppose."

"Home, then, if you please."

"Very peaceful. It's hard to predict what these freaks are going to do, but they were fine," Haddi grumbled, annoyed by the disturbance to his normal routine.

"Oh, come on. It's not as if we have a problem with these people. I'd rather deal with this lot than the Saturday night drunks."

"No, not me. Give me drunks any time rather than these weirdos. When you're dealing with pissheads, you know exactly where you stand."

"Haddi, you're getting old. There's no hurry back, we'll just keep behind them and make sure there aren't any stragglers. All right?"

Skúli composed his piece in his mind for the Sunday edition. This would be a front page, "reports Skúli Snædal, crime correspondent", he thought.

Dagga and Lára walked ahead, wondering where their support car had gone.

"Good photos?" Dagga asked.

"Not bad at all," Lára replied, scrolling through them and holding the camera up so that Dagga could share them.

"He's good-looking, isn't he?"

"Who?"

"Kolbeinn, the juggler guy," Lára said. "Didn't you notice him? I couldn't stop taking pics of him without his shirt on. Gorgeous, I thought."

"Passionate type," Dagga agreed. "Great-looking and has no idea of it. Hey, Skúli, what do you think? Lára was saying that juggler is just luscious. She reckons he can leave towels all over her bathroom floor whenever he wants."

"Well, I wouldn't know . . ." Skúli muttered, flushing and dropping back behind in embarrassment.

"Well, I don't know," he heard Dagga say. "I like that young policeman you had the pics of this morning."

"Gummi? Very young and innocent, I thought."

"Nothing like teaching a young dog new tricks. I was hoping he'd take my name and address."

Skúli rolled his eyes and let himself drop even further behind.

As the marchers made their way home and night began to fall, heavy cloud rolled in off the Atlantic and settled low, shrouding the hills and hugging the mountainsides. It was almost fully dark as two figures emerged from the hillside overlooking the construction site, hauling themselves from shallow hiding places scooped in the ground where their friends had half-buried them.

They silently made their way to the part of the fence where security cameras had the most awkward angles to cover and quickly snipped at the wire until a hole big enough to crawl through had been made. Inside the compound they vanished, returning without the backpacks they had set out with. They rapidly patched the fence to hide their tracks and vanished back up the slope where they unearthed a pair of mountain bikes that had been hidden for them in the loose gravel. Swinging legs over, they bounced down the track towards Hvalvík.

They were long gone when flames began to lick hungrily at the row of trucks and bulldozers, as well as the site manager's new Landcruiser, which the activists had felt was just as legitimate a target.

CHAPTER SIXTEEN

Sunday, 14 September

The site manager could hardly speak through his fury. The previous day's demonstration had cost a day's work, but at least it had been peaceful. He had been called out in the early hours to find that his fleet of vehicles was wrecked and the security guards had seen nothing. His first phone call had been to the agency that had supplied them and his second had been to Spearpoint to demand a more reliable replacement.

Gunna arrived with Haddi from Hvalvík to find Björn already at work. A couple of uniformed officers were looking over the burnt-out vehicles and Haddi went to keep them company. Björn was sitting in the site manager's office interviewing the latest in a procession of the site staff.

"Hi, Björn. How goes it?"

"Ah, Gunna. At last," Björn replied, turning away from the miserable-looking man sitting opposite him. "Make us some coffee, will you? And a few doughnuts wouldn't come amiss."

"You, dear friend, can kiss my arse and make your own coffee."

"No offence, Gunna. We few remaining male chauvinist pigs have to try and make a stand now and again."

"None taken. How are you getting on?"

"Bloody terrible. They're all Polish or Portuguese, or some such foreigners. Their Icelandic is as good as my Swahili, so it's all in English."

"Your English is all right, isn't it?"

"My English is fine, but theirs isn't," Bjössi grumbled. "Anyway, any luck your side?"

"Not a peep. Nobody saw a thing last night between here and Hvalvík. I've spoken to every farmer along the way and there's not a thing. Even that old nosy parker Jóhann at Fremribakki, who's up at five every single morning in case he misses out on something, says he hasn't seen or heard a soul since the march went past yesterday."

Bjössi jerked a thumb at the door and the man sitting opposite him scuttled out without a backward glance.

"So, what have we got, then?" Gunna asked, examining the office noticeboard.

"Nothing, it seems, unless forensics find something around the wreckage. I reckon they just used good old-fashioned rags soaked in petrol, lit a fire under each one and then got out quick."

"So, no witnesses, because the security guards were playing poker in one of the sheds all night, and not a hope of finding footprints or anything that could be definitely linked to these guys, not after the number of people who were tramping around here yesterday."

"It's going to take a while, this one," Bjössi said with satisfaction, leaning his bulk back on two legs of the site manager's chair so that it creaked in protest. "I expect we'll come across them sooner or later, but it won't be through anything we do here. Someone will blab or want to settle a score eventually."

"You know, I'm wondering how they got clear without being seen. The fires started around midnight, so it was pretty dark. It's a good long walk from here even into Hvalvík. If we can find out how they did that, we'd be a step or two closer."

"Hm. If you think so. Ach, some idiot'll have a drop too much to drink soon enough and spill the beans," Bjössi said with conviction. "Anyway, I'd better carry on with these numbskulls who see and hear nothing and don't know anything either."

14-09-2008, 2006

Skandalblogger writes:

What's that freedom thing about, Grandad?

The march was exciting, wasn't it just? The papers and the TV are telling us how peaceful it was, with Kolli Sverris doing his juggling and all the colourful people getting in tune with nature before they return to civilization in their 4 × 4s in time for the footie.

But a little bird whispers to the Skandalblogger that not everything went as sweetly as we're being told. Just how did the fire in the InterAlu compound start? You know, the fire that nobody's talking about that burned out every piece of heavy machinery on the site? What?

You mean you didn't know about it? All the news guys were there, even our cousins the Norwegians were good enough to send a TV crew, but unfortunately they'd all gone back to their hotels by the time the real business started.

And what happened to the overseas activists who were quietly herded off to one side at Keflavík, kept for a couple of hours and just as quietly deported without even leaving the terminal?

Well, damn me for a cranky old liberal with some strange ideas about freedom of speech and the right to protest, but I'd have thought that there might be a bit more to this than meets the eye.

Keep taking the pills, and watch this space!

Bæjó!

Vilhjálmur Traustason hesitated, sparking Gunna's curiosity. In spite of what she saw as his numerous failings, the man could generally be relied on to get straight to the point.

"I, er, wanted to mention to you the investigation into the young man who was found outside Hvalvík."

Gunna could imagine him twisting his fingers into knots as he spoke.

"And? What? The lad was identified quite quickly and we're making progress. At the moment it's all about finding out how he got there from a bar in Reykjavík, even though Sævaldur reckons he has a suspect."

"Yes, of course. Precisely. You don't agree with him?"

"Nope. Gústi the Gob may be a nasty piece of work, but he's not going to kill someone for a few credit cards. Why, what's your problem?"

"Ágúst Ásgeirsson has been bailed. No murder charge has been made, only theft and fraud."

"Aha. I told you he wouldn't get it to stick."

Vilhjálmur sighed. "I don't want you to allocate too many resources to this case. I have asked Reykjavík to leave Sævaldur in overall charge of the case and to liaise with you as and when."

Gunna stopped her jaw from dropping. "Are you telling me to drop this?"

"This isn't a murder inquiry. The man drowned while drunk."

"He was pushed."

Vilhjálmur continued as if Gunna had said nothing. "I'm instructing you not to put any effort into this. The city force will follow it up. You're going to have enough to do with the InterAlu work going on in your area."

"So Reykjavík are going to be looking after this?"

"Yes. That's it."

The phone clicked as the connection closed.

Matti was about to call it a night and go home to get some sleep when the door opened and a florid young man slumped into the passenger seat.

"Where to, mate?"

"Kópavogur."

The young man slumped back in the seat and fumbled with his glasses. Matti caught the whiff of alcohol and the urge for a drink swept over him.

"Women, they're rubbish," the young man slurred. "You married?"

"No. Not any more."

"Good for you, mate, good for you. They're just . . ." He floundered for words. "They're just, rubbish. You know?"

"Know what you mean. Girlfriend chucked you out, has she?"

"Fuck, no. Worse."

The taxi hummed past the lights at orange on to Sæbraut.

"Who d'you work for?

"Himself? Nonni the Taxi."

"Well, mate. Just you be glad you work for a bloke. That's all I'm saying," he said with bitterness in his voice, rooting through the pockets of his jacket and bringing out a half bottle of vodka from an inside pocket.

"Not in the taxi, please," Matti mumbled, every fibre of his body aching for a drink as the man spun off the top and swigged.

"What? Oh, sorry. But, yeah. Bloody women, specially when your boss is a woman. Nothing worse, specially a bloody ball-breaker like mine. Evil cow."

"Where d'you work, then?"

"Spearpoint."

"What's that?"

"Never heard of it? What planet have you been on? PR and stuff, consultancy, project management."

"Right."

"I've got two weeks' holiday. Flights to Florida booked and paid for. Scuba diving by day and pina coladas by night, and then the evil old bitch tells me today that I'm needed next week, and that's that, no arguments."

"Must be something big to take your holiday off you."

"Ach. It's those fucking bunny-hugging do-gooders. They set fire to those trucks and stuff out at Hvalvík and we have to try and clear up the mess, set up press jaunts, show people around, sort out new agencies, all that shit."

The desire for a drink subsided as Matti took better notice of what his passenger was saying.

"So. Who's this ball-breaker you work for?"

"The Minister's Lady," the man replied through even greater depths of bitterness. "The lovely Mrs Sigurjóna Huldudóttir, CEO of Spearpoint, evil, nasty bitch woman," he slurred.

Normally he would have kept drunks like this one at arm's length, but now Matti pricked up his ears.

"Couldn't say. Never met the lady."

"She's bloody everywhere, going on about her house in the country or some fucking charity gig she's organized to collect a few quid for orphans in Africa and make herself look like some kind of a fucking saint."

"I know who she is. I've just never met her, so I couldn't say. All right?"

"Well, all I'm saying is she's a cow and even though her husband's a twat he doesn't deserve her, running his life for him and then shagging her staff as well."

Although Matti was getting tired of the man, he paid attention all the same.

"What's that? Bit frisky, is she?"

"Ach. Shit. Never mind. Better keep quiet."

Drops of spit were beginning to collect on the dashboard as the man sat forward in his seat and snarled to himself.

"Bloody woman," he slurred. "We all ought to get together and sue the arse off her for harassment. Y'know, if she was a man, she'd never get away with all the shit she gets up to."

"Yeah?"

Matti's pulse was set racing by anything even mildly salacious, but he struggled to mask his curiosity, hoping that a show of indifference would bring out more details.

"Yeah. Sigurjóna and her studs. Every trip she takes an assistant." He spat out the last word with more venom than Matti would have thought possible.

"Assistant?"

"Yeah. Personal assistant. Bloody woman. Very personal assistant."

"What? Taking notes? Carrying bags?"

"And the rest. And she changes assistants more often than she changes her knickers. Hell, I'd better keep my gob shut. Said too much already."

"Where are you going?" Matti asked, slowing down as he passed a speed camera.

"Scaramanga."

"Righto. Still doing the business there, are they? Or have all the strippers gone now?"

"Dunno. Gonna find out. It's been a fucking shit day with that old witch and I've got to do something to make it a bit better."

"I can, er, help you out with that. If you're looking for some company," Matti ventured.

"What?"

"If you're looking for a lady to look after you for an hour or two."

"OK," the man said slowly. "Tell you what, give me your number and I'll give you a call if I don't get lucky."

"Sorry, mate. One time offer only. Not an offer to be passed up."

"How much?"

"Negotiable. Depends what you're looking for."

"No, hell. I'll sort myself out. I can always go and jump on the bloody boss if I get really desperate."

Matti slowed, hauled the car off the main road and past the sprawling Smáralind shopping complex, slowing for lights and taking several more turns before pulling up in front of a nondescript building with only a single bright light over its door, where a thickset man in black stood guard.

"Here we are. That'll be six thousand five hundred."

The man dropped a handful of notes on the seat as he struggled to stand up and get out of the car.

"Want me to wait for you? In case they don't let you in?"

Matti shrugged as the man found his feet and set his course for the door without answering.

"Not my problem if you've got to walk back to town," he muttered to himself as he scooped up the notes and trousered them. It was just as well he hadn't bothered to set the meter running.

CHAPTER SEVENTEEN

Monday, 15 September

"Snorri?"

"Yup."

"Hi. Busy?"

"You know," Snorri replied guardedly.

"Listen. You remember the car that was in the dock at Sandeyri?"

"Blue one, yup."

"Stop saying yup, will you? You sound like a teenager."

"Sorry."

"Look, I have something I'd like you to look into. I have to go out to the InterAlu place again now and I don't have time, otherwise I'd be doing it myself."

"All right?" Snorri said dubiously.

"Now, remember what I told you about cultivating a suspicious mind? This Egill Grímsson character was run down on the ninth of March. If this car is the one that was responsible, I'd bet anything you like it was in the dock at Sandeyri within a few hours."

"Go on," Snorri said.

"I'm sure it went from Grafarvogur out to Sandeyri and someone must have had a sight of it."

"All right. So what do you want me to do?"

"Just a bit of digging through traffic records. See if there's a speed camera that may have caught it, anything like that. Shouldn't take you long."

"That's a bit of a while ago now."

"I know. I'm not expecting miracles, but do what you can."

"Fair enough."

"I might knock off once I've been to the compound, so you can drop in and see me when you're done. If I'm not here I'll be at home. OK?"

Snorri grunted in agreement and Gunna jingled the second-best Volvo's keys as she left him to get back to his computer. Egill Grímsson irritated her. But what irritated her even more was that the case had been mothballed and that it had taken place where the Reykjavík force would hardly welcome interference from outside.

15-09-2008, 1448

Skandalblogger writes:

Cosy Moments will not be muzzled!

Things are getting serious, boys and girls. It's just like the movies, only this is real life. Real life, people, just to remind you, is what happens right after you select Shut Down.

We understand that there's a price on the Skandalblogger's head. We hear there's corruption and skulduggery afoot. We hear that there's (whisper it!) money in the kitty to get our fingers broken one by one. We hear that there are respectable people in high places who want us shut down, so obviously we've been doing something right, especially if our hit stats for the last month are anything to go by. Maybe we should start selling advertising space?

But seriously, folks, who's the tough guy who visited a computer communications consultant Skandalblogger has never met or heard of, on the same day that the poor man had a fatal heart attack and unaccountably broke his own arm in the process? Is it the same hardnut who may or may not have driven a dead-drunk Einar Eyjólfur Einarsson off to an out-of-the-way harbour and rolled him into the water to drown quietly? Isn't it time we had a few answers?

But just so as you sad people can have your fill of filth and revel in the misfortunes of your elders and betters . . . Excuse us, did we say elders and betters? Of course we didn't mean that, what we meant to say was the rich and morally bankrupt, maybe even genuinely bankrupt if the tales of panic we hear from our financial friends have a grain of truth . . .

Anyway, beware, ladies, and especially gentlemen. If you go for the little blue pills that help with a certain problem down below, then watch out, as Skandalblogger is reliably informed that there's a duff batch on the streets. Right size, right shape, right colour, right price. But no trade. You pay your way, pop your pill, and the lady's still looking at a night with Mr Floppy.

You pays your money and takes your choice!
Bæjó!

Gunna returned from what she felt was an entirely wasted trip to the InterAlu compound, cursing the waste of an afternoon on what was little more than assuring the site manager that there would be no more demonstrations outside his gates.

She emptied the Co-op shopping bags into the fridge and the cupboards, hummed as she swept the kitchen floor for the first time in days, cleared the debris from the fridge and bagged it ready to go in the bin before deciding that the bathroom could wait for its birthday. Something to grapple with put Gunna into a detached frame of mind that allowed her to do mundane chores she would normally put off, leaving her free to turn things over in her mind while cleaning the flat on autopilot.

She recognized her own symptoms and resigned herself to the fact that she would have no peace until she found some kind of conclusions. She brewed coffee and sat down at the kitchen table to read through her notes, as well as the printouts she had made of Clean Iceland's web pages that included a lengthy obituary of Egill Grímsson.

She was startled when the doorbell buzzed. At the door she looked through the frosted glass to see Snorri still in uniform outside, looking a little uncomfortable.

"Come in," Gunna said with an unaccustomed cheerfulness, swinging the door aside.

Snorri grunted a greeting, bent down to pull off his shoes, padded behind her into the kitchen and sat down in the chair against the window without needing to be asked. Scanning the papers scattered across the table, he picked a mug from the window sill and automatically held it out to be filled.

"I stopped off at the station, but Haddi said you'd gone home. So here I am."

"Laufey's supposed to be home from her trip today, so I ought to be here for her.

"Another trip?"

"Work experience, which she managed to wangle at a stable near Ólafsvík, the cheeky thing. Her grandmother lives up that way so she's been there for the weekend and she should be back any minute. Now, young man, there's something I wanted to talk over with you without any curious ears listening in."

"You're not up to anything dodgy, are you?"

"Don't talk like a daft old woman."

"All right, I just don't have long before my lesson."

"What lesson?"

"Jói Ben's daughter."

"Silla Sjöfn or the other one?"

"Silla Sjöfn."

"And what's she supposed to be teaching you?" Gunna asked, mystified for a moment before she remembered that Snorri had begun to supplement his modest police salary by giving driving lessons. The tips of Snorri's ears glowed pink.

"I'm teaching her," he said lamely. "To drive."

"Sorry. Slipped my mind."

"And you were about to say something unladylike as well."

"Me? Come on."

Snorri slurped coffee and looked at the papers on the table with curiosity. "And?"

Gunna took a deep breath. "I'm convinced there's more to all this than meets the eye."

"I thought that the moment we saw the film of that bloke stealing the jeep," Snorri admitted. "Very professional, only took a couple of seconds. But if you're going to steal a car, why nick an old crate like that?"

"An old heap is unobtrusive. I'm sure there's a link between the jeep and Egill Grímsson and I wouldn't be even slightly surprised if our body in the dock wasn't part of the story as well."

"I know it's unusual and suspicious, but what makes you think there's a connection?"

"What it boils down to is that Egill Grímsson was the motivator behind getting this Clean Iceland Campaign off the ground to start with. Clean Iceland organized that march up at the InterAlu compound. My guess is that Einar Eyjólfur was feeding information to Egill, and Einar Eyjólfur was working for Spearpoint."

"Which is that bunch who are bringing in all these Poles and Portuguese to work up at the Lagoon?"

"Right first time, young man. There's certainly a bit more to this can of worms than meets the eye."

She decided not to mention that Spearpoint was owned by a minister's wife, while Snorri rolled the empty mug between his hands.

"So, have you found anything out?" Gunna asked. But the front door opened before Snorri could answer, banged against the wall and brought a gust of cool air with it before slamming shut again.

"Mum? You home?"

"In here, sweetheart."

Laufey swung a backpack on to the floor. Her face was drawn with fatigue, but shone with excitement.

"Have a good time, did you?"

"It was brilliant, Mum, brilliant. We went riding every day. Who's this?" she asked, staring straight at Snorri.

"This is Snorri, one of the policemen from the station. Snorri, this is my darling daughter, Laufey Oddbjörg."

Laufey wrinkled her nose. "Laufey Obba," she said with decision. "I don't like Oddbjörg. Mum, can I have a horse?"

Snorri snorted as he stopped himself from laughing.

"What's so funny?" Laufey demanded, nose in the air.

"Sorry. Nothing."

"Laufey, my love," Gunna said patiently. "Look, I'm a bit busy right now. Can you put all the clothes that need washing in the basket? I'll get dinner soon."

"We had great food at the farm, meat soup like Grandma makes only not the same and all sorts, and there were pancakes —"

"Laufey, please. Ten minutes, OK?"

"All right," she conceded, dragging her rucksack by the shoulder straps to her room and shutting the door behind her.

"Enough to put you off having kids, isn't it?"

"She can come out to the stables and ride one of my horses if she wants," Snorri said shyly.

"You're one of these horsey types as well? I'd never have guessed you had a screw loose, young man."

"I'm afraid so. My brother farms near Eyrarbakki and he keeps some horses. It's in the blood, I suppose."

"That would be fun for her and Eyrarbakki's not that far," Gunna mused. "Now, what have you found?"

Snorri grinned. "Nothing from traffic. No speeding, no running red lights, nothing at all."

"Oh well, it was a long shot," Gunna conceded.

"Ah, but there's more. You know the big filling station by the roundabout has CCTV over its forecourt? They even have a webcam outside that shows everything that goes round the roundabout. So I went and asked nicely if they had records of everything, and there it all was. There's only one road out to Sandeyri, so it had to go past there, and I have to say, you were absolutely right."

"Of course, young man. You don't get to be sergeant by being wrong," Gunna said warmly. "Now, what does this tell us?"

Snorri scratched his head and thought. "Well, not a lot really, nothing that could stand up as evidence. Can't see any registration numbers or the colour of the jeep, can't make out the driver. All we can see is that a jeep of that model went out to Sandeyri at 22.18 on the ninth of March and there's no sign of it coming back."

"Are there any gaps in this webcam?"

"Only in the winter when it can freeze up, the guy at the filling station said, but there wasn't a frost then. So it's all there."

"So that jeep couldn't have come back along the same road after the ninth and we wouldn't know about it?"

"That would mean sitting through hours of recordings to be sure."

"OK. So what we have here helps, but it's never going to be evidence. Still, excellent work, young man."

"But that's not all."

"Oh?"

"I watched the whole sequence from that evening. There's only a few dozen houses at Sandeyri, hardly anyone lives there. There's practically no traffic at all out there in the evenings. But that night there was this."

Snorri dropped another printout on the table. It showed a large car leaving the roundabout along the exit leading to Sandeyri. Gunna picked it up and looked at it carefully.

"Time 22.44. Can't make out the registration number," she said dubiously.

"Have a closer look."

"At what?"

Snorri pointed. "There. A taxi plate. And there's this."

He placed a second printout on top, showing an identical vehicle entering the roundabout from the same turnoff.

"He comes back at 23.31. That would fit nicely. Our man drives out to Sandeyri when it's quiet. You can't see the dock from any of the houses because it's behind the sea wall, and nobody's likely to be looking out of the window at that time of night anyway. He rolls his car off the dock, calls a taxi and waits to be picked up."

"Very neat," Gunna decided. "Right. Can we trace the taxi?"

"Easy enough. It's a Mercedes, dark colour, and if you look at that picture of it coming off the roundabout, you'll see that the front wing is dented as well."

"Snorri, my boy, I think you can imagine what I'm going to ask you to do next."

"As it happens, I've already done it."

"And?"

"The taxi is owned by a company called Radio Taxis, which is in turn owned by a gentleman called Jón Gunnsteinn Hannesson."

"Otherwise known as Nonni the Taxi and old friend of the police, as they say in the cop shows," Gunna said grimly. "Know him of old, I'm afraid. That's excellent, Snorri, much more than I'd hoped you'd come up with. But, there's one thing."

"Hm?"

"I'd prefer this to be kept very discreet."

"Riiiight?" he said slowly, both his tone and eyebrows rising as he said it.

"Look, it's not secret, but I don't want it all over the place yet. If we dig into the Egill Grímsson case, we're in danger of stepping on the city force's toes to begin with, and . . ."

"And?"

Gunna felt awkward but steeled herself to admit what she had been hoping was not the case. "I get the feeling this is all being sidelined. I'm sure it's being quietly dropped."

"Shit. Who?"

"Couldn't say. I'm being leaned on by Vilhjálmur not to put too much effort into this."

"What? The Emperor?"

"Excuse me? Why do you call the chief inspector the Emperor?"

"Bára Gunnólfs said it first. Haven't you noticed he looks like a Roman emperor?"

"You cheeky bastards," Gunna guffawed. "I'll bet you youngsters all say rude things about me as well."

"No. We like you. But we do wonder about your toyboy, though."

"What?"

"You know. The one from *Dagurinn*."

"Skúli? He's a good lad, just a bit bewildered at the real world, I reckon. He's only been out of school a few months."

"He seems a strange character."

"That's what a sheltered upbringing and years of university do for you, I suppose."

"The opposite of us, then?"

"Yup, I'm afraid so. Anyway, say a word out of turn and I'll tell Vilhjálmur what you lot call him and you'll find yourself transferred to Grímsey before you know it."

* * *

Lára looked up and frowned as she parked outside. She remembered leaving the kitchen window of her flat open so the cat could jump out on to the balcony, but she hadn't left it that wide open.

On the stairwell something whispered to her that things weren't quite right. She wrapped a hand around the rape alarm that nestled in the bottom of her bag, hoping that it would work if she needed it, wondering if any of the mostly immigrant occupants of the other flats in the block would hear it or even take any notice if it were to go off.

Her key slid into the lock and she swung open the door as quietly as she could, wincing to herself as it creaked. Stepping inside and leaving the door open, she looked carefully around the living room and bedroom, satisfied herself that there was nobody hiding behind the shower curtain in the tiny bathroom and only then noticed that the place had been ransacked.

Every drawer and cupboard was open, with contents spilled on to the floor. Her underwear was in a heap on the bed, jeans and tops piled on the floor. Books and papers had been hauled from shelves and the kitchen cupboard that contained her cameras had been rifled, but nothing appeared to be missing. Lára sighed with relief that she had taken her laptop with her that morning and finally put down her bags in the remaining clear space in the middle of the living room.

A sudden rattle in the kitchen made her nerves scream in alarm, until the black and white cat jumped from window sill to kitchen table with an inquiring look on its face.

"Hi, Kisi. What happened here, then?" she asked it, but the cat only stared back at her.

Hunched under the sink, she fumbled for the panel under the sagging kitchen unit and triumphantly brought out a handful of disks that she knew contained most of her recent work.

Relieved, she unclipped the phone from the ragged patch of denim on the waistband of her jeans and dialled 112.

CHAPTER EIGHTEEN

Tuesday, 16 September

Gunna felt self-conscious in Reykjavík. The city had changed so much since she had been on the Reykjavík force that she even found herself taking wrong turnings along the new roads that seemed to sprout up every time she ventured into town.

Radio Taxis had a yard at the back of an industrial area not far from the main road. On an overcast morning Gunna nosed the police Volvo through grey puddles between drab workshops until she found Radio Taxis' offices, a shed that looked slightly better on the inside than the ramshackle exterior.

A couple of bare bulbs lit up the yellowing walls. A woman glanced up briefly from her desk as Gunna entered and then looked up a second time with a flash of panic as she noticed the uniform.

"Good morning," Gunna offered cheerfully, recognizing the woman's discomfort.

"Hi. Nonni's not here at the moment," she replied.

"That's a shame. Know where he is?"

"Playing golf, I expect," the woman sniffed. "He seems to have better things to do than spend time here these days."

"Not to worry. It's just a routine call. I'm Gunnhildur Gísladóttir from Hvalvík police. And you are?"

"I'm Eyrún Jónína. Routine? What about?" the woman demanded suspiciously.

"Mercedes taxi," Gunna said, placing a slip of paper with the registration number on the counter between them.

"Yeah. That's one of ours. Is there a problem?"

"Nothing special. Our computer flagged up this vehicle's registration and this is just to tidy up our records," Gunna lied. "I see this car had a collision on Snorrabraut a few months ago. Has that all been settled with the insurance company now?"

Eyrún Jónína sat at her desk and leafed through a bulging folder. "Yeah. That's all settled. Some yuppie's caravan fishtailed across two lanes and bumped the wing. His insurance paid up, no questions."

Gunna pretended to make notes. "That's fine. The reason the computer flagged the vehicle up is that there was a road traffic accident in my area last week."

"That idiot's not had another dent, has he?"

"No, nothing like that. A witness mentioned that a Mercedes taxi had been in the vicinity at the time and there are only a few cars like this in the country registered as taxis. I'd like to identify the driver as a potential witness."

"That's all right. Just as long as he hasn't screwed up one more time." Eyrún hauled another binder from the shelf above her desk. She leafed through it and pulled a sheet of paper from a plastic sleeve in the middle, placing it on the counter.

Gunna frowned in irritation and surprise as she looked down at a photocopy of the driver's licence.

"Know him, do you?" Eyrún Jónína asked with a short laugh. "Matti drives that taxi all the time."

"I know most of the taxi drivers," Gunna muttered, scanning through the details even though there was no need to. She wrote down the licence number and shook her head sadly as she peered again at a youthful version of Marteinn Georg Kristjánsson glaring truculently back at her.

CHAPTER NINETEEN

Wednesday, 17 September

17-09-2008, 0119

Skandalblogger writes:

So everyone knows, a memorial service for Einar Eyjólfur Einarsson will be held at the church in Mosfell at 4 on Saturday 27th, so don't be late. It's now three weeks Einar disappeared and there's three weeks' silence on what happened to him.

All right, so we know he died incapable, cold and alone. But how come he drowned a hundred kilometres from where he was last seen? It's not so much a case of did he fall or was he pushed, rather, did he walk, or was he driven? And as it would have taken him a week to walk there, who the hell was driving? Whatever the police may think, this was no accident, so just who did this terrible thing?

Come on, Keflavík police Führer Vilhjálmur Traustason! This is on your patch! When are you going to get to the bottom of this one and let us know what did happen to this young man, who Skandalblogger can now reveal was very much one of us?

See you all on the day . . .

"The taxi is used on a permanent basis by a driver called Marteinn Georg Kristjánsson, born in Vestureyri on the eighteenth of September nineteen sixty-seven," Gunna announced when Snorri asked if she had found out anything useful.

"He's from Vestureyri? You know this guy, then?"

Gunna nodded. "Fat Matti, he's called. He has a record of petty thievery, mostly cars, numerous instances of public drunkenness and the odd punch-up," she told Snorri, wondering at the same time whether or not to tell him quite how long she had known Matti. "He spent a long time in Canada until they picked him up a few years ago and sent him home by parcel post with a stamp on his arse. Oh, shit." Gunna sighed and Snorri looked up from the computer at her in surprise.

"He's something of a troublemaker?" he asked, pointing at the screen. "I've got his record here and it looks that way."

"Snorri, my boy, you don't know the half of it. Matti's one of my many cousins from the west and he's never forgiven me for joining the force. He's always made a point of being as awkward as he possibly can without actually being arrested, and I reckon I spent my first few years in uniform hauling the silly bastard out of trouble here and there."

She hunched her shoulders wearily. "Damn and blast. That's all we bloody needed, Fat Matti having something to do with all this."

"Right," Snorri said, at a loss for what to say next.

"It's OK. It might be fun to catch up with the old fool again. He might have found God or something in the meantime."

"Nope." Snorri shook his head, scrolling through Matti's record. "In the last two years there's speeding, max points on his licence, public drunkenness, some minor violence and a few other odds and sods."

"Not to mention what's not on record," Gunna added. "There was a narcotics case a few years ago, but he wriggled out of it and someone else did the time for it."

She hung her head and sighed even more deeply, then swore quietly under her breath. "The upside of it is that as Fat Matti's a relative of mine, I'd prefer not to have to arrest him. So if he shows up anywhere around Hvalvík, you or Haddi can do the honours."

"I'll look forward to it," Snorri said with a smile.

"You do that. If you see him, bang him up and call for me."

Matti was worried. He was more than worried, he was scared. The sight of the tall man with the wispy hair and the glasses whimpering in agony over his smashed arm stayed with him in the days following the terrifying drive back to Reykjavík. Hardy had sat in the passenger seat enjoying the sunshine, humming to himself and cracking the occasional joke that Matti couldn't appreciate. The man seemed more relaxed than Matti had seen him before, as if his swift act of controlled violence had released a tension in him.

The big taxi's wipers swept drizzle from the windscreen as Matti dropped a customer off outside one of the big office blocks on Borgartún. It was mid-afternoon and he decided to head back to Reykjavík airport to see if a fare could be picked up from one of the domestic flights. Pushing through the mid-town traffic he almost crashed into the rear end of a bus halfway through Channel 2's three o'clock news bulletin.

A man had been found dead at his home just outside Borgarnes, where Mýrar County police were treating the death as suspicious and appealing for witnesses.

"Shit. Shit. Shit," he swore to himself.

He was due to collect Hardy at four thirty from a meeting in Kópavogur. Matti wondered whether or not he would have heard about the man's death.

Sitting outside the airport he watched a couple of Fokker Friendships land and the passengers start to trickle out of the terminal, suitcases and small children at their feet. Country people, he thought, not used to a big city like Reykjavík and looking forward to seeing the place for a few days before going back to Akureyri or Húsavík.

He looked at his watch as a hard-faced woman with two shell-suited children and a clutch of suitcases in tow tapped on the window.

"Can you take us to Kópavogur?" she rasped.

"Yeah, I'll open the boot," Matti agreed unwillingly. It was too short a fare, leaving him too much time to wait for Hardy to come out of his meeting and not enough time for another fare in between. But he lifted the woman's cases into the boot and ushered the children to the back seats and ordered them to put the seat belts on.

"Don't I know you?" she demanded suddenly as Matti swung the car out on to Hringbraut.

"Don't think so," Matti grunted.

"I do. You're Matti Kristjáns, used to live in the flat over the bakery. You must remember me, surely? Kaja Jóakims?"

Matti's heart sank. He put his foot to the floor and breezed through a set of lights a fraction of a second after they switched to red.

"Nah. Not me," he said unconvincingly as the woman looked sideways at him through narrowed eyes.

They finished the trip in record time and an uncomfortable silence as Matti resolved never to wait outside the airport when flights from Vestureyri were landing. There was too much chance of running into someone from home, an unwelcome face from the old days. Admittedly he did now recognize the red-faced woman as the modern personification of the pudgy girl with pigtails and a shrill voice from over the road, but the last thing he wanted to do was to start comparing notes on who was living where these days.

Outside the large detached house that was Kaja Jóakims's destination, he mumbled as he fiddled with the meter.

"Four thousand," he said.

"Discount for old times' sake?" Kaja Jóakims asked shyly.

"Already included," Matti muttered.

With notes in his hand, he lumbered from the car and opened the boot to retrieve their cases, while a young woman emerged from the house and embraced his passengers in turn. He was quickly back at the wheel and ready to go when he noticed that the young woman and Kaja Jóakims bore an uncanny resemblance.

"See you later, Matti," she cooed and waved as he drove away, swearing out loud now that he had an empty cab and more than half an hour to kill.

"Kaja Jóakims a grandmother," he grumbled to himself. "Who'd have thought it?"

He cruised slowly into Kópavogur with the For Hire sign off and parked in the centre to get a coffee and a roll from a bakery. He ate it outside, resting his rear end on the car's bonnet and enjoying the warmth of it. He reflected that half an hour to kill was actually just long enough for a snack between fares. It was a shame that the weather was wet and there was a shortage of young women in thin summer clothes about to improve the view.

Hell, you can't have everything, he decided and his mood darkened as he remembered that Hardy needed to be collected and probably didn't know that his victim was now a dead man.

Outside modest offices sandwiched between the tiny Kópavogur harbour and a yard where bulldozers roared constantly as they filled trucks with sand and gravel, Matti pulled up a minute before he was expected, just in time to see Hardy shaking hands with a beefy man who looked as if he was still wearing the suit he had been confirmed in. He watched them exchange a few final words, smile at each other and part.

"Good afternoon, big man. Right on time, I see," Hardy said with a shadow of a smile as he settled himself in the taxi's passenger seat.

"Part of the job, being on time," Matti grunted. "Where to?"

"Hverfisgata, by the bus station will do."

"The one by the police station?"

"That's the one."

They drove through the city in silence, Hardy with his hands folded as he admired the view. Matti hunched over the wheel, wondering whether or not to tell him what he had heard on the news. By the time they reached the city bus station, he had decided to keep quiet for the moment.

"What's the matter, big man? Seen a ghost?" Hardy asked cheerfully.

"Could be," Matti replied. "D'you need me tomorrow?"

"Not sure yet. Might need you at short notice."

"Yeah, that's OK. I'll be on the rank tomorrow. Won't be going far, so just give me a call if you need me."

Hardy nodded and slipped silently from the car. Instead of driving away, Matti picked up a stack of receipts from the pocket in the door and pretended to look at them, watching Hardy in the mirror as he receded from view. As soon as he was far enough away, Matti dropped his paperwork and craned his neck around in time to see Hardy step quickly sideways into an alley.

Matti gunned the taxi's engine, swung it round in an illegal U-turn and bumped it down an entrance into the parking lot belonging to a block of offices. In the corner he killed the engine, jumped out and vaulted over a low fence into a yard, then along an alleyway into Lindargata. He was just in time to see Hardy disappear round another corner, doubling back on himself.

Matti retraced his steps and found himself puffing with more than exertion going uphill. He couldn't understand why Hardy had walked in a circle until he was back in the parking lot next to the taxi and caught a glimpse of his pale leather jacket as he punched a code into the lock on the back door and let himself in.

"Shit. Should have bloody known better," he cursed.

Matti wasn't sure if Hardy had seen him on his heels, but he was sure that he would have seen the taxi parked there. As he took his place behind the wheel, he wondered what Hardy was doing in a block of offices that housed a Christian radio station, several lawyers, a photographer's studio and a hypnotic healer.

But what really concerned him now was how Hardy would react if he suspected he was being tailed, however inexpertly — and whether or not Hardy had actually seen him.

CHAPTER TWENTY

Thursday, 18 September

"Gunnhildur," Gunna replied, picking up the phone on its fourth ring.

"Hi, it's Skúli. Just wanted a quick word if that's OK?"

Gunna leaned back in her chair and stopped herself yawning. "I'm off out in a minute, so it will have to be a quick word."

"Fine," Skúli gabbled. "I'm just after an update on the Einar Eyjólfur Einarsson case. Is there anything new?"

"Why are you asking?"

"Y'know, just keeping on top of things."

"As a conscientious newshound should."

"That's right. Is there anything?"

Gunna wondered where Skúli's sudden interest had come from.

"Progress is being made, young man, but that's all I can tell you," she replied guardedly.

"And off the record, is the guy you've charged the right one?"

"You're not recording this, are you?"

"No, of course not, off the record."

"Skúli, over the phone, everything has to be on the record. If you want an informal chat, you'll have to come out here," she replied.

"Oh. OK. But that's all you can say?"

"That's all I can tell you right now. Progress is being made. A man has been charged with a related offence, but you know that already."

"Yeah, but he hasn't been charged with the murder, has he?"

"All I can tell you is that a man has been in custody and has now been bailed and that he is helping with inquiries. If you want a cosy chat, it'll have to be face to face."

She could sense his disappointment through the crackling phone line.

"Have you seen Skandalblogger's latest?" Skúli asked suddenly.

"What's that?"

"Come on. Surely you must have seen the Skandalblog?"

"No, I'm afraid I haven't. We're a bit behind the times out here in the backwoods, you know."

"I think you ought to have a look. Is your computer running?"

"Now? No, just switched off. I have to be in Reykjavík in half an hour."

"Will you have a look when you get back? I'll email you the link if you like?"

"All right. You do that, if you think it's important."

"OK. I really think you need to see this. I'll do it right now, and I'll call you back later, unless you have time to meet, since you're on your way over here anyway?"

"I'll have to wait and see how long I spend sitting around at Hverfisgata. You can call my mobile around three if you like, and we'll see then. OK?"

"So that's official, then? It stinks?"

"Absolutely reeks, dear girl."

Jonni and Dagga were hunched over her laptop perched on a tall table at a café not far from *Dagurinn*'s offices.

"It's a real story," Dagga mused. "Something that would make some waves."

Jonni sipped his lukewarm coffee. "A homegrown Icelandic scandal of the kind that we've seen so many times before."

"Meaning?"

"It goes on all the time, but nobody talks about it. It's well-connected people cashing in on their connections. Look, this company, what's it called?"

"ESC, Energy Supply Consultation."

"Or whatever they're called. It's been done before and there's nothing new about it. You set up a state-owned company with taxpayers' money, let it run quietly for a good while without actually doing much or letting anyone notice, until it becomes part of the scenery. With me so far?"

Dagga nodded.

"That's the easy part. Then comes the trickier bit. Privatization is king, so eventually the company is privatized, sold off."

"Understood. So what's wrong with that?"

"It's basically a form of insider trading, the whole thing set up in advance with some decent government contracts, a healthy injection of cash — yours and mine, I might add. Then it floats and there's an influx of cash and you go to the bank and they'll match it and maybe a good bit more. The whole thing is boosted, there's a scramble for stock in the company, so you and your mates who bought into it on the cheap can sell and make a killing, or sit on it and hope for a bigger killing later. Bingo, it's pay-day."

"OK," Dagga said slowly. "Unethical, but illegal?"

"Does it matter?" Jonni leaned back and gazed out at the rain with the satisfied look on his face of a man who has already done enough work before lunch to allow him a relaxed afternoon.

"Of course it matters. It's in the public interest, surely?" Dagga asked.

"Certainly. The public absolutely, definitely should know."

"So, are we going to tell them?"

Jonni shrugged. "Dear girl, you don't know the half of it yet. Go on, join the dots."

"All right," she sighed. "ESC is due to be floated on the stock exchange. The people who have share options grab and sell, making a fat profit."

Jonni leaned forward, unwittingly planting his elbow in a puddle of cold coffee. "Now, who stands to gain?"

"The people with share options."

"Who are?"

"There's plenty of them."

Jonni stretched and upended the remains of his coffee down his throat. "It's not that simple. If you like, you can go to Reynir Óli and tell him you have a cracking story about government corruption at the highest level, with a minister presiding over the selling off of state assets to a coterie of selected friends, or even himself, come to that, and see what happens."

"Come on, Jonni. Tell me. I'll be your best friend."

Jonni sighed and stood up. Dagga closed her laptop and stowed it away in her bag.

"Just follow the money."

"OK," Dagga replied slowly. "Come on, tell me more."

"Who owns *Dagurinn*?"

"There are several owners."

Jonni shoved open the door and they emerged into the street. He buttoned his coat and shivered. It was cold for late summer.

"Yeah. But who's the big boy?" he asked, ploughing through puddles while Dagga stepped from side to side to avoid them and tried to keep up with Jonni's pace.

"Rich Golli, Ingólfur Hrafn Ormsson. Does he have a stake in this as well?"

"Dagga, my dear. Rich Golli has fingers in financial pies everywhere. I have no idea if Our Glorious Leader has an interest in ESC, but you can be pretty sure that he has friends who have, and he's unlikely to want to piss them off, unless, of course, there's a grudge he wants to get off his chest. Hard to say."

"So what do we do?"

"Up to you. Take it to Reynir Óli and see what happens, if you like."

"Jonni, if it's such a good story, why aren't you following this one yourself?" Dagga asked suspiciously.

A grin began at the corner of Jonni's mouth and spread slowly across as his face lit up.

"Excellent, Dagga. Now you're thinking like a real journalist, cynical and suspicious," he said, angling forward the elbow of his right arm for her to put a hand through it. "You shouldn't imagine that your old uncle Jonni doesn't have something up his sleeve. When you've given Reynir Óli a shock that'll give him palpitations, I'm going to give him a shock that might well put him in intensive care." He smiled slyly. "Intrigued?"

"Of course I am."

"Don't worry. It'll come out soon enough. Come on, let's get out of the bloody rain."

It had already been a long night and Matti began to doze until he heard knuckles rap on the roof of the car above his head. He opened his eyes, opened them even wider when he realized what he was looking up at, and wondered if they would go away if he were to let his eyelids slide down again.

Knowing they wouldn't, he wound the window down an inch.

"Jæja, Matti. Haven't seen you for a while. How've you been keeping?"

"Gunna. What've you got to say for yourself?"

He looked in the mirror to see a young policeman step back and get into the squad car parked right behind his taxi, while Gunna walked around and opened the passenger door to drop herself carefully into the seat beside him.

"Well, cousin Matti. How's tricks?"

"Cousin Gunna," Matti said stiffly in mock formality. "What have I done to deserve this honour?"

"Not sure yet. Maybe I was just wondering why I'm not on your Christmas card list any more."

"So this is just a family visit? Who's dead?"

"Matti, this isn't a family matter, unfortunately. What have you been up to this time?"

"Look, I've been keeping out of trouble and I'd prefer it if the police could leave me in peace, like the Reykjavík crowd do at the moment. What are you doing here, anyway? I thought you were out to pasture in Hvalvík now?"

It was a bright day and sunshine sparkled between banks of cumulo-nimbus that idly threatened to rain on the opera house construction site opposite and the squat black mass of the Central Bank building. Matti had turned into the half-empty parking lot to take a quick nap before going back to the taxi rank across the road. He liked to be close to the harbour, even though it accommodated more cruise ships than trawlers these days.

"Just checking up on you. Had an inkling that you might be involved in something slightly shady on my patch, so we decided to have a look round and see if you had time for a quiet chat."

Matti scowled. "I'm busy. I'm working."

"You were snoring."

"Just resting my eyes. But now I have to get back to the rank. This is a working taxi and I have bills to pay. Nonni isn't running a charity, y'know."

"Come on, Matti. Let's keep this friendly, shall we? If needs be, we can go to the station."

Gunna could almost sense the cogs ticking over in Matti's mind as he stared through the windscreen at the queue of lunchtime traffic idling impatiently at the lights.

"All right, then. I've got ten minutes, then I need to be back on the rank."

"Tell me about March, will you? Were you working?"

"That was bloody months ago!" Matti exploded.

"The ninth of March. Where were you then?"

"How the hell should I remember that far back? Of course I was working, busy time of the year, that was, before everything started to go quiet."

Matti's fingers fidgeted in his lap, thumbs circling each other nervously. He fumbled in the pocket of the car door and shook a cigarette from its packet.

"Open the windows if you're going to light up, will you?" Gunna asked sharply.

"Yeah. Nothing like an ex-smoker, is there?" Matti retorted even more sharply, lighting up and blowing smoke out of the now wide open window.

"March, Matti. What were you up to?"

"Hell, I don't know. Ferrying drunks around in this thing, probably."

"All right," Gunna said in her calmest voice. "I'll jog your memory. What was this taxi doing in Sandeyri on the ninth of March?"

If Gunna hadn't been looking directly at him, she would have missed seeing Matti's eyes bulge slightly for a moment.

"Er. Might have had a fare. I can't remember. I go all over, I'm often out there round the airport."

"All right," Gunna said calmly. "Let's jog your memory a bit further, shall we?" From her jacket pocket she extracted fresh printouts of the webcam pictures that Snorri had obtained, unfolded them carefully and passed them across to Matti, who held them up, shaking his head as he did so.

"Nope, sorry. Can't see the number. Not my taxi."

"It's your taxi. It's the only Mercedes taxi of this model in the entire country. And if you look carefully at that second picture, you'll see the dent in the wing that you got from a scrape with a yuppie's caravan on Snorrabraut last summer, which you still haven't bothered to get fixed."

"Yeah, well. It's Nonni's car, so it's his problem. He can get it fixed."

Matti's phone squawked. He picked it up and squinted to read the incoming number before stabbing at the phone to reject the call.

"So. That night in March. Tell me about it."

"Look, Gunna, I remember now I had a day off and Nonni let one of the other lads take this car out that night. It was my birthday. I had a night off and a couple of drinks."

"Cousin Matti, don't try to bamboozle me. I know perfectly well your birthday's in September and with you there's no such thing as a couple of drinks. It's a week or nothing."

"Hell, Gunna," Matti groaned. "Get off my back, will you? I've got to get back to work."

"When you tell me what this is all about."

"Look. It's nothing illegal, all right? A bit dodgy, maybe, but nothing bad. OK?"

"Tell me more."

"OK, OK. Look, sometimes I take ladies for a drive. They want a ride and I don't ask what they do when they get there. This one wanted to go to Sandeyri. I dropped her off outside the shop and picked her up there a bit later. Don't know where she went and what she did there is her business."

"And I assume it was business?"

"I don't know. I don't ask and I don't get told lies. All right?"

Gunna flipped open a notebook and wrote down a few lines, more to add to Matti's discomfort than to aid her own memory. "And this, er, lady's name?"

"No idea. Like I said, I don't ask."

"Was she a local?"

"Dunno."

"Don't bugger about. Icelandic or foreign?"

"Foreign."

"From?"

"Dunno. East. Russia or somewhere like that."

"If I were you, cousin Matti, I'd make an effort to remember this girl's name and see if you can find her."

"Like you think I can find her again?"

Gunna yanked the door handle and swung a leg out. "You might need the alibi. See you soon, Matti."

He grunted and started the engine, then leaned his head back on the rest and ran a hand over his eyes. In the mirror he could see Gunna standing by the squad car talking to the young officer sitting inside. After a moment's thought, he put his head out of the window and twisted his neck around.

"Hey, Gunna."

She looked up, said a word to the officer in the car and walked slowly over to him. "Yes, Matti?"

"Well," he muttered, embarrassed, "I was, y'know, sorry to hear about your bloke. Bit of a rough old time for you, I reckon."

"Thanks. You know. You get over it."

"Yeah. Look after yourself," he grunted, sliding the big car into drive.

"And you. Behave yourself, Matti."

Gunna got into the squad car's passenger seat, shaking her head.

"How'd it go?" Snorri asked, pulling out into the traffic and stopping at the first of many sets of lights before the open road over the heath to Hvalvík.

"Well, my cousin has always had a problem telling the truth, and this time is no exception."

* * *

Birna heard the screech as soon as the Minister put the phone to his ear. She felt briefly sorry for him but the feeling soon passed. Politicians are like pets, a senior official had told her in an expansive moment when she joined the civil service's fast-track scheme as an outstandingly bright but nonetheless raw graduate.

"Think of them as cute little puppies, it makes it so much easier to deal with their tantrums," the short of breath and soon-to-retire senior head of division had explained. "They come here keen and bright-eyed and wagging their little tails, anxious to please. Then they disappear to higher things or they just disappear. So there's no point getting fond of them."

Since then, she had classed incoming and outgoing ministers as those destined to disappear upstairs or those destined to disappear back to their rural constituencies for good. Privately she felt that Bjarni Jón Bjarnason deserved to disappear into obscurity, but had a nagging feeling all the same that the future would bring him bigger, but not necessarily better, things.

Bjarni Jón waved hurriedly at Birna to leave the room, but she was already on her discreet way out before he had even raised his hand.

"What is it now?" he grated into the phone and held it away from his ear to avoid premature deafness as Sigurjóna yelled with all the force of her considerable lungs into his ear.

"Have you seen that fucking Skandalblogger? Have you? Have you seen what that fucking arsehole has said about my sister? Have you?"

"No . . . Should I? It sounds like he's been rude again, or am I getting mixed signals here?"

This time Bjarni Jón grimaced and held the earpiece even further away as a tirade erupted from it.

"Jóna . . . Jóna, Sugarplum . . ."

"How dare you? Call yourself a fucking minister? You're a fucking useless piece of shit who can't even shut up some lying bastard scumbag . . ."

"Jóna. Calm down, please. Talk to me, will you?"

On the other end of the phone there was a respite as Sigurjóna's sobs could be heard down the line and Bjarni Jón took a deep breath, relieved that she had at least shut up.

"Jóna, my love? Are you listening to me?"

"I'm here." She was back, steely again with her bout of tears quickly over.

"I keep telling you, I'm doing everything I can. I've had meetings with the National Commissioner, the Minister of Justice, the Minister of Foreign Affairs, you name it, I've badgered them about it. I've had briefings from the head of the computer crime division, our own techno-nerd department and everyone apart from the receptionist downstairs. And I can't get any further."

"This has to stop." Sigurjóna's voice had gone as cold as a winter's night.

"I agree, but I can't see how."

"Offer the bastard money."

"What?"

"You heard what I said. Buy the bastard off."

"How? If nobody can find him, how?"

"Find a way."

Bjarni Jón groaned. "Jóna, my love. Leave it. Let it ride. Ignore it. It'll stop sooner or later. It isn't as if we haven't heard gossip before."

"Find a way, Bjarni."

The phone went dead in his hand. Bjarni Jón took a deep breath and typed the Skandalblogger's URL into his web browser. He gasped when he finished reading the latest entry, then a smile galloped around his face and he laughed out loud.

"Bloody hell. How do they find out this stuff?" he asked himself, pressing the buzzer for Birna's desk.

"Minister?"

"Birna, would you make me an appointment with the National Commissioner, please?"

"Again, Minister?"

"Yes, again. And as soon as is convenient," he said, wondering if Birna and the rest of the department would also be logging on to the Skandalblogger's page to read the latest titbit that had upset the Minister's wife.

CHAPTER TWENTY-ONE

Friday, 19 September

19-09-2008, 0223

Skandalblogger writes:

You do the hokey-cokey and . . .

And now for the sexual aberration of the week. Which well-known and highly exclusive city hairdresser to the rich, especially to the rich, has a penchant for back door fun with a difference? What is it with these sisters and their arses? Anyway, this lady likes it rough and Skandalblogger is reliably informed that she asks her gentlemen friends to use the following recipe.

Step 1. Roll on heavily ribbed condom, any flavour.

Step 2. Sprinkle todger with finest organic marching powder.

Step 3. Get stuck in.

Word has it that if the fun dust does to her arse what we're told it's already doing to her nose, she's going to be crapping in a bag long before she gets shunted off to the old folks' home.

. . . and you shake it all about . . . !

"Hi. Skúli."

"So I hear, young man. And just why are you calling at this time of night? Sorry, didn't have time to meet you in Reykjavík yesterday."

"That's all right. Didn't wake you up or anything, did I?"

Gunna laughed hollowly. "It's all right. I've only just come in. Been round the village to make sure the local bad guys are all behaving themselves."

"OK. Have you got the TV on?"

"Why?" Gunna asked curiously.

"I think you ought to watch the news. And buy a paper in the morning."

Something in Skúli's voice told her that he was serious and she rooted through the pile of old newspapers on the table for the TV remote control, jamming her phone between shoulder and ear while she did so. "Something important, is it?"

"Yeah. Einar Eyjólfur Einarsson? I reckon you'll need to see this. It was on the 19.19 news, but I reckon it'll be on the ten o'clock news in a few minutes as well, and it's our front page tomorrow."

Gunna looked at her watch. "Right. That gives me ten minutes to find the remote and when the news is over I'm going to get some sleep."

"Hope so. I'll see you next week, I expect."

"Goodnight, young man."

"G'night."

Gunna put the phone down and finally found the remote on the floor under the table. The TV flickered into life and she sat back to watch the news, easing her boots off and putting them neatly by the side of the armchair. She wondered briefly why Skúli had said he would see her next week.

As the news bulletin began, the screen filled with a blurred picture of Einar Eyjólfur Einarsson, wearing a colourful shirt and a goofy smile. He was the main story and as the newsreader switched to an item about forthcoming local elections, she heard the phone start to ring again.

CHAPTER TWENTY-TWO

Saturday, 20 September

"Gunnhildur, you're here because this is your area and your case," began Vilhjálmur Traustason, still shaken from last night's TV report. Everyone in the room remained silent and waited for him to continue. A police station on a Saturday morning is no less busy than at any other time and phones could be heard ringing in other rooms and traffic hummed past outside the window.

"What we have is a somewhat untrustworthy allegation that the death of this young man who was found unfortunately deceased in —" he peered at the report in front of him — "the harbour at Hvalvík, was deliberately perpetrated."

Vilhjálmur Traustason spread his hands flat on the table in front of him and squared his shoulders. "Having gone over the reports in detail and read carefully through the information from forensics and pathology, to my mind it is absolutely clear that the young man suffered death by drowning while intoxicated."

"I don't disagree with that," Gunna broke in. "But what we didn't manage to establish was how he managed to get, dead drunk, from Reykjavík to be found floating in the dock at Hvalvík, especially after our investigation came to an end and Sævaldur took it over."

Vilhjálmur looked at Gunna as if she were a recalcitrant child and sighed audibly. "There are other factors involved, Gunnhildur. We have to tread a delicate path on occasions and we also have to allocate resources where they are most needed. I don't have to remind you that we are facing a very different enforcement environment to the one you might remember from before you took over in Hvalvík. Hm?"

"That's as may be, but now we have to reallocate some resources to this matter," broke in Ívar Laxdal, the National Commissioner's deputy, who had been silent until now with a sheaf of newspapers in front of him, topped by a front page bearing the same picture of Einar Eyjólfur Einarsson as had already been on every TV report. Gunna knew Ívar Laxdal, who had already been a senior officer when she joined the force, only by his reputation for blunt speaking. Now he voiced everyone's thoughts.

"This Skandalblogger's allegations have been picked up by the media and splashed over the front pages. Regardless of the circumstances of the case, it hardly reflects well that this could have been investigated more thoroughly at the time," he continued. Vilhjálmur Traustason looked hurt, as if he had been punched in the kidneys by a trusted colleague.

"So what are we doing?" Bjössi asked with ill-concealed irritation. Gunna could see that he was desperate to go outside for a smoke and sympathized with him.

Ívar Laxdal stood up. "There will be a press announcement this afternoon and I need you there for that, Vilhjálmur. I expect to see progress by the end of the day. I need to have an evaluation this afternoon, please," he said brusquely, putting on his gold-braided cap. "I'm sure I can leave you to organize everything and I'll see you at headquarters at one. Email it through to me when you're ready."

He swept from the room, leaving Vilhjálmur pale with suppressed anger as he swiftly detailed three of his own officers to liaise with Gunna and CID, and followed his superior's example by sweeping from the room, after having called a further meeting for that afternoon.

The tension relaxed as the door banged shut in his wake.

"Right, then. So what the hell are we going to do?" Bjössi asked, looking at Gunna. "You're the man here with the experience, sweetheart."

Gunna looked at Bjössi and Bára, the young woman Gunna had chosen Snorri over for secondment to Hvalvík.

"How many people do we have to play with?"

"Us," Bjössi said. "As well as your guys from Hvalvík, plus whatever Reykjavík decides to help us out with. We've already set aside an incident room."

"We can call on a couple of the guys here when they're available for legwork," Bára added.

"OK. Let's start with Reykjavík, we need liaison straight away with the computer crime division to try and track this oddball down. What is it he calls himself?"

"Skandalblogger."

"Ideally we need to contact the person behind it and find out what else he or she knows. We need to go through the records of the original investigation and find out more about Einar Eyjólfur's background. Bára, you can pull my reports off the system so you're not going over the same ground twice. We already know quite a lot, but we haven't gone as deep as we ought to. Anything on friends, colleagues, whatever. His girlfriend's name is Dísa and she lives in Vogar. No idea if she still works at Spearpoint; find out. I have her full name and address at the station in Hvalvík and I can email those to you later."

Gunna drew breath. She was already enjoying the buzz of running a team, wondering how long it would be before someone more senior would be assigned to the case.

"Bjössi, will you please do your thing as far as you can with what's available? Go through the pathology again and the forensics, then come back and tell me where the holes are. And if you feel like it, you can get on with that right now and go for a puff on the way."

Bjössi needed no second invitation and was out of the room before Gunna had finished speaking.

"Bára. Clean Iceland. Do we have any contact with these people? Do we have any intelligence on them? I'm sure there's something, but it's a question of which department is holding it. Einar Eyjólfur was involved with Clean Iceland, so we need to speak to them. Find out who to talk to and talk to them, who's driving that bunch and what exactly was our boy's role."

Gunna's words came out in a torrent and she could not restrain a fizz of excitement at the activity she was kicking off.

"You all have a couple of officers to make use of, so make use of them. Delegate. Ask questions. All right? Now let's get on with it. The trail's gone cold, but that shouldn't slow us down too much. You know what number to find me on and I'll be back this afternoon."

Gunna clapped her hands once and found herself in an empty room. Outside, she ran into Björssi sheltering from the stiff breeze in the lee of the building and grinding the butt of a cigarette under his heel.

"Hi, Gunna. What d'you reckon on all this, then?"

"That's better."

"What is?"

"Less of the sweetheart for the moment."

Björssi laughed and coughed. "Ach, you know I don't say it to wind you up. Hey, what about Vilhjálmur, then?"

"Got his bollocks in a vice."

"Well, let's hope they don't stay there. Because when the people at the top are suffering, they tend to squeeze the bollocks of the people underneath them. Not that you have bollocks, sweetheart, but you do, if you know what I mean."

"Point taken, and coming from you, I'll treat that as a compliment. But all the same, this wasn't investigated properly and that was Vilhjálmur's decision."

"Under pressure."

"What do you mean?"

"What I mean is that Vilhjálmur was being pressured from higher up not to make it a priority. He's been expected to put as much effort as possible on narcotics, and that's what he's done."

"All right, so he's not such a bad guy, just misguided."

"He's always done everything by the book. Just following orders, is what he'd say, and rightly so. Hey, where are you off to?"

"I feel like a day off," Gunna shot back as she started the second-best Volvo.

Matti was worried, more worried than he had been the time he'd been stranded in Grimsby after failing to reach his ship just as the last Cod War broke out, more worried than the time his first — or second? — wife's brothers had threatened to pay him a visit when he'd staked and lost her parents' house on what should have been a cast-iron winning hand.

This could be serious. Although Matti had watched Hardy carefully on their various journeys together over the summer around the south-west, acting as a combination of guide, driver and interpreter when necessary, he was still wondering just what Hardy's business was about. He speculated that Hardy was American, disguised with a neutral enough accent to pass as a European. He felt sure that Hardy's business was something to do with the spate of heavy industry projects springing up around the country, but this hardly concerned him. He knew that while Hardy paid on the nail and treated him with the respect due to an equal, his passenger in the understatedly expensive clothes was not someone to tangle with lightly. The air of authority and the hidden menace were unmistakable to someone with a professional interest in gauging the desires or the gullibility of the person in the passenger seat.

At the time he had thought nothing of the trip to pick Hardy up on the dockside at Sandeyri in March. The man had wanted to go to many unlikely places at odd times and had been dropped off and collected from several unfamiliar places that Matti had been forced to search for when the time came.

But he had to admit to himself that he was intrigued when the TV news had shown a short item about a car being recovered from the dock at Sandeyri. He wondered idly about it and put it from his mind. But now he had something to be concerned about — the possible loss of a valued client and an excellent source of tax-free, back pocket earnings.

Sitting in the morning rush hour traffic waiting for the lights to change at the Miklabraut junction, Matti turned down the radio, abruptly silencing yet another round of Channel 2's celebrity gossip, and drummed the wheel with his thumbs. After weeks of driving Hardy back and forth across the south of Iceland, he still had only a hazy idea of what the man's business was. The only point of contact was an anonymous mobile number, and Hardy rarely asked to be collected or dropped off at the same place more than once. This time their meeting place was on the Grensás taxi rank where Matti bullied the big car into a space on the end. He was starting to feel uncomfortable in the Mercedes since Gunna had questioned him. Normally he wasn't inclined to worry too much about the law, but this time he felt as if everything on the road was watching him.

As usual, Hardy appeared within a few seconds, dropping into the passenger seat with the nearest he came to a smile.

"Where to, boss?" Matti asked.

"Out of town today."

"OK. East? South? Which way?"

"Hvalvík."

Matti's heart almost missed a beat and he was sure that Hardy immediately sensed it.

"Hvalvík it is, then," he grunted, coaxing the car out into the road and scraping the bumper of the car double-parked in front.

They sailed through Reykjavík's sunshine. It was a warm day and the dust rose thickly in the heat. Hardy was dressed as usual in spite of the temperature, the pale leather jacket making him look slimmer across the shoulders than he really was.

"Everything all right, big man? You're quiet today," Hardy said pleasantly as they left the city behind and began to climb the heath.

"That guy. The one you went to talk to near Borgarnes. He's dead."

Hardy lifted an eyebrow. "How do you know?"

"It was on the radio. Heart attack, they said."

"So? You didn't see anything, did you?"

"Not a thing," Matti assured him.

"Then there's nothing for you to worry about, is there?"

Hardy looked relaxed as he admired the landscape around him. His hands lay idle in his lap with fingers twined together.

"You know, Matti," he said eventually. "The guy you work for?"

"Nonni?"

"No, big man. Not the taxi man. The other guy you work for, the one you need to be particularly discreet about."

"You, you mean?"

Irritation flashed over Hardy's face. "No. The one with the establishment."

"Him? Why? I don't do much for Mundi Grétars these days."

"Ah, but I'm sure you do. I have a little word of advice for you."

"Like what?" Matti demanded.

"It might be an idea to distance yourself from those activities for a little while."

Matti did his best not to be angry. With the police already snooping into his business, he found it hard to accept that Hardy was also aware of his other sideline.

"What's this about, eh?"

"I just thought you ought to know that your friend may have some problems in the next few weeks and that it might be useful if you're not too closely involved with him and his ladies for a while."

Bloody hell, Matti thought. The bloody man seems to know everything there is to know.

"Especially the lady that you're such good friends with. We wouldn't want her to be in any trouble, would we?" Hardy asked with an unmistakable note of iron in his tone.

Matti drove in shock and silence while Hardy examined his fingernails. Neither of them spoke until Hvalvík could be seen as a bundle of houses clustered around the shallow curve of its bay in the paler sunshine of the south coast.

"Where to now?" Matti asked gruffly, butterflies fluttering under his belt at the thought of Gunna or that other cop noticing his taxi going though the village.

"This time we're going out to the Lagoon site," Hardy said and Matti sighed with relief as this meant at least going straight through the village and out the other side without needing to stop. But his peace of mind was cut short as the fuel gauge light blinked red as they passed the "Hvalvík welcomes careful drivers" sign.

"Shit. Bastard."

"What's up?" Hardy asked quietly.

"Ach, nothing. Just got to diesel up."

The car rolled to a halt in front of the pumps outside Hafnarkaffi. Matti hurriedly pumped fuel, cursing the slow pace of the machine and staring out over the roof of the car to scan for anyone who might recognize him.

"Shit. Fuck," he continued to mutter to himself as the pump clanged to a halt and he hurried inside to pay at the counter where there was nobody to take his money. For a moment he was tempted to jump back in the car and leave, but thought better of it. In a one-horse dump full of nosy parkers, somebody would be bound to notice.

"Sorry, my love. Been waiting long, have you?" cooed a woman who appeared suddenly behind the counter.

"Er, no."

"Not a local, are you?"

"No."

"Oh. And I was sure I recognized you from somewhere. Can't for the life of me say where, though. From Reykjavík, are you?"

"Yeah," Matti grunted, willing her to move faster as she tapped buttons on the computerized till.

"I'll never get the hang of this thing," she warbled. "The old till's so much easier, but progress is progress and I suppose I'll have to get used to it sooner or later. That'll be six thousand two hundred, my dear."

Matti dropped notes on the counter and made for the door. As he stepped out, a police car cruised up the street towards them and Matti swore to himself, looking down at the ground as he opened the car door.

Hardy looked out from his seat at the police car as it passed by. Matti lifted his head to follow his gaze and was relieved to see that rather than the cousin he definitely had no wish to run into, the driver was an older man with a kindly face who looked over at them curiously, but didn't bother to stop.

“Right. Let’s go then, shall we?”

Hardy pointed. “There’s a café there. Do you want to eat?”

“No,” Matti said brusquely. “Let’s get out to the compound, shall we? It’s a real dump, that place,” he added lamely.

Dagga coaxed the television next to her desk into life as a sober newsreader was halfway through his item on the 19.19 news.

“. . . morning and we are taking you straight over live to the press briefing that is already taking place.”

“Smári Geir doing well for himself on TV, I see,” Dagga observed as the young man’s face vanished and was replaced with a trio of senior police officers sitting behind a row of microphones.

“We consider that, in the light of this serious allegation from a highly unusual source, a further investigation is justified,” one of them read out from a prepared statement. Skúli stared at the group, his eyes going from the man speaking to one of the others next to him, and back.

“These allegations are of an extremely grave nature, claiming that a very serious crime has been committed against an innocent young man, culminating in his death. We are issuing a general appeal for witnesses to come forward and to place at the disposal of the police any information that may identify the alleged perpetrator,” Vilhjálmur Traustason read out in a tone as morbid as the grave.

Flashes flickered and he blinked repeatedly.

"We have already identified persons who may or may not be involved in this incident. At present we are eliminating persons who are known to have been at or near the scene on the day in question. That is all. Questions?"

There was an immediate chorus that was cut short as the broadcast returned to the studio.

"No statement on their website yet," Dagga said, looking up from her laptop. "I've emailed and asked for the text and I suppose it'll be here soon. What are we doing on this, Jonni?" she asked.

"We can cobble most of it together from the statement when it comes and the TV reports, but I suppose we'd better find a few comments. Any ideas, Skúli, as you're our crime man?"

"What's Reynir Óli's take on this?"

"Oh, the usual." Jonni yawned. "Play along with the others, make it a front page if we can get an angle no one else will have."

"Like what?" Dagga asked.

"Well." Jonni smiled cruelly. "I was thinking Sigurjóna Huldudóttir. She's been on the receiving end of Skandalblogger more than most people, so I'm sure she'd love the chance to sound off. It's just a question of which one of you two darlings wants to go and listen to her ranting. Make it early, though. She's normally a bit pissed by mid-afternoon."

At the Keflavík station Gunna had already banged the doors aside when she realized that she didn't know where her own incident room was, but catching sight of Bára at the end of a corridor she set off to follow her.

"How goes it?"

"Fine. I have two guys chasing up Clean Iceland and I'm off in a minute to talk to the guy who calls himself the strategic director."

"Good. Play it cool, will you? We don't want to alarm anyone. Now, is everyone here? I need to speak to you all together."

The incident room was just a large office with a few desks, phones and PCs. A planner pinned to the wall showed the dates when Einar Eyjólfur had been last seen and when his body had been discovered.

Gunna stood before it with the sheaf of notes she had picked up from the station in Hvalvík, along with Snorri, who had been given the whole story in a staccato barrage on the way after they had left a bewildered Haddi in sole charge at Hvalvík.

"Right, ladies and gentlemen." She looked around at Bára and Björssi. "Where's Snorri?"

"Here, chief," he said apologetically, slipping in around the door.

"I'll keep this quick," Gunna announced, pinning the passport picture of Ström staring blankly out of it to the wall board. "This man is someone we need to eliminate. We don't have anyone else at all. Einar Eyjólfur appears to have had no enemies at all, everyone liked him, so there doesn't seem to be anyone anywhere who would have wanted to harm him."

She tapped the noticeboard with one finger.

"Name of Ström, presumed Swedish national, has probably been to Iceland more than once. I have established that he rented a car of the kind seen on the dock that night, a BMW X-three jeep with JA in the number. Don't worry," she warned, seeing the expression on Bára's face. "I've spent a day already eliminating every vehicle that doesn't fit. We need to know what his business is, who he is, why he's been here and what his movements have been."

"Is this man a suspect or a witness?" Bára asked.

"Initially a witness. We've placed him provisionally, time and place, where Einar Eyjólfur was found. Also, we have a possible link to him and the stolen blue jeep that was lifted from Sandeyri harbour. Now, Bjössi, will you investigate, assuming the jeep hasn't been disposed of? If we link this to Egill Grímsson's death as well, as I firmly believe we can, then we have something uncomfortably big on our hands."

Bjössi looked pensive for a moment. "Fuck. You mean this guy's killed two people?"

"It looks that way to me," Gunna agreed.

He whistled. "Vilhjálmur and Ívar Laxdal are going to love you. Iceland hasn't had a double murder since . . .?"

"I suppose since Gréttir did his stuff. So, I want this investigated as a priority. Bjössi, I want you to start by contacting Stockholm. Then Interpol. Snorri will email you the picture of our boy to send out."

She put the sheaf of documents from Swiftcars on to the desk in front of him.

"His passport, driving licence and credit card details are all in there, so hopefully our herring-munching friends in Sweden can tell us something straight away. Get on to Visa. The credit card trail might help us as well." Gunna took a long breath. "We don't know if he's still in the country. We have no idea if he thinks we might be on to him. We can only assume he's dangerous and not to be approached. OK? That's all for now."

The group scattered, leaving Gunna and Snorri behind as they all hunched behind phones and computers or disappeared from the room.

"What now, chief?" Snorri asked.

Gunna thought. "I want to know where Matti Kristjáns is in all this. He was nowhere to be found yesterday, so you'd better be off to Reykjavík for the afternoon and see if you can track the old bastard down. Have a quick look at the taxi ranks and if he's not there, get straight down to Nonni the Taxi's place. Be as heavy as you like if they don't cooperate."

"OK. I can do that."

"It's getting on for one now, and there's the briefing with Vilhjálmur Traustason at five, so hopefully I'll have something for him by then. You'd better be off and see if you can find anything out before then."

With everyone else busy, Gunna tapped a computer until it awoke from its sleep, typed "Clean Iceland" into a search engine and waited impatiently for the machine to do her bidding.

A list of choices appeared, Gunna clicked on the most obvious one and instantly the website of the

Clean Iceland Campaign emerged in front of her. She saw that it was largely in English and began to pick her way through the panels of information, starting with news. Here she scrolled down to the beginning of the year, quickly found a bulletin on Egill Grímsson's death and read through a short biography of the man, detailing his commitment to the cause of opposing heavy industry in Iceland and his devotion to his family, alongside his dedication to his job as a schoolteacher in the grey Reykjavík suburb where he had lived for most of his forty-four years.

Gunna made a few notes, including that he had been one of the founders of the movement and had lobbied the Ministry of Environmental Affairs tirelessly, while being involved in an international campaign of protests outside Icelandic embassies across the developed world in cooperation with environmental groups abroad that formed a loose network across much of Europe, North America and some Asian countries.

She closed the window on the screen and sat back.

So, he was a bit of a firebrand on the quiet, was our Egill, she mused.

CHAPTER TWENTY-THREE

Sunday, 21 September

This time Matti Kristjáns wasn't just worried — he was frightened. He ran the conversation with Hardy over in his mind as he packed those of his meagre possessions that he didn't dare leave behind.

"Meet me in an hour and we'll talk it over," Hardy had said nonchalantly, too nonchalantly, Matti thought. Had it been a mistake to tell Hardy a little bird had whispered in his ear that the police were looking for him? Although no stranger to a little persuasion himself, Matti couldn't forget Hardy's coolness after having so effortlessly broken the wrist of the man in the farmhouse outside Borgarnes.

Rooting under his bed, he hauled out a seaman's canvas kitbag and stuffed clothes unceremoniously into it, dirty clothes and clean going in together, and a sleeping bag on top of the lot. From the drawer in the bedside table he took a few papers, driving licence, health insurance card, passport and a couple of bank cards, all of which he stowed in the inside pocket of his jacket.

Sadly he surveyed the stack of glossy pornography peeking from under his bed. Antiques, some of these, he thought with a pang, recalling that the airbrushed nudes had been with him through plenty of tough times without a word of complaint.

Matti shoved the stack back under his bed and clicked the door shut on his way out. At the bottom of the stairs he paused and listened for the TV in the living room. A daytime soap meant that the old woman was in. In fact, she wasn't older than Matti, but years of hard living had taken a grim toll.

"Tóta! Going out for a bit," Matti called, hoping she wouldn't hear him, but the door swung open and the heavy-set woman stood in the doorway leaning on the frame.

"Going to be long?" she demanded without taking the cigarette from her lips.

"Day or two," Matti lied.

"Paid up, are you?"

"Yeah, I think so," he lied again as Tóta's eyes narrowed, and he knew that she could smell something wrong. Set a thief to catch a thief, he thought bitterly.

"Well, if you're not sure how long you're going to be, then I'd better have another month's rent so's I can be sure," she said in a sandpaper growl.

Matti knew when not to argue. He pulled a handful of notes from his trouser pocket and handed them over.

"That's all I've got right now. Nonni's supposed to be paying out at the end of the month for the booking work and we'll square up then if that's OK."

Tóta thumbed through the notes, counting under her breath.

"All right. That'll do for now," she said as her face broke into a gap-toothed smile. "I won't rent your room out straight away, though I reckon I could put four Poles in there tomorrow if I wanted to. Tonight, even," she cackled, and promptly dissolved into a fit of coughing. Matti made his escape as Tóta's face was beginning to go a colour he wasn't comfortable with.

The big car's engine whispered into life and within seconds he had made up his mind and was out on the main road, heading through the late morning traffic of Reykjanesbraut to Kópavogur. He drove through the centre of the town in a hurry, but not enough of a hurry to attract attention. He kept his eyes peeled for the police, half expecting to see his cousin Gunnhildur creeping up on him with that sinister lopsided grin of hers.

Matti shuddered at the thought that Hardy was now probably aware that he wasn't going to meet him, and he waited for his phone to ring as he swung off the main road and swerved to take the speed bumps of the suburban streets as painlessly as possible. He stamped on the brake and stopped in front of a terraced house at the bottom of a cul-de-sac. He leaped out of the car, bounded up the half-dozen steps and was inside the door as he hammered on it.

"Marika!"

"She sleeping," a tall woman in a coarse towelling dressing gown said sourly, appearing from the kitchen with a plate of toast in one hand.

"But she's here?" Matti demanded. "Alone?"

"She alone," the woman replied sharply. "We not work here," she added, by which time Matti was at the top of the stairs and knocking at a door. Before a sleepy questioning reply was heard, he was already inside the room.

"Marika, get up. We have to go."

"What? Matti?" The girl in the bed looked out from under her duvet in bewilderment, black hair twisted around her face.

"Marika, listen," Matti panted. "We have to get away from here. Just for a few days. There's trouble."

Marika sat up in bed, one hand scratching under her outsized Fatalagerinn T-shirt.

"Trouble? What you mean, trouble? Police trouble?"

"Yes, yes, police trouble. You come with me, OK?"

"OK, Matti. Tell me what trouble? All of us in trouble?"

"No, just you, me trouble. Just a couple of days. Then we come back here."

Marika yawned and snapped into wakefulness. "Matti, you tell me what problem is. Then we go. Sit here." She patted the bed.

"No. Get dressed. I'll tell you while you put clothes on."

"OK. You tell. But turn round."

Marika slipped from the bed and waited for him to turn his back before hauling the voluminous T-shirt over her head.

"Matti. Tell. Not look in mirror," she admonished.

"Look. I have a problem, a bad man is looking for me, wants to maybe kill me. He has seen me with you in the car. He knows Kaisa and some of the girls, maybe he knows this place, and he knows Mundi, says Mundi is going to have trouble."

"You turn round now," Marika instructed, buttoning a plain blouse. She raised her arms and tied her hair back in a bun before starting to drop things haphazardly into an open suitcase. Matti wanted to yell at her that the car was parked outside where Hardy would be able to see it, that the street was a dead end with no hope of escape except on foot through someone's garden, but he held his breath and sat on his hands.

"Ready. We go," Marika announced brightly, at last, and Matti grabbed the case and was downstairs before she had closed her mouth.

At the doorway Marika and Kaisa held a loud conversation, not a word of which could Matti understand. Kaisa banged the door behind them as the car pulled away and Matti sighed with relief.

"Matti, where we going?"

"Out of town. West."

Marika seemed satisfied and filed her nails on the way through Reykjavík, on to the main road. Only when they had cleared the city and were bowling past the well-kept gardens and stables of Mosfell did she look up and take notice, as if seeing the scree-sloped hillsides for the first time.

"Matti?"

"Yeah, sweetheart."

"This man. Policeman?"

"No."

"Criminal man?"

"Yes."

"Pity." She shrugged.

"Why's that?"

"Police no problem."

"How so?"

Marika sat back and folded away her nail file. "Sometimes policeman come to us and say he make trouble. OK, Kaisa take him upstairs, be nice to him for half an hour. No more trouble."

Matti rocked with laughter. "Always Kaisa?"

"Always Kaisa look after policeman."

"But why her?"

"Don't know. Maybe policeman like very tall. Maybe Kaisa just like police."

"This policeman, he comes to the house, or to the club?"

"Club. Always club."

"In uniform?"

"No, of course not uniform. Don't be stupid."

"So how do you know he's a policeman."

"Because he smell like a policeman," Marika said with decision. "He walk like policeman, he have clothes like policeman."

"You don't know his name, do you?" Matti hazarded.

"No, of course not. Not real name. Anyway, who would want to make trouble for Matti?"

"You've seen him once or twice at the club. The tall guy with blond hair. Always wears that leather jacket."

Marika nodded. "Swedish man."

"Swedish? No, I thought he was American?"

"Swedish," Marika said firmly.

"How do you know?"

"Maret tell me. He speak when he sleep. He speak Swedish when he sleep."

While Matti was grimly hugging the big car's wheel as it growled up the long slope of the heath on the road north and Marika filed her nails, Gunna sat back and simply enjoyed the feeling of being out of uniform for a few hours.

It hadn't stopped her from calling in at the station to see what progress Bára and Bjössi were making. Bára looked surprised to see her, while Bjössi made it clear that her presence wasn't wanted and that she should make the most of an afternoon off duty now that she finally had one.

After a visit to the supermarket in Keflavík, she drove Gísli's rusting Range Rover through the achingly slow Sunday afternoon traffic in the town to the museum that overlooked the small boat harbour and parked in the sunshine.

She pulled down the shade, peered carefully at herself in the mirror and didn't entirely like what she could see. She looked tired, and older than she ought to. Fine lines were starting to appear at the corners of her eyes and fatigue was entrenched in her face. She had long ago given up make-up, having been told many times by Raggi that her fresh complexion didn't need it.

Gunna frowned and her mighty eyebrows fused into a dark bar across her forehead. For a moment, she thought about crying off and going home, but brushed aside the idea of a grown woman being nervous about what was not even really a date.

She fussed for a moment with her hair, decided that this week she really would have to get it cut before it became so thick that it would be beyond control, and swung herself down from the Range Rover.

He was sitting alone at a table by the window in the corner of the room, gazing down at one of the small boats leaving the little pontoon dock. Outside a group of children on the café's balcony waved frantically at the boat as it chugged past and whooped with delight when the man at the tiller waved back at them.

"Waiting for someone?" Gunna asked.

Steini's head jerked up and he grinned with what Gunna saw was obvious relief. He quickly stood up and took her by surprise by leaning forward to peck her cheek.

"Don't you know I could arrest you for that?"

Steini held out both hands, wrists together. "Go on, then."

"Sorry. I'm off duty," she apologized, sitting down opposite him. "Anyway, how are you?"

"Fine."

They sat in awkward silence for a moment.

"The Salt House was good," he ventured finally.

"It was. Shall we do that again some time?"

"I think we ought to," Steini replied seriously and waved for the waitress to bring a menu.

Gunna made her choice in seconds flat and laid her menu down again while Steini pored over his a little longer. She felt guilty, enjoying the colours outside, cobalt sky and the bright green of the autumn grass clinging to the basalt outcrops surrounding the little harbour, while Bára and Bjössi were on duty.

"Aren't you hungry?" Steini asked.

"Do I look like the sort of girl who doesn't enjoy her food? Of course I'm hungry."

Steini grinned and waved to the waitress, who stood there with her open note pad and waited expectantly.

"Ready to order?" the girl asked finally, as Gunna and Steini each waited for the other to go first.

"Fish of the day," they both suddenly said simultaneously.

"Two fish," the waitress said. "And to drink?"

"I have to drive, so water for me," Gunna said, looking at Steini.

"Same here," he added, handing back the menus. Gunna sat back and stretched her legs out beneath the table, basking in the warmth of the afternoon sunshine on her face. Steini let a smile run around his face while his fingers tugged at the end of his moustache.

"How goes it? Work and everything?"

"Ah, really busy right now. I shouldn't be here at all."

"Well, there's no point overdoing it. You don't get paid any more for it and I don't suppose you'll get thanked either."

"Y'know, you're probably right," Gunna agreed, trying to imagine Vilhjálmur Traustason with anything other than the usual disapproving look on his long face. "It'll blow over soon, I hope."

"Is that all the work around that aluminium smelter they're building?"

Gunna sighed. She had hoped to get away from work for an hour or two. "Partly. We have an unusual murder investigation in progress that's taking all my time right now."

"Murder? In Iceland?" Steini's eyebrows lifted in surprise.

"Yup. It's a serious one and I'm afraid that's about all I'm able to say. Case in progress and all that, has to be kept confidential."

"Understood. Ah, food," Steini said with his interest on the waitress, striding towards them with a plate in each hand.

Gunna hadn't realized quite how hungry she was until the aroma of the generous portion hit her senses.

"*Bon appétit*," Steini said seriously, setting to with gusto.

They ate in silence. Gunna felt that Steini was not completely at ease and wondered why, while she found herself to be more relaxed than she had expected. Steini seemed to be the kind of person it was easy to spend time with, without a need for chatter. The case was still preying on her mind and it irritated her that she could not clear thoughts of work even for a few short hours.

"Good fish," she said finally when her plate was almost clear.

"Can't beat it," Steini agreed, his plate already shining. "Coffee?"

"Let me finish, at least."

"Sorry. It's force of habit, not being able to eat slowly. It's all those years of having half an hour to wake up, eat your dinner, drink a cup of coffee and be out on deck on time."

Gunna smiled wryly. "Don't think I don't know. My dad and my brothers are just the same and Raggi always finished before me as well."

Steini nodded. "How are your kids? Your lad's at sea, isn't he?"

"Yup. Deckhand on *Snœfugl*."

"Not a bad berth. Has he been there long?"

"Since January. He tried college but couldn't get on with it. Then one of his uncles, you must know him, Stefán Jónsson, had a word and got him a berth to see how he'd like it. Gísli took to it straight away. I wouldn't be surprised if he applies for navigation college in a year or two."

"Send him to me if he needs any coaching," Steini smiled.

"I might do just that. But we'll see," Gunna replied absently. She shook herself quickly, realizing that her thoughts were drifting unconsciously back to Matti and whether or not to try and hunt him down in the morning.

She looked up to see Steini gazing quizzically at her.

"Sorry. Miles away," she said, irritated with herself.

"Work on your mind?" Steini asked gently.

"Unfortunately," she admitted, wondering at the same time if she should mention the offered promotion that would also entail moving to the other side of the country. "Until this is sorted out, I'm afraid it's going to be on my mind. But I ought to be on my way home soon. Laufey's gone riding and I'd better cook a meal for us this evening for once."

Steini waved for the bill until the waitress placed it in front of him and sauntered away.

Gunna reached for it. "My turn."

"No, come on. I invited you."

"I know, but you paid last time," Gunna said firmly and Steini shrugged. Gunna stood up to walk over to the bar. She rested her elbows on the counter and dug through her purse, lifting one foot to place it on the brass rail that ran along the foot of the bar. Steini smiled quietly to himself as he admired Gunna's figure in the loose cheesecloth trousers that he felt did her so many more favours than uniform.

"Ready?" she smiled, returning to the table. Steini stood up and followed her outside.

"Well, thank you for a pleasant lunch," Gunna said as she dug in her pocket for the Range Rover's key and dangled it from a finger.

"Yours?" Steini asked, patting the big car's bonnet.

"No," Gunna said, laughing. "It's Gísli's. He's wanted one of these since he was about five. So as soon as he'd saved up enough, that's what he bought. The insurance was costing him a fortune considering he's at sea four weeks in five, so now he splits the insurance with his old mum and I use it as well when he's away."

"That's very generous of him," Steini said and Gunna had a sudden image of a tongue-tied teenager in front of her. "You know, Gunna, you're a highly attractive lady and I'd like to see more of you," he said quickly.

Taken by surprise, Gunna took a few seconds to reply.

"That's very kind of you to say so, Steini. I wouldn't mind seeing a bit more of you as well, but I've a lot on my plate right this minute and I don't know . . ." She took a gulp of air. "I'm sorry, you've caught me on the hop."

Steini smiled slowly. "I'm sorry. Didn't mean to startle you. I'll give you a call in the week if that's all right?"

His face was one big question as Gunna nodded.

"Do that. I'm going to be busy, but give me a call when you have time," she said firmly.

He hesitated for a moment and finally leaned forward to peck her on the cheek.

"See you soon, then," he said and strode away to the van that Gunna recognized from the day they had spoken on the dock at Sandeyri.

Gunna sat in the Range Rover's driving seat and waited for her stomach to settle.

"Good grief," she grumbled to herself. "I should be past all this stuff by now. Like a lovesick bloody teenager."

CHAPTER TWENTY-FOUR

Monday, 22 September

The second-best Volvo hummed through Hafnarfjördur in the morning sunshine, with the faintest dusting of white on Esja's slopes in the distance above Reykjavík a reminder that the short days of winter weren't far away. Gunna had always had misgivings about what she saw as the mountain's brooding hulk and had never understood the fondness people born in its shadow always professed for it. Gunna found Esja less than impressive compared to the dramatic sheer slopes of her childhood home.

She toured a few of the taxi ranks at Grensás and Lækjargata, near the shopping centres and the big hotels, and cruised slowly down Raudarárstígur to the Hlemmur bus station and across past the police station to the main road into the town centre, looking out for Matti's green Mercedes, wondering as she did so if this was the right thing to be doing.

She headed out of town, and stopped at the Höfdabakki traffic lights next to Nonni the Taxi's yard, scanning the car park outside for the green Mercedes. Gunna wondered whether or not to go in and ask for

Matti's whereabouts, but decided against it, unwilling to send him a message that could be misunderstood if not delivered personally.

Gunna checked the time and decided to take a round trip through the Bakki district and Kópavogur before a final look through Matti's normal haunts in the old western end of the city.

Lunchtime traffic thickened as she gunned the Volvo out of Kópavogur and on to Kringlumýrarbraut back towards the city. Passing the airport, she wondered idly how the billionaires with their little summer houses around Skildingarnes would be preparing for the invasion of their territory if the city were to have its way and close the airport to make way for more building south of the city centre.

"It'll happen. Money talks its own language, as Mum used to say," Gunna grunted to herself, pulling up at the lights at Lækjargata for the second time that day and seeing that the taxi rank there was empty.

"Hell. Lunchtime, I suppose."

She drove slowly past the slipways and the remnants of the old town, where rusting houses clad in corrugated iron were gradually being replaced with steel and glass, and past Kaffivagninn. She thought of stopping there, but since office types had discovered the old dockers' eatery on the quay, it had gone upmarket and lost some of its attraction.

Further along and beyond walking distance from the office district, she pulled up on a patch of waste ground opposite Grandakaffi among a cluster of taxis, pickup trucks and a bus at the end of its route. For a moment she admired the trawlers in their blue-and-white Grandi livery at the quayside and listened as a group of men in paint-spattered overalls engaged in a friendly argument in some Eastern European language as they made their way from a half-painted ship over the waste ground towards the café. They fell silent as they noticed her uniform, nudging each other as they passed her. Gunna walked behind the men, trying not to look as if she was following them to the café, but she could sense their discomfort.

In the sunshine half a dozen men sat over large meals and newspapers around rickety tables and Gunna scanned the faces quickly, catching the eye of a thin-faced elderly man who looked as if a square meal coming his way was a rarity. He nodded imperceptibly as she passed, and carried on with his bowl of soup.

The group of workmen were at the counter, bargaining with a tiny Asian woman in broken English. As Gunna approached, the woman looked past them in relief. Gunna wondered what had brought her to Iceland.

"What're y'looking for?" the woman asked in perfect Icelandic that marked her down as a second-generation immigrant.

"Coffee and a ham sandwich," Gunna decided. There was a palpable relaxation of tension among the group of men as they realized that she was there to eat. The woman put a sandwich on a plate on the counter and pointed to the coffee urns.

"Six hundred."

Gunna fished in her pocket for coins and finally came up with a crumpled thousand krona note.

"Have you seen a green Mercedes taxi around?" she asked, handing over the money.

"What? Big Matti?"

"That's the guy."

"Not for a day or two. Want me to take a message?" the woman replied, handing back a handful of coins.

"No. It's all right. Nothing urgent."

Gunna took her sandwich and coffee outside into the sunshine and looked around before planting herself down opposite the narrow-faced man.

"Well then, Baddi. How's life? Keeping yourself occupied?"

"Little Dodda, isn't it?"

Gunna nodded and bit into her sandwich. Hearing the Dodda name, only remembered by a handful of family from Vestureyri, took her home and back thirty years with a jolt. "Not so little these days."

"Not so bad, y'know. Keeping busy."

"Good to know," Gunna said. She understood the older generation and their need to be working all the time. "I thought you'd have been retired by now, Baddi."

"Ach. You know. I tried for a while but my Magga didn't like having me under her feet all day long, so I do three days a week now. Enough to keep out of the old woman's way."

Gunna nodded. "Working for Nonni?"

"Yup. Just weekdays. Can't be having with the drunks. There's a young feller drives the cab nights and weekends. He makes a packet and works hard for it, and Nonni's got his car working day and night. I do a few days, so we're all happy. And how's your mum these days?"

"She's the same as ever. Greyer. Still complaining. How about your boys?"

"Nothing but trouble. Gummi's still at sea, just. Beggi's got himself married again. Fourth time, or maybe the fifth. I've given up counting. Filipina girl this time, half his age, at least. So, did you just happen to be passing?"

"Sort of," Gunna admitted. "Looking around for our Matti."

"Ah," Baddi said with satisfaction. "Now there's a lad who never got round to growing up."

"But have you seen him about? He's driving a green Merc for Nonni."

"I knock off in an hour or two, so the young lad can get on with the evening shift. I recall seeing Matti last week, but not since."

"And I take it you'd normally see him about?"

"Normally, yes. On the rank at Lækjargata, or around town. We Icelanders don't like to think so, but our island's only a goldfish bowl," he said gravely. "You see everyone sooner or later."

"That's odd. I've been looking about for Matti, and I haven't seen him."

The old man frowned. "What's the boy done this time? If you can tell me, that is?"

Gunna upended her mug and drained the last bitter drops of coffee while there was still a little warmth in them. "Y'know, Baddi? I'm not sure and I'd tell you if I did know. I have a nasty feeling he's tangled up in something deeper than he's used to this time . . ."

"And you don't want him getting into any real trouble again? Dodda, my girl, you're soft."

"Ach. Family and all that. Matti's a pain in the arse, but he's a good sort at heart, and I did promise his mother years ago that I'd keep an eye out for him."

"Well, some days he's not about at all. Our Matti always keeps busy, and from what I've heard, he's been running some foreign business chap about. Cash in the back pocket and no questions asked."

Gunna extracted a pen from her top pocket and scribbled her phone number on a napkin. "Will you give me a call if you hear anything?"

"I'll do that."

Gunna stood up, ready to leave. Baddi looked at her squinting into the bright sunshine that lit up every crease and wrinkle in his lined face.

"You might try where he lives."

"Where's that?"

"Not sure. I think it's one of those old houses in Flókagata that was split up into flats years ago. He rents a room from a couple who seem to rent out most of their flat, live in their own living room and drink the rent. Anyway, he's always moaning about the landlady. Ugly Tóta, he calls her."

"Ah, thank you, Baddi. That rings a bell or two right away."

"Hope that helps. I'll let you know if I hear something."

"Do that." Gunna straightened her cap and left Baddi as he lifted and opened that day's *DV*, showing her the "BJB to step down?" headline emblazoned across the front page over an unflattering picture of the Minister and Sigurjóna caught unawares by a photographer's flash.

As far as Dagga could see, Sigurjóna Huldudóttir was a model of sobriety, good nature and sparking health on a fresh Monday morning. Her hair fell in a shining blonde curtain to her shoulders in a way that was both fashionable and practical, her understatedly expensive suit said business, while showing just a hint of enhanced cleavage.

"You've seen all this shit that Skandalblogger has been publishing? I mean, not just about my husband and myself, but about a whole host of other prominent people as well?" she asked.

"No, not all of it," Dagga lied, wishing she had dressed more smartly for this interview.

"Then you're not as well prepared as you ought to be," Sigurjóna said mildly.

"Well, I am here at short notice, and personally I don't spend time digging into other people's dirty linen."

"Pleased to hear it. Well, what do you want to talk about, now that you're here? You're from *Dagurinn*, right?"

"That's right. I wanted your opinion on this blogger, and on blogging in general."

Sigurjóna sat back behind her vast desk, empty but for a closed laptop, a neat pile of papers in a wire cage and a few tasteful trinkets, artfully distributed. Dagga could see a reflection of Sigurjóna in its highly polished surface and she concluded that the desk's owner probably didn't do a great deal of paperwork at it.

"Blogging has become a huge part of the Icelandic way of life," she began. "I'm probably right in saying that there are now more blogs here than there are Icelanders, so there is certainly a measure of overkill."

"Blogs that nobody reads?"

"Exactly. Plenty of blogs nobody reads, a lot that are dormant, and also plenty of blogs that have a limited set of readers. You know what I mean, ones that have plenty of traffic but within a small group of friends or classmates or work colleagues. Then there are some that become enormously busy, generally for a limited time before they disappear again."

"Like Skandalblogger?"

"Yes," Sigurjóna said without a trace of the sour anger she felt at the mention of the name. "It's something that isn't going to go away. This is more than a passing fashion. Blogging has become enormously important, especially to the younger generation. Don't you have a blog yourself?"

"No, actually I don't," Dagga lied again.

Sigurjóna looked quizzical.

"But I know you have your own blog and I've read some of it," Dagga added hurriedly.

"It's rubbish," Sigurjóna said airily. "Only don't quote that. It's got to the point where everyone has a blog, even government ministers. It's part of the PR machine. We advise our clients to have a blog and to update it regularly, and of course I'd prefer you to not mention that piece of information either."

Dagga smothered her irritation. Surely someone so expert in dealing with the media would know better than to say something and then ask for it to be kept quiet?

"But on the record — are you prepared to tell me about Skandalblogger?"

Sigurjóna looked pained. It was something that she had practised in front of a mirror along with the winning smile that made clients feel they could trust her with their children's lives.

"Of course. But there isn't a lot to tell that isn't already well known. This blog started up about a year and a half ago. It's completely anonymous. Some of us who have been on the receiving end of this particular brand of poison have made a study of it and it's our opinion that there's one person who writes not all, but certainly much of it, and the information seems to come from several different sources."

"So this is a group effort?"

"Certainly. One person would hardly have access to so much information — and misinformation, as a great deal of what appears on this blog is absolutely false. If you were to publish this kind of story in *Dagurinn*, I can assure you that you would be sued for every penny you have, and more."

Dagga desperately wanted to ask if the story about the Heathrow sex marathon and Sugarplum were true, but didn't want to be thrown out, at least not quite yet.

"And have you tried to track down this person? Or persons?"

"Naturally. The police computer crime division is also working on it and I'm sure that every newspaper in Iceland — yours included — has had a crack at finding whoever is responsible for this blog. Am I right?"

"You're right," Dagga admitted. "Our internet whizzes had a try but couldn't get very far. It's hosted in South America somewhere, isn't it?"

"It comes and goes. It's on a server in some central Asian republic at the moment, as far as I'm aware."

Dagga checked the red light on her recorder. "Returning to the personality actually behind this blog, do you have any ideas, any clues as to who it may be?"

Sigurjóna raised her hands, palms upwards, by way of reply.

"Is there anything that can be done?"

"Probably not. If the person or persons ever surface, there will be a good few people who will undoubtedly have grievances they will want to obtain damages over, but there could be huge problems in establishing proof," she said, flashing the smile again.

"Is this an issue of free speech?"

A spasm of anger passed over Sigurjóna's face and Dagga was sure that asking about boob jobs would probably mean the end of the interview.

"Of course it's not about bloody free speech," she said with irritation. "It's about the right of ordinary, honest people to live their lives without being slandered in a hideous and hurtful way, without being able to refute all kinds of awful, untrue allegations."

"I take it there's no truth in any of the allegations that Skandalblogger has put forward?"

Sigurjóna's voice rose in pitch and volume. "Certainly not. It's all spiteful fabrication, pure lies."

"As for your husband and the allegations about his relationship with ESC and InterAlu —"

"As I said, it's all lies and fabrication."

Although she was keeping her famous temper in check, Dagga was sure that Sigurjóna was about to explode. Dagga saw her eyes flicker over the desk and settle for a moment on the tiny recorder with its red light. She suddenly calmed and returned to her normal manner.

"I'm terribly sorry. You must forgive me, but you have to understand that the last few weeks and months have been . . . stressful, shall we say?"

"I understand that it's been difficult for you and for quite a few other people. Your husband —"

"Isn't here," Sigurjóna interrupted. "He will have to speak on his own behalf and I'm sure he'll be happy to do so. But I can say that he is deeply disturbed and hurt by allegations that he has behaved less than entirely honestly."

"And InterAlu? They have been portrayed very unfavourably. As Spearpoint is InterAlu's public relations agency, surely you can comment for them?"

"I'll have one of my staff email you a statement this afternoon," Sigurjóna replied with an icy dismissiveness in her voice that Dagga realized indicated the interview was almost at an end.

"Before we finish, I'd like to ask about the young man Skandalblogger alleges was murdered a few weeks ago?"

"An extremely unfortunate matter. The police investigation, as far as I'm aware, has found nothing to indicate any kind of foul play."

"You don't believe he was killed deliberately?"

"Of course not. I'd like to know how he found his way out there to that place in wherever-it-was . . ."

"Hvalvík," Dagga supplied.

"Wherever. But that's all the mystery there is. Look, the internet and the blog world are full of all kinds of conspiracy theories and lunatic ideas. It's not a great source for a journalist from a serious newspaper to be using for research."

Well, meow, Dagga thought. "And Skandalblogger's comment that he was 'very much one of us'? He was a Spearpoint employee, wasn't he?" she asked, imagining that she could hear the enamel on Sigurjóna's perfect teeth being ground to dust.

"I'm sorry," Sigurjóna said, barely controlling the urge to let fly. "That's something that has already been commented on, and out of respect for Einar Eyjólfur Einarsson's family I would prefer not to comment further. Now, if you'll excuse me, I'm very busy."

Dagga picked up her recorder and they both stood up. Sigurjóna came around the desk, fury gone, smiling again.

"Thank you so much. By the way, are you happy at *Dagurinn?* Hm? You know, I started at the ground floor in journalism as well, and it's a great way to begin."

"I know."

"Of course, I can see you've done more research than you wanted to let on. Let me know when you feel like moving on from *Dagurinn*, won't you?" Sigurjóna added archly, shaking Dagga's hand. "And you'll send me a draft of your article? Just to check. I'm sure you understand."

It was only when Spearpoint's door closed behind her that Dagga checked her recorder and saw with relief that it was still running.

Gunna looked the old house up and down. With three storeys clad in corrugated iron and perched on a concrete basement, it was typical for the area, which was gradually becoming fashionable once again. Doubtless it would be sold sooner or later to an entrepreneur who would tear it down and replace it or else fill the old house with pine and dimmed lights.

But today Gunna was interested in the list of names on the array of doorbells and doubted that any of them would work. One of the fading slips of paper had been altered in the not too distant past, with the occupant's real name scratched out and "Ugly Tóta" scrawled across instead.

Gunna guessed that the flat the bell belonged to would be in the upper part of the house. She pressed the button, heard nothing and shoved the door, which, unsurprisingly when she saw the smashed lock hanging by a single screw, opened in front of her.

The stairs were dark and the first landing showed her a row of closed doors, but when she heard the sound of a television from behind the first one, she rapped at it. She heard the springs of a sofa complain inside and shuffling feet approach. The door opened and Gunna recognized Tóta immediately.

"What?" Tóta demanded, smoke from the stub of cigarette between her lips curling past half-closed eyes.

"Good morning, Tóta. I'm sure you remember me. This is what you might call a friendly visit."

"Since when have coppers been friendly's what I want to know?"

"Well, you were happy enough every time we carted that lad of yours off to cool down in the cells."

"Yeah, well. He was a bit high-spirited when he was younger, my Pesi was. Anyway, what does the law want round here?"

Gunna looked over Tóta's shoulder at the dingy room behind her, curtains drawn to keep out summer sun, and a large flatscreen TV gabbling to itself in the corner, the only new thing in the room. "Aren't you going to ask me in, then?"

Tóta shrugged. "Suit yourself."

Tóta settled herself back in the corner of the sofa that fitted her snugly and finally took the cigarette from between her lips. "This can't be anything that serious, otherwise there'd be two of you," she growled.

"Like I said, just a friendly visit. I'm looking for Matti Kristjáns. I understand he's living here at the moment."

"Yeah, Fatso lives here."

"And where is he now?"

Tóta shrugged and lit another cigarette from the glowing stub of the first. "Dunno. He went out."

"When?"

Another shrug. "Yesterday, maybe?"

"Was it or wasn't it?"

"Dunno. Can't be sure."

Gunna took a deep breath and counted to ten. "So, Tóta, has your bloke still got his little hobby going in the cellar, or has he given that up?"

Tóta looked away from the TV for the first time and glowered. "You're not going to make trouble for an old man, are you? What difference does a bottle of moonshine here and there make?"

"Hard to say. I might not look too closely here and there. Depends how helpful you are. Where's Matti?"

"Dunno. He went out yesterday. Paid his rent and was gone. That's all."

"All right. So now you're sure it was yesterday. Early? Afternoon? Evening?"

"Morning," Tóta said. "Morning-ish. I don't know."

"Any idea where he went?"

Tóta didn't even shrug, just spread her hands wide. Gunna levered herself thankfully from the chair.

"Right. I need to see his room."

"Upstairs." Tóta pointed vaguely towards the door.

"Show me."

Tóta trudged ahead of her up the flight of narrow steps, slippers a size too big flapping against cracked heels, and fished for a set of keys in the pocket of her housecoat. She tried several before the right one clicked into the lock and the door swung open.

"You ought to have a warrant," Tóta said dubiously as Gunna snapped on surgical gloves and went into the room.

"If you want a warrant, I can get one of my colleagues to be here with one in half an hour and I'll wait in your living room until he gets here. If that's what you want? Hm?"

Tóta lapsed back into insolent silence and watched from the doorway, scattering ash on the carpet.

"Have you been in here since Matti left?"

Tóta said nothing and Gunna pulled the drawers of a small dresser open to find only dust inside. Some of Matti's clothes were draped over the back of a chair and the creaking wardrobe was empty apart from a raincoat that might have gone out of fashion a generation ago.

"I said, has anybody been in here since Matti left?"

"Look under the bed."

"Why?"

"Just look."

Gunna swept aside the hem of the duvet and bent down to peer at the dust and a noticeable dust-free square patch underneath.

"Nothing there."

"Then the old man's been in here and nicked Fatso's porn mags. So he's been in here."

"Tóta, do you have any idea where Matti is? I'm not going to bugger about here. This isn't something trivial."

"I don't know," Tóta whined. "He paid his rent, he went out."

"Did he say when he would be back?"

"No."

"Do you expect him back, considering he's taken most of his stuff?"

"Maybe. Maybe not. If he isn't back by the end of the month, I'll rent his room out to someone else. I could get three Polish in here, easy," she said, brightening at the prospect.

"Let's try again. Do you know who he was going about with? Any friends who visited him here? Anyone looking for him? Did he mention anyone in particular?"

"No. Nothing. He whinged all the time about Nonni the Taxi and the bloke at some club he did business for. Some foreigner, he said. I reckon Fatso was a bit scared of him, didn't want to upset him."

Gunna shut the door behind her, but decided to keep the surgical gloves on until she was out of the house. "What sort of business?"

"Don't know. Didn't ask. But Fatso had plenty of money. Lots of money."

"Where from, d'you know?"

"Ask Fatso when you find him. I'll bet he won't tell you either."

At the front door, Gunna rolled off the gloves, taking her time as Tóta was clearly anxious to get back to her television.

"Thank you for your assistance. If you hear anything about Matti, I'd appreciate it if you let me know. That way I won't have to look for him down in your cellar, if you get my meaning," Gunna said as Tóta scowled through the crack of the door.

* * *

Dagga decided to take the stairs instead of waiting for the lift. As she reached the first landing, she heard the lift hiss and open above and behind her, but shrugged and decided to carry on anyway.

Hardy stepped from the lift and dialled a number on his mobile, letting it ring until a disembodied voice told him in soothing tones that the number was either switched off or out of range. He cut the voice off before it had a chance to ask him to try again later and stepped quietly into Spearpoint's offices.

Dísa looked up as the door opened and recognized him. Without a word spoken, she buzzed through to Sigurjóna.

"What?" Sigurjóna snapped through the intercom.

"Mr Hardy is here to see you," Dísa replied.

"One minute, please, Dísa. Then show him in."

"Sigurjóna will be right with you," she said in her careful English, looking back up at Hardy who simply nodded in reply.

Hardy stood impassive at the desk. Dísa found the man sinister. He said little, but what he said was always polite. On his rare visits to Spearpoint's offices, he always looked the same, always dressed in the same way come rain, shine or snow. As she waited for the minute to pass, Dísa thought to herself that what really made Hardy sinister was the impassive look that gave no clue as to what he was thinking.

The intercom light flickered in front of her and Dísa looked up to where Hardy was standing at the window, hands folded together behind his back and rocking almost imperceptibly on the balls of his feet.

"Sigurjóna's free now," Dísa said to his back. Hardy twisted round soundlessly, nodding at Dísa with a hint of a smile.

Sigurjóna was sitting at her desk, watching a TV news channel with the sound turned down low. She glowered as Hardy came in and padded across the thick carpet.

"It's started again," she said, without bothering with a greeting.

"The blog?"

"Last week. I thought you had stopped it when it went quiet. I thought you'd found someone who was responsible for all this?"

"A message has been sent. I'm sure it will be effective."

"Yeah," Sigurjóna spat. "And do you know what that stupid Skandalblogger is saying now?"

"No. I haven't read it."

"All right. It's saying that someone who drowned in Hvalvík harbour was put there deliberately."

"Is that so?"

"I hear the police are asking questions again."

"I see."

"I thought I could trust you after Horst said that you could fix anything?"

Hardy wondered how many drinks Sigurjóna had already had at this early hour of the afternoon. He felt that drinking while concentration was required was the sure sign of an amateur, or someone in deeper than they could cope with.

"Some tasks take longer than others, I'm afraid. But the important work is progressing well. I understand that Horst is satisfied with progress at the site in Hvalvík and that the Lagoon site is also coming along well."

"Yeah. That's all on schedule. I have well-paid staff to look after the details, so they do just that," Sigurjóna said. "Now, I'm wondering if you're going to finish the little job I asked you to do before?"

"It's in hand," Hardy assured her. "It's not often that something like this can be done overnight. But I have to ask for your help with another matter as well."

Sigurjóna smiled a touch more broadly than she would have done without access to the vodka bottle in the cabinet. "In that case we'll help each other out. But why do you need help with anything from us?"

"I need to locate someone and, as I don't have local knowledge, I need assistance from someone who does."

"I'm sure one of my people can help. But what about the driver who was fixing stuff for you? Can't he help you with whatever you're on the lookout for?"

"That's the person I need to locate."

Without looking away from Hardy's face, Sigurjóna pressed a button on the intercom console on the desk in front of her. "Dísa, would you ask Jón Oddur to come and have a word with us, please?"

She released the intercom button. "By the way, Mr Hardy, what are you doing on Friday night?"

CHAPTER TWENTY-FIVE

Tuesday, 23 September

"You're on your own again, Haddi. Anything you need?"

Gunna leaned over the desk and peered at the monitor as Haddi appeared in the doorway. "Keflavík again?" he asked. "Taking Snorri as well?"

"I'm afraid so. I hope this isn't going to take too long, but it is something a bit out of the ordinary," she added as the computer chimed to indicate new messages.

"Bloody hope not," Haddi grumbled. "I've got enough on my plate as it is with all this traffic and whatnot going through the place. As for paperwork . . ."

His voice dropped to a mutter when he realized Gunna's attention was on the computer as she quickly scrolled through her messages, deleting as she went.

Hi Gunna,
The article's almost finished and I have just a couple of points I'd like to go over with you before I hand it over to the editor. Can we meet in the next few days? By the way, I've attached a few of Lára's photos that we'd like

to use with the feature. Can you let me know if these are OK? If there's any you really hate, I'll make sure they're left out.

Thanks, regards, Skúli.

"Hey, Haddi," Gunna called. "Come and have a look. We're going to be famous," she said, clicking on the icons one at a time to open the picture files.

Haddi bustled in and stood behind her as she ran through the photos of the station, Haddi and Snorri sitting at their desks, both of them being briefed, Snorri manning a speed camera with Gunna scowling behind him.

"Good grief, Gunna, my girl, you look like you've had a bag of sour lemons for breakfast there." Haddi guffawed.

"And you look like one of the Keystone Kops."

"That's a good one."

"I like that, the way they've got the whole village in the background."

"She's bloody good with a camera, that girl is," Haddi had to admit.

Gunna clicked on the final picture and brought up an image of herself taken during the march on the InterAlu compound, from a low viewpoint and with the hills and some of the marchers reflected in her mirror sunglasses.

"So's that. Makes me look like a proper mean old cow. I hope they use that one."

Haddi took off his glasses, polished them on his tie, put them back on and peered at the screen.

"I've seen that bloke," he said, pointing to a man among the crowd behind Gunna's shoulder in the picture, who was staring directly at the camera. She peered at the screen and found herself looking into the eyes of a man she had last seen on a car park surveillance camera.

"Him?" she asked, pointing.

"That's him. Fair-haired feller, the one in the pale leather jacket."

"All right. When did you see him?"

"Saturday morning, I think. He was down at Hafnarkaffi, getting out of a taxi with a big fat bloke."

"Any reason you noticed him?"

Haddi scratched his head. "Not really. You don't often see a Reykjavík taxi round here, that's all, and the driver looked a right shady sort of character, didn't like the look of him at all. I was going to check his tyres, but I'd just been down the quay and it would have made me late for coffee here. So I didn't bother."

"A Reykjavík taxi? Did you get a number?" Gunna asked sharply.

"No. Didn't bother. They were probably going to the aluminium place and stopped off to get petrol or something."

"What sort of car was it?"

"Mercedes," Haddi replied instantly. "Green, station wagon. Dent in the passenger side front wing. Why do you ask?"

"Just wondering. What about the driver? Big guy?"

"Big, well, a fat bloke anyway."

"Big tache? One of those seventies ones like the Smokey and the Bandit guy?"

"That's it. Didn't like the look of him at all."

"Not to worry, Haddi. Not to worry," Gunna said, reaching for the phone and stabbing at numbers.

"Skúli Snædal, please," she said crisply to the receptionist who answered. "Yes, it is important. This is Gunnhildur Gísladóttir at Hvalvík police and I don't care in the least if he's in a meeting."

Matti opened his eyes and looked at the lumps on the ceiling that took him back to being a small boy again when he had been dispatched to Álfasteinn every summer, until he was precocious enough a teenager to spend the summer baiting lines and watching the slate-grey halibut flop over the gunwale instead.

He reached out, expecting Marika to be curled in a ball beside him, but his hand found only a cold depression in the mattress.

"Marika!"

"What?"

Matti hauled on his trousers and made his way blearily to the bathroom where he peed loudly and with great relief. "What are you doing?"

"Nothing," she replied from the next room.

In Álfasteinn's long kitchen, she sat in a ragged armchair with a large black and white cat perched on its arm. Both of them looked at Matti as he appeared, face puffed and the hair on one side of his head standing on end. Marika put the book she was reading on the other arm of the chair.

"Where's Lóa?"

"Gone out."

"Going to be long, d'you know?"

"She say she be quick. An hour, maybe. She is nice lady, your cousin."

"Ach, she's all right, is Lóa. A bit of a monster sometimes. Any coffee?" he asked through a yawn.

"On cooker." Marika picked up the book and returned to it.

"What are you doing?"

"Reading."

"Reading what?"

"English book. *Grapes of Wrath*."

"Good?"

"Yes."

Matti shuffled over to the stove and poured coffee from the pot. He yawned again, scratched and drank. Marika looked up for a moment and shook her head briefly. Matti switched on the radio over the sink and listened for a minute to an announcer reading out a list of forthcoming funerals before he switched off again and wandered to the window to look out over the sea. Marika turned a page and carried on reading.

Suddenly the cat jumped down to the floor and went to sit expectantly by the door. Matti watched it drowsily and wondered if it had seen a mouse, but the door creaked open and a large collie loped in, greeting the cat before lying down on a square of carpet under the window. Behind the collie came the stocky figure of Lóa, kicking off rubber boots at the door and padding in thick socks into the kitchen.

"Ah, Matti my boy, so you've finally managed to drag your fat arse out of bed, have you? The whole bloody house was shaking, you were snoring so loud."

"Yes, Lóa, dear cousin."

She heaved a bag on to the worktop and a chunk of meat oozing blood could be seen inside.

"What's for dinner, then?"

"Hallgrímur over at Einarsnes shot a seal yesterday and this is my share of it. Good of him, I think."

She lowered herself with a groan into a chair.

"Bad back still?" Matti asked.

Lóa nodded. "Now and again. Well, what brings you up here this time?"

"Ach. You know. Needed to get away for a while."

"In trouble again?"

"Sort of."

"What sort of?"

"Nothing much. Just need to let the dust settle."

"That's not what I gathered from your young lady."

Matti goggled. "But . . .?"

"But what?"

"You don't speak English or Romanian or whatever it is she speaks."

"Well, Matti, it may have escaped your notice, but Marika speaks quite passable Icelandic."

"Bloody hell."

"Language, please."

"Sorry. I never noticed. We just speak English together."

"And now you can speak Icelandic as well. At least she doesn't use all those awful slang expressions you use all the time."

"Bloody hell."

"Language, Matti."

"Sorry."

Lóa stood up and banged the kettle on to the stove. "Matti, you always come up west when you're in the soup, and I'm not going to ask again what it is this time. I'd like to know if it's serious, though, and if the police are looking for you."

"Well, yes."

"Serious, or police?"

"Both."

"Silly boy. You can't stay here long without being found, you know. Hallgrímur's wife saw you in the shop in Hólmavík yesterday. If she knows you're here, then sooner or later everyone else will."

"I know," he admitted.

Lóa's voice dropped to a murmur. "Your young lady, Marika. Seems like a nice girl. Got her head screwed on. You ought to hang on to her."

"Ach. She's all right."

"Not your type, I'd have thought. Skinny little thing. Does she work?"

"Yeah, in a club."

"So I assume that's where you met, is it? Some dive?"

"Sort of."

"What sort of work does she do?"

Matti sighed and knew that the truth wouldn't do, although not telling the truth to Lóa could be a dangerous business.

"She dances," he said finally.

"Oh, I see. What kind of dance?"

"The sort where you take your clothes off and people watch."

Lóa's brow furrowed in a way that reminded Matti uncomfortably of their cousin Gunna.

"Bloody hell," she said finally.

It was late in the afternoon and they had a meeting room to themselves. Skúli thought Gunna would be impressed as they sat in their glass cage at *Dagurinn*'s offices, but she didn't seem to have realized what a feat he had achieved. He could see Jonni and Dagga looking curiously at them, and turned back to the computer screen.

"Is this all the pictures?" Gunna demanded.

"It's all the ones I have, but I suppose Lára might have more."

"And this is the highest quality you can get?"

"I think so. Lára didn't compress the files, so this is as they were taken."

Gunna peered at the picture of herself on the screen, jaw set firm, sky and mountains reflected in the mirrors of her sunglasses. "Zoom in, will you?"

"On what?"

"There." She pointed to the man in the middle distance looking directly at the lens from behind her.

The man's face filled the screen, impassive blue eyes and a day's worth of stubble on his cheeks. A very ordinary face, Gunna thought, nothing special about the combination of features, but unmistakably the face of a strong-willed character used to getting his own way.

"Skúli, my boy, I'd very much like to get more pictures of this man if it's possible. Can you get hold of the photographer?"

Skúli opened his mobile and thumbed buttons before holding it to his ear.

"Hi, Lára? Skúli at *Dagurinn*. Yeah, fine, thanks. And you? Cool."

Gunna sat and listened to Skúli's half of the conversation, fascinated at the way his entire manner changed when speaking to someone of his own age.

"Yeah, er, Lára. I need a favour if that's OK? I have someone here who wants to see any pictures you have of the march at Hvalvík. Yeah, it was a great day, wasn't it? Just wondering if you're on the way over here at all?"

Gunna frowned and motioned to Skúli for him to pass the phone to her. He frowned back.

"Er, Lára, just a moment," he said, and held the phone in the palm of his hand. "She says she has more pics, but wants to know who wants to see them?"

"Let me speak to her."

"Er, OK."

He handed the phone across with a second's reluctance.

"Good morning. Lára? This is Gunnhildur Gísladóttir, Hvalvík police. I'm working on an investigation and need to identify someone in one of your pictures of the march. Could you help out?" Gunna asked in a tone that clearly expected a positive reply.

Lára's voice crackled through a poor line. "Yeah, that's OK. I can bring my laptop and you can go through all the pictures I took if you want."

"Excellent. When?"

"Depends where you are? Are you in town or out at Hvalvík right now?"

"I'm in Skúli's office at the moment."

"No problem. I'll be right with you. Five minutes."

"Good. Thank you," Gunna finished, snapping Skúli's phone shut. "She'll be here in a few minutes."

"She's here already," Skúli said, looking over Gunna's shoulder. She swung her head round to see Lára's gangly form approaching, lopsided with a camera bag slung over one shoulder. She stopped at Dagga's desk, where some exaggerated air kisses took place as Jonni scowled.

"You know," Skúli said, looking at the image on his computer screen, "I spoke to this man at the march."

"What? Why didn't you say so before?"

"Should I have?"

"Ach, I'm sorry, Skúli. Now, tell me more."

"Well, not much really. He came and chatted for a minute, and then he was gone. Didn't think much of it."

"What did he say?"

"Not much. Asked if I was a journo and I said yes. He said he was working for a German magazine called

Eco Zeit, but I googled it afterwards and it doesn't seem to exist."

"Did he say his name?"

"No, don't think so."

"And is he German or what?"

Skúli thought. "Sorry, I don't know. He spoke English very well, better than I do, but I couldn't tell you if he had an accent or not."

There was a tap at the door and Lára appeared, grinning.

"Hi," Skúli responded with a warmth that told Gunna he was more than a little pleased to see her. "That was quick."

"Wasn't it just? I was upstairs. Been doing some pictures for *Home and Garden* magazine on the next floor," she said, unfolding a laptop and tapping it into life. She quickly located a folder of image files, swiped across them and opened the whole series.

"These are the pics from the march. That was a pretty good day, I even sold some photos of it in Denmark and Sweden. Now, what was it you wanted to look at?"

Skúli turned his computer towards her and pointed to the man's face behind Gunna's shoulder.

"Oh, that creep," Lára said.

"You spoke to him?"

"Briefly. He asked for my phone number and said we ought to meet for a drink sometime."

Gunna was amused to see Skúli bridle visibly.

"A bit too smooth, I thought," Lára continued.

"Where did you think he was from?"

"Not from here, at any rate. He spoke English, but he could be from anywhere. Not England, though. His English was too precise, too perfect. Y'know what I mean? Like he'd learned it at school."

"Lára knows. She studied in England," Skúli butted in.

"What were you studying? Photography?" Gunna asked.

"No. Human resource management, actually."

"What?"

"Well, I wanted to study abroad, but to get a student loan it had to be something that isn't offered in Iceland. So I went for human resource management."

"And now you're a photographer?"

"That's right. I trained to manage a big department, and now I work for myself. Good, isn't it?" Lára asked brightly.

"OK, good. But if you're sure this guy wasn't a native English speaker, that helps. Now, any photos?"

"Yeah, there are a few more of him somewhere. What's he done?"

"Not sure yet, and as it's an ongoing inquiry, I couldn't tell you anyway at the moment," Gunna grunted, hunched over the screen as Lára tapped the space bar to toggle between pictures.

"There he is again, behind those guys who didn't want to let anyone pass."

"That's him," Gunna agreed. "Any more?"

They scrolled through the several hundred pictures and found half a dozen showing the man's face, each time at the periphery of the march and never far from the police presence. Lára copied the picture files and handed them to Gunna on a disk.

"Here you are."

"Thanks. It's not a problem to let me have these? Journalistic integrity and all that?"

"Hell, no," Lára replied. "As long as you're not stopping me doing my job, it's not a problem. I'm happy to help the police, and I'd be even happier if they found the bastard who burgled my flat."

"Where do you live?"

"Breidholt."

Gunna thought for a moment. "Sævaldur Bogason's patch, I think. I'll remind him when I see him. Anyway, Skúli, I'm afraid I might have to ask you not to publish the photo of me with our man in the background, or at least to crop him out if that's possible. If he is someone we're looking for, then I'd prefer not to spook him. When does it all go to print?"

"Week after next, I think."

"Right. I'll let you know. Give me a day or two. Lára, thank you for your assistance, it all helps."

CHAPTER TWENTY-SIX

Wednesday, 24 September

Although Gunna had seen the County Sheriff before, she had never had a reason to speak to him. Seated in the incident room in front of her and flanked by Vilhjálmur Traustason and Ívar Laxdal, he looked surprisingly youthful in faded jeans and an open-necked shirt instead of his usual office wear.

"So, what do you want to tell me about?" the Sheriff asked as Gunna stood up in front of the whole group. Bjössi, Bára and Snorri sat behind them and waited.

"I have some information about the person who may have been in the vicinity when Einar Eyjólfur Einarsson was murdered —"

"Allegedly," Vilhjálmur broke in.

"Allegedly," Gunna repeated. "But I felt that in the light of what we've been told, I'd best call you all together to save myself from having to repeat this later."

Vilhjálmur fidgeted while the Sheriff nodded. Gunna took a deep breath and thumbed copies of a series of pictures to the wall.

"The team have been in touch with police forces in the UK, Germany, Sweden, Denmark and Norway.

Sweden came up trumps and this is the man we want to talk to."

"And he is?" Vilhjálmur asked querulously.

"Gunnar Ström. He's been identified as having hired a car that appears to have been on the quay at Hvalvík the night Einar Eyjólfur died. He bears a striking resemblance to the person who stole the jeep that is likely to have been used to murder Egill Grímsson. We are absolutely certain he was present at the march on the InterAlu compound at Hvalvík."

"A lot of coincidences?" Ívar Laxdal asked quietly.

"Plenty of them," Gunna agreed, feeling her shirt start to stick to her back and wishing she had taken off her uniform tunic. "But considering this man's background, I feel we need to concentrate on him."

"Go on," Ívar Laxdal prompted.

"Not a pleasant character. Several sentences for violent crimes, involvement with narcotics, and a big car theft operation that exported stolen cars to West Africa from Scandinavia via various Baltic States. It seems he's broken quite a few kneecaps in his time and he's suspected of nastier things, including at least one disappearance and a very unpleasant incident with someone's fingers and a hammer and chisel, but not much that can be proved. The man's a pro."

"Is that all?" Vilhjálmur asked, his face pale with horror.

"His background is that he's a Norwegian national, aged forty-two, naval PT and unarmed combat instructor until dishonourably discharged. Resident in Sweden since 1993, half a dozen stretches including a five-year sentence for grievous bodily harm, which was the hammer and chisel thing."

"Good God," Vilhjálmur whispered.

"His real name's Gunnar Hårde, with a little circle over the A, so I suppose he might be related to the Prime Minister, but I doubt it somehow."

"A proper Norwegian conspiracy?" Bjössi shot in. For form's sake, Gunna frowned at him and smothered the urge to laugh.

"Something like that. Anyway, our man's been a good boy for the last few years, travels under his own name, listed in the Södertälje phone book. But Special Branch in Sweden have been keeping an eye on him and he's been back and forth to Estonia and Latvia quite a bit in the last few years. No idea what he's been doing there, but he's been declaring income from what's described as work as a security consultant, and paying his taxes like a good boy. Still waiting to hear back from Oslo."

"Good. Did you run the Gunnar Ström name past them in Sweden?"

"Yup. He's used that name before, but a long time ago. Other names he's used are Ekström and Angström. They're checking with their passport office for any valid passports in those names that might fit our boy. But the fun part is that Sweden says our man is retained as a security consultant for InterAlu, which means he's on our doorstep. He may well be in the country right now."

Gunna surveyed the three men sitting in front of her in silence. Vilhjálmur looked aghast.

Ívar Laxdal's expression was impassive and the County Sheriff looked thoughtful.

"What do you need, Gunna?" he asked quietly. "More people?"

"Not right now. I need cooperation straight away from other forces and some quick backup when it's needed. I may need to upset some people in high places, but I don't reckon that's something that can be avoided if we're to get to the bottom of this."

"That can all be arranged, can't it, Ívar?"

Ívar Laxdal nodded and grunted, his chin in one hand.

"And as this guy is clearly dangerous, I want access to the Special Unit if some strong-arm stuff looks likely."

"As this appears to be a unique case for Icelandic policing, I feel a more senior officer should be handling it," Vilhjálmur said abruptly.

"I was wondering when this was going to occur to you," Gunna murmured.

Ívar Laxdal and the Sheriff frowned in unison.

"Gunnhildur is a highly competent officer. I don't see a problem with her taking charge of this investigation, particularly as she has been with it from the outset," the Sheriff pointed out.

"This is an exceptional case," Vilhjálmur responded stiffly.

"And in my view Gunnhildur is an exceptional police officer," Ívar Laxdal said. "She's familiar with every aspect of the investigation so far and we risk losing time by handing over to someone more senior. Do you have another officer in mind? Do you feel you should be in personal charge?"

Vilhjálmur opened his mouth and closed it again, while Gunna wondered when they were going to stop discussing her as if she were in another room. Unlike the three men sitting in front of her, she could see frowns on the faces of Bjössi, Snorri and Bára behind them. There was silence for a moment until Ívar Laxdal broke it.

"This is something you're confident to handle, isn't it, Gunnhildur?"

"It is," she answered hoarsely.

"That's settled, then," Ívar Laxdal said with satisfaction. "Now, where are you taking this?"

"As low-profile as possible for the moment."

She turned to the desk, picked up Matti's picture and one of the green taxi and added them to the row of photographs on the wall.

"I would very much like to track down this character, Marteinn Georg Kristjánsson, known as Fat Matti. He's a taxi driver and small-time criminal who we understand has been ferrying Ström/Hårde, whatever we decide to call him, around the country. Matti has disappeared and I'm concerned for his safety. I'm hoping that he hasn't been quietly disposed of, as he may well be able to provide some information about Hårde's activities."

Ívar Laxdal nodded. "I think the best we can do is to leave you to get on with it. Agreed?" he asked, turning first to the Sheriff and then to Vilhjálmur before shoving his chair backwards as they all rose to their feet.

"If you need anything, call me," he said as the door swung shut behind them.

"Well done, sweetheart," Bjössi announced, breaking the silence and clapping his hands slowly. "Knocked 'em dead. Now what?"

Gunna sat down and felt her legs turn to jelly. "Snorri, I'd like you to start with a quick scout around Reykjavík and see if you can find Matti anywhere before we put out an alert for him. Bára, anything from Clean Iceland about Egill Grímsson and Einar Eyjólfur?"

"Nothing concrete. Supposed to be meeting them this afternoon."

"All right," Gunna decided. "Keep to that, but let me know. Bára, would you check to see if Fat Matti's taxi has been picked up anywhere and check all the flights as far back as you can for Ström or Hårde? That's it for now. I have to get back to Hvalvík for an hour and I'll see you all here in . . ." She craned her neck to see the clock on the wall. "In two hours."

Reynir Óli scowled. Sometimes *Dagurinn*'s editor felt that a little discipline could be applied to Jonni Kristinsson, but a feeling that he would be unlikely to come out of it well had always held him back.

"Well? What do you have?"

Jonni looked sideways at her as Dagga took a deep breath.

"ESC," she said.

Reynir Óli's head jerked up, eyes wide. "What?"

"Energy Supply Consultation."

"I know what it stands for," he snapped. "What's the story?"

"It's to do with that Hvalvík aluminium project, the one that went quiet when National Power decided not to sell them electricity."

Reynir Óli had recovered his composure, but had a nasty taste in his mouth and was sure that Jonni was scrutinizing him. He nodded slowly. "And?"

"I understand that it's about to be floated on the stock exchange now that it has a contract to supply InterAlu with electricity."

"And?"

"ESC were granted a special concession as a public-private partnership to build an autonomous hydro-electric plant in the hills above Hvalvík, so they can dam the river there to produce electricity and supply it to InterAlu."

"Isn't this just rumour?" Reynir Óli asked. "Is this really a story that we can use?"

"Good grief, man. If that isn't a story, what is?" Jonni exploded, pulling off his glasses and pointing them at Reynir Óli. "Public money used to set up a dodgy company that then gets floated while all the scumbags in the know get share options. They get a fat contract through some shady back-door deals with other government departments, side-stepping a state monopoly in the process, and the moment the contract with InterAlu becomes public knowledge, their share value will go through the roof."

“Channel Three’s already sniffing around it,” Dagga added. “I don’t know how far they’ve got, but they’ll run it as soon as they can get a handle on the scam.”

Panic flashed behind Reynir Óli’s rimless glasses. “I need to see something absolutely cast-iron before we can run this,” he said doubtfully. “Look, guys, we don’t want to upset too many people too early. So, look, er, keep this very discreet and, er, I’ll do some consultation. OK?”

Without pausing to listen to a reply, Reynir Óli was gone.

“Like a scalded cat,” Jonni observed with satisfaction. “Did you make that up about Channel Three being on to all this?”

Dagga nodded.

“Master stroke. Excellent.”

Skúli looked from one to the other and back again. “Is all this true?”

“Is what true?” Dagga asked.

“All that about ESC and InterAlu and Hvalvík?”

“Absolutely,” Jonni replied. “According to some of my finest unattributable sources of government gossip, our young lady here is right on the money.”

CHAPTER TWENTY-SEVEN

Thursday, 25 September

"Seen him?" Gunna demanded as soon as Snorri came in.

"Not a whisper of him anywhere."

"Bloody man. Where the hell is he?"

"No idea, chief. He's just vanished."

"Right. Tell me where you went."

Snorri sat down and opened his folder of notes, with everything carefully logged. His finger followed the trail down the page.

"Started at the taxi ranks, Hafnarfjördur, Kópavogur, Grensás, then Lækjartorg, Tryggvagata, the usual places. No sign. Spoke to a few of the taxi drivers and nobody's seen Fat Matti about. Then his flat, bedsit, whatever you call it. Ugly Tóta — is she really called that?"

"Ugly by name and ugly by nature. She used to be a terrible hell-raiser in her younger days, which weren't that long ago. I've bundled her into the back of a squad car more than once."

"Ugly Tóta hasn't seen him. Nothing more than she told you the other day."

"So he hasn't been back?"

"Not that she's aware of, and there's hardly anything in his room to come back for anyway, you said."

"OK. Didn't expect anything else. How about Nonni the Taxi?"

"Nothing there either. Nonni was there himself this time and he's not happy."

"He's not a cheerful character at the best of times."

"Even less cheerful now. Matti's actually one of his best drivers and he does quite a bit of his contract work, and for that they like to keep the same faces as much as possible. He says that when Matti's not well, by which I suppose he means pissed, then he always calls in. Never fails. But now he's disappeared and so has the car."

"In that case I can understand. A newish car, isn't it?"

"Yup. No car and no driver to drive it. Like the man said, there's payments to be made on the vehicle whether it's earning money or not."

"Did you come over heavy?"

"Did my best. Nonni was a bit reticent until I pushed him and made it clear that this is a murder inquiry we're dealing with, and he came clean."

Gunna just raised an eyebrow instead of asking.

"It seems that some of what Matti does by way of contract work is for Mundi Grétars."

"Scaramanga?"

"That's the one. Evil place, a real rip-off. They have some, um, exotic dancers there who apparently do more than just dance, all foreign girls."

"Prostitution?"

"Who knows? The policy is that whatever the girls do outside working hours is up to them. It seems that some do and some don't. But it's common knowledge that Mundi doesn't discourage them from doing business, as it keeps the punters coming in. Matti and a few of the other drivers ferry them about to wherever they're supposed to be working."

"Which is where?"

"Parties sometimes, or mostly private houses for special customers. They work at hotels in town as well."

"Bloody hell, the stupid bastard. If his mother wasn't still alive and kicking she'd be turning in her grave."

"Nonni says he's heard that one of the girls has gone missing as well. That's all I can tell you. He wouldn't let on any more and I got the feeling he didn't feel safe having told me what he had."

Gunna rose to her feet. "Well done, Snorri. Did you get a name, description?"

"The girl's called Marika and it seems she and Matti have had something going for a while."

"Matti? Good grief," Gunna muttered.

"The woman's Romanian, like the rest of that bunch, and Nonni thought there were four or five of them living in one of the terraced houses somewhere in the Smárar district. He didn't know exactly where, but I'll bet we can lean on one of his drivers and find out easily enough."

"Or we could lean on Mundi Grétars, which could be a pleasure in itself. You'd better get your report done as soon as possible so we can keep on top of all this stuff. We'd better liaise with Reykjavík on this one, get Scaramanga looked into properly and see if we can track down this bunch of exotic dancers or whatever they call themselves. I don't like the sound of all this at all."

She shooed Snorri away to a spare computer terminal and went outside the building. Standing by the back door she was surprised to see the afternoon sun lighting up the brightly painted fishing boats on the slipway and realized that it was getting late in the day.

She felt tired, more tired than for a long time, but exhilarated that the case was making progress at last — faster than she had anticipated, as well as opening up other avenues that clearly also needed to be investigated.

Gunna fished an almost empty packet of Prince from her pocket and lit up, sucking down smoke as the door clanged open and Bjössi appeared beside her with two mugs of coffee.

"Here y'are, sweetheart," he mumbled with an unlit cigarette in his mouth that Gunna lit before taking the mug from him. "By the way, Borgarnes are investigating a suspicious death on their patch."

Gunna raised an eyebrow. "Anything to do with us?"

"The guy was a computer programmer, a real über-nerd. Seems he had a heart attack, but managed to break his arm at the same time."

"Right, we'll put someone on to it to find out the details. Bára, maybe?"

"Bára's busy enough as it is, but it's up to you, sweetheart. You're the man in charge."

"For the moment, anyway."

"It didn't look right at all," Officer Unnur Matthíasdóttir at the Borgarnes police station said, shaking her ponytailed head and grimacing.

"What happened?"

"Well, it seems that the man's wife had been away for a week on a shopping trip in London. She came home on the Saturday morning, which was the thirteenth and found her husband sat up against the inside of the front door, stone dead. She had to go round the back of the house and get in that way."

"All right, so what was the cause of death?"

"It's all on the sheet and the body's still at the National Hospital if you want to go and have a look for yourself," she said wearily. "The cause of death was a heart attack, plain and simple."

"But there's more to this?"

"Hell, yes. Didn't find that out straight away, though," she sighed. "His wife went nuts, called an ambulance and was in a proper state by the time they got there. So she was sedated, as the ambulance crew could see the bloke was past helping. They took her off to hospital and came back for him."

Gunna leafed through the case notes she had downloaded from the police network. "He'd been dead for a while?"

"That's right. The post-mortem results put the time of death at thirty-six hours previously, give or take half a day. So, round about Tuesday the ninth, something like that. What's suspicious is that the man had a broken arm that would definitely have been extremely painful and the pathologist reckoned that it's not a break that could be achieved easily by falling over. He reckoned the arm had been forced."

"Deliberate, then?"

"Yup. Somebody broke his arm, and then the poor chap had a heart attack, either in front of the attacker or after he'd gone. Most likely afterwards, considering he was sitting with his back to the closed front door."

"Arngrímur Örn Arnarson. Fifty-five years old, ran his own company," Gunna read from the notes.

"Right enough," Unnur confirmed. "An odd sort of bloke. Lived in Borgarnes about five years and kept to himself, although his wife was a bit more sociable. He did some sort of computer, internet stuff. Called himself a consultant. Anyway, what's your interest in this one?"

Knowing the question would come, Gunna had already wondered during the two-hour drive from Keflavík how much she should say.

"We're investigating an unpleasant sort of character and we have confirmation that one of his associates was around here on that Tuesday. It's too much of a coincidence to ignore."

"How do you know?" Unnur asked.

"Paid his toll at the tunnel and the number was recorded. Came back later the same day."

Gunna placed a picture of Matti's taxi on the desk. "That's his vehicle. And it may have gone through here quite a few times. We're actively looking out for this car now, as quietly as possible. But if there's no response in a day or two, we'll have to run a TV and radio appeal."

Gunna placed pictures of Matti and Hårde on top of the taxi. "And if you can find anyone who has seen either of these, then we'd definitely be on to something."

Unnur nodded. "All right. We'll see what we can do."

Gunna tapped Hårde's face. "This guy is dangerous. Extremely dangerous."

Unnur looked taken aback. "What are you looking for him in connection with?"

"Well," Gunna said grimly, "if he's responsible for Arngrímur Örn Arnarson's death as well, then we're looking at three killings."

"Bloody hell," Unnur whistled.

25-09-2008, 1044

Skandalblogger writes:

Oops! Rule one . . . even if you don't tell the truth, do tell your wife . . .

Bjarni Jón, we're feeling all warm and fuzzy today because we enjoyed your performance on Kastljós so much. However, we hear that your performance afterwards wasn't so hot. Look, a word of advice here. We all know about ministers not bothering to brief their secretaries, aides, advisers, etc, but forgetting to let your good lady know that you were looking at chucking it in was, shall we say, a little lacking in foresight, especially as she trades so heavily on having a husband in government and the ear of the guy at the top.

We hear that the recording went pretty smoothly, a lot more smoothly than the blazing row you had with the lovely pouting Sigurjóna in the ministerial jeep.

Click here* for the video clip, and if anyone who can lipread would like to send us their interpretation of what the delightful Sigurjóna had to say, please email the Skandalblogger. We can have a pretty good guess at what was being said, considering that instead of being in hubby's arms, the succulent Sigurjóna scuttled off afterwards for a girls' night out with little sister, celebrity strimmer Erna, but we'd like to be sure.

Anonymity guaranteed!

Bæjó!

Gunna already knew that the third item on that evening's TV news would be all about Matti. Laufey lay with her head on her mother's shoulder and didn't wake as Gunna lifted the remote control from her hand to increase the volume.

". . . Police are concerned about the whereabouts of Marteinn Georg Kristjánsson and are appealing for information. Marteinn Georg was last seen on Sunday morning, wearing dark blue tracksuit trousers and a blue polo shirt under a dark brown leather jacket. He was last seen in the Smárar area driving a green Mercedes station wagon, number . . ."

Gunna muted the TV as the phone rang and at the same moment a picture appeared on the screen of a considerably younger Matti looking like a gangland hoodlum with his swept-down moustache.

"Gunnhildur."

"Hi. It's me."

"Skúli, how goes it?"

"Still at work getting the morning edition together."

"Good. You've got enough to make a decent story about Matti? I'd appreciate it. It's urgent that we find out what's happened to him."

"That's fixed. The story's on an inside page, but there's a box on the front with a 'Have you seen this man?' caption. Er . . ."

"Yes? What is it, Skúli?"

"Well, actually it's a bit embarrassing."

"Come on, lad, out with it."

Gunna heard him breathe deeply as if summoning all the courage he had. "I wanted to ask you about Vilhjálmur Traustason."

"Fire away. We've known each other for a long time, although we've never got round to forming a mutual admiration society."

"All right. I could see there was a bit of tension between you two. But what I was wondering about was a story that the Skandalblogger came up with some time ago, about a police officer who had, quote, formed a happy working relationship with a Baltic beauty who dances nearby. End quote."

"And? Some sort of connection with Vilhjálmur? Anything that I need to know about?"

"Well, yeah. This is the awkward bit. I was doing a story about prostitution that hasn't been published yet, and I interviewed one of these girls in a room at Hotel Gullfoss. And as we were leaving the room, I saw your boss going down the corridor with another girl."

"Skúli, you're sure?"

"Absolutely, no doubt. Walked straight into them. When I saw the guy at the hotel I thought it was a bit creepy, but it wasn't until I saw him at the press conference I realized it was the same person."

Gunna held the receiver in the palm of her hand to muffle it. She didn't know whether to laugh or shout with rage. She saw that the news item about Matti was over and the screen now showed an airliner on a runway somewhere warm.

"Skúli," she said at last, "you're still there?"

"Yeah, of course."

"I'd ask you to be very careful with what you've just told me. As far as I'm aware, no crime has been committed and all you've seen is him accompanied by an unknown woman. Right?"

"Yes, that's right."

"So if this were to get into other hands, you could destroy the man's career, not to mention his marriage. You're sure about this?"

"I'm dead sure."

Gunna cursed silently and wondered how, if ever, she would be able to broach the subject with Vilhjálmur Traustason. "Skúli, can you keep this under wraps?"

"I can. But if I've noticed, then other people will as well."

"I'll talk to him when I can. All right?"

"OK," Skúli said dubiously.

"Thanks, Skúli. I owe you a favour."

Gunna put the phone down and Laufey stretched out on the sofa, eyes open.

"Mum, who's Skúli?"

"Skúli's a journalist on a newspaper who's been writing a story about your old mum."

"So he's not your boyfriend or anything, then?"

"I hardly think so, young lady."

Laufey yawned and kneaded her eyes with the backs of her fists. "That's all right, then."

"Why do you ask?"

"Nothing. Just some of the kids at school said that my mum's got a boyfriend at last and I said no she hasn't."

Gunna sighed. Dinner with Steini had been a pleasure. They had both enjoyed themselves and Gunna had forgotten for a few hours much of the weight she felt she had been carrying since Raggi's death. Steini had called again but she hadn't had time to do more than promise vaguely to meet.

"Laufey, my darling. One day you'll understand that a young man like Skúli is hardly likely to be interested in an old lady like me."

"You're not old," Laufey said, swinging her legs down to the floor. "And Finnur says his dad said he'd give you a portion. What does that mean, Mum?"

Gunna spluttered as she choked back laughter. "And who is Finnur?"

"A really stupid boy in my class."

"All right. Who's Finnur's dad?"

"I'm not sure. I think he works for the council."

"Thank you. I'll look out for him and see if I can give him a parking ticket."

"All right. I'm going to bed now."

"But don't you tell Finnur that tomorrow, will you?"

Laufey yawned again, pulled off her socks and dropped them on the floor.

"In the basket, please," Gunna pointed out as Laufey scowled in perfect facsimile of her father's face, giving Gunna a sudden pang. "I have to go early tomorrow, so you'll be all right to get yourself up for school, won't you?"

"Sure, Mum. I'm not a kid, you know."

CHAPTER TWENTY-EIGHT

Friday, 26 September

Clean Iceland's offices were two rooms between an artist's studio and a health food shop a street back from Mýrargata and the slipways of Reykjavík harbour. Looking out of the window behind Kolbeinn Sverrisson's head, Gunna could see the masts of the whaling boats that had been there for a decade without putting to sea.

Bára stood by the door while Gunna took the only other chair in Kolbeinn's cramped and crowded cubbyhole of an office. Every surface was covered with snowdrifts of paperwork, folders, books and papers. The floor could only be seen in the shape of a corridor threading its way between boxes of more files.

"It's a mess," Kolbeinn sighed. "We only moved in here last week and there hasn't been time to sort anything out yet. We don't even have phones connected yet."

"How many of you are there here?" Gunna asked.

"Just two of us. Me and Ásta full time, then there's loads of people who donate a few hours a week to the cause."

Kolbeinn Sverrison was a raw-boned man with cropped dark hair and an open, engaging face cross-hatched with several days' worth of stubble. Gunna had seen him in the distance at the march and wondered if the anger and passion he had shown then were far below the surface. He looked different, more vulnerable than the clown-like figure she had seen in his outsize green hat at the head of the march and later addressing the crowd with a fury that had left him drained.

"Are you here to donate a few hours to Clean Iceland?" he asked wryly, pouring coffee from a thermos into three cracked cups on the edge of his desk.

"No, sorry. Do you have the pictures, Bára?" Gunna asked, swivelling in her seat. Bára passed forward a folder and Gunna extracted pictures of Egill Grímsson and Einar Eyjólfur Einarsson. She placed them one by one alongside the row of cups.

"Anyone here you recognize?"

"Could be."

"And?"

Kolbeinn's brows knitted in a frown as he lifted a cup and sipped.

"Why do you need to know?" he asked finally.

"Because, as you must be aware, these two people are dead and we'd like to know why and who's responsible."

"InterAlu is responsible," he said flatly.

"Would you care to explain?"

"Both of these men were close to us here at Clean Iceland. Egill was one of the founders of the movement and one of our most energetic campaigners. He poured a huge amount of energy into lobbying politicians and government departments, highlighting illegal acts, generally making himself a nuisance to InterAlu and all the other aluminium manufacturers who want to set up shop here."

"But particularly InterAlu? Why?"

"Because it's just so fucking blatant. The environmental survey was a sham to begin with. Then there was the issue of power, when the National Power Authority refused to supply them. So they went ahead and started building their own hydro-electric plant in a nature reserve, after they had bribed or bamboozled the government into declassifying the reserve and allowing the power station to be built. The pollution will be horrendous when it's finished. It's crooked government. It's worse than that. It's stupid government being diddled by a pack of crooks."

Gunna felt that she was seeing a burst of the same passion: the man's presence had gone from quiet to electrifying in a matter of seconds. "And Einar Eyjólfur?"

The passion vanished as soon as it had appeared. "Ach. Einar. He was a great guy."

"You knew he worked at Spearpoint and that Spearpoint is involved with the power plant?"

"Involved? Don't you know that the owners of Spearpoint also own fifty per cent of ESC, the company that's building the power station? They're more than just involved and it's even more of a fucking scandal if you remember that one of these people is a government minister," Kolbeinn spat. "But yes, we were fully aware that Einar Eyjólfur was working at Spearpoint and he was an invaluable source of inside information. I have no doubt this is why he was killed."

"Why haven't you contacted the police about this?"

Kolbeinn laughed. "What? And you think anyone would believe us? Come on."

Gunna picked up the pictures from the desk and replaced them with one of Gunnar Hårde. "Recognize this guy?"

"Nope. Who is he?"

"OK. And this one?"

This time she placed a picture of Arngrímur Örn Arnarson on the table.

"I know this one. He's a computer programmer who did some work for us years ago. In fact, he set up our first website in the nineties. Haven't seen him for a long time. I thought he'd moved away?"

"Not far. He moved to Borgarnes. We believe he was murdered a couple of weeks ago and that he could be linked to Egill and Einar Eyjólfur. Do you know anything of Arngrímur's activities?"

"Shit. No."

"When did you last see him or have any contact with him?"

Kolbeinn looked briefly at the ceiling. "I'm not sure. Probably six, seven years ago. To be honest, I wasn't too comfortable around him, always got the feeling there was something dodgy he was up to. Know what I mean?"

Gunna nodded. "Perfectly. It's part of the job description. But can you be more precise? What was it made you uncomfortable?"

"It's hard to say. He was a highly competent systems guy and a very clever programmer. But he was one of those people who would do any kind of work for the right price. I don't think he had much in the way of principles. He made our website and kept it secure, as we certainly had a good few hacking attempts that Arngrímur did his best to trace. But we had to pay him the going rate, even though this isn't a rich organization and it's supposed to be on a non-profit basis."

"So what happened?"

"He was too expensive for us after a while. That was that."

"Who took over his work?"

"Egill, mostly, to begin with. Actually my little sister is our webmaster now but we have a much simpler site that's easy to maintain and we have a series of blogs and a Facebook presence instead."

"When did you see Einar Eyjólfur last?"

"Months ago. Not long after Egill died. I could tell he was worried then, but he wouldn't talk about it. Who's this guy?" Kolbeinn asked, tapping Hårde's picture with a forefinger. "A suspect, maybe?"

"He's someone we want to trace. That's all I can tell you. How come Einar Eyjólfur was working at Spearpoint? Did you plant him there?"

"Not at all. He applied and got the job on his own merits. It wasn't until he had been there some time that he got in touch with us. We'd been friends since we were at university. Drifted apart when he went off to the US to do his master's. He called one day and suggested we meet, about two years ago. That's when he told me all about the Hvalvík smelter plans and he essentially became our mole."

"So do you think his employers were aware of what he was doing?"

"Eventually, yes. I'm certain of it and I think that got him murdered. Not the people at Spearpoint — the ones who manage InterAlu. They are absolutely ruthless."

Kolbeinn waved a hand at the mass of papers. "Somewhere in here I have a file on their business activities in Central America and in the Philippines. Breaks your heart, some of it."

"So who do you believe is responsible?"

"For Einar Eyjólfur's death? You're the detective. You tell me."

"I'm asking you as an expert in your field."

Kolbeinn looked Gunna directly in the eye. "Ultimately, global capitalism. But immediately, I'd say it was one of InterAlu's people, a man called Horst. I have no doubt he was the one who gave the instructions. But who actually did the deed, I have no idea. Maybe this guy here?" And he looked sideways through narrowed eyes at the picture of Hårde on the desk.

* * *

Everyone watched as Gunna brooded. She wondered briefly if Björssi or any of the other older officers had mentioned anything about her background to these young police officers who had started their careers well after her return from extended sick leave to take over the quiet backwater of Hvalvík.

"Any sightings of Matti Kristjáns?" she demanded, brushing aside irrelevant thoughts.

"Nothing so far," Snorri said. "According to Nonni the Taxi, Matti has two phones, one of his own and one that he uses for taxi work. Both are switched off. There have been no sightings that we're aware of, except that the taxi went through the Hvalfjördur tunnel last Sunday and hasn't been logged coming back."

Gunna breathed a sigh of relief. "Our Matti has a long history of taking to his heels when it comes to trouble. We can assume that he's at least still alive and is somewhere outside the city," she replied, aware that the others would now be wondering how she knew so much about a taxi driver's personal habits. "I might even hazard a guess as to where he's gone. Bára, Borgarnes?"

"Nothing yet. The Borgarnes force is still knocking on doors in the area, but unfortunately they're a bit stretched right now."

"Just like every bloody force," Björssi said sombrely.

"Yeah, but they've also just found a dope farm and investigating that is taking a good bit of their time right now."

"Now," Gunna continued. "Progress on our man, the elusive Mr Hårde. What do we have? Snorri?"

"His credit cards are all in order. He's been here quite legally as an EU citizen and he seems to travel under his own name and on a valid passport. We have no idea where he is right now."

"What else?" Gunna asked, seeing a smile forming at the corners of his mouth.

"I was up at the Lagoon site yesterday to go through the traffic schedule and as I was talking to the foreman there, I thought I'd show him the picture of our man. And what do you think? He's working there as some kind of security adviser. Turns up unexpectedly every day or three, makes a few phone calls and then disappears again."

"Right under our noses? Bloody hell."

"Yeah. Seems he's pretty discreet about his movements. But the foreman reckons he's British or American, calls himself Hardy with a Y on the end. Shouldn't we put a full-scale search into action and see if he can be flushed out?"

Gunna tapped the table with her fingertips in an irregular rhythm. Only Bjössi smiled at the reminder of Gunna thinking hard that he hadn't seen for a long time.

"No. I don't want to spook him, and it's not as if we have the manpower to sustain a full-scale search for more than a couple of days. Great if it works, but a disaster if it doesn't. The man knows what he's doing and I'm concerned that if we put pressure on, he'll vanish."

"How?" Snorri asked. "There's only one airport and we can keep watch on all the flights."

"There may only be one airport, but there are plenty of ways in and out of this country, particularly for someone with this man's experience and links to a company like InterAlu. They're the next people we need to have a word with. Snorri, would you investigate and set up a meeting?"

"Actually, I already have," he said shyly. "Investigated, that is. InterAlu themselves aren't part of the picture at all, except as shareholders. The smelter is owned by a company called Bay Metals, which they own forty-nine per cent of and possibly more under other guises as there are quite a few foreign shareholders. The biggest local shareholder is a trading company called Spear Investments, which is owned by —"

"Sigurjóna Huldudóttir?" Gunna asked.

"Well, her and her husband. The same company's also the largest single shareholder in ESC and the Hvalvík Lagoon power plant."

"You know, we keep coming back to this bloody woman all the time. I think it's time we had another chat with her."

"Shall I arrange it?" Bára asked.

"No. I feel it might be better to just show up unannounced tomorrow morning. Snorri and Bára, I'd like to have both of you with me on this one."

"You know who her husband is?" Bjössi asked dubiously.

"I'm very much aware that she's married to the Minister for Environmental Affairs, but I've dealt with more unpleasant people than him in the past," Gunna replied, to sharp intakes of breath from around the table. "But I'm also sure that if anyone has an idea where our Mr Hårde is, then she does."

Sigurjóna stepped through the Gullfoss Hotel's side door with her sister Erna unsteady on her feet at her side and Hardy padding silently behind.

He kept to one side as they were greeted with flurries of kisses. Hardy flinched as cameras flashed and he watched as liveried waiters brought trays of glasses, choosing fruit juice for himself while Sigurjóna and Erna made short work of successive deliveries.

Boredom was something Hardy handled well. Military training had taught him to keep quiet until something needed to be said, and in prison he had learned to keep within his own thoughts for as long as necessary. Hunting for prey of four- and two-legged varieties had given him patience greater than that of any prey he had outwaited. Sitting at Sigurjóna's and Erna's table at an awards ceremony was not quite the same thing, but he still was able to call on old skills as the people around him chattered in Icelandic interspersed with odd English words, occasionally breaking into shrill laughter.

The food was acceptable, although cold, and in a restaurant he would have sent it back. But prison and the military had taught him not to pass up a meal, so he ate the fragrant but rapidly cooling lamb and potatoes, sipped his drink and enjoyed the sight of Sigurjóna, Erna and the rest of their group becoming progressively more raucous as the bottles of wine on the table were systematically drained. He wondered how capable Jón

Oddur, the sweating young man detailed to assist him, would be in the morning.

"Are you enjoying yourself, darling?" Erna yelled into his ear, draping an arm loosely around his neck and pummelling his shoulder with her free hand.

"Of course," Hardy replied smoothly.

"You're not drinking?"

"I don't drink. At least not alcohol."

"Drying out?"

"No. I just don't drink."

"Everyone drinks. Unless they're drying out," Erna said with finality.

Sigurjóna's name was called out and she lurched upright to walk falteringly towards the stage where a young man with a head as shiny as his suit was waiting for her and clapping.

"What's the award for?" Hardy asked Erna, who had a hand on his shoulder again.

"I don't fucking know. Best advert for decaffeinated yoghurt or something like that. Nobody goes away from here without a prize," she yelled back at him over the storm of applause that greeted Sigurjóna's arrival on stage.

Sigurjóna grabbed the microphone ahead of the shiny-suited compère and launched into the impromptu speech that one of the office staff had carefully crafted for her that afternoon. The room quietened as she began, but the speech lasted a long time for something made up on the spur of the moment and the level of chatter rose steadily, moving gradually forward from the back tables.

"What's your sister saying?" Hardy asked.

"Just bullshit. She's thanking everybody she's ever met, including the postman, the girl she sat next to in primary school, her personal trainer, and her husband."

"Where is he tonight?"

"Hell, I don't know where high-and-mighty Bjarni Jón is," she snarled. Hardy was interested to see she disliked her brother-in-law and filed the information away for future reference.

"Was he supposed to be here?"

"You're sitting in his seat, honey," Erna said, attention on Sigurjóna who was winding up her speech. "Oh, how sweet! She thanked me as well! Big sister!" she squawked in delight, reaching for a bottle from the middle of the table and upending it into her glass.

Sigurjóna tottered back with applause and whistles ringing in her ears, a black glass statuette of a pair of elongated praying hands under one arm and a wine bottle held by the neck in her other hand.

"She's great, my big sister, isn't she?" Erna declared to Hardy in a voice that carried over the conversation around them. "Her tits are better, but at least mine are real."

Hardy felt the phone buzz in his pocket and put a hand inside his jacket to take it out. He looked at the number displayed and stood up quickly with the phone flashing in his hand.

"Excuse me just one minute," he said quickly and marched towards the lobby.

"Don't be long, honey! Bjarni Jón's not here and we girls need at least one man around!" Erna yelled after him.

The elegant statuette by a well-known artist had become a collection of slivers of black glass that shuffling feet had dispersed across the floor of the ballroom, providing a nightmare mess for the staff of the Gullfoss Hotel to clean up in the morning. With the ceremony long over and already forgotten, a few couples gyrated jerkily across the dance floor and groups of dazzling people, much the worse for wear, sat in alcoves around the edge, some on the point of passing out.

"Where's my sister?" Sigurjóna demanded, shaking Jón Oddur by the lapel of his silver-grey suit. She took a long draw on the joint in her other hand as Jón Oddur's eyes opened blearily.

"Dunno. She just went. Haven't seen her," he slurred.

"Where did she go? Was she alone?"

"Don't know. She was dancing with that foreigner."

"Which one? There's plenty of foreigners here."

"Er. The tall guy. Y'know. Had a meeting with him today. Yesterday," he corrected himself. "Hardy?" Sigurjóna sat down hard on the chair next to Jón Oddur and ground out the joint on the table top. "Did you get a room here?"

"I booked four," he said proudly.

"Shit. My fucking sister," she cursed. "Come on. Where's your room?"

CHAPTER TWENTY-NINE

Saturday, 27 September

"Good morning."

Erna opened one eye and lifted her head from the pillow, dropping it down again as sunlight filtering through gaps between the curtains pierced her eyeballs. She quickly screwed her eyes shut again.

"Hi," she mumbled.

"Your head hurts?" Hardy inquired gently.

"Yeah. Sleep more," she mumbled.

Hardy nodded, swung his legs from the bed and padded from the room. Erna vaguely took in the sound of running water as she drifted back to sleep.

An hour later he returned to wake her, mugs of fragrant tea, two aspirins and slices of toast spread with honey on a tray that he balanced in one hand as he slid back into the bed alongside her.

"Good morning again."

"And to you."

"Feeling better now?"

"Yes, thanks."

Hardy put the tray down on his lap and passed her one of the mugs.

"My mother told me not to accept drinks from strange men."

"Maybe I'm not a strange man any more?"

Erna sipped and gulped down the two little white tablets.

"What time did we get back here?" she asked.

"Around two."

"An early night, then. What time is it now?"

"Ten."

"Have a good time last night?" she asked, crunching toast over the tray to catch crumbs.

"Of course. I take it you mean the ceremony, or do you mean the party afterwards?"

"Was there a party afterwards?" Erna asked blankly.

"The party that you and I had here."

"Oh, that."

"Both of them were pretty good."

"That's good." Erna yawned, curling back beneath the covers and sending exploring fingers towards Hardy's thigh. "I need to get up but I'm too lazy. It's great to stay in bed for a change."

"When are you usually up?"

"Never later than seven on normal days. Maybe eight on a weekend. Depends on the kids."

"How many do you have?"

"Two." Erna yawned again.

"They're not here today?"

"They're with their fathers for a change for a couple of weeks. One lives in Chicago, the other one's here in town."

"Peace and quiet then?"

"For the moment. But I'll miss them soon, I expect. How about you? Children? Girlfriend? Wife, maybe?"

Hardy chuckled. Erna placed her head on his chest and could hear his laughter deep inside.

"Nothing. Nobody. There's just me. A single man with no ties."

"Then there must be something wrong with you if no woman has snapped you up yet."

The hair of his chest tickled her nose and she ran a hand through it.

"I like this," she said softly. "Icelandic men shave everything. They think it's sexy but some of us like a man who has some hair. It's more, y'know . . ." She struggled for the English word. "Like a cave man, you know what I mean?"

"Primeval?"

"I guess so. Hey, I have to shower. Do you want to fuck again before or after?"

Bára cupped the phone in her hand, pursing her lips in irritation. She shook her head as Gunna lifted a questioning eyebrow.

"Yes, I am fully aware of that," Bára continued. "And no, I didn't know that the PR Federation awards were held last night. Look, I'm sorry that your boss may have a hangover, but this is an important investigation into a serious matter . . ."

Bára paused and listened for a moment to a flood of complaint before she cut through the voice again. "Excuse me, but this is a police investigation. I need to speak to Sigurjóna Huldudóttir urgently. Now, are you going to tell me where I can find her?"

The voice chattered into Bára's phone and she lifted it up, shrugging her shoulders. She waited for it to go quiet before she continued.

"Excuse me, I repeat, this is a police investigation. Look," she said quickly, pre-empting the voice on the other end before it began to complain again. "You need to speak to my superior officer. Hold on, please."

Bára covered the mouthpiece with her hand. "I can't get any sense out of this woman at all. She just yells at me that Sigurjóna's not in the office today, refuses to release her mobile number and then said something about harassment. Will you speak to her?"

Gunna stood up and walked around the desk. She picked up the handset, pressed the loudspeaker button and put the handset down, leaning forward to speak to the machine in the middle of the desk.

"Who am I speaking to, please?" she asked as smoothly as she could.

"This is Ósk Líndal, Sigurjóna's personal assistant," a haughty voice crackled through the speaker in reply. "She's not here today and isn't contactable."

"Fine, now listen, Ósk. This is Gunnhildur Gísladóttir and I'm at the Keflavík police department," she said, her voice hardening gradually. "I understand that my colleague has been trying to reach Sigurjóna Huldudóttir this morning without much success, which I also understand is due largely to a lack of cooperation on your part."

"Do you really think this is something so serious that it warrants my ignoring her explicit instructions to leave her alone?" the voice snarled back.

"If it wasn't important, it could wait until Monday. But it is and it can't," Gunna snapped back. "So, are you going to tell me where she can be reached, or better still, where she is right now, or is the wife of a government minister unwilling to cooperate in an investigation that carries the highest priority?"

"Wait," the voice replied submissively. They could hear papers being shuffled and a mobile phone beeping quietly.

"Here it is," Ósk Líndal snapped, and Gunna gestured to both Snorri and Bára to write the number down. "I suppose I may as well tell you that last night Sigurjóna stayed at the Gullfoss Hotel. I don't know her room number, but the company booked four rooms."

"Thank you. You've been a great help," Gunna said, back to her smooth voice again.

"Yeah. Well, if you need any other information, then don't call me," the voice grated, with the phone banging down on to its rest at the other end as the last word spilled out.

"Nice one, chief. That's the way to make friends," Snorri said with a wide grin on his face that almost matched the one on Bára's.

Sigurjóna's head throbbed. Swathed in a voluptuous white dressing gown and with hair awry, she sat in a deep armchair in one of the Gullfoss Hotel's finest suites.

"Do you know where all your staff are at the moment?" Gunna asked her gently as Jón Oddur, bare-chested and pink-faced, appeared from the bedroom with a handful of tablets and a glass of water which he put on the coffee table in front of Sigurjóna.

"Of course not. I employ a human resources manager who does that."

"Ósk Líndal?"

"That is one of Ósk's duties."

Gunna opened the slim briefcase she had borrowed from Snorri and took out copies of the photos of Hårde that had come from the Swedish police. She placed a picture of a stubble-faced, younger-looking Hårde on the table.

"Do you know this man?"

"Should I?"

"You tell me."

"Yes."

"Tell me about him."

Sigurjóna frowned in irritation. "His name's Graham Hardy. He works for InterAlu as their site integrity consultant for the construction of the Hvalvík Lagoon plant."

"And if I were to tell you that he has convictions for assault and grievous bodily harm, what would your reaction be?" Gunna asked.

Sigurjóna's face was expressionless. "So? Our connections with InterAlu on a day-to-day basis are generally via Hardy and he's given us no cause for concern. He's very efficient, very well organized. What he may have done in the past isn't relevant. He does his job well and that's all that matters."

"Where is he now?"

"Why do you want to know?"

"All I can tell you is that it concerns an ongoing investigation and it isn't a trivial matter. Locating your Mr Hardy is a priority."

Sigurjóna yawned and leaned back in the armchair. "Isn't there any coffee? Jón Oddur! Order coffee, will you?"

The young man put his head briefly round the door, nodded and bobbed quickly back to the bedroom.

"I'd prefer it if this conversation could be kept confidential from your staff," Gunna said acidly, emphasizing "staff".

"Close the door, then."

Gunna nodded to Snorri, who walked over, gently shut the bedroom door and sat back down again on the plush sofa next to Bára.

"Can you tell me about the work Hardy does?"

"Why don't you ask him yourself?"

"If I knew where to find him, I would. What does he do?"

"I told you. He's in charge of security at the Hvalvík site on behalf of InterAlu and at the Hvalvík Lagoon site on ESC's behalf."

"Your company?"

"So you read newspapers, inspector?"

"Sergeant. When I have time," Gunna replied. "I have to say, I was rather hoping that you would be more cooperative."

"Good God, you wake me up on a Saturday morning after an awards party and expect me to be cooperative?"

"I would expect the wife of a minister to cooperate with a murder investigation."

"Murder? Who?"

There was a knock at the door and Gunna said nothing.

"Shall I?" Snorri asked.

Sigurjóna nodded. Snorri opened the door and took a tray of cups and a silver thermos of coffee from a black-waistcoated waiter. He put it carefully on the table and sat back down on the sofa where Bára was taking notes.

"You still haven't answered my question," Gunna reminded Sigurjóna as she poured coffee for herself.

"What question?"

"Where's Hardy?"

"I have no idea where he is. As you know, until a quarter of an hour ago, I was asleep. Anyway, you haven't answered my question either."

"You mean the one I expect you know perfectly well that I can't answer?"

"Yeah. Who's been murdered?"

"Like I said, I can't say anything about an ongoing investigation."

"It's that silly boy Einar Eyjólfur, I suppose. Look, he must have been drunk, got a lift with somebody and lost his way somehow. For such a smart guy, he was an idiot in some ways."

"I can't comment at the moment. But it's important that we speak to Hardy soon. Where's he living?"

"Don't know."

"He's working for you and you don't know his address?"

"Strictly speaking, he doesn't work for me. He's an employee of InterAlu and we purchase their services in some fields, some of which happen to be carried out by Mr Hardy."

"How about a phone number?"

"I contact him when I need to at the compound in Hvalvík. Jón Oddur has the number."

"No mobile?"

"Probably. But I don't have a number for him," Sigurjóna lied.

"I assume you must have a record of when Hardy has been in Iceland, in which case I must ask you to let me have a full list of his stays here."

"I'm not sure we would have that." Sigurjóna yawned again. "You could ask Ósk. She might know."

"You're paying for this guy's services and you don't have a record of the work he has done for you? That hardly sounds plausible."

Sigurjóna's face frosted over. "Are you accusing me of lying, sergeant?"

"No," Gunna replied sharply. "Merely a suspicion on my part that you might not be as helpful as you could be. Failure to cooperate with a police investigation is a crime in itself, you know."

"I am aware of that. If you want any information, you'd better call Ósk. Now, if that's all, I have calls to make this morning, including one to my lawyer."

Gunna stifled the smile that leapt to her lips.

"Give him my kindest regards, would you? We'll leave you to catch up on your sleep," she said, noticing the bedroom door open a crack. She stood up and handed the keys of the Volvo to Snorri.

"You drive this time," she said to him and turned back to Sigurjóna. "Thank you for your time, and apologies for disturbing you at such an early hour of the morning."

"What do you think, chief?" Snorri asked as the lift swooped groundwards.

"Bullshit from start to finish, I reckon."

"She knows where Hårde is and how to contact him. Body language. Every time she tells a lie, her face goes blank for a fraction of a second and then relaxes," Bára said. "What next?"

"Hell, I don't know. It's getting on for midday, so I'll buy you both lunch at the bus station. Then we'd better get back and see what's happening at the nerve centre. Then someone had better call that bloody woman again."

"The one who said not to call her if we needed to know anything?"

"That's the one. And if she doesn't answer the phone, send someone to bang on her front door. But first we'd better find the manager of this place."

Bára nodded to herself while it took Snorri a moment to catch on. Gunna extracted the Swedish police's photo of Hårde from the file and put it in Snorri's outstretched hand.

"I'd like you two to go and chat to a few of the staff. Show them the pic and ask if they've seen him about. He could be under our noses in a suite of his own right here."

"Gotcha, chief," Snorri grinned.

"I'll go and do the same with the manager. Then it might be lunchtime."

Sigurjóna cursed. She paced back and forth across the thick carpet of the suite with her phone at her ear. She swore again as the voicemail kicked in.

"Hi, this is Erna's phone, I can't take your call right now, so just talk after the squawk. Bye!"

Sigurjóna stabbed her phone's red button to end the call and hit redial.

"Jón Oddur!" she yelled as it began to ring, and his head appeared round the bedroom door. He stood expectantly as Sigurjóna listened to Erna's voicemail message again.

"Hi. It's me. Hope you had a good time last night. Call me. OK? Bye," she intoned into the handset and clicked it shut.

"What is it?" Jón Oddur asked from the door.

Sigurjóna stepped towards him, opening the dressing gown.

"I need a shower. Order breakfast from room service, will you?" she snapped as she strode to the bathroom, shrugging the dressing gown from her shoulders and draping it over his outstretched arm as she swept past.

Her fingers caressed the hard whorl of scar tissue that ran diagonally across his shoulder.

"I'm sure there's a story behind this," Erna whispered huskily.

Hardy gently rolled on to his back and the scar disappeared from view. "Yeah. Not a nice story, though."

"Tell me one day."

"Maybe I will. Why do you have different names?" Hardy asked.

Erna settled herself across the bed with her head resting on Hardy's chest and one ankle hooked over the opposite knee. Hardy lay back with one hand behind his head and the other across Erna.

This time her fingertip traced the outline of a blurred fouled anchor tattooed beneath the coarse hair of the forearm lying on her chest. "What do you mean?

"You and your sister. You're Daníelsdóttir and she's Huldudóttir. So why don't you have the same surname?"

"It's not a surname. We don't have surnames in Iceland."

"Some people do."

"Yeah, a few people do. It's a bit stuck-up. Here everyone takes their father's name. Dad's Daníel Jónsson — that's Daníel the son of Jón — and I'm Erna Daníelsdóttir, Erna the daughter of Daníel. My son's called Jón, after my dad, but he's Jón Bergsson, because my ex-husband's name is Bergur. See?"

"I figured that out. But why aren't you and Sigurjóna both Daníelsdóttir? Are you half-sisters?"

Erna untangled her legs and rolled over on to her side to look along Hardy's torso at his chin. He pulled a pillow under his head to look down his chest at her and extended a hand to stroke her side with his fingertips.

"It's complicated," Erna began.

"How complicated?"

"Well, not really. Our father's name is Daníel and our mother's is Hulda."

"Go on."

"In the old days, if someone's father wasn't known, if he'd run away, or refused to admit a child was his, or was a foreigner or something, then the mother's name would be used instead."

"Sounds reasonable."

"Yeah, but it was very unusual, didn't happen often that someone's dad was just completely unknown. But in the last couple of years it's become a lot more common. Y'know, people splitting up all the time and hating each other afterwards. So a lot of women got fed up with having their kids carrying around the name of some deadbeat guy they'd rather forget and used their own names instead."

"OK, I get it. Ditch the husband and his name as well, understandable."

Erna stretched and inched herself forward as Hardy's fingertips grazed her hip and wandered along her thigh.

"What was I saying? Yeah. Well, it got a bit sort of, y'know, fashionable as well. There are women who fell out with their dads who took their mothers' names instead. It's all very feminist and a bit smart to carry your mother's name now."

"So is that why Sigurjóna is Huldudóttir? Did she have a disagreement with your father?"

"No, not really. They've never got on all that well, but they haven't fallen out either. I think she saw it as a career move more than anything else, looks good with all that cultural mafia crowd she hangs out with. Do you know what, Mr Hardy? You're quite a nice man really. We should go away together. Get to know each other properly."

She heard Hardy's chuckle again deep in his chest.

"You really think so? Where?"

"I do. Spain, maybe. Or Morocco. While the kids are off my hands."

"Can you do that?"

"Yeah. The girls can run the salon easily enough. They don't even need me there a lot of the time. Can you get away from your work for a few days?"

"I should think so, if it's something important."

"I think it could be something important, don't you, Mr Hardy or whatever your real name is?"

"I'd have to talk to Sigurjóna, make sure she doesn't need me for anything at the Lagoon."

Erna stretched like a well-fed cat and readjusted her legs, putting his hand in hers to lift and place it in just the right spot. Hardy listened for a moment.

"Is that a phone ringing?" he asked.

"Don't know. Don't care," Erna hissed. "Want me to have a word with your boss? But right now, keep doing that and I'll see what I can do."

27-09-2008 1551

Skandalblogger writes:

Oh, people! O tempora, O mores, as the poet said and as a very few of Skandalblogger's classically educated readers will recognize. The rest of you, just google for it.

Sigurjóna, what were you thinking with that post-awards bash in someone else's suite at Hotel Gullfoss? And there was us thinking that white powder was going out of fashion. Which high-ranking Ministry official, which well-known media guru and which fashionable designer were photographed enthusiastically partaking of Sigurjóna's largesse with the cheese grater?

Click here* for the photos — a few details obscured to protect the guilty. Or here* for the video clip of Sigurjóna dropping and smashing the exclusive and ludicrously expensive award statue, an individually handcrafted glass artwork by Hanna Kugga.

And where's the old man? Gallivanting overseas again at the taxpayers' expense? But, hell and damnation, that's what we pay our politicians for, to get the hell out of the country for as long and as often as possible so the staff can get on with running the show without interference.

Still, who knows? He's supposed to be there for the full week, but Skandalblogger hears on the grapevine that there might well be a good reason to come scuttling home early from the conference in Berlin where he's holed up in the Bristol Hotel, definitely a step up from the Gruesome Gullfoss and its Latvian hookers. At least at the Bristol there's a bit more variety to choose from.

Well, Bjarni Jón . . . See you on . . . Wednesday? Maybe Thursday?

The call icon winked on the screen of Bjarni Jón Bjarnason's laptop. Birna raised a questioning eyebrow and he nodded to her. She silently stood up from her side of the vast dining table scattered with papers.

Bjarni Jón clicked on the accept call button and Sigurjóna's voice erupted through the speaker at the same time as an imperfect image of her appeared in a box below the internet phone's control panel. He could see that she was dressed smartly, as if for the office.

"Hi, darling. How are you? Everything OK at home?"

"Of course," Sigurjóna snapped back. "Are you alone? Why can't I see you on-screen?"

Bjarni Jón sighed. Birna looked at him inquiringly from the sofa on the far side of the suite where she had retreated with a pile of paperwork. The inquiring look asked if she should leave them to speak privately.

"Birna's here. We're preparing for the meeting with Horst. You can't see me because I don't have a camera on this computer."

"All right. Listen."

Bjarni Jón could make out his wife's pinched features. "What is it, love? How did the awards go? I take it they gave you something?"

"Yeah. Most forward-thinking company, or some such crap. There was a hideous statue that came with it, so I dumped that," Sigurjóna said quickly. "Listen, I can't get in touch with my sister. She doesn't answer her phone."

Bjarni Jón drummed the desk with his fingers. "So? There's nothing new about that."

"And I've had the police here this morning asking about Hardy. They want to question him about that boy who was found dead in Hvalvík. I'm worried about this and I can't reach Hardy either."

"Shit," Bjarni Jón hissed to himself and fumbled for a headset that he plugged into the computer. Sigurjóna's voice broke into his ears and would at least keep half of the conversation private. "Have you called the compound?"

"Of course I did, and his mobile," Sigurjóna snarled. "I'm not an idiot."

"I never said you were," Bjarni Jón said hastily. "Where did you see Hardy last?"

"At the awards last night."

"He was there? Why?"

"Because I invited him."

"Good grief."

"The police have some idea that he has a violent past."

"We knew that already. Horst told us."

"Not directly."

"No. He hinted. He said that Hardy was very competent," Bjarni Jón said, looking over the top of the screen to see if Birna was paying any attention, but she appeared to be engrossed in paperwork now spread across the sofa.

"Where are you, anyway?" Sigurjóna demanded.

"Hotel Bristol."

"Yeah, but where?"

"Berlin."

"Again?"

"Yup, again. Environment Ministers' conference."

"God."

Bjarni Jón could see Sigurjóna's face on the screen looking down at the keyboard as she typed. She looked strained, he thought, more tense than usual. He peered at the image of her beamed from the camera on top of her laptop.

"Are you all right, Sugarplum?" he asked tenderly.

"What?"

He saw her sit up straight, startled.

"Are you all right?" he repeated.

"Yes, yes," she replied quickly. "You're meeting Horst this afternoon?"

"Tomorrow."

"Anything special?"

"Not that I'm aware of. Just a routine chat, I suppose. He asked for this meeting. What do you want me to do about — you know?" he asked, avoiding mentioning the police out loud with Birna in the room.

"Will you call Lárus?"

"Lárus Jóhann? Again?"

"Yes."

"And talk about what?"

"Just call him and ask him what's going on."

"Look, how can I?"

"He's the Justice Minister. He ought to have some bloody clue about what his police force is doing."

"He's done us a lot of favours already. It's not even as if we're the same party. I can't call on him too often."

Bjarni Jón saw Sigurjóna's face grimace with anger, fuzzed by the time-lapse imaging of the internet phone.

"Just do it, will you?" she snapped and Bjarni Jón was relieved that he had had the foresight to plug in the headset.

"I'll do what I can," he replied smoothly for Birna's benefit, suppressing the irritation building up inside.

"OK. Do that. I'm going to try Erna again. It's not like her to not answer me."

"All right, darling, let me know, won't you?"

"Yeah. And you'll let me know when you've spoken to Lárus. Bye."

The stop sign appeared in the connection box on the screen and Bjarni Jón wondered what he was going to say to the Minister of Justice.

CHAPTER THIRTY

Sunday, 28 September

"Hell, I'd just take the money and say thank you in your position," Bjössi said firmly. "I wouldn't even consider turning that kind of thing down."

"Yeah, but it's the moving part I'm not so keen on."

"Why? Cheap housing in the east and you can rent out your place here to some yuppie couple who can't afford to live in Reykjavík. You'd be quids in, especially with an inspector's pay grade. And the job might be more fun."

Gunna had discouraged opinions from colleagues who had managed to hear of the offer of promotion and the transfer that would go with it. Bjössi was the latest and also the most forthright in his advice.

"I know. But it's Gísli and Laufey I'm concerned about. I really don't want to uproot her from school, especially as she's doing well and seems happy enough there."

"Gunna, my dear, I'm sorry to break this to you, but Gísli's a big lad and he'll want his own place soon enough. All right, Laufey's thirteen, so how long do you think she's going to want to stay with Mum?"

"But Bjössi, I like living in Hvalvík. It suits me. It's comfortable."

Bjössi wanted to stamp his feet. "Just right. It's too bloody comfortable, Gunna. You're getting old and set in your ways before your time."

"Are you trying to get rid of me, or what?" Gunna retorted. "To be honest with you, I had been wondering about leaving the force and giving something else a try."

Bjössi laughed. "And do what? Gunna, I can't see you working on the meat counter in the Co-op."

"Don't talk such crap. My widow's pension keeps the wolf from the door, and there's security work, insurance claim stuff, that sort of thing."

Bjössi stood up and shrugged himself into an outsized overcoat that Gunna had told him many times made him look like a flasher. "Well, it's up to you. But times are going to be bloody tough in the next few years and working for the public sector at least has a bit of security about it. You'd be bloody mad to turn it down. Up a pay scale, a shift to plain clothes if you want it, cheap housing. Even if it's just for a year or two, it'd be worth it," he said heavily. "Come on, apart from this case, what's the most interesting piece of work you've had in the last year? Was it when Sigga Vésteins broke into the pharmacy and you had to follow the footprints in the snow to find out which low-life it was, or was it when you had to bust Albert Jónasson for 300 kilos of over-quota cod?"

"Ach, Bjössi, I don't know."

"Gunna, look, either take the job or get yourself a boyfriend. You deserve a little excitement for a change."

"Where are you?" Sigurjóna demanded immediately the phone was answered.

"Reykjavík," Hardy replied. "Is there a problem?"

"The police have been here looking for you. Where are you at the moment?"

"Let's just say I'm in Iceland. It may be best if you don't know exactly where I am."

Sigurjóna paced up and down the black quarry tiles of her rarely used designer kitchen, and noticed that the cleaner had left smears on the stainless steel hood over the six-burner gas stove. She made a mental note to have words with the girl. "They know about you and are looking for you."

"That's understandable. Do you know what information they have?"

"No. They were very cagey and wouldn't say anything except that it's high-priority."

Hardy looked up from the armchair enclosing him and listened to Erna singing tunelessly to herself in the bedroom. He was amazed at the woman's energy. There was definitely something about these sisters, he thought to himself.

"Listen, have you seen my sister?" Sigurjóna demanded suddenly.

"Why?"

"I can't reach her and I haven't seen her since the awards. Did she go home with you?"

"She's fine." Hardy chuckled. "I'll ask her to call you."

"Shit. Well, that's a relief anyway. At least I know why the randy old cow's not answering her phone. I hope she hasn't completely tired you out?"

"Tell me about your visit from the police. What did they want, exactly?"

"To know where you are. That's all they'd say."

"A senior officer?"

"There were three of them. A sergeant and two officers."

"Plain clothes or uniform?"

"Uniform."

"Do you have the man's name?"

"It's a woman. Gunnhildur. She used to be quite well known. She's tough."

"We'll see. I'm sure we can fix something," Hardy said with a chill in his voice. "Now, if you'll excuse me, this isn't a secure line and I have some things to arrange."

"OK. But get Erna to call me, all right? Hardy?"

"Yes?"

Sigurjóna was silent for a moment.

"Was Einar Eyjólfur's death anything to do with you?" she asked, almost whispering the words and listening to Hardy's silence.

"That's an unpleasant question," he replied eventually, smoothly. "But I take it his disappearing was useful for you?"

"Well, it was. Yes."

"Then don't worry about it."

* * *

Bjarni Jón Bjarnason was learning how shock feels. His fingers and feet were numb, and he found himself observing his own reactions to the news with a detached objectivity that surprised him.

"Jeeesus," he whispered silently to himself.

Horst meshed his fingers delicately together and planted his elbows on the glossy tabletop, so perfectly polished that his whole image was mirrored in the surface.

"Are you all right, Mr Bjarnason? I am, of course, sorry to have to bring you such unwelcome news. Would you like a drink?"

"Er, no thanks," Bjarni Jón stumbled, trying to keep an outward semblance of composure. "Can I ask the reasons for this?"

"Certainly," Horst answered smoothly. "This seemed like a very positive project at the time when others were setting up geothermal and hydro-electric systems for powering smelters. We definitely saw this as a possibility, but when our Norwegian friends pulled out for reasons of their own —"

"Ethical reasons," Bjarni Jón added sourly.

"Exactly, ethical reasons."

"Surely you weren't all that concerned about ethics?"

A narrow smile flashed across Horst's face. "Not particularly, but our parent company, as you know, is looking at the long term and they are concerned about adverse publicity, as well as other aspects. To be quite blunt, we do not have confidence in your economy and we understand that the financial sector in your country is weakening."

"What?" Bjarni Jón demanded. "Our banks are in a very strong position. I think you're on the wrong track here."

Horst's face gave nothing away. "If you think so, Mr Bjarnason. But we have very reliable information to the effect that your bank does not have the funds to support your company's activities."

"That's absolutely ridiculous. There have been a few minor exchange rate problems, but our financial sector is one of the strongest in the world."

"We are fully aware of who your bankers are and what their real position is. If I were in your position, Mr Bjarnason, I would be concerned."

Bjarni Jón realized that there was no menace in Horst's voice. He had the feeling that he was being given unwanted advice by a wise uncle.

"I assure you, we are not badly positioned and everything is set to go ahead with the last phase of the finance for the Hvalvík Lagoon project."

"Yes, of course. I believe this represents some eighty per cent of your company's contribution?" Horst asked.

"You know it is."

"Then I think you may be disappointed. I hope not, but I believe you will be when you meet your bankers."

"Ridiculous," Bjarni Jón repeated.

"Between ourselves, it is much easier for us to do our business in the developing world. Developed countries such as yours present obstacles that we are not used to dealing with, and frankly, we do not want to deal with. We don't find joint ventures particularly comfortable."

"So you're just going to walk away?"

"Precisely. We are withdrawing from the project. There will be a question of some compensation that will have to be arranged, but we can deal with that when your lawyers contact ours. It might take a few weeks."

"They certainly will."

"Of course. That isn't a problem. We would appreciate it if you would instruct them to do so as soon as is convenient, as InterAlu would prefer to have everything concluded as rapidly as possible."

Bjarni Jón stood up now that feeling had returned to his feet. Horst did the same and walked around the table, offering a hand to shake. Bjarni Jón debated with himself for a second whether or not to accept it before limply grasping Horst's hand.

"Doesn't this reflect badly on you, Mr Horst, as you were in charge of the project?"

"Quite the contrary," Horst said, smiling. "I was dubious about it from the start and warned the directors of our parent company of the difficulties I expected we would be presented with in Iceland. As it happens, I was quite right, so actually it reflects rather well on me personally."

Bjarni Jón couldn't keep the bitterness out of his voice. "So you come out of it all right and we have to pick up the pieces?"

"I am aware that this is a significant disappointment to you and your wife, Mr Bjarnason. Please be assured that there is nothing personal in this, but I really do think that your bankers have a great many questions to answer."

"It's just business," Bjarni Jón said, trying not to sneer, wondering how he was going to break the news to Sigurjóna. "Have you announced this yet?"

"Exactly. Business. We haven't made an announcement and I don't expect we will. InterAlu prefers a low profile. Please give my kindest regards to your wife and we will be in touch with her people after the weekend. I'm sure she can issue a suitable press release," Horst added with a hint of a grim smile.

Gunna parked the jeep outside *Dagurinn*'s offices. Normally she would never have used a private car for police work, but Skúli had been so insistent they meet that she borrowed the keys to Gísli's Range Rover and made the hour's drive to Reykjavík in ten minutes less than usual, even with the detour to drop Laufey off with her friend on the way.

"So what did you want me to see, young man? And why the hell are you still at work at eight thirty on a Sunday evening?" Gunna asked as they made their way in single file through the maze of workstations. She thought the young man looked tired. There were black bags under his eyes and his hair stood on end where he had repeatedly run his hands through it.

Although every light was on, *Dagurinn*'s office was deserted. A pair of tiny Asian women were slowly dusting each desk in the background, clicking off desk lights as they went.

"I'm still at work because I have a ton of stuff to get through and also because I wanted to make sure Reynir

Óli wasn't here when I show you the proofs of Tuesday's *Hot Chat*."

"*Hot Chat*? What's that?"

"God, Gunna, where have you been? *Hot Chat's Dagurinn*'s answer to *Seen & Heard*," Skúli said. "It's pretty shit, actually. It's just the same as *Seen & Heard*, but it's got a bit more raunchy as the competition got tougher."

"Which did?" Gunna asked, confused already.

"Well, both of them did. They're both garbage. Lots of gossip and celebrity scandal."

"And that's what you want to show me?"

"Yup. Come on."

Skúli threaded through the quiet desks and the two cleaners soundlessly stepped aside to let him pass, looking at Gunna, still in uniform, with fearful eyes. She tried to smile at them, as if to send a message that she wasn't remotely interested in their immigration status, but their expressions remained impassive as she followed Skúli.

At the far end of the row of desks, he sat down and started up one of the computers. He tapped at the keyboard and paused. A page of newsprint and pictures appeared gradually, scored with red guidelines, and Skúli scrolled downwards.

"The guy you're looking for, the foreign tough guy. You know, the one who was at the march in the spring. Is that him?"

He pointed at the screen and Gunna fumbled for her glasses. She peered at the image of four people sitting round a table with a cluster of wine bottles in the middle. Hårde had a smile on his face and his left arm round the back of a statuesque blonde woman. On Hårde's right side sat the pink-faced young man Gunna had seen at the bathroom door in the Gullfoss Hotel suite and next to him sat a regal Sigurjóna in a low-cut black dress, all of them with their attention on something out of camera shot.

"Bloody hell. What's all this?" Gunna asked.

"I'll print it out for you."

Skúli's fingers flickered and a printer hummed somewhere behind them.

"It's the PR Association Awards, held the other night. The design guy did these pages today and I saw the proofs this afternoon."

"But it's Sunday. Don't you people ever take a day off?"

"The guy who did the story is a freelance, and freelancers never stop working. The page make-up guys are on flexi-time, so if they want to, they can work twenty hours straight and take two days off. I guess the one who did these pages was in today because it's the last page of the mag and I don't expect he'll be in again until the middle of the week."

Skúli swung his chair round and picked a crisp set of proofs from the printer under the bench behind him. He smoothed the sheets and spread them on the desk.

"That's Sigurjóna Huldudóttir." His finger paused at Jón Oddur. "Don't know who that guy is. That's the foreign guy."

"Hårde, his name is, but you don't know that."

"OK, that's Hårde." His finger moved on. "And that's Erna Daníelsdóttir."

"Who's she?"

"Celebrity hairdresser, Sigurjóna's little sister."

"Good grief. You can see the resemblance."

She inspected the double page spread with its "PR Practitioners Pull Out the Stops!" headline. Another picture showed Sigurjóna with a blissful smile on her face accepting an award. Gunna skimmed over further photographs of grinning people in formal finery sitting at tables or standing on a platform accepting their own awards.

"Looks like quite a party. Who took these pictures?"

Skúli pointed to the by-line at the top of the page. "There."

Under the headline she read "Words and pictures: Ármann J."

"Right. Where can I find this Ármann character?"

Skúli shut down the computer. "I'll find his number for you."

Back at his own desk, Skúli skimmed through the post-it notes adorning the monitor and copied the number on to a scrap of paper.

"Thanks, Skúli. I take it I can hold on to this?" She brandished the pages he had printed out.

"Yeah. But I'd appreciate it if you didn't let on where they came from."

He yawned and closed the laptop on his desk.

Gunna pressed her phone to her ear and listened to it ring.

"Snorri? Hi, Gunna. Yup. No, it's OK, nothing wrong. Something's come up, so we'd better be early tomorrow. Pick me up at six outside my place and can you call Bára and the others, and ask them to be there for a meeting at seven?"

Skúli pulled on the jacket that was draped over the back of his chair and looked expectantly at Gunna as she spoke.

"That's all right. Yeah, sorry to disturb you," Gunna continued. "No, I'll call Bjössi and let him know as well. Thanks, Snorri. Goodnight."

She snapped the phone shut and dropped it back in her pocket.

"Thank you, Skúli. I think I can forgive you for dragging an old lady out on a Sunday evening."

"I hope it's some use to you. But you'd have seen it anyway on Tuesday."

"I doubt it. *Hot Chat* isn't exactly at the top of my reading list. But thanks again, young man."

"No problem. Er, Gunna?" he asked diffidently. "Any chance you could give me a lift home?"

Gunna parked Gísli's Range Rover and sat in the driving seat, listening to the engine tick, continuing to run things through in her mind.

She was still muttering to herself as she opened the front door and kicked off her boots, flexing stiff toes that had been cooped up far too long. She noticed instinctively that Laufey's trainers were in their place.

She peered past Laufey's bedroom door and heard her breathing softly. In the kitchen she poured coffee and water into the percolator, and hung her cap on the door before hauling off her uniform jacket and slinging it over the back of the sofa. In the shower she let the scalding sulphur-smelling water run until the knotted muscles across her shoulders gradually untied themselves and she could hardly see for steam, and wondered what linked Arngrímur Örn Arnarson's killing to those of Egill Grímsson and Einar Eyjólfur Einarsson.

The bloody man hadn't been involved with Clean Iceland for years. So why knock him off? she asked herself.

Gunna wrapped herself in a dressing gown that had seen better days, but since she had stolen it herself from a hotel in Copenhagen on the honeymoon with Raggi all those years ago, it had enough sentimental value to be kept. She retrieved her glasses from her jacket pocket and perched them on her nose to flip through the Sunday newspaper that had been lying on the doormat since early that morning. Although she had called Snorri to bring the morning meeting forward, she deliberately hadn't asked what progress he and Bára had made in chasing Ósk Líndal for information.

"Bloody shame, really," she muttered to herself. "Bloody good coppers those two. But I'd bet any money they're both out of the force in two years."

She reached for her mug on the table and realized that she had leafed through the paper automatically without taking a single thing in, so she sipped coffee and leaned back in the flat's only comfortable chair to run the faces through her mind again.

"Mum?" Laufey inquired drowsily, padding softly into the room and dropping on to the sofa to wriggle under Gunna's arm.

"Hi, sweetheart. All right?" Gunna asked tenderly, suppressing a pang of guilt at having been out for so long.

"Yeah. I went to Sigrún's and had dinner there and then I came home and did my homework," she said carefully.

"All your homework?"

"All of it."

"I'm sorry, my love, things are really busy at work at the moment."

"I know, Mum. You are going to catch this murderer, aren't you?"

"How do you know?" Gunna asked in surprise.

"Mum," Laufey explained patiently, "I do watch the news and I hear it when you're on the phone. And Finnur said that when you catch him, he'll get life. Is that right?"

"We'll see. I hope so," Gunna said as her mind flashed back to Einar Eyjólfur. "Come on, you'd best be off to bed again. I have an early start tomorrow, so you'll have to sort yourself out in the morning. Did Sigrún say you could go to her for lunch again tomorrow?"

"Hm. Yup," Laufey mumbled.

"Go on, sweetheart. Off to bed. I'm going to sleep soon as well."

Laufey dragged herself to her feet and shambled back to her room. Gunna heard the creak as she lay down and within a minute her thoughts were back to the case.

She was delighted to know that Matti Kristjáns had run for shelter and had a good idea of where he had run to. The thought of her cousin being another victim would have been hard to bear. In spite of the rancour between them, she felt genuinely fond of Matti as one of those people who had always been part of the family scenery for as long as she could remember.

Gunna glanced at her watch on the table in front of her and saw to her surprise that it was almost eleven. She lifted her feet on to the coffee table and laid her head back in the chair on the headrest, intending to close her eyes for a minute.

Three hours later the front door clicked and she snapped awake. She realized that she had fallen asleep in the chair and her legs were aching. She lifted them stiffly to the floor as the living-room door swung silently open and the shadow of a tall figure appeared in the doorway.

She felt entirely helpless, wearing only a dressing gown and her mind fogged with sleep. The figure dropped a bag on the floor and stooped slightly to avoid cracking his head on the lintel as he stepped into the room.

Gunna sighed silently with relief and delight.

"Hi, Mum. Thought you'd be asleep."

"Gísli! When did you get in?"

"Docked an hour ago. Is there anything to eat?"

CHAPTER THIRTY-ONE

Monday, 29 September

Gunna's head was aching. She should have gone back to sleep, not let herself be tempted to spend an hour in the middle of the night talking with Gísli as he devoured sandwich after sandwich and a jug of coffee. She was overjoyed to see him home after a month at sea and had a good idea he would spend much of his ten days ashore in Reykjavík, only returning to the house in Hvalvík for sleep and laundry.

"What do we know that we didn't know yesterday?" Gunna asked to set the ball rolling once Ívar Laxdal and Vilhjálmur Traustason had taken their seats at the back of the room.

Bára, wide awake, answered first. "Marteinn Georg Kristjánsson walked into Hólmavík police station last night."

"Excellent. I thought he might do something like that," Gunna said with satisfaction. "Where is he now?"

"Hverfisgata. Hólmavík police drove him as far as Brú and Reykjavík sent a car to pick him up from there."

"Right. I'll go and talk to Matti as soon as we've finished. What else?"

"Arngrímur Örn Arnarson. Death certainly not accidental, but no indication of how or who as yet. The man was a computer whizz of some kind, ran his own company called Tenging. Snorri knows more about this kind of stuff." Bára looked sideways at Snorri.

"He specialized in security, firewalls and things like that, stopping hackers and prying eyes from looking too closely into systems," Snorri offered. "I reckon he was setting up systems for people who are doing things that aren't entirely legal and placing them overseas somewhere in countries where things aren't looked at too closely."

"Porn, scams, that sort of thing?" Bjössi asked.

"Could be."

"Skandalblogger, maybe?"

"Who knows? Maybe we'll find out when our own über-nerds get in there."

Gunna looked around the table. "Right then. Ósk Líndal. Any joy?"

Snorri grinned. "There's someone who isn't a happy bunny on a Sunday afternoon."

"Explain," Gunna instructed sharply.

"She didn't answer the phone, so we paid her a visit. She lives in one of those terraces at the top of Mossfellsbœr, so it was easy enough to drop in on the way back from Borgarnes," Bára explained.

"And?"

"She was as unhelpful as she could be without slamming the door in our faces."

"Well, I reckon we interrupted some kind of party," Snorri grinned.

"She was even less pleased when we got her to go and open up the Spearpoint offices so she could look up what we wanted."

"She was in some kind of kimono thing and had to get changed so she could go out," Snorri added. "She's a biiig lady. A seriously strange woman."

"OK, what did you get?"

"She had all the info there that we wanted. All the dates that Hårde has been here from the middle of last year onwards," Bára said, handing over a computer printout. "As you can see, he was in Iceland when Einar Eyjólfur disappeared and also in March when Egill Grímsson was killed. And apart from a couple of breaks, he's been here almost all summer."

"That figures," Snorri added, speaking for the first time. "The site manager at the Hvalvík compound confirmed that Hårde had only been there once or twice a week, but after the fire on the night after that march, he's been around pretty much all the time."

"Did you make any progress on finding whoever started that fire, Bjössi?" Gunna inquired.

"Nah. No fingerprints. No identifiable footprints. No witnesses. Nothing to go on at all. They'll show up sooner or later, but how much evidence there might be towards a conviction when that happens is anybody's guess."

"Airlines, anyone? Any progress there?"

"Sorry, chief. Only got one pair," Snorri said sadly, with both of his large hands on the table in front of him.

"Not to worry. That's next, please, ladies and gentlemen. Anything from the nerds in Reykjavík?"

"Yes. Er, there's a new entry on Skandalblogger's page, posted on Saturday. Has anyone seen it?" Bára asked.

Heads were shaken around the table.

"It's about the awards thing that Sigurjóna Huldudóttir attended, alleging large amounts of cocaine being present."

"Nothing new there, then," Snorri said. "Is that something worth chasing, d'you think?"

"Don't know. We have enough to be getting on with as it is," Gunna mused. "I'll let the Reykjavík drug squad know and they should be able to investigate."

"But that's not all," Bára added. "There was a strange comment to say that Bjarni Jón Bjarnason should have good reason to be on his way back to Iceland early from this conference he's at in Berlin. No more details. Maybe Skandalblogger knows something we don't?"

"I'm wondering if maybe we ought to be having a quiet word with the Minister for Environmental Affairs," Gunna said quietly, as if to herself, placing Skúli's printout on the table and spreading it out. At the back of the room, Vilhjálmur Traustason's eyes widened in horror. "And we need to find out about this, immediately."

"What's this?" Snorri asked, looking at Gunna with surprise. "I didn't think you read this sort of thing."

"I don't. It was passed to me last night. This is what Tuesday's *Hot Chat* is going to look like. But you'll have to wait until tomorrow to buy your own copies of *Hot Chat*."

Gunna said *Hot Chat* as if the very words themselves smelled like a public toilet on a hot day.

"Is this from your toyboy?" Bjössi smirked.

"That would be telling. If you look, you'll see that these pictures were taken by a freelance hack called Ármann J, real name Ármann Jens Helgason. His phone number's there. One of you can chase this guy up today and squeeze what you can out of him. Snorri, I'll leave that to you. Now, if we look at these photos, incidentally taken at the Gullfoss on Friday evening during that bullshitmongers' jamboree, we will see the lovely Sigurjóna, her PA or whatever he is, Sigurjóna's sister Erna the hairdresser, and a certain Mr Hårde."

"Bloody hell," Bjössi said and whistled.

"The cheeky cow." Bára seethed. "She knew exactly where he had been the night before and certainly didn't bother to tell us that."

"Ah, but we didn't ask where he had been, only if she knew where he was when we spoke to her. So another visit to the delightful Sigurjóna might be in order. OK, boys and girls. Grab yourselves a coffee, then get to it, please," Gunna said, noticing with discomfort as he stood up the new lines that had appeared on Vilhjálmur Traustason's long face, making him look a few years older than he had at the end of the previous week.

"Ah, Gunnhildur. A word, if you would be so kind."

Hårde drove faster than usual out to Hvalvík, talking for most of the way to the voices that came through his mobile headset. His room at the guesthouse he had been staying at was tidy, and still occupied for a few more days as far as the owners would be concerned. The bed was made and there was still a toothbrush in the bathroom, but the locked suitcase on the bed was empty.

After three conversations in three languages, Hårde passed the "Welcome to Hvalvík" sign in a cloud of dust that hung in the still air behind him, warming in the morning sun.

The phone bleeped a fourth time. He looked down at the display and raised a finger to touch the button on his headset.

"Good morning, Herr Horst," he said gravely, in English this time.

"Good morning, Gunnar."

"Is everything confirmed?" Hårde asked.

"Of course. It's just as we discussed. You are able to disengage?"

"I'm not sure yet. There might be some difficulties in leaving the country."

"If you need an alternative route, then call me on this number." Horst's gravel voice rattled in his earpiece. "But I'm sure you'll be all right. If I don't hear from you, I'll assume that we can meet here in a few days?"

"A week, maybe."

"A week? Is there some delay?" Horst asked in surprise.

"Just a few days' holiday for a change."

"Of course. I think you deserve a break," he said, chuckling. "Call me if there's a hitch."

"I will."

Hårde clicked the connection shut as the car cruised around Hvalvík, past the harbour area and along the road to the compound, where he sounded the horn for a guard to open the gate.

The room emptied quickly as Vilhjálmur Traustason stalked the length of the room, hands behind his back. He did not speak until the last one, Bjössi, winking at Gunna as he shut the door behind him, had left the room.

"Just wanted to let you know I'm watching your progress and you're doing a fine job," he said. Gunna could only look at him in disbelief.

"What's this for, Vilhjálmur? You're not usually one for patting people on the back."

"That's as may be. But you are making progress and the team is performing very well under your management."

"Where's this going?"

"Your promotion, and posting. I need to have a decision this week."

"Hell. I'd forgotten all about that."

"The Egilstadir force has requested you, Gunnhildur. Informally, of course," he added hurriedly.

"I'll think about it and you'll have my decision next week."

"Excellent. Now, there's another matter we need to discuss."

Vilhjálmur Traustason stood and looked out of the window at the queue of morning traffic collecting at the roundabout outside. "I've had a communication from Lárus Jóhann Magnússon."

"What? The Minister?"

He nodded gravely. "The Ministry of Justice is concerned about the level of attention being focused on Bjarni Jón Bjarnason and his family and has requested a clarification."

"You mean Sigurjóna Huldudóttir has yelled at her husband, who has bleated to Lárus Jóhann?"

"The Ministry has taken notice, shall we say?"

"Look, Vilhjálmur. This woman is as crooked as they come. One of her staff was undoubtedly murdered and she is doing nothing to help the investigation — quite the reverse, in fact. I have a bloody good mind to haul her in for questioning on the basis of what she carefully didn't tell us."

A look of fury, quickly suppressed, passed across his face. "Please, Gunnhildur, consult me first if you do. I have to say, to an extent, your promotion could ride on this case."

"Oh, so if I screw this up and embarrass someone with big friends, then I'm not going to be flavour of the month? Come on. There's something extremely unpleasant going on here and I could really do with your backing. Just how serious is the Minister's interest?"

"What do you mean?"

"Bjarni Jón Bjarnason is a lad and belongs to the Independence party. Lárus Jóhann is Progressive and he's an old fart. They're not in the same party. They don't even like each other. So what's going on? How serious is this pressure you feel you're getting from the top?"

"I'm sure I couldn't tell you. There was simply a concern over possible undue harassment of Sigurjóna Huldudóttir."

"What I'm wondering is this: is Lárus Jóhann just passing on Bjarni Jón Bjarnason's whining for the sake of form? Or is there really something here they might be concerned about?" Is it my promotion that's at stake, or does yours depend on this as well, Villi?" Gunna asked gently.

This time the look of distaste on Vilhjálmur's face was replaced by a brief flash of anger, rapidly erased.

"We all depend on a certain success rate to see ourselves receiving the promotion we deserve, Gunnhildur," he said smoothly.

"But are you going to back me up? This bloody woman is in it up to her neck and it's going to look a lot worse for all of us in the long run when it all comes out and it turns out that we didn't look hard enough."

Vilhjálmur stood stiffly and his face went entirely blank as he gazed over the long stream of cars snaking along the main street outside.

"The wife of a minister . . ." he muttered to himself.

"Villi . . .?"

"All right. Do what you need to do."

"And support from my superior officer?"

"Of course. As long as you have evidence to substantiate everything."

"Ah, that means you'll back me up if I can prove everything and you'll drop me in the crap if I put a foot wrong?"

"That's it, in a nutshell," Vilhjálmur snapped.

Erna walked on air and life seemed to be trying to be really good to her for the first time in months. Leaving the house that morning to run a few errands, she had given Hardy a long kiss that fizzed with passion and threatened to drag the pair of them back inside for another half an hour, until he pulled back, tapped the end of her nose with one finger and told her sadly that he couldn't avoid going to the site.

At the salon, the girls had noticed something about her, giggling and whispering among themselves. It was only Marta, the salon's manager, she spoke to, but she assumed that by now all the girls would be in on the secret that Erna was taking a week off and taking a new man with her.

Sitting at the traffic lights waiting to turn off into Bústadavegur and into town, Erna squeezed her thighs together and tingled in anticipation of a week in the sun, running her mind over everything already packed and ready.

"Had a good time in the country, Matti?" Gunna asked cheerfully.

"Yeah. S'always good to get away from the tarmac for a while."

As he wasn't under arrest, merely helping the police with inquiries, Matti wasn't being held in a cell. They sat in an interview room at the central police station on Hverfisgata.

"How's Lóa?"

"Ach. She's fine, the same as usual."

"Still got the goats?"

"Yeah. Same goats."

"Why did you walk into the police station in Hólmavík?"

Sitting on his hands and with the hangdog expression Gunna remembered from the teenager who had always been in trouble, Matti looked wretched.

"Lóa told me I should. She said old Hallgrímur's missus had noticed me so it was only a matter of a few days till you found me, so I might as well go over to Hólmavík and have done with it."

Gunna nodded sagely. "Lóa is nobody's fool."

Matti nodded back, head still hanging.

"What happened to your girlfriend?"

"Marika? Still at Álfasteinn, for all I know."

"This bloke you've been going about with, tell me about him."

"Hardy?"

"If that's what he calls himself."

"What about him?"

"Everything, and be quick about it."

"He's a right hard bastard."

Gunna waited until Matti looked up, and she stared him straight in the eye. It's a shame he grew up to be such a slob, she thought to herself. It's a shame he went through life constantly on the back foot, considering what a pleasant boy he had been when someone gave him a little attention.

"Look, I need to find this bloke before he kills someone else and I don't have a lot of time to do it, so tell me what you know and please get on with it."

"So he really has killed people?"

"Two that we're sure of, possibly one more."

Matti went pale. "I knew he was a hard fucker, but I didn't think he was that nasty."

"You don't know the half of it. Where is he, Matti?"

Matti shook his head. "No idea."

"Come on. You must have some idea. Where did you usually meet him?"

"He always called and told me where to pick him up. Normally by the side of the road somewhere, or else on the rank somewhere. Grensás or Lækjartorg normally. Down at Grandi sometimes. He liked to eat in Kaffivagninn, said it was a homely sort of place."

"Do you think he was living somewhere downtown?"

"Yeah, probably."

"Come on, Matti. Think, will you? He's bumped off two people already."

"All right. It's in Hverfisgata, the other side of the crossroads. There's a block of offices with a dodgy photographer on the ground floor. At the top of the place there's a couple of little one-room flats. He lives in one of them. I followed him one day and saw him go up there," Matti announced proudly.

"You mean he's been just over the road from here?"

"Yup."

"Stay here."

* * *

Gunna and two burly officers emerged from the tiny flat, leaving a pair of technicians to dust painstakingly for fingerprints.

The place was scrupulously clean, minimally furnished with little more than a narrow bed, a small closet and a threadbare chair in the single room, with a tiny bathroom off to one side. It reminded Gunna of a cell as she looked through everything, the photographer from the ground floor who owned the three flats standing at the door and wringing his hands.

"So, who lives here?"

"Just people passing through. A few days now and again. Never very long."

"Yeah, but who?" Gunna asked, pulling off the surgical gloves she had worn inside the flat to pick through the sparse contents of the kitchen cupboard.

"I don't ask too much. If someone wants a room for a while . . ." He shrugged.

Gunna squared her jaw and shoulders, putting on her grimmest expression. "And who's in this one?" she growled.

"Big guy. Don't know his name. Only saw him a few times."

"When did you see him last?"

"A while ago."

"How long a while?"

"Not sure. Before the weekend, anyway."

"Name?"

"Dunno."

"He rented a room and you don't know his name?"

The photographer looked deeply uncomfortable. "Well, yeah. I don't ask too many questions, y'know?"

"No, I don't. That's why I'm asking. Don't make this harder than it has to be," Gunna said quietly while the other officers were out of earshot. "Look, you come clean on this and I won't have to say anything to anybody about tax-free income. OK?"

Beaten, the photographer looked at the floor and twisted his hands. "All right. The place is rented by a guy called Jón Oddur for some foreign guy to use. He pays every month on the dot in cash. I don't know the guy at all. He was at school with my brother, that's how he came to me."

"Good man. What's this guy look like?"

"Jón Oddur? Beefy. Short hair, thin on top. Goatee. Always looks nervous. Only saw the foreign bloke a few times, tall guy, fair hair, quiet."

"Well done. That wasn't so hard, was it? Now, when's the rent due next? Because I think you might be disappointed."

At the station, Matti had laid his head on the table and was fast asleep. He jerked it sharply up as Gunna slapped the tabletop with the flat of her hand.

"Now that you're awake, Matti, and I have your full attention, tell me why you did a runner."

Matti kneaded his eyes with his knuckles as he struggled to make it back from sleep. "Scared, y'know? He's a scary bloke, is Hardy."

"How so?"

"He's just . . ." Matti fumbled for words. "He's quiet. Doesn't say much. He's cool. But when he tied some guy up in knots and broke his arm, bloody hell, that opened my eyes a bit."

"Explain."

"That was a while ago. One moment he's just stood there chatting to this bloke and the next the feller's on the ground screaming. Hardy says to the guy: 'This is a message to your friend to make it stop.' And he's stood there smiling with one hand through the guy's arm, twisting it. The poor feller was like a sack of spuds when Hardy finally let him up."

"Any idea who this was?"

Matti shook his head.

"Do you know someone called Arngrímur Örn Arnarson?"

"Should I?'

Gunna placed a blow-up of the man's national archive photo on the table. "Lived at a place called Grund, just outside Borgarnes."

Matti hesitated. "Well, I did take Hardy there," he admitted finally. "But I didn't go in. Just waited by the car."

"When was this?"

"Not sure. Week before last?"

"So why did you run for it?"

"Scared. When I rang him up and said the coppers had been checking up on me, he went all quiet and said we should meet, and I don't know why, but it didn't seem right, so I thought, shit, best get out of the city for a while," Matti explained, words tripping over themselves as they tumbled out.

Gunna glanced at her watch and Matti continued. "I knew he'd seen me with the girls, y'know, driving them to places and that. And I know he knew me and Marika, y'know, sometimes . . . So I thought he might go and scare her, so I went and got her, told her it was a bit of a holiday, so off we went."

"To Auntie Lóa at Álfasteinn?"

"Yeah."

"Sorry, Matti, I have to go. Look, you're free to go later when you've made a statement, but I need to be able to reach you, so don't go too far."

"I can't," Matti said bitterly. "The taxi's still in Hólmavík because your lot brought me down here in a cop car. Now I'd better go and tell Nonni the Taxi why his car's not here."

"You do that. You're living at Ugly Tóta's still?"

Matti groaned. "If she hasn't filled my room up with Latvians. Unless I can stay in a cell here for a day or two?" he asked with hope in his eyes. "Like, until you've caught him?"

"Is he really your cousin?" Bára asked. They were standing outside in the car park, having left Matti to go back to sleep in a cell.

"He is, I'm afraid," Gunna admitted. "And he's been a pain in the arse to everyone around him since the day he was born. Now, you heard what he said: 'This is a message to your friend to make it stop.' Egill Grímsson and Einar Eyjólfur were both killed discreetly, if we can describe it that way. But Arngrímur was different. I don't think Hårde intended to kill him at all, just provide a painful message. Do you get the impression that this was maybe a message for someone else?"

"Hard to tell. Who is this a message for, do you think?"

"What do you think?"

"I'd say Skandalblogger," Bára said with conviction.

"Why?"

"We know Hårde's worked for Spearpoint. Sigurjóna Huldudóttir and Bjarni Jón are constantly being skewered by the blogger, and the whole country reads it."

"Fair enough," Gunna agreed. "In that case, I'd like you to get back in there and put some pressure on Matti to get as much detail as he can remember on who this guy was that Hårde wanted to frighten. Could be a lead to this blogger and to Arngrímur's associates."

Bára nodded. "When do you want me back in Keflavík?"

"Whenever you're done. I'll get Snorri or someone to come and pick you up unless one of them here can run you back to us. You can tell Matti from me that Cousin Gunna will make his life hell if he doesn't cooperate."

"What going on here?" Bára asked as Gunna stopped the car outside the glass and concrete block where Spearpoint's offices occupied a floor near the top.

Every parking space was full, with faces behind the windscreen of every car. A camera crew was in the process of setting up its equipment on the forecourt outside the building, to the consternation of the huddles of people on their way home through the crush of the evening rush hour traffic.

Gunna double-parked across the row of spaces reserved for directors and they made their way slowly through the gathering crowd. Gunna scanned for a familiar face and eventually alighted on Jonni Kristinns, sitting in a tired grey Skoda parked in a disabled spot. She tapped on the window and Jonni looked around and grinned at her. The window hissed open.

"Gunna, my dear. Good to see you."

"And you, Jonni. What the hell's going on?"

Jonni tapped the side of his nose theatrically. "Ah. That's what we'd all like to know."

"Come on. Spill the beans, old lad," Gunna instructed. "No bullshit, now."

"Rumour has it that InterAlu is pulling out of its deal with Spearpoint. Nothing's been confirmed and nothing's been denied. Not a word so far."

"Big news, then?"

"Oh, yes," Jonni said, licking dry lips. "Top story. Timing's just right as well. Too late for the TV news and not too late for our morning edition."

"Is Sigurjóna in her office?"

Jonni shrugged. "No idea. We're just waiting to see what happens. It's a hell of a story if it's true."

"Won't this leave her in trouble?"

"And how. They have some colossal financial commitments and if their partner has pulled out, it means that Sigurjóna and her unpleasant husband have been royally shafted up their collective back passage. Of course, it could just as well be that the bank has run out of cash and is doing the same, without the benefit of lubrication, as one of my colleagues put it rather graphically this morning."

"Of course, now you'd never say anything as disgusting as that, would you, Jonni?"

"Well, not in print, anyway. Hello," he said, looking up. "Got to run, Gunna, looks like something's happening."

With a speed that surprised Gunna, Jonni was out of the car and at the forefront of the scrum that formed around the door as Jón Oddur, red-faced and sweating, appeared to face a barrage of questions.

Gunna and Bára stood at the back of the group to listen as Jón Oddur floundered.

"Quiet, please. Quiet," he pleaded with the crowd of microphones in his face and the staccato rattle of questions being fired at him. He pulled a sheet of paper from the inside pocket of his jacket and unfolded it, blinking as flashes went off in his face.

"I have a prepared statement to read. I am not authorized to answer any questions afterwards. I will read this only once."

He looked around him at the microphones, raised the sheet of paper and read in halting, careful English: "Spearpoint values its ongoing business relationship with InterAlu and is fully confident that this is set to continue to our mutual benefit. We are at present engaged in cooperative negotiations with InterAlu and its partners to extend and expand our current partnerships across the business environment."

Jón Oddur paused and looked up at the expectant faces around him before taking a deep breath. "Spearpoint's senior management has built up a positive working relationship with the heads of InterAlu's European business development division and we fully expect this to continue. Speculation of a rift between Spearpoint subsidiaries ESC and Bay Metals, and InterAlu is completely unfounded and has no basis in actuality. As media professionals ourselves, we are fully aware of the need to respond to unfounded rumours and we would ask our colleagues at the front line of news reporting for a level of circumspection in reporting unverified and unverifiable hearsay. Message ends. Thank you."

"Jón Oddur, what's InterAlu's take on all this?"

"Is Sigurjóna going to make a statement herself?"

"How many jobs are going to be lost when InterAlu pull out?"

"How much money does Sigurjóna personally stand to lose on this?"

The questions came thick and fast, while Jón Oddur slowly turned and began to make his way back to the door, carefully avoiding eye contact with anyone in his way.

"Jón Oddur, what are the implications for the Minister's position? Will he have to resign?"

"What about the allegations of intimidation and bribery? What's Spearpoint's response?"

The barrage fell silent as the glass door swung shut behind him, and Jón Oddur could feel rivulets of sweat running down his back as he made for the lift at the trot.

"Bullshit," Jonni Kristinns announced with delight as he returned to his car. "Bullshit from start to finish."

"Why do you say that?" Bára asked.

"What else could they say? He didn't say anything at all that says anything. No facts, no information, just business as usual. I reckon it's a smokescreen to keep the lid on things while they salvage what they can from the wreck," he said with satisfaction.

Gunna nodded and looked up at Spearpoint's windows high above. "It doesn't sound right, does it? Is denying everything flatly like that normal practice, Jonni?"

"Yeah. It's the normal bullshit. This has to be a face-saving exercise while they try to keep the stock exchange happy. Spearpoint is privately owned, but I'll bet you a shag to a bag of shit that ESC's share value is going to plummet."

"Er. No thanks, Jonni. Maybe later, all right?" she said as he launched himself into his car and beat the unwilling engine into life. "Jæja, Bára. Maybe we should have brought Snorri along as well. He would have enjoyed all that. Come on, let's see if we can track down Sigurjóna."

Ósk Líndal was more imposing than Snorri's description of her had even hinted. She stood two metres tall in flat shoes, looking down at Gunna and Bára. Her arms were folded underneath a bosom that jutted alarmingly into free space. Robustly built herself,

Gunna felt pleasantly petite standing opposite her and Bára's slight frame was little more than a wisp alongside the two of them.

"Sigurjóna is not available," Ósk announced sternly. "I thought your officers had already been given all the available information they asked for yesterday."

"They were," Gunna replied equally sternly. "But we have some more questions for Sigurjóna."

"I'm here in her place while she's out of the office. You can ask me anything relevant to the company."

"What exactly is your role here?" Gunna asked.

"I am the operations manager. I handle the day-to-day running of the company. If you have questions, I can do my best to help," she barked, looking anything but helpful.

"Where is your boss right now?"

"She's not here."

"I wasn't asking where she isn't."

"I'm not at liberty to divulge her whereabouts."

"You would be if I come back with a warrant."

"In that case, our lawyers will be waiting for you."

"If that's the way you want to play it, that's fine with me. Now, I want to speak to some of your staff."

"Who?"

"To begin with, I want to talk to that boy with the red face who was outside just now."

"We don't have a meeting room available right now."

"In that case he can come down to Hverfisgata and we can talk there, and you can send the rest of them down at thirty-minute intervals."

Gunna lifted herself to her maximum height, bringing the top of her head level with Ósk's nose.

"It's past five o'clock. People will be going home shortly," she protested.

"Then you'll just have to tell them that they can't."

"All right. You can use the canteen if you must. I'll ask the receptionist to clear it for you and make sure nobody disturbs you."

"Is that Dísa?"

"Dísa? No, she left. Ill health, depression."

Jón Oddur had not recovered from his ordeal outside. The office lights weren't doing him any favours, she noticed. The man's skin looked blotchy and there were bags under his eyes.

"Tell me about the party," Gunna prompted.

"What about it?"

"Who was there. What went on."

He groaned and slouched back in his chair. "All right. It was the PR Practitioners' Awards night. Sigurjóna was slated for an award, so we needed a presence."

"So this is a PR company, right?" Bára asked. "How come Spearpoint is involved in managing a construction site?"

"It basically evolved into a project management operation. Sigurjóna had been doing PR work for a long time and when she got involved with InterAlu, she was asked to lay on fixers and interpreters. It all snowballed from there and the company has been growing really fast over the last year and a half."

"All work with InterAlu?"

"Yeah, and ESC, and more foreign companies are coming to us all the time now."

"ESC and Spearpoint aren't the same thing?"

"The offices of both are here. But Spearpoint is privately owned and ESC is a limited company."

"Owned by?" Bára asked.

"Sigurjóna, her husband, a few other people, and InterAlu."

"And if InterAlu pull out, Spearpoint loses its biggest customer?" Bára asked and Jón Oddur nodded again.

"And ESC becomes worthless. Worse than worthless, actually," he said, squirming in his seat.

"Look," he groaned finally. "You didn't hear this from me, but you'll hear it soon enough anyway. On Friday Glitnir Bank will inform the Central Bank that it's unable to service its debts. It's not ESC's bank, but that one isn't in any better position. It's just a case of when."

Startled, Gunna wondered what to say, but settled for glaring into Jón Oddur's face.

"They probably won't announce it until after the weekend, but just wait and see. Everyone knows something big's about to happen after the currency's been on the slide for months. It's only a few of us know what's really happening."

"And this affects ESC?"

"Of course it does!" Jón Oddur yelped. "It affects every business in the country! But ESC is due to be financed for the big phase of the Hvalvík Lagoon project by the bank, and some of us know that the bank doesn't have anything left to lend."

Gunna drew a deep breath. "Well, young man. I hope you're wrong."

"So do I. But this isn't just happening in Iceland. This is all over the world. I tell you, Iceland is looking at unemployment and inflation, big time," he added gloomily.

"In that case, I'm sure that the police force will be able to fill a few vacancies," Gunna said tartly, shocked at Jón Oddur's prediction and forcing herself to keep her mind on the job. "Now, the awards night."

Jón Oddur deflated and slumped in the chair. "OK. There were half a dozen of us from here went to the ceremony. We booked rooms at the hotel and there was a party afterwards in Sigurjóna's suite."

"Who attended?"

"Er, me, Sigurjóna. Ósk was there but she left early. Sigurjóna's sister was there as well and a few other guests," he gabbled as Bára scribbled down names in her folder.

"And the one you haven't mentioned?" Gunna said gently.

Jón Oddur was suddenly on the defensive. "Who's that?"

"This guy."

Gunna placed the printout of the pages from *Hot Chat* on the table. Jón Oddur looked up and then down again in surprise at seeing the photo of himself.

"Oh, him. Yeah, he was there as well. Sigurjóna invited him. This is . . . where did you get it from?"

"You didn't mention him. Why?" Gunna demanded, ignoring Jón Oddur's question.

"I don't know. Just forgot. We don't normally have anything to do with him anyway."

"Tell me about this man. Do you know where he lives?" Gunna probed.

"No. We don't know anything about him, really. I know he's one of the InterAlu people but he reports direct to the boss."

"Hverfisgata? Above Sindra Foto?"

"Oh. That place. Look, I pay the guy every month and he keeps the flat free for whoever we need to put in there. I suppose Sigurjóna must have told him to stay there," he said quickly.

"I don't believe you. I think you knew very well that he was staying there. What happened at this ceremony? Where did he go afterwards?"

"Why? What's he wanted for?"

"Can't discuss it. All I can say is that it's a major investigation."

"I'm not sure where he went. Erna was all over him and I think they disappeared about the same time. They were both there at the awards but I don't remember seeing either of them at the party in the suite upstairs."

"What time did the party begin?"

Jón Oddur hung his head and twisted his fingers in circles. "I don't know. I was quite wrecked, just like everyone else there. Two, maybe. Something like that. Look, haven't I told you enough yet?"

"Not until you've told us everything," Gunna said sharply.

Jón Oddur rested the back of his head in his hands as he looked up at the ceiling. "All right. The awards were OK, just what everyone expected. Sigurjóna got her award, made a speech, blah, blah, got her glass thing and that was that. More awards, lots of speeches. So, by midnight everyone's pretty fucked up. Sigurjóna dropped her glass award and she was furious, accused me and then Ósk of breaking it. Anyway, it calmed down and there was some crappy seventies band on that only the old people wanted to dance to. Then we all went up to the suite and we had a little party there, about ten people, something like that. It's a bit hazy," he admitted with a nervous smile.

"All people from Spearpoint?"

"Yeah. No, well, mostly I think. There were some women there I didn't recognize. Foreign. And there were quite a few people who came and went."

"Then what?"

"Hell, I don't know. I woke up in my room at about six in the morning next to Sigurjóna. I still had my tux on. She'd lost her dress somewhere, though. I don't remember anything between the party and waking up. That's it. Then you banging on the door's the next thing I knew."

Gunna tapped the picture on the table in front of her. "When was the last time you saw him?"

Jón Oddur's brow furrowed as he fought to remember. "It's all really hazy, y'know. I reckon at the end of the dance in the ballroom. The last I saw of him was at the table, I suppose. I don't think he drinks. But

Erna can really put it away and she'd draped herself all over the poor guy."

"Are you saying that they might have left together?"

"Could have. Don't know."

"All right, Jón Oddur. That'll do. Now, where's Sigurjóna today?"

Jón Oddur shrugged. "She's not here today, which is fine with all of us. We get a lot more work done when she's out of the office."

"So she's where?"

"No idea. At home, maybe? Ósk always knows where she is."

"Where's Sigurjóna?" Gunna growled.

Ósk began to rise to her feet but stopped halfway at the sight of the expression on Gunna's face. "She's not here today."

"Phone number? Address?"

"I'm not at liberty to divulge that," she repeated angrily. Gunna could see the blood rising across her neck and into her face.

"You will be if I come back with a warrant."

"If you do, our legal team will be waiting for you."

"Look, I won't come back with a search warrant, it'll be a bloody arrest warrant."

"For what, may I ask?"

"You may well ask, and it'll be for possession of and intent to supply a class A drug, and I'll alert every officer in the country to arrest her on the spot and haul your boss to the nearest police station until I get there.

While you're at it, I want her sister Erna's address and phone numbers as well."

Ósk scribbled phone numbers and addresses on a slip of paper and passed it across.

"You didn't get that from me," she snarled, her face flushed and this time rising to her full imposing height.

"We'll see. I'm warning you not to let her know that we're on the way. If she's not at home, I'll be back and you'll be charged with obstructing a police investigation. Let's go," Gunna snapped, striding to the door with Bára, fumbling to answer her phone, at her heels.

"That was fantastic," Bára said in admiration once the door had slammed shut behind them.

"Bloody woman," Gunna rumbled as she ignored the lift and took the stairs three at a time. "I'm going to drop you at the Gullfoss and I want you to go through the staff who were on duty on Friday night. Find out who was there, and especially when Hårde left, and if he left with Erna. Find out where they went. They must have got a taxi if Erna was as pissed as Jón Oddur reckons."

"Right," Bára puffed, wondering how someone built on generous lines could have so much energy.

"Seven thirty tomorrow. Let me know then what you've found out."

CHAPTER THIRTY-TWO

Tuesday, 30 September

Birna Ólafsdóttir lay back as far as she could and closed her eyes, but she kept the seat fully upright out of consideration for the people in the row behind. The rest of the party were scattered around the aircraft, the price of having changed their arrangements at short notice. She was relieved to be seated between strangers, away from colleagues and their need to discuss work.

She was not unhappy to have the trip to Berlin cut short, although she carefully made no outward show of it. A civil servant is just that, she felt, a servant with a role to play during working hours. What her personal opinions were did not come into the equation and she also took a quiet pride in maintaining a distinct separation between her career and her personal life.

The ministerial party had not been due to return to Reykjavík until Friday, with a morning flight after the obligatory cocktail party scheduled for Thursday evening and the formal dinner that followed. This was something that she would have been excused, leaving the Minister to consume rather too many liqueurs and smoke the cigars she knew his wife did not allow him at home. Birna had not scheduled anything for her Thursday evening in Berlin beyond a room service meal and an hour or two in front of the television after a long bath.

But a walk along Kufürstendamm yesterday morning and coffee, as if by chance, with some old friends while the Minister was still clearing his head of the previous evening's brandy had been enough of a pleasure to make the trip as a whole enjoyable.

A police car was already in the drive of Sigurjóna and Bjarni Jón's discreet mansion in Seltjarnarnes when Gunna parked behind it. Gunna scowled to herself, wondering what was happening as she scrunched up the gravel path in the first frost of the autumn to ring the bell.

A young policewoman answered the door. Gunna recognized her and racked her memory for the girl's name.

"Edda, isn't it?" she hazarded.

"Yeah, I'm Edda Sif. And you're from Hvalvík, aren't you? Gunnhildur? What brings you here?"

Gunna stepped back and motioned for Edda Sif to step outside as well.

"What's going on? This is Sigurjóna Huldudóttir's place, isn't it?" she asked when they were out of earshot of the mansion's gaping hallway.

"That's right. She's inside with my partner. We had a report of a missing person and were sent here to get a statement straight away. It helps when your husband's in the government," she added.

"Who's the missing person?"

"Her sister, Erna Dan. You know, the hairdresser?"

"OK, give me the gist of it."

"The call was an hour ago. It seems her sister hasn't been seen since Friday night."

"But it's only Tuesday now. We're not talking about a child here."

"Yeah, I know, and it's not as if the sister doesn't have a history of vanishing for a few days now and again. I checked our system and she's on that as well."

"What for?"

"Drunk and disorderly, mostly. A few fights, just handbag waving, really. Always booze-related."

"Married? Kids?"

"Two kids, separated. One child's father lives in Grafarvogur, the other's is in the US. Both kids with their fathers at the moment, due back to be with their mother in two weeks."

"And Sigurjóna?" Gunna asked. "What's her theory? Does she have a basis for believing her sister to be missing?"

"So it seems. Says she went off with some foreign guy called Hardy and hasn't been seen since, and now she's not answering her mobile."

"Checked anywhere else?"

"No answer at her home either."

"Ah. In that case I'd better have a word with the lady."

"Do you have an angle on this?" Edda Sif asked curiously.

"Bloody right. It's Hårde I'm after."

* * *

Sigurjóna's tearful presence occupied the whole of the expensively furnished room. She sat on a leather sofa overshadowed by a huge abstract painting in blocks of primary colours, sniffing as a young policeman probed with gentle questions.

Gunna marched in and looked Sigurjóna directly in the face. She stared back with hostility in her eyes.

"You? What are you doing here?" she asked as anger and some colour began to seep back into her face, carefully made up in spite of her tearful demeanour. A tiny rivulet of mascara had begun to flow southwards from the corner of one eye.

"Olli, isn't it?" Gunna asked the young policeman, perched with an open notebook on a corner of a deep armchair. The young man nodded.

"All right. Leave me with this lady for ten minutes, would you? There must be a kitchen here somewhere, and I'm sure Sigurjóna won't mind if you put some coffee on."

At a loss at Gunna's unexpected appearance, Sigurjóna nodded mutely.

Gunna perched on the edge of the deep chair that Olli had vacated to search for the kitchen.

"Where the hell is Hårde?" she demanded.

"I don't know," Sigurjóna wailed and dabbed at her eye with a tissue.

"All right. Tell me what's happened. Quickly, please."

"I don't know. Erna was with us all at the awards party —"

"Hårde as well?"

Sigurjóna nodded.

"How come he was there at a party for PR people?"

"I invited him," Sigurjóna admitted and hesitated.

"Go on."

"He was dancing with Erna and they disappeared about the same time. Quite early. I think they may have gone home together."

"To Erna's home?"

"I expect so."

"Have you been there? Called her?"

"I've tried to call, but just get her voicemail and she doesn't call back."

Gunna watched Sigurjóna carefully. As far as she could make out, the woman's concern for her sister was genuine. "Where does she live?"

"Skólagata twelve."

"Where's that?"

"Kópavogur. Up the hill from Smárinn."

"Olli!" Gunna called and the young man came in from the kitchen with the aroma of coffee behind him.

"Yes?"

"Get on the radio. I want a squad car at Skólagata twelve in Kópavogur in five minutes flat. Tell them to check the place out quietly. Don't knock, don't be too obvious, don't approach any men who might be on the property. I'll be there in a minute, all right?"

Olli ducked back and they could hear him talking in the other room as his set buzzed.

"Sigurjóna, I have every reason to believe that you have been rather economical with the truth so far. I believe that this man you think your sister has disappeared with is an extremely dangerous character. I believe he's responsible for at least two murders here in Iceland and probably more elsewhere. Now, where's he been living?"

"It's a guesthouse in Mjósundsvegur. Can't remember the number. Right at the end near the old church."

"Do you have any phone numbers for this guy?"

Sigurjóna picked a mobile phone up from the black glass coffee table in front of her where Olli had just placed a mug of black coffee for Gunna.

"They're on their way," he reported quietly while Sigurjóna scrolled through her phone's stored numbers.

Gunna nodded at him without her eyes leaving Sigurjóna.

"Here it is," she said quietly, holding out the phone.

"Write the number down, Olli. Get on to the phone company and find out every bit of information you possibly can, and whether it's switched on, and if possible where it is. Bully them if you have to. This is on the National Commissioner's authority if they quibble," she instructed as Olli retreated.

"Sigurjóna, now. Your sister. Tell me about her. Has she done anything like this before?"

"Plenty of times. She's hopeless with guys. She finds one she likes and she's like a little puppy and can't keep her hands off him. Then after a week or two there's a row and she hits the bottle. It's happened time and again, and she always ends up here crying on my shoulder. I've always been able to reach her and she tells me everything. But this time I can't get hold of her at all. It's just not like her."

"When did you last speak to Hårde?"

"Saturday."

"What?"

"Right after you left the Gullfoss. I told him you were looking for him."

"You told him? Bloody hell," Gunna exploded and quickly contained her anger. "What else did you tell this psycho?"

"Not much."

"So, what then?"

"That you're in charge of the investigation," Sigurjóna said.

In disbelief, Gunna sat back and thought in silence, ignoring the buzzing of the phone in her top pocket. She stood up suddenly, decision made, pulling the phone from her pocket to see who had called.

"Edda! Olli! Here, now."

The two young officers tumbled into the room from the kitchen.

"Any luck?" Gunna asked Olli.

"Not yet. They're on to it and are calling me back. They want to verify my status as well."

"You can do that at the station. This lady is going to Hverfisgata with you, right now."

Sigurjóna half rose to her feet and began to protest. "Why? What is this for? I want my lawyer here right now, this instant —" she crowed before Gunna cut her off.

"You are going to Hverfisgata to be questioned properly about your role in assisting a wanted felon in evading custody, to begin with. Then there's your role in the deaths of Egill Grímsson and Einar Eyjólfur Einarsson, and I'm sure there're a few things to be found out there."

"I knew nothing about that," Sigurjóna snarled.

"And then we can move on to the fact that you've knowingly hindered an investigation. From there we can go on to possession of a proscribed substance with intent to supply. How's that?"

"You fucking evil fat lesbian bitch," Sigurjóna hissed. "Arresting me, you'll fucking suffer for this. You know who my husband is."

"Yeah. A soon-to-be ex-Minister. You're not being arrested. You're being taken into custody for your own protection. You've five minutes to put some clothes on."

Edda and Olli took unsure steps forward.

"Take her to Hverfisgata and let her sober up a bit before we start talking to her. Her lawyer can be called, but don't hurry any more than you have to. If she kicks up, cuffs. All right? Get a move on then," she ordered, as Edda stepped forward and gripped Sigurjóna's upper arm to bring her to her feet.

Erna decided that she had time for an hour at the gym and a visit to the salon before her flight. As she stopped at the junction to turn left, a police car came fast along the main road, slowed sharply and turned into her street. She wondered what it was doing in such a quiet neighbourhood and decided they would probably be looking for one of the neighbours' teenage kids. She'd find out when she got back, she thought, grinned to herself and patted the shoulder bag on the seat beside her.

Erna had packed no more than a change of underwear, shorts, a couple of T-shirts and a minimum of toiletries, as well as her laptop and an old address book. Hand baggage only this trip. If she needed anything else, hell, there were shops in Morocco as well, she decided, not that she was planning on wearing too many clothes. Her stomach fluttered in anticipation of seven days at the secluded villa in M'diq, a sleepy resort an hour's drive east of Tangier still known only to a discerning few.

She had booked the flights and the hire car online, and called to let Hardy know to meet her in the departure lounge. She listened to his deep chuckle with a pleasure that bordered on the sensual, recalling listening to that rumbling laugh through his chest.

Hårde's rented car rolled out through the compound gate and along the road back to Hvalvík. At the crossroads outside the town, he turned away from the main road and took the old unmade track that he knew would be noisy and uncomfortable, but would take him unobtrusively to Keflavík and the airport where Erna would be expecting to meet him in a few hours.

Outside the town and on a curve that was out of sight of prying eyes, Hårde pulled off the road. There were several hours to wait since his work at the compound had been simpler than expected. He had decided not to tell the site manager about InterAlu's decision — they'd find out soon enough.

Hårde closed his eyes and kicked off his shoes. He drew his feet up into the closest approximation he could manage of a lotus position and concentrated on each breath, forcing himself to be calm.

Bjarni Jón Bjarnason fretted in club class. With the aircraft in flight, he was cut off from phone, email and the exchange rate, and hated it.

He hailed a passing stewardess, asked for a brandy and admired the woman's muscular bottom as she bustled away to fetch it.

The meeting with Horst had left him numb. He could see little more than the whole edifice crashing about his ears. Spearpoint would be left high and dry by the bank with crippling commitments and no customer to buy the power it was due to start producing at the end of the year — if they were even to get that far.

Maybe he could pull strings and get the National Power Authority to absorb the project — in return for a quiet payoff of some kind that would settle outstanding debts. Nationalizing it could be the answer. ESC could become public property, with Spearpoint's holding quietly transferred somehow, which would look good at any rate, he thought idly, and caught himself as his thoughts drifted back to Sigurjóna.

Maybe it was time for a change, a quiet parting of the ways and a smooth divorce? But he knew that, with Sigurjóna, nothing was likely to be quiet or smooth. A husband in government was a major asset to her that she would be unlikely to let go easily.

He sympathized with her. Spearpoint had been doing extraordinarily well on the basis of her undoubted personal skills and their combined access to the right people. They both felt they had worked hard to get this far. But Sigurjóna was certainly hard work. A sweet little thing who would do as she was asked, give him a brood of children and not spit venom every time he lit a cigar would also be nice.

And what about her lunatic sister? Bjarni Jón groaned to himself out loud. The stewardess with the magnificently toned behind looked at him with momentary concern as she delivered his brandy with a flashing smile, and he smiled wanly in return. No rings on her fingers. He quickly considered asking for her phone number but decided against it.

But Erna, bloody hell, what a mess. Two out-of-control kids, two failed marriages, numerous smashed cars and a discreet spell in rehab, not to mention bailing her out of a cell once or twice after screaming matches in the street. Bjarni Jón was fully aware that Sigurjóna and Erna were close, but the woman was a liability he could do without. So where the bloody hell had she got to this time? It wasn't as if she hadn't disappeared for a day or three before, but this time Sigurjóna was clearly more worried than usual. Hell, he'd worry about it when he got home, he thought, allowing his eyes to drift back to the stewardess's buttocks as she backed down the aisle with the trolley of drinks yet again.

* * *

Hårde opened his eyes. The sun was higher in the sky than it had been when he had closed them. His mind was calm. The dusty surface of the road told him that nobody had passed while he had thought.

The time he had spent concentrating on every breath, guiding his attention back to counting each slow inhalation whenever his thoughts wandered, had cleared his mind.

He picked up the mobile phone that he had switched off at the InterAlu compound and opened it. He deftly lifted out the SIM card, dropped it out of the car's window into the grass at the roadside and replaced it with another that had been wrapped in a twist of paper in his wallet. He switched on and scrolled to one of only a few numbers in the directory.

"Horst," the gravel voice answered.

"Hårde."

"Problem?"

"Not sure. I need an alternative route off this island."

"You are mobile? Car?"

"For the moment. I may have to get rid of the car soon."

"Call me back in twenty minutes. I'll have something for you," Horst said, ending the call abruptly.

She watched Sigurjóna sit defiantly in the back of the squad car, handed the keys of the house to Edda for safekeeping and shut the door behind her. Pacing Sigurjóna's gravelled path with a Camel, Gunna returned Snorri's missed call.

"You called. What is it, lad?"

"Hårde, I think. There's a pair of seats booked on a flight to Madrid at five thirty this afternoon. Names of Erna Daníelsdóttir and Gunnar Hadre."

"Madrid? Erna as well? You know she's been reported missing?"

"Maybe she's not that missing after all."

"Obviously not," Gunna pondered. "It might be a smokescreen of some kind. I don't like it. The man knows he's being looked for. I want a team up there to grab him if he does show up for this flight, but I want surveillance up there straight away. Get on to the airport force, will you? Tell them what's happening."

"Yeah, of course, chief."

"Is Vilhjálmur about?"

"In his office, I think."

"OK. I'll call him there."

She dialled again and listened to the ringing tone with impatience.

"Vilhjálmur," announced the expected measured tone.

"Gunna. There's plenty going on and now I need you to do your bit."

"Ah, Gunnhildur. Making progress, I assume? Excellent —"

Gunna cut him off abruptly. "Vilhjálmur, listen. Sigurjóna Huldudóttir's in custody at Hverfisgata."

"What? The Minister's wife? You're certain?" he demanded through a sharp intake of breath.

Gunna could feel the tremor of fear in the voice on the other end. "Of course I'm bloody sure, and I can find grounds to hold the miserable cow if she makes a fuss. Now, listen, and you'd better write this down. I want you to get on to Reykjavík now, straight away. I need a car in Mjósundsvegur with at least two officers before I get there."

Vilhjálmur was silent, but she could hear the scratch of his fountain pen.

"Mjósundsvegur. Number?" he asked to her relief.

"Don't know. It's a guesthouse at the top end by the church. That's where our man's been staying. I doubt he's there, but I don't want to chance it alone."

"Quite right," Vilhjálmur replied. "I'll get it fixed for you right away."

"Ask forensics to get there as well. If there are any prints, I want them. As soon as I'm done there, I'll be on the way out to Keflavík again. Things are happening at the airport, I reckon, so I want you to get on to the most senior officer there and brief him. Snorri can tell you more. All right?"

Vilhjálmur Traustason had the fleeting feeling that Gunna had been promoted over his head.

"Nine five five zero, zero three five five."

Gunna's communicator buzzed and she pressed the button on her headset to reply.

"Zero three five five, nine five five zero."

"Olli here. The phone company just got back to me. The number is an ordinary pay-as-you go SIM card that was never registered. It's the sort you can pick up at petrol stations. Nothing special about it and no hope of identifying the user."

"Not to worry. It was worth a go."

"Hang on. It's been switched off for about two hours."

"Any idea where?"

"The last connection was through the mast at Lækjarbakki."

"Outside Hvalvík?"

"That's the one."

"Two hours ago?"

"Last connection was 10.05."

"OK, thanks, Olli. Make sure the number's monitored in case it comes up again, and will you ask the phone company to call me direct if there's any activity?"

"Will do. We checked Erna Dan's house as well, all quiet, no sign of anything unusual and the intruder alarm says it's active."

"Good," Gunna said. "Sounds like nobody home there."

They were back around the incident room table, ignored computer screens lighting the room with their dim glow. There was a chill in the room now that the sun had travelled far enough west by midday for its rays to leave their side of the building in shadow.

"What do we have?" Gunna demanded, without bothering to greet anyone and hauling off her jacket as she sat down.

"I went to the Gullfoss like you said," Bára began. "Tracked down a doorman who saw Hårde leave with Erna at about two in the morning. They left on foot and he didn't see them take a cab or get in a car."

Vilhjálmur shimmered silently in. Gunna looked up at him inquiringly, but he held both hands up palms outwards to indicate that he did not intend to take part other than to listen.

"Who spoke to the snapper, Ármann?"

"Me, chief," Snorri replied quickly. "Nothing much to tell, really. He didn't notice Erna and Hårde particularly, just snapped off the photo of every table and got as many names as he could."

"Nothing, then?"

"Nothing we didn't know already. He showed me the whole file of pictures he took, and our two can only be seen in a couple of them. He left before the party really got going. But he said he saw all the awards being presented and also Sigurjóna dropping hers on the floor."

"How did that happen?" Gunna asked.

"Just pissed, I think. Ármann also did some video and he admitted he'd posted the clip of Sigurjóna dropping her statue on to YouTube, the one that Skandalblogger linked to."

"Any significance there? Does this guy have a link to the Skandalblogger?" Gunna asked.

"Could be. But if so, he's not saying anything, which is hardly surprising. Is that relevant at this stage?"

"Probably not," Gunna decided. "Making a fool of yourself in public generally isn't a criminal offence. I just want to know where that bloody Hårde is and if Sigurjóna's fruitcake sister is still in the land of the living. Who dug up the flight ticket info?"

"Me again, chief," Snorri's hand went up. "17.35 flight this afternoon to Madrid, booked in the names of Erna Daníelsdóttir and Gunnar Hadre."

"Hadre?"

"Well, close enough to Hårde. I checked back with the airline. It was booked over the net using a credit card that checks back to Erna Dan."

Gunna leaned back and stretched her legs out in front under the table. "What I'm wondering is this, did Erna book this and maybe type in Hårde's name wrong? Or did maybe Hårde book this using her computer and credit card? I have to admit, I'm getting a nasty feeling that we're going to find a seriously dead Erna somewhere sooner or later."

"Ah, I'll see if I can check," Snorri said. He seated himself in front of one of the semi-dormant computers and tapped at the keyboard to wake it.

"What does anybody think?" Gunna asked. "I reckon it stinks."

"Why's that?"

"The man knows we're looking for him."

"How would he know that?" Vilhjálmur asked quietly.

"Because Sigurjóna bloody Huldudóttir told him so. Anyhow, it seems too easy. Watch the airport and wait for him to show up. It's too simple. A man like Hårde doesn't get caught out like this."

"Where else could he go?" Bára asked.

"Hell, I don't know. There are private aircraft coming in and out, more than ever now that Iceland has more billionaires per square metre than anywhere else in

Europe. There are other airports, shipping, the ferry in the east. Or he might lie low until the heat's off."

"Where, though? He'd be noticed, surely?" Snorri suggested.

Gunna opened her mouth to speak, but closed it as the door banged open and Björssi came in.

"I thought you were at Hverfisgata practising police brutality on Sigurjóna?" he said, as Gunna watched deep disapproval register on Vilhjálmur Traustason's face.

"Gave up. She flatly refuses to say anything at all without her lawyer present. I left her in an interview room with old Viggó Björgvins to bore the crap out of her."

"That'll do the trick. People have been known to admit to all sorts rather than listen to that old fart drone on for hours on end," Björssi agreed. "Oh, and there's a young man down in reception, wants to speak to you and says it's urgent."

"What? Who's that?"

"Don't know. Said his name's Skúli. Does that mean anything to you?"

"Ah. Yes. In that case, ten minutes for a coffee and a fag for the puffers. Back here at . . ." She looked up at the clock, registering that any chance of a lunch break had been and gone. "Back at five past."

"Getting anywhere, Snorri?" Gunna called across the room as she opened the door.

"The technical bloke at the airline says he's sure enough that the flights were booked using the Icelandic version of the web page. Also, whoever booked it got all the accents right in Erna's name, but got Hårde's name wrong."

"Well, I suppose that indicates Erna was alive when the flights were booked," Gunna rumbled.

"Yeah, but that's not all. There's a Gunnvald Ström booked on a flight to Billund this afternoon as well."

"Bluff? Coincidence? We'd best have a presence at the airport and look out for Mr Ström and hopefully eliminate him."

Skúli was sitting in the police station's lobby with Lára at his side.

"What brings you here?" Gunna asked as she sat down next to them.

"The guy. We've seen him."

"Which guy? Who do you mean?"

"The one you're looking for. The one on the *Hot Chat* pages I showed you."

"Hårde?"

"I don't know his name. But the one who was sitting at the table in that picture."

"He was on the march," Lára added.

"Where? When?"

"About twenty minutes ago. At the check-in desk at the airport."

"You're sure? What was he up to?"

"He was in the queue to check in for a flight, I suppose."

"Bloody hell. What were you doing up there, anyway?"

Skúli grimaced. "A shot in the dark. Bjarni Jón Bjarnason was arriving from Berlin. We were supposed to try and get a comment from him if we could, now that the InterAlu withdrawal seems to be happening, but he must have been whisked away through the VIP lounge. Which is what we'd expected anyway. Instead of going straight back, we decided to go for a coffee in the café by the departure desks and Lára almost walked into him."

"Did he see either of you?"

"Don't think so."

"Would he recognize either of you anyway?"

"I doubt it. We only spoke for a few minutes."

"Good. Right. I have to run, as you can imagine, Skúli. I can't tell you how grateful I am for the information, and if this comes off, I owe you an enormous favour."

Skúli grinned broadly. "No problem."

"By the way," she murmured in a voice that wouldn't carry, "maybe you ought to know that a certain prominent political figure's wife is in a cell at Hverfisgata, not that you heard that from me."

Skúli grinned. "Great. Thanks, chief."

"Call me tomorrow. OK?" Gunna shot at him, departing at a trot.

"Vilhjálmur!" Gunna bellowed, bursting back into the incident room. "Where the hell is the bloody man when you need him?"

"Here, Gunnhildur. If you'd slow down for a second, you'd find me right behind you," he said tartly.

"Right. No time to fart about," she said briskly as the rest of them appeared, having heard Gunna's bellow echo through the building. "Our man's at Keflavík airport right now."

"And you thought he wouldn't be?" Snorri mumbled through a mouthful of sandwich.

"I may be wrong. So fire me. I'm told he was at check-in twenty minutes ago, so he's probably checked in by now and waiting for his flight. Vilhjálmur, I want the airport force alerted straight away."

"They're already on standby for this person, but it hasn't helped with the Minister going through and all the press they expected."

"I don't give a stuff about the Minister. He's long gone by now. Get them back on the ball and tell them that our man is probably in the building. Remind them he's dangerous. Now, please, Vilhjálmur."

Vilhjálmur Traustason left the room at the closest to a run anyone had seen since he had been in the police handball team twenty years before.

"Snorri, Björssi, you're with me. Bára, I want you to stay here and hold the fort. Get on to the airport and explain what the hell's going on."

"Isn't Vilhjálmur doing that?"

"Vilhjálmur is safely out of the way talking to his opposite number at the airport. I want you to communicate with us and with the guys on the ground. Make sure they know what's happening before we get there."

"OK. Will do," Bára said, parking himself at a computer screen and placing a headset over one ear.

"Come on. Snorri, you're driving," Gunna said, tossing the keys to the second-best Volvo high in the air.

Hårde didn't believe in disguise. A confident approach, preferably with a discreet smile, was his preferred way of staying inconspicuous, although it wasn't always easy for a man of above average height.

He was unhappy with the airport while being unable to put his finger on precisely what was wrong, apart from Sigurjóna's having told him that the fat policewoman was looking for him. The check-in queue moved quickly enough and the concourse area was crowded enough for him to meld into the throng. He looked carefully at the queue ahead of him and singled out a couple of possible targets, men of roughly his own age and build, travelling alone.

He knew he would be ahead of Erna and had to admit to himself that he was looking forward to seeing her again, even though they had only parted that morning. He forced himself to think objectively and not to let the thought of her writhing beneath him cloud his judgement. Women come and women go, he reminded himself.

He watched the girl at the check-in desk for reactions that would betray that his name had been flagged up by the computer system, but she was mercifully bland.

"Have a nice flight, Mr Ström," she smiled, passing him his boarding pass.

He passed security painlessly as a bored guard waved him through to pick up his X-rayed hand baggage.

Inside the departure lounge, he drank a coffee at the bar and made his decision.

Ib Torbensen was bored and tired. His business trip to Iceland had been successful enough, but the small company representing his employers' products had exhausted him. The evening before they had taken him to dinner and a few drinks that had become a crawl through some of the noisier parts of downtown Reykjavík, ending in a raucous bar only a few hours before he needed to be awake at a meeting that he had not been able to stop yawning through.

He drank coffee, but didn't feel well enough to eat. His coat was making him too hot and he regretted not having packed it in his luggage. After three cups of coffee, he stood up, dropped some notes on the bar and wandered idly among the shops until the need to pee became too strong to fight.

He found a toilet on the far side of the concourse. Standing at the urinal and watching the yellow stream hit the bowl, he vaguely registered the door open and someone else enter the toilets.

When Hårde's right arm snaked around his neck, Ib Torbensen tried to shout. But Hårde's left arm quickly connected with his right hand, trapping the arm around Ib Torbensen's neck in the crook of the elbow, while the flat of Hårde's free hand forced his victim's head forward. As Ib Torbensen collapsed into unconsciousness, Hårde caught him and hauled the body to a cubicle, shutting the door behind them both.

Five minutes later, Hårde emerged, leaving an unconscious Ib Torbensen on the cubicle floor, having divested him of all his travel documents, passport, money and every piece of identification.

He walked smartly back across the concourse to the bar and saw Erna perched on a barstool. He hesitated for a moment, and made a second decision.

He dropped a hand gently on her shoulder. "Don't say anything, Erna."

She turned to him in surprise, but kept quiet.

"You said you thought I was a dangerous man?"

Erna nodded, eyes wide.

"I'm not coming with you."

"What? Why?" she couldn't help demanding, eyes wide.

"Listen. I have to fix something and you haven't seen me."

He squeezed her shoulder gently with the hand that had nearly killed lb Torbensen. "You haven't seen me since yesterday. Go to M'diq as planned. I'll see you in a few days."

"How many days?"

"A few. That's all I can say."

He squeezed her shoulder once more as Erna looked at him with a mixture of sorrow and fury. "OK, Mr Dangerous. Make it soon."

"Soon," Hårde said, his eyes wrinkling at the corners with a suppressed smile, and in seconds he had melted back into the crowd around the bar.

He walked purposefully but not too fast towards the long walkway leading to the departure gates and passport control. Halfway along, he spied a noisy group of people coming towards him from an arriving flight, laughing and joking among themselves. Hårde took a step to one side to make way for them and turned to double back, following until they reached the top of the steps for arriving passengers to go down to the baggage reclaim.

He stood behind an elderly couple on the escalator. At the bottom, he took a deep breath and walked past the carousels to the Nothing to Declare channel, where he was waved straight past and out, back on to Icelandic soil.

At the car hire desk, he thought the girl might recognize him, but with a queue to deal with, she simply asked him to sign in the right boxes, photocopied Ib Torbensen's passport and swiped his credit card before handing over the keys.

In the rental car lot, Hårde smiled grimly to himself as he heard the distant wail of sirens and prepared to drive on to the road, pausing at the exit to allow an ambulance followed by two squad cars to hurtle past and halt to disgorge a group of uniformed police officers led by a broad-shouldered woman.

There were uniforms everywhere, customs officers, airport officials, two paramedics and police officers from both the town and the airport.

One of the customs officers explained to Gunna and Snorri, while a groggy Ib Torbensen was revived by the paramedics and Bára went with one of the security staff to examine CCTV data.

"Who are you?" Gunna asked as soon as Ib Torbensen appeared to be awake enough to answer a question, but he shook his head in reply.

"Icelandic? English?" Gunna barked.

"I'm from Denmark. It's OK to speak English," Ib Torbensen said slowly.

"What happened to you?"

Ib Torbensen thought as he raised his hands to his throat and massaged his neck.

"I do not know," he said drowsily. "I went to piss, and woke up in the lavatory when someone was shaking me."

"When did this happen?" Gunna demanded, reverting to Icelandic.

"He was located at 16.35 in the departure lounge toilets," one of the security men replied.

"And when's he supposed to be flying, and where to?"

"Billund, he says, and he's missed his flight. It's closed."

"What's your name? Can I see your tickets and passport?" Gunna asked, switching to unwilling English, attention back on the forlorn Ib Torbensen, now massaging the sides of his head with the palms of his fat hands.

"My name is Torbensen. Everything has been taken from me, everything."

He rooted in the pockets of his coat and jacket, and hauled himself upright to check the pockets of his trousers.

"Nothing. Everything gone," he announced.

"You'd better see if you can stop that flight from leaving and be quick about it," Gunna told the airport security officers. "There might well be someone on that plane masquerading as this gentleman. Snorri, you go with them and have a look. Be careful. This guy's nasty."

Snorri and the security men loped away, muttering into microphones on their lapels.

"What worries me is if he isn't on that flight," she muttered to herself. "Otherwise the bloody man could be anywhere by now."

In the airport's operations room, Gunna growled every time unwelcome news came in. Nobody had used Ib Torbensen's seat on the flight to Billund. In fact, there were two empty seats, Ib Torbensen's and another in the name of Gunnvald Ström.

The flight to Madrid had already departed on time, with Erna Daníelsdóttir on board. But nobody by the name of Hadre, Hårde, Hardy or Ström had boarded and the Hadre Erna appeared to have booked a seat for failed to check in for his flight.

Gunna was even more gloomy when she realized that in the furore around Ib Torbensen, she had overlooked searching Erna out and preferably questioning her for long enough for her to miss her flight.

Ib Torbensen was taken off to hospital in Keflavík for questioning and to be met by hastily summoned staff from the Danish Embassy in Reykjavík, while Snorri accompanied the groaning man, his neck in a brace, to get a statement. Gradually the crowd thinned.

"Where did the bastard get to?" Gunna fumed. "The bastard," she emphasized. "The bastard outflanked us. Never, never, never underestimate these people." She glared balefully at Bára.

"He checked in as Ström," Bára announced.

"What?"

"He checked in," Bára repeated. "We've worked it all out. It's all on CCTV. Come on, I'll show you."

At a computer terminal in the operations room, she showed Gunna what they had been able to piece together from the CCTV data.

"He checks in here, hand baggage only. OK?"

"Yeah, got that."

"So, next we see him, he's here. That's Hårde, isn't it?"

Gunna peered at the screen and nodded. "That's him."

"Right. Next we see him, he's here, near the bar in the departure lounge, and it seems he sits there for a while. Now, this is the interesting part," Bára said, fingers flickering over the keyboard as she scrolled forward and called up material from other cameras. "He's here in the walkway that leads to passport control, but he never gets there."

"How does that work?"

"Who knows? You can't get to the departure gates and the flights without going through passport control, and he doesn't. The security chief spoke to all the duty officers and our man didn't go through."

"So if he's not on a flight, he's either hiding somewhere in the airport, or else he's sneaked out and is still in Iceland," Gunna said, thumping the table with her fist. "The sly bastard. Knocking that poor Danish guy out cold and letting him be found was just a diversion to take the attention off him while he did a runner."

Hårde felt numb. He had not been happy about using the international airport, the only route off this weird island, he reflected. Creating a diversion may have been what was needed to get him away from the airport, but it would undoubtedly have spurred the amateurish Icelandic police into even more efforts to locate him. Hårde took a deep breath and reminded himself that no adversary should ever be underestimated — that way lay complacency and errors of judgement.

At a petrol station in Reykjavík he bought sandwiches and calmly ate one over a plastic beaker of gritty coffee while he looked through the phone book. Matti had shown him how to find virtually anyone in the country — and there she was: "Gunnhildur Gísladóttir, police officer, Hafnargata 38, Hvalvík." Sigurjóna had described her as the fat policewoman. Even though he knew the woman's name and had seen at the airport as she disappeared inside the building that Sigurjóna's description had been less than kind, he still thought of her as the fat policewoman.

The anonymous Toyota sprang eagerly into life and he sat in thought with his hands on the wheel. Horst had done his best, but even a man with influence can hardly work miracles, so this gave him a couple of days to lie low before he could make an exit. He wondered if it would be better to hide away, if somewhere suitable could be found, or if it would be worthwhile trying to derail the search for him.

Without having consciously made a decision, he swung the little car on to the main road and followed it for a short distance before slowing to take the exit road that would take him through the lava fields towards the coast.

Outside the station, Gunna puffed a hurried Prince cadged from Bjössi with her phone at her ear.

"Sigrún? Hi, Gunna."

She waved Bjössi away as he appeared through the fire door, mugs in one hand, a cigarette packet in the other.

"Sure. Yup. Thank you, Sigrún, that's very kind of you. Yup, something of a panic right now and I can't begin to tell you anything about it. Top secret."

Bjössi held out a mug and Gunna took it in her free hand.

"OK. Thanks. No problem, I'll see you in the morning. I'll speak to Laufey and let her know. Great, bye." She thumbed the red button and finished the call with relief.

"All right, sweetheart?" Bjössi asked with concern.

"Yeah. Nothing that can't be sorted out. Just fixing up childcare."

"Laufey? How old is she now?"

"Thirteen."

"Teenager yet?"

"Getting there, but I'm sure there's worse to come."

"You could send her to us if you need to. Dóra wouldn't mind at all."

"Thanks, Björssi. I might well take you up on that."

She took a gulp of coffee. "But Gísli came home yesterday and he's got ten days off, so Laufey thinks that big brother is all the supervision she needs and the two of them will rub along just fine without Mum."

"And can't they?"

"Björssi, my old and dear friend. Gísli is nineteen and he's been at sea for weeks. I'm sure you can imagine that babysitting his little sister is not his top priority right now."

"Sorry. Should have known. The boy probably has beer and girls on his mind."

"Exactly. Now, if you'll excuse me I'll call Laufey and try to explain that to her and why she's staying with Sigrún down the street until Mum's little panic at work is sorted out."

Darkness was starting to fall as Hårde parked the Toyota outside the deserted school and waited without being sure what he was waiting for. There was no car parked outside the terraced house, although there were tyre tracks in the mud. No lights could be seen at Hafnargata 38 and Hårde decided to leave it until it was fully dark before making a move.

He huddled low in the seat and was sure he was unlikely to be observed as a woman in a heavy coat and rubber boots splashed up the street and went direct to number 38, opening the door and stepping inside without having to unlock it. Hårde waited and wondered if this were the right house, or if the new arrival were a friend or a relative, or even the fat policewoman's girlfriend? It wouldn't surprise him, he thought with a dark smile.

The door swung open again and this time the woman walked back down the street, accompanied by a gangly teenage girl with a schoolbag under one arm. This time Hårde stepped from the car and followed at a discreet distance, observing as the pair walked downhill, clearly enjoying a lively conversation, before disappearing into a low-slung house set back from the road behind an untidy garden of stunted trees.

Hårde smiled to himself and walked back in the growing gloom of the evening. Warm lights appeared at most of the windows in the street and he could make out television screens behind most of them. This was reassuring, as people who are busy watching a soap opera don't tend to look out of their own windows.

He opened the door of Hafnargata 38 with a single swift movement of a strip of flexible plastic and stepped inside, clicking the door to behind him.

It was close to midnight when the whole team assembled again in the incident room. Bára, Snorri and Gunna were haggard after the long day.

Bjössi was his usual self. He always looked as if he had just woken up, regardless of whether he had been on his feet all day or had just started his shift.

Gunna was surprised to see Vilhjálmur Traustason still on his feet. His face was paler than usual and Gunna guessed that he hadn't closed his eyes either.

"So," Gunna began, flexing her fingers in front of her and yawning. "He's given us the slip. He was undoubtedly at Keflavík airport this afternoon and either we didn't get there in time, or else he saw us coming and slipped away. We're pretty sure we know how and I'm positive that half-strangling that poor Danish bloke was a red herring. With Vilhjálmur's agreement —" she gestured towards Vilhjálmur Traustason standing by the back wall near the door with the brooding presence of Ívar Laxdal at his side — "we have informed the media and a report was carried on every TV news report this evening, with a photo of Hårde, and an announcement that members of the public should not approach him. It'll be in every newspaper in the morning as well," she added. "Anything else?"

"We've interviewed everyone we could get hold of at the airport," Snorri said. "We're fairly sure our man's still in the country, but no idea where."

"We need traffic surveillance ramped up as much as possible overnight. If he's not within a few kilometres of the airport, then Hårde must have got hold of transport somehow. I can't imagine him not being mobile, judging by the way he's worked up to now," Gunna concluded.

"And Erna Daníelsdóttir?" Vilhjálmur asked quietly.

"Landed safely in Madrid, and jumped on a transfer to Tangier." Bjössi yawned.

"Tangier?"

"That's it, Morocco. The Madrid airport police questioned her at our request, but nothing useful. We'd like her to come straight back and answer a few questions, but as she hasn't committed a crime, it's not as if we can have the woman shipped home. We just have to wait until she comes back. Unless there's a chance of a trip to the Mediterranean to interview her, in which case, I'd be happy to volunteer. I know it's a tough job, but someone has to do it."

Vilhjálmur blanched, until he realized that Bjössi was joking.

"All right, back here tomorrow, please, ladies and gentlemen," Gunna announced. "Bjössi and me at six. Snorri and Bára, I don't want to see you here before ten."

"Do you want a lift home, chief?" Snorri asked.

Gunna thought briefly and brightened inwardly at the prospect of seeing Gísli for an hour or two. Then she remembered that Laufey would be at Sigrún's house and Gísli would hardly be likely to be waiting for his mum to come home when he could be in Reykjavík with the girlfriend he hadn't seen for weeks.

"No. I'll just get my head down here tonight, if Vilhjálmur has an empty cell I can use. But thanks anyway."

Hårde left his shoes by the door and padded from room to room, trying to decide his next move. One room was clearly a child's, probably the one he had seen walking down the street, with bunk beds, posters on the walls and a row of neglected fluffy toys looking down from a high shelf. A smaller room looked like a guest bedroom, sparsely furnished but obviously recently used.

A third small bedroom was the domain of someone older and Hårde could see that the clutter of washed but unironed clothes on the dressing table belonged to the whole family. The double bed that filled much of the room was unmade and smelled both musty and inviting as Hårde remembered just how tired he was after a short night in Erna's demanding company followed by a long day.

He shook himself, reminding himself as he did so that he had to find two days of seclusion and that this was not the place for it. He left the fat policewoman's bedroom and scanned the long living room. He peered at pictures placed between books on the shelves along one wall, first of a smaller version of the girl he had seen walking down the street, then at a black-trimmed formal photograph of a man in some kind of military uniform, looking serious but with the same impish look of mischievous good humour that was evident in the girl's face. A second set of pictures showed a heavily built young man at varying ages with a tousled head and freckles, who was trying to look at ease and failing.

Hårde nodded and made his decision. In the L-shaped kitchen he found a carrier bag and loaded it with a bottle of wine, another of water and all the fruit and pastries he could find before slipping back into his shoes and over the road to the car, clicking the door behind him.

As he started the engine and let the little car roll forward down the slope, a heavy Range Rover roared to a halt and parked outside number 38. Young people stepped down from it, a young woman with ginger hair in a loose bun and a broad-shouldered young man whom Hårde instantly recognized from the pictures on the wall.

He drove away unobtrusively, taking the westbound road out of Hvalvík. He was relieved that he had not been interrupted in the fat policewoman's house and pleased that he had not needed to make certain of the young couple's silence, but annoyed with himself for giving in to curiosity and taking a chance of being seen without good reason.

CHAPTER THIRTY-THREE

Wednesday, 1 October

Gunna surfaced from sleep unwillingly. Something behind her eyeballs throbbed and told her not to open them. She forced her eyelids apart and the light immediately stabbed deep.

"Morning," Bjössi called cheerfully. "Wakey, wakey, sweetheart."

"Belt up, will you?" Gunna snapped back before the thought occurred to her that maybe Bjössi wasn't going out of his way to be unpleasant.

He sat down on the bed in the station's cellar in a room that was halfway between a cell and a storeroom and patted Gunna's thigh under the heavy duvet that was wrapped around her.

"Y'know, Gunna, my love? If that's the way you are in the mornings, I can only say I don't regret never having got you into the sack."

"Sorry, Bjössi. Didn't mean to be short with you. What's the time?"

"Almost six."

He held out a mug of coffee and Gunna took it with both hands as she sat up, Bjössi shielding his eyes in mock horror.

"It's all right. I'm decent enough," she growled. "I don't suppose I've got anything you haven't seen before."

"Possibly. But not as big," Björssi answered seriously, ducking a swipe from the hand not clasped around the mug.

"What's been going on?" Gunna asked with the first mouthful of coffee helping parts of her mind recall what had happened before she had closed her eyes a few short hours before.

"Looks like we've pretty much traced our man's movements up to when he left the airport. He's in a hire car on our Danish guy's credit card."

"I suppose Torbensen isn't anything to do with Hårde?"

"Nope. Like you said, he's a red herring. The man's a salesman for an agricultural equipment manufacturer in some backwater in Jutland. Spoke to his managing director and he's worked there for twelve years. The local company they supply confirmed who he is and that he's been with them pretty much all the time he's been in Iceland, all three days of it."

"So that's him ruled out."

"Plenty of people think they might have seen Hårde at the airport, most of them aren't sure though. Apart from the girl behind the bar who thinks he might have spoken to a fair-haired woman who was sitting there, but again, isn't sure. The woman at the car hire desk reckons she'd recognize him if she saw him, but Ib Torbensen's credit card and driving licence pretty much nail him down there anyway."

"And his phone?"

"Still switched off."

"The man knows what he's doing. I'll bet you anything you like he's ditched that phone and he's using another one by now. Right, Bjössi, my man. Are you going to get out and let a lady dress in peace and quiet?"

She gestured towards her shirt and uniform trousers folded over the back of the cell's only chair.

"I suppose so," Bjössi sighed. "Of course, if I'd known you were scantily clad under that duvet, I'd have crawled in before I woke you up."

"Get away, you randy old goat," Gunna retorted. "If I didn't know better I'd think your Dóra wasn't giving you any."

Ten minutes later they met again in the incident room. Vilhjálmur Traustason put his head around the door and withdrew quickly.

"What do we know?" Gunna asked, yawning.

"Last sighting of our man prior to the airport yesterday was at the InterAlu compound in Hvalvík. The operations manager there said he left before eleven. Maybe he went there yesterday to deliver the bad news."

"Bad news?"

Bjössi put morning newspapers on the table and spread them out in a fan. Each one had a picture of Bjarni Jón Bjarnason on the cover, except for *Dagurinn*, which carried a picture of a tearful Sigurjóna shielding her face from the camera, with the police station on Hverfisgata in the background.

"Has that bloody woman been let out?" Gunna demanded.

"I'm afraid so," Björssi confirmed tentatively. "Orders from high up, or so we're told. It's handy to have friends in high places."

"Shit," Gunna cursed as the door opened and Vilhjálmur Traustason came in soundlessly. "Vilhjálmur, those idiots in Reykjavík have let that bloody woman out."

It wasn't a question and Gunna's tone made it into an accusation.

"No choice in the matter. She's not to leave Reykjavík, though."

"Lárus Jóhann?"

Vilhjálmur Traustason allowed himself the thinnest of smiles.

"No," he said softly. "I have a feeling that Bjarni Jón Bjarnason's influence isn't quite as strong as it was a few days ago. Sigurjóna Huldudóttir's lawyers made a case for release that we couldn't give a good reason for opposing. However, I have passed on your information to the narcotics squad and it's being investigated. That's all I know right now."

"I hope they hang the bloody woman out to dry," Gunna grated.

"Are you telling me, Gunnhildur, my dear, that you don't care for the lady?" Björssi asked with exaggerated courtesy.

"Quite right. Now, business. Where's Hårde now?"

"Still in Iceland," Bjössi said. "We can be sure that unless he managed to disguise himself pretty fantastically, he didn't leave through the airport yesterday and it's so heavily monitored now that he daren't even try."

"How good is the monitoring over there? I'm wondering how long he'll have to lie low before things cool off and he can try again? Or try another route? Where do we look next?"

"Do we need to?" Bjössi asked.

"What do you mean?"

"The man knows what he's doing, but he has to have some kind of contact with other people. The longer he's in the country, the more chance he'll show up or at least be noticed. He's not a local and as soon as he opens his mouth he certainly can't pass for one. His face was all over the TV last night and today it's all over the papers. If he's not aware of that already, he will be soon and he'll know someone's going to recognize him."

"So, you're saying that he'll have to move quickly?"

"Exactly," Bjössi said thoughtfully. "We may have forced him to act faster than he would have wanted to."

He carefully spread out the sheaf of newspapers across the table. Alongside the main news of the day, including Bjarni Jón Bjarnason's early return from a conference overseas to face the growing financial crisis, Hårde's face could be seen somewhere on every one, leading to a story inside.

Only *Dagurinn* had Sigurjóna on the front cover, with Lára's by-line under the picture and "Skúli

Snædal — crime correspondent" right under the headline. Gunna felt a warm glow and suppressed a smile as she stood up and the others followed suit, taking it as a signal that the meeting was about to close.

"Right. I want everything watched that can be watched. We'll have every force in the country alerted about Hårde, especially anywhere with an airfield. I'd like to see some additional monitoring at Akureyri and Egilstadir airports as I believe there are a few international flights from there, aren't there?"

"Yeah, one or two a week, I think," Vilhjálmur hazarded.

"And Reykjavík airport as well. There are all kinds of oddballs going in and out through there what with all the private jets and whatnot. I'd hate to think of him getting away in a private jet."

"That it?" Bjössi asked, making notes on a pad in front of him.

"I want every port authority warned as well, not that there are all that many to worry about. Keep on top of all the shipping movements, everything that's going to an overseas port, no need to worry about fishing vessels, just cargo, especially anything going short-haul to Europe."

As Bjössi took notes, Gunna spied Vilhjálmur, hands behind his back, looking doubtful. "Problem, Vilhjálmur?"

"Costs. This is a level of activity that is normally handled by a larger force and I'm concerned that we cannot sustain it for long without possibly requesting additional funding. The overtime costs are already far too high."

"Can you talk to the Sheriff?"

"I will do so this morning."

"Please do. I honestly don't think this is going to take long. Our man's in the open now and I'm sure he'll be noticed soon enough if he's still in the country. If he's not here . . ." Gunna shrugged and didn't bother to finish her sentence.

"What d'you reckon, Gunna?" Bjössi asked when Vilhjálmur had left the room.

"Hell, I don't know. It's like nothing we've ever had to deal with before."

"I reckon it'll all be over by the weekend," Bjössi announced confidently and Gunna looked sideways at him.

"You reckon?"

"Yup. Unless he's gone camping in the highlands and wants to live on berries and songbirds until the heat dies down. He has to be noticed by someone sooner or later. It's a small country, Gunna. You can't hide in Iceland."

"Yeah. I suppose you're right. I hope you're right."

Sigurjóna sat huddled in the armchair with the 24/7 television news on in front of her. She was again swathed in her dressing gown, hair greasy and red cheeks puffing her face.

Rain hammered on the windows behind the TV set from a pewter sky and the room was half dark. On the screen an elegant newsreader dropped her smile and announced that Minister for Environmental Affairs Bjarni Jón Bjarnason had returned unexpectedly early from a conference in Berlin to face the growing financial crisis.

The screen cut to a clip of Bjarni Jón alighting from a black official car outside the Ministry to be greeted by a knot of microphones.

"I have no comment to make as things stand. You can expect a statement when I have discussed these issues with the Prime Minister," he snapped at the expectant throng, shaking raindrops from his coat as he disappeared into the maw of the building.

"And have you issued a statement yet?" Sigurjóna asked blankly without looking round as her husband appeared behind her.

"Of course not. Managed to get away from the Ministry without being seen by the scum."

He knelt at her side and put an arm awkwardly around her shoulders. Sigurjóna shook him off in irritation as the elegant newsreader returned, set her face to neutral and continued.

"It is reported that aluminium conglomerate InterAlu has withdrawn from its provisional agreement with entrepreneurial company Spearhead and its power generation subsidiary ESC. Twenty-four Seven News was told by InterAlu's Berlin office earlier today that there was no comment to be made and referred us to ESC, where phones were not being answered yesterday afternoon. Chief executive Sigurjóna Huldudóttir was today unavailable for comment due to other commitments, according to a Spearhead spokesperson a few minutes ago."

"Jón Oddur or Ósk?" Bjarni Jón asked.

"Don't know," Sigurjóna replied in a bleak voice. "Is it all over?"

"All over? Who knows?" Bjarni Jón groaned. "It's not just us that's in the shit, if that's what you mean."

"How do you mean?"

"This week the Central Bank will get a visit from Glitnir to tell them formally that they can't service their own loan payments. We're discussing what to do. The old man may be prepared to bail them out using foreign currency reserves, but I don't know. Or he may want to hang on to the cash as it seems there's worse to come. At the moment it's anybody's guess. After that, it's still anybody's guess."

"This is going to be bad, then?"

"Jóna, this is going to hurt everyone. But after Monday, I think we can be fairly sure that nobody will be even slightly interested in Spearpoint or ESC."

Sigurjóna's back straightened and the line of her mouth lifted. "And what did the Prime Minister say? Are you stepping down?"

"Good grief, no. He wouldn't hear of it. We all have to stand together in tough times."

"Have you told Lárus Jóhann?"

"Of course not," Bjarni Jón cackled. "I'll let him think he's being shifted upstairs for a few more days. Mind you, the treasury at a time like this is a poisoned chalice."

Again the newsreader cut away to a clip, this time showing a red-haired young woman nodding to a microphone. Bjarni Jón groaned as she appeared on the screen.

"Good grief, Ingunn Sverrisdóttir. Just what I need now," he moaned, reaching for the remote control that Sigurjóna whisked out of his reach.

"I want to hear this," she snarled, increasing the volume.

". . . absolutely," the red-haired woman said, caught in mid-sentence. "On behalf of the Left-Green Alliance, I want to make it plain that there is every indication of completely unacceptable conduct from the Member of Parliament concerned and we will definitely be inquiring with the Prime Minister's office as to when a full public hearing into Bjarni Jón Bjarnason's conduct is due to be held."

"You're referring to the collapse of the InterAlu project in his constituency?"

"That and more," Ingunn Sverrisdóttir assured the camera in a clear, clipped voice. "I'm talking about conflicts between the national interest and the Minister's own personal business interests. I'm talking about a full Parliamentary inquiry into misappropriation of public resources. I'm talking about a man elected to Parliament to look after the interests of his constituents who has blatantly misused his position to enrich himself."

"Strong allegations from Left-Green spokesperson Ingunn Sverrisdóttir. Thank you for your input and now back to the studio," a young man holding a microphone said as the camera swung back to show him and the red-haired woman standing outside the Parliament building.

Bjarni Jón Bjarnason closed his eyes and collapsed in a heap on the sofa. "Bitch. That's totally unfair. The fucking bitch."

"What the hell do you expect from some stupid lesbian communist fuckwit? You can't expect them not to stick a knife into you now they have a chance, not after the way you've treated them in the past," Sigurjóna sneered.

"It'll be forgotten on Monday," Bjarni Jón said with satisfaction, levering himself to his feet to pour himself a hefty drink. "Want one?"

"No," Sigurjóna said with determination, standing up.

He poured a stiff vodka and brought the bottle with him to the table. Sitting down, he extracted a small cigar from an inside pocket and put it between his lips.

"Oh, for fuck's sake. You're not going to smoke that in here, are you?" Sigurjóna demanded, scowling at him.

"Yes, I bloody well am," Bjarni Jón replied airily.

"In that case I'm going to the office."

"Do whatever the hell you like," he said, lighting up and contentedly blowing smoke towards the expensive abstracts on the walls for the first time. "You always have done, so why change now?"

He felt happier with the arrangements for his fall-back plan. The airport had been too carefully watched and the hours in the air would have been too dangerous, leaving too much time for him to be noticed, calls to be made and a discreet tap on the shoulder at the destination airport where security would be tight in these days of international terrorism. He wondered how the unfortunate Ib Torbensen was feeling. Probably being waited on hand and foot in an Icelandic hospital.

He stretched out in the narrow bed, extending his feet past the end of the heavy duvet that was made to suit someone twenty centimetres shorter, and wondered what time it was.

Late in the evening he had tucked the little grey Toyota away behind the unobtrusive tarred wooden shed set well back from the road but with a view through the rattling windows of rain-laden skies to the west. The back door had opened with the same piece of plastic he had used on the fat policewoman's door, only even more easily. Weeks before he had scouted out the area, noting the locations of remote summer cottages in case he might need to disappear. It wasn't something he expected might happen, being a respectable employee of an international company, albeit with a false passport, but he'd done it anyway out of force of habit.

He had two days to wait for Horst's ticket off the island, two full days to lie low and stay out of trouble. Normally he would have relished the prospect of two days of solitude to spend watching a little TV, stretching and meditating, but this time Erna sashayed in front of him every time he closed his eyes, grinning as she peeled off her clothes.

The car would have to be dumped, he decided. The fat policewoman would certainly by now be aware of the number and make of the car rented on the Danish guy's credit card, so sometime during the day he would need to replace it discreetly. He wondered about laying a false trail for the fat policewoman to follow, even a strike of some kind to give them something else that would overload the country's tiny police force beyond being able to seek out a single person making a quiet departure.

"It's all right, Mum," Laufey said. "I don't mind staying with Sigrún."

Sprawled in an armchair, she returned her attention to Facebook and Gunna gave up.

Sigrún leaned on the door frame with folded arms and grinned. "Don't worry. She's fine here."

"Well, if you're sure," Gunna said fretfully.

"It's all right," Sigrún said soothingly. "Is it that bloke who was on the news yesterday that you're after?"

"Yes, it is," Gunna admitted.

"Then don't worry about it. She's fine here for a few days."

"Thanks, Sigrún. I owe you a huge favour," Gunna said, turning up her coat collar as close as it would go to her cap to trot the hundred metres uphill through the rain to her own house.

She threw herself through the front door. Inside, she shook rain off her jacket, took it off and hung it on the door before kicking off her boots. Although the place felt empty without Laufey, it had a feel of habitation about it.

"Hello!" she called out loudly, striding to the kitchen to look around. Plates and dishes that she had not used were stacked on the draining board. In the living room, an empty wine bottle stood on the table.

Gunna cast about, called again and went over to look at the sofa, rearranging the scattered cushions with swift movements. Spotting something white peeking from under a cushion in the corner, she pulled at it gently.

"Hi, Mum."

A towel tied around his waist, Gísli rubbed his eyes as he emerged from his room to find Gunna sending a wry half smile towards him as she held up a lacy white bra.

"Well, my lad. It's definitely not one of mine," she said. "Far too small."

"Sorry, Mum."

"Company?"

"Yeah. She's still asleep."

"All right. I won't disturb you. I've just nipped in for a shower and a change. Got to be back at the station soon again anyway."

Gísli grunted and went past her to the kitchen, and soon the flat was filled with the aroma of brewing coffee.

For some reason she couldn't put her finger on, her bedroom felt different, as if there were a fleeting aroma of someone else that she couldn't quite catch hold of. Gunna threw clothes in a corner of her bedroom, wrapped herself up for Gísli's benefit and made for the shower. A few minutes later she was towelling off vigorously, and was soon feeling properly awake again in a clean uniform shirt at the kitchen table as Gísli poured fresh coffee into a mug.

"Mm, hello. The smell woke me up," a small voice behind her said.

Gunna turned to see a round freckled face and flood of red hair streaming over the shoulders of one of Gísli's shirts.

"Mum, this is Soffia," Gísli announced with sheepish pride.

"Hello, Soffia, pleased to meet you. I'm Gísli's witch of a mum, but you call me Gunna."

"I know who you are. Gísli said you were in the police," she said slowly, sitting on Gísli's knee and moulding herself to him.

"When are you sailing, Gísli?" Gunna said, draining her mug.

"Not until next week. There's no hurry since they cut the bloody quotas again."

"Fine. Are you staying here? It's up to you. I've no idea when I'll be back."

"We'll stay here for a while, I think," Soffia said carefully. "If that's all right with you?"

"No problem. I'll be back sometime. Just make sure my lad washes up after himself, won't you?" she said, standing up and making for the door, by which time the young couple were already wrapped precariously around each other.

In the lobby, she half closed the door and bent to pull her boots on again, looking out through the narrow window by the door to see that the rain was beating down outside harder than ever.

* * *

He drove slowly through Hafnarfjördur, down the hill from the town's southern entrance and stopped at the lower quayside, thought about going into the café on the dock where he had eaten several times with Matti, but decided against it.

With the wipers struggling to clear water from the windscreen, Hårde drove slowly up the slope and along the southern edge of the harbour area, through a small industrial estate crowded with fork-lift trucks, badly parked vans and large plastic tubs of fish waste along the sides of the road. Looking for a suitable opportunity, he carried on past the industrial zone, before taking a U-turn to double back, this time passing the bay towards the town itself.

Confidence, that's the key, he reminded himself. A man with a smile and a purpose doesn't normally get asked what he's doing.

He parked neatly in a bay in the town centre and got out of the car to reconnoitre on foot, the collar of his jacket turned up, hands deep in his pockets. The small precinct of shops where he bought a couple of pastries had a few people walking around, but both the post office and the bank in particular were busy with longish queues. Chewing a sweet roll, he timed a middle-aged lady as she entered the bank — it took her an encouraging eleven minutes to get her business concluded and leave. He went back to the car, where he sat watching the passers-by while he ate a second roll and drank the carton of fruit juice he had bought.

He unfolded the free newspaper he had picked up without looking at it carefully and was jolted awake at the sight of a photo of himself at the bottom of the front page, one that he recognized as the Swedish police's mug shot of him.

He swore, anger rising inside him until he carefully stifled it. Only the woman serving at the shop counter had seen him clearly, and she had been a foreigner as well, not likely to read an Icelandic newspaper. Nobody else would need to see him anyway, so the photo in the paper needn't be an issue.

What had caught him off guard was that the fat policewoman was obviously further ahead of him than he had imagined. Maybe that stupid taxi driver had told them something? Or Sigurjóna, a person he would never be able to trust.

He looked back at the paper and saw to his surprise that Sigurjóna was there on the cover too, one scarlet-taloned hand shielding a sour pout from a photographer's flash, and he chuckled grimly to himself, well able to imagine what would be going on now that InterAlu had dropped its Icelandic partners.

Ágúst Vilmundsson wasn't having a good day. He had been late for work that morning, one of his men hadn't turned up and he had had to reorganize the whole schedule for the day to fit in the six jobs that seven men would have to do between them, knowing full well that finishing four jobs of out of six would be good going.

After the coffee break, he left the first job with two of the lads getting on well with the old lady's new floor and decided that he would have to go and give a bit of moral support to the two finishing off fitting a kitchen in Kópavogur, but on the way he remembered that the sheaf of bills on the passenger seat would have to be paid and now was as good a time as any to stop off at the bank.

Ágúst Vilmundsson cursed the rain as he drove into Hafnarfjördur, cursed it as he tried to find a spot to park and cursed yet more as he hurried across the car park to the bank with the rain fogging his glasses.

Ten minutes later, he stepped back out into the rain, reminding himself for the hundredth time to get internet banking set up so he could pay bills in the evenings instead of having to do it when it didn't suit him.

At first he thought the drops of rain on his glasses were playing tricks on him, so he took them off and peered myopically about the car park. There was no doubt about it. He perched his glasses back on his nose and peered about him, spying a police car in the distance making sedate progress along the road between the bay and the rows of shops. He ran as fast as he could towards the road, crashing through sparse hedging plants along the road and waving.

The police car drew to a gentle halt beside him and a window hissed down.

"Got a problem?" the young officer inside asked, looking over at him.

"Some bastard's stolen my truck," Ágúst Vilmundsson announced bitterly, as if the day hadn't been miserable enough already.

* * *

Sightings of Hårde trickled in, with each report filled and passed over to Gunna's team. By late morning they had chased up a dozen leads, liaising with police in Reykjavík to coordinate inquiries in and around the city.

"No, that's perfectly all right. Thank you for your help." Gunna heard Snorri finishing a call and swearing under his breath the moment the receiver was on the hook.

"What was that?" she asked as Snorri scrawled "No further action" across the report sheet in big letters.

"Ach, you know how it is when there's an appeal on the TV. That was an elderly lady in Húsavík. It seems there's a Polish fishworker living in the flat above her who she thinks might be Hårde. The guy's been living there for the best part of a year, he's short and fat with a black beard, but as he's foreign she thought it might be him in disguise."

"Sure you don't want to check it out?" Bára asked sweetly.

"Please . . ." Snorri said as the phone trilled again.

Bára followed Gunna outside to the smoking spot by the back door and watched as Gunna lit up, frowning.

"If you were in a strange country and needed to stay out of sight for a while, what would you do?" Bára asked her.

Gunna inhaled deeply and thought. "I've no idea off the top of my head. What about you?"

"I reckon either somewhere very unobtrusive, right off the beaten track, or smack in the centre of things. If

I was trying to stay out of sight and didn't have to worry about cash, I'd book into the smartest hotel I could find. You remember how snobby and unhelpful they were at Hotel Gullfoss?"

Gunna nodded. "You're quite right, although I can't see our boy checking in there somehow. But it fits. The man does have a certain style," she admitted.

Gunna ground her half-smoked Prince beneath a heel and they walked back towards the incident room where Snorri was watching his computer screen while carrying on a conversation through the headset clamped to one ear.

"Thank you, yes. We'll follow that up. Goodbye," he said, hanging up.

"Anything useful?" Gunna demanded.

"Petrol station attendant on Hringbraut. Reckon he sold Hårde a hot dog and a bottle of mineral water last night. Worth a visit, d'you reckon?"

"Definitely. You'd best get on with that right now and check on that report from the girl in Hafnarfjördur who saw him this morning while you're at it. But first, Snorri, tell me something."

"Chief?"

"If you were on the run and wanted to keep a low profile, what would you do? Come on, let's think about what one of us might do in Hårde's position."

"Me?" Snorri said slowly. "I'd just live in the car for a couple of days, park up here and there, keep moving around. Maybe find a shed or something to lie low in, or maybe a boat somewhere. There's plenty of decommissioned boats around that aren't going anywhere. It depends how long," he finished.

"That's just it. It depends how long for," Gunna mused. "People get noticed around harbours now that they're so quiet. I'm inclined to go along with what you said, Bára."

"Which was what?" Snorri asked.

"Do it in style. Check into the priciest hotel in town. Bára, as it was your idea, you'd better see to this. Go round all the hotels within spitting distance, do all of them."

Bára nodded and went to her desk to pick up the phone as Snorri pulled his jacket and squared his cap on his head.

"Bára, you can ask Sævaldur — sorry, *tell* Sævaldur we want three or four of his people to help out with this and see if you can get round the whole lot before midnight. Organize it for lateish this evening, so it takes in people checking into hotels tonight as well. All right?"

"Yup," Bára said, looking up as Snorri stepped out of the room, holding the door wide for Vilhjálmur Traustason accompanied by the brooding form of Ívar Laxdal.

"Progress, Gunnhildur?" Vilhjálmur asked gently, while the National Commissioner's deputy cast his eyes around the room.

"Bugger all, actually. Hårde's been seen in practically every part of Iceland in the last twenty-four hours, and most of them we can discount entirely once we've spoken to the person calling in. A couple of sightings in

Reykjavík and Hafnarfjördur, one from a petrol station on Hringbraut that sounds convincing, and then there's a girl who works in a coffee shop in Hafnarfjördur who says she sold him a couple of Danish pastries. That's convincing as the girl's from Estonia and said the way the man spoke sounded familiar. Snorri's on his way to interview her and see if there's any relevant CCTV footage anywhere. That's it for now. We're organizing a sweep of hotels this evening in case he's booked himself in somewhere."

"You think that's likely?" Ívar Laxdal asked forbiddingly.

"I'm not convinced," Gunna admitted. "But I think we have to check. I feel it fits in with the man's character. He does things in style."

"Up to you. But I've read the file from Sweden as well. He's a military man and used to roughing it. Don't rule that out."

"Point taken," Gunna agreed. "But I'm following Bára's idea of the hotels in the first instance. I have the feeling that this might be a way of wrong-footing us as something we wouldn't expect, so it's worth a look. If nothing comes of it this evening, we'll think again."

Gunna pursed her lips in irritation. "The problem is," she went on, "we don't know what he's waiting for. Does he have a deadline? We don't know if he's waiting for anything in particular other than a chance to get the hell off this island. We don't know if he's on his own or if he has friends helping him out. I'd really like to haul Sigurjóna over the coals one more time on this. If she's not helping Hårde, she'd have a damn good idea who might be."

Vilhjálmur Traustason looked worried. "She is a minister's wife," he reminded her.

"A bent minister," Gunna retorted.

Ívar Laxdal opened his mouth to speak when Bára interrupted. "Gunna! Chief!" she squawked, hand over the phone.

"What is it?"

"The car's been found."

"The rental car?"

"Yup. It's in Hafnarfjördur. A traffic warden saw it had been there past the time limit, wrote out a ticket, then she checked the number and it flashed up as missing. No doubt about it."

"Right. Snorri's on his way, right? Tell Reykjavík to get a technical team and a dog on to it right this minute, and I don't give a stuff if they say they're busy."

"Lárus Jóhann."

"It's me. I need a favour."

"Bjarni Jón. I hardly expected a call from you."

"Yeah. I have a lot to deal with right now," Bjarni Jón Bjarnason murmured into the phone. He tried to keep his voice as low as possible and was hoping that he could make a few necessary calls without alerting Sigurjóna, still sitting blank-eyed in front of the 24/7 News.

"All right. There's not much I can do for you, my boy."

"Look. This is me doing you a favour as much as the other way around."

"One hand scratching the other, you mean?"

"Yeah. Sort of."

"And what do I get out of it, whatever it is?"

"You get some grateful people who could be in a position to be extremely helpful."

"Helpful, how?"

Bjarni Jón took a long breath. "You know that things are changing?"

"Ah, the old man's not going to let you tough it out?"

Lárus Jóhann chuckled grimly at Bjarni Jón's silence. "Don't worry, my boy. It'll all blow over soon enough. Did you think I was born yesterday? Look, there'll be another scandal along next week, and by the time elections come round again, it'll all be forgotten. You need a little patience and a thick skin to stay in politics, my boy. Look at Árni Johnsen."

Bjarni Jón sighed. "If it happens, I hear you're tipped for the treasury, or am I wrong?"

Lárus Jóhann could hardly keep the flush of pride from his voice. "I don't know what you're talking about, young man."

"Yes, you do, you old fox."

"Nobody's tipped for anything at the moment. My guess is that when the financial situation is announced after the weekend, the old man will want to show a united front, which means nobody will go anywhere — you included."

"But . . .?"

"When the dust settles, then there'll be a round of musical chairs. Until then, I suggest you keep your head down and jump when the old man cracks the whip."

"In that case, a word to the wise."

"What are we talking about?" Lárus Jóhann asked sharply, and Bjarni Jón knew he had his full attention.

"If you don't know, I'm not going to say anything."

"Come on, play the game, will you?"

"Lárus, this is just a piece of advice that helps you far more than it helps me. Listen, there's a ship docked at Skarfanes."

"What, at that fishmeal factory?"

"Yes, Lárus, the one your wife owns forty per cent of. That one."

"Go on, Bjarni."

"This ship needs to leave on Friday without anything untoward happening. No customs, no inspections, nobody looking too closely at the crew. You understand?"

"Not entirely, but I assume you'll explain soon enough."

"When the ship's gone, I'll tell you everything you need to know. Just whisper in the right ears."

"I'm intrigued."

"Just do it, Lárus."

"But you give me your word you'll tell me what this is all about?"

"I'll tell you what I know. You're in Parliament on Saturday?"

“I’ll be in my Parliamentary office until twelve. Come and see me before that.”

“Right. See you then,” Bjarni Jón said, and the phone went dead.

It was still blowing gusts heavy with the tang of seaweed, but the rain had stopped and sunshine was making valiant attempts to break through broken banks of grey and black cloud scudding across from the west.

The lunchtime rush hour was at its peak and the anonymous grey Toyota sat forlornly in the car park, surrounded by the comings and goings of shoppers looking for places to park. A stream of curious onlookers were delighted to have something to watch as they waited in the burger van’s queue as the furore around the little car grew.

Helga Karen Finnsdóttir was still bewildered by the storm she had unleashed by reporting the little grey Toyota. First the pleasant young policeman who said his name was Snorri had asked her some questions and then asked her not to go further than the coffee shop in the precinct as his sergeant would want to talk to her as well.

Then all hell was let loose. A van full of people in white overalls had arrived, and a mechanic with Toyota emblazoned on his overalls who had opened the car for them. Then a policeman came with a dog on a lead that sniffed the car and then appeared to go around in circles before snuffling back to a spot away over on the far side of the car park, almost as far as you could get from the grey Toyota.

Finally the rude policewoman had appeared, fired off a dozen questions and then joined the dog handler before coming back.

"Right, what time was it when you booked the car?" Gunna asked abruptly.

"I already told your colleague, it was five minutes to twelve."

"And how long had the car been here?"

"I took a note of its number about nine thirty."

"So it had been here almost three hours when you gave it a ticket?"

"Well, yes," Helga Karen admitted.

"What's the time limit here?"

"Well, it's supposed to be two hours, but I don't like to issue a ticket right on the two hours. I normally give people a few minutes. It's easy enough to get held up."

"That makes you a very generous warden," Gunna observed, warming to the woman. "How long have you been doing this job?"

"About a year. Just over."

"How often are you supposed to check each car?"

Helga Karen thought for a moment, huddled deep in her bright yellow waterproof uniform coat, a size or two too large for her.

"It's supposed to be around every hour or so," she said.

"And in practice?"

"There's just too much to get round in an hour," she said helplessly. "We have targets and they're quite hard to reach. I suppose normally I can get around everything in an hour and a half. But I'm on my own today as Jóga who works the shift with me is off as her little boy's ill and she couldn't get anyone to sit with him."

Gunna was beginning to get impatient. "All right, tell me exactly how long this car could have been parked here."

"It was there just before ten when I did my first round, but it wasn't there when I finished at four yesterday."

"So it was parked here between four yesterday afternoon and around ten this morning? Is that what you're saying?"

"Exactly."

"Thank you. That's what I was after," Gunna said, turning and striding away.

CHAPTER THIRTY-FOUR

Thursday, 2 October

Hårde parked the grey Mercedes a street away and walked up the hill with his bag over his shoulder. The car's owner, who had made the mistake of driving down the rutted track to check on his summer house, was now lying in a heap in his own garden shed and would have no further need of either car or summer house.

From old force of habit, he had cleared up behind him, washed the dishes he had used and even hung the wet dishcloths on a rail behind the kitchen door. The magazines he had read went back to the rack next to the bed and the remote back to the plastic holder on the TV set. His brief sojourn in the shuttered summer house next to its own black-sand beach had been restful and had given him a chance to sleep, stretch and catch up on the news. There had been nothing on local TV about the hunt for him, and he assumed that this either wasn't news any more, or else the gathering financial storm was overshadowing everything else. A computer and an internet link would have made things even better, but live football on satellite TV almost made up for it.

Letting himself in through the back door of Erna's darkened house, he wondered just how soon the Mercedes' owner would be missed. The elderly man who had spluttered with fury when he found Hårde watching his TV wore a wedding ring, so presumably his wife would raise the alarm sooner or later. Presumably finding the white truck parked behind the summer house would put the police on to the trail of the Mercedes, but that couldn't be helped. The system alarm bleeped its warning and Hårde quickly punched in the number to disarm it. Without turning on any lights, he made his way through the house, taking in the aroma of Erna that he could smell everywhere.

The spacious bathroom sat at the middle of the house, the only room with no outside windows. Hårde clicked on the light and shut the door before turning on the hot water and opening one of the cabinets to survey the rows of jars and bottles jumbled on to the shelves.

Late in the afternoon and everyone was tired. The search was in progress for Ágúst Vilmundsson's scruffy pickup. The reported sightings of Hårde had slowed to a trickle. Snorri was back at the airport checking flights and working with the airport police on monitoring the hundreds of people passing through the departure lounge.

Bára yawned to herself, aching to sign off and sleep for a few hours.

"All the prints match up," she told Gunna. "All the fingerprints from the guesthouse in Mjósundsvegur, the flat in Hverfisgata and the Toyota rental car. All the same person."

"The cheeky, impudent bastard."

Vilhjálmur Traustason appeared silently, accompanied again by Ívar Laxdal, hugging a slim briefcase to his chest and sporting a military-style black beret instead of his usual uniform cap.

"Progress, Gunnhildur?"

"Ach, our man pops up and then he's gone by the time we get anywhere near him. The phone he was using is dead, I reckon, so no chance of tracking him through that. He had a rental car that he ditched in Hafnarfjördur and we're as sure as we can be that he stole a white pickup and drove off in that. The search is on for that, but he may have switched cars twice more since then, for all we know."

Gunna ran a hand through her hair, leaving it sticking up at angles. "I'm telling you, Vilhjálmur, this is one sly bastard. We've never had to deal with anyone like this before. He's a real artist."

"What do you think your chances of apprehending this character are?" Ívar Laxdal asked quietly, and Gunna thought quickly.

"The longer he's running about, the better the likelihood of picking him up. Iceland's not a big place and there are only so many ways out. But this guy has some highly placed friends somewhere."

"Do you mean the company he was working for here?"

"Something like that. Although with the news we've seen of their business today, I'd imagine they have other fish to fry right now."

She drummed her fingers on the desk, wondering whether or not to tell him that deep down she had little hope that Hårde would now be found.

"I don't doubt that as long as he's in Iceland we'll find him," she decided. "Assuming he is still in the country, he can't stay that many steps ahead for long and even a pro like this guy will make a mistake or be unlucky sooner or later. What really worries me more than anything is if he's confronted by a police officer without backup, how far is he prepared to go?"

"Meaning what?"

"This guy has murdered three people already and could easily have killed that Danish guy if he'd wanted to. I'm convinced he didn't kill him because he was a better diversion alive than as a corpse so that while we buzzed around like flies, he had a breathing space to run for it."

"What are you asking for, Gunnhildur?" Vilhjálmur said.

"I need an armed response team I can call on when I need them."

"I see. Excuse me for a moment," Ívar Laxdal said as the mobile phone in his top pocket chimed. He checked the display and answered in an undertone. He looked up quickly at the group.

"One minute. I'll be right back," he said as he clicked the door shut behind him, phone back at his ear.

"I don't know if I have the authority to mobilize the Special Unit," Vilhjálmur said. "Is this man armed?"

"I doubt it, although it's possible. He seems dangerous enough without a gun."

Vilhjálmur pursed his lips. "I'll see what I can do."

"I'm sure laughing boy in the corridor can mobilize the toy soldiers easily enough," Gunna said. "Anyway, I have things to do."

"Where are you putting your effort now?"

Gunna wanted to tell him that any slight lead would be welcome, but refrained.

"Right now we're checking every kind of transport link there is. Snorri's liaising with the international airport. We've got flights monitored for anything unusual scheduled to leave the country. Luckily all the squillionaires seem to be hiding at the moment, so there aren't that many private jets on the move."

Vilhjálmur looked sour at the reference to the conflicting reports that had been scattering the news all day on the deepening financial crisis.

"The rest of us are watching shipping at the moment," she continued.

"Trawlers?"

"Hardly, Vilhjálmur. Short-haul commercial shipping mostly. There are still a few yachts and cruise ships about, but I don't think they're likely."

"Why's that?"

"I'm not too worried about the cruise ships. Port control in Reykjavík is pretty strict and we can worry about that tomorrow anyway. I'm not too fussed about Hafnarfjördur, as the port is so trussed up by security and CCTV that unless he has a cast-iron way into the area, there should be alarm bells ringing in our guy's head."

Gunna rested her chin on her hands and tried to think clearly as Ívar Laxdal returned to the room, his phone stowed back in his top pocket.

"Sorry. I had a few calls to make. Now, were you saying something about armed response?"

"Yes, Vilhjálmur and I were discussing it."

"Fine. It's authorized. You have seventy-two hours in which you can alert a six-man team. Echo Squad are already on manoeuvres not far from here, so they can respond fast. I have already alerted their commanding officer."

"Bloody hell, you work fast," Gunna said appreciatively.

Clearly not used to being addressed with such familiarity by a provincial sergeant, he opened his mouth and then closed it with the words unsaid.

"Keep me posted, please. Check with me within forty-eight hours if you need an extension," he finally said frostily, sweeping from the room with Vilhjálmur close behind him.

CHAPTER THIRTY-FIVE

Friday, 3 October

Rain again threatened to break through. Hårde enjoyed the sight of the majestic grey and black clouds rolling across the morning sky just as Gunna looked at them with annoyance and wished the bloody rain would let up for an hour or two.

In the mirror he critically examined the dark tint that his hair had taken, courtesy of a tube of hair dye from Erna's bathroom. The expensive sunglasses he had found in her bedroom would only go dark in bright light. He didn't like the dark hair, but an all-over crop in a few days would take it out.

Dry weeks followed by a break in the weather had left the Icelandic air sparkling with clarity. The greens of fields and the brown and grey tones of the rocks and hillsides glittered with a new life. Hårde was even enjoying the drive through the jagged lava fields in the smooth Mercedes. It wasn't his ideal choice of car, but he had to admit it was comfortable. He sped through enough puddles to plaster the number plates with a respectable layer of mud.

He approached following Horst's instructions, leaving the main road along a wide but barely visible track that looked at first glance like little more than a flattened area of ground where the black lava had been pounded down.

The track widened and swung away from the main road down towards the coast where a long swathe of rock had been cleared, shovelled aside and flattened to make way for the long sheds of the factory squatting by the sea. Hårde frowned as an indefinable yet powerful aroma drifted even through the car's closed windows. Passing by the long building where there was no indication of any activity, nor any cars parked by the door at the end marked Office, he found a quiet spot between some containers and an expanse of ground strewn with the detritus of industrial fishing. Pumps, nets packaged into huge bales, coils of rusting wire and assortments of anonymous stainless steel equipment lay stacked on pallets against the day that something might possibly come in useful.

Hårde left the key in the car, reasoning that there was no need to put the unfortunate owner's heirs to any additional inconvenience. Briefly he toyed with setting fire to it, figuring that it would cover his tracks more efficiently. He immediately dismissed the idea as impractical — a fire would attract attention and he admitted to himself that he just liked the idea of a bonfire.

He checked quickly that he had everything, shut the car door and walked past the buildings on the seaward side where a long quayside was deserted apart from a small freighter moored at the far end. A generator rattled and the belching mouthfuls of oily black smoke from the funnel told him that the main engine was being started up.

The ship was low in the water. Hårde swung his holdall on to his back and took the gangplank in a few long strides before looking about to see where any of the crew could be found. He heard a door slam above him and a bearded face under a peaked cap appeared at the bridge wing.

"Gunnar?" the man demanded fiercely.

"That's me."

"Good. Come up. Go through the door there and shut it behind you."

The ship's bridge was deceptively small. A single chair occupied the centre overlooking the radar screens, and there was a stool near one of the windows for a lookout.

"I'm Terje," the man in the peaked cap said, shaking Hårde's hand firmly. "You're our new second engineer for this trip?"

"That's right. Where are we bound, and what are you carrying?"

"Fishmeal, going to Rotterdam, calling at Stornoway. Or so I'm told." He smiled. "Been to sea before?"

"Yup, but it was a long time ago."

"In that case I take it you know your way around an engine room, so you'd better go below and sort yourself out. There're only four of us on board. Follow the smell of food and you'll find the galley. Trude's the cook. Tell her I sent you and she'll show you a cabin. But keep your hands off her. She's married to the mate and we want to keep this a happy ship."

Terje's eyes twinkled with suppressed curiosity. "I'm not asking any questions," he added. "And if anyone asks, you're the new grease monkey and I know nothing about you. OK?"

Hårde grinned. The shipboard smells of salt, paint and the lingering aroma of burnt lube oil were already bringing his navy days back to him.

"Absolutely fine by me, Terje. When are we sailing?"

"As soon as the engineer tells me everything's warmed up and ready to go. So you'd better be ready to chuck off the ropes in ten minutes. If that's all right with you?"

The question was asked in a reserved tone, as if Terje were not entirely sure whether to treat Hårde as a passenger or one of the crew.

The door at the back of the bridge opened and banged back against the bulkhead. A dark man in an overall that had once been white appeared.

"OK?" Terje asked.

The man just grunted and left the way he had come.

"That's Kalle, our chief engineer. Actually, our only engineer. On deck in half an hour. Trude'll get you some wet weather gear as well. We've already eaten, but I expect she'll find you a bite once we've sailed," Terje said with finality, indicating that Hårde's induction into the crew was over as far as he was concerned.

Apart from the buzz of conversation and ringing phones elsewhere in the building that permeated the thin plasterboard walls, the incident room was quiet. Snorri and Bára were at their computer terminals, trying not to disturb Gunna, who growled down every attempt at conversation. The evening before they and officers from the Reykjavík force had been to every hotel in and around Reykjavík and come away with nothing.

"Come on then. Is there anything?" she demanded, finally breaking her own silence as the other two almost sighed with relief.

"Nothing, chief," Snorri admitted. "No sightings that can't be accounted for."

"It seems the bloody man's disappeared," Gunna grumbled. Her head was aching and she was certain she had the makings of a cold coming on. She wondered idly if Gísli and his girlfriend were still at the house in Hvalvík. This one seems a bit more serious than the others, she thought. Seems a pleasant enough girl, but a redhead? That means temper.

"Any news?"

"What?" She spun her chair around to find Vilhjálmur standing by the door that he had opened silently. "Sorry, Vilhjálmur. Didn't hear you come in."

"Just wondering if you have any news?" he asked softly. "The Minister has asked to be kept informed."

"No, I'm afraid everything's gone cold. The truck we're sure our boy disappeared in has vanished. We haven't had a sighting anywhere that can't be explained in two minutes and frankly we have nothing to go on."

"That's unfortunate." He cleared his throat softly.

"Excuse me, sir," Snorri said, stepping up to where Vilhjálmur was standing in front of the large whiteboard on the wall. He set to work with a marker, reading information off a sheet of paper in his hand and filling in the gaps.

"What do you have there?"

"Shipping movements," Snorri replied without stopping.

"Very good."

"That's about all we have to go on," Gunna explained. "What is there, Snorri?"

"There's *Starlight*, a freighter sailing from Grundartangi at midnight," he read out, still writing. "There's *Beinta*, a Faroese trawler leaving Hafnarfjördur at ten tonight and a couple of Russian trawlers, also in Hafnarfjördur, which haven't decided when to leave yet," Snorri read off the screen. "Then there's a freighter called *Juno Provider* docked at Skarfanes last night, no information on when they're leaving, and a yacht that called at Hvalvík this morning and is still there. There's a reefer called *Wilhelmina* due in Grindavík at six tomorrow morning, due out at six in the evening, and there are three cruise liners calling at and sailing from Reykjavík in the next forty-eight hours, the last ones of the year, I reckon. Want me to look any further afield?"

"All foreign shipping?" Vilhjálmur asked.

"There isn't any Icelandic shipping any more," Gunna said, yawning. "It's all flagged out these days. Snorri, how about flights?"

"Nothing out of the ordinary, as far as air traffic control is aware. They've been asked to alert us as soon as there's anything other than routine commercial traffic."

Vilhjálmur coughed again. "Without putting pressure on you and your team, Gunnhildur, we will have to scale back soon if there are no results."

Normally Gunna would have wanted to argue from the sheer force of habit of wanting to hear the chief inspector's voice go up an octave, but she thought better of it.

"Probably right, Vilhjálmur. If he doesn't show up soon, we can be sure he's slipped past us. I'd like to keep this running to the middle of the week, if that's OK with you and the accountant? But in the meantime, I really want a word with Sigurjóna Huldudóttir again. I'm convinced she knows how and where to find Hårde."

"We'll look at costs on Monday," he said frostily. "Are you certain that Sigurjóna can tell you more?"

Gunna fumed inwardly at the man's trepidation. "I'm bloody positive. She's the kind of woman you'd know was lying even if she only said good morning. Look, if she's going to put in a formal complaint about harassment, we may as well make it worth her while. She's the only real link we have to Hårde, apart from her sister, who's sunning herself somewhere warm."

"If you absolutely have to," he snapped back, turning to make for the door. "But you don't have my approval. It's absolutely your responsibility," he added as a parting shot.

"Snorri, can you check on that yacht in Hvalvík harbour?" Gunna asked.

"Yup. Will do."

"First get on to Akranes and ask them to get themselves out to Grundartangi and check on . . ." She consulted the list of shipping movements on the wall. "*Starlight*. OK? And it wouldn't do any harm if customs could give it an extra going over. The same goes for the reefer docking in Grindavík tomorrow."

"What about the other shipping?" Bára asked.

"I'm not too worried about fishing vessels, especially the Russian ones, unless our man wants to spend three months on Flemish Cap."

"Shall I check out the one at Skarfanes, Gunna?" Snorri asked. "It looks interesting."

"Why?"

"It's just along the coast. There's only the fishmeal plant there and nothing else. Nobody ever goes there except the staff. It's pretty busy during the capelin season, but that was over months ago and it's probably quiet now."

"How do you know all this?"

"My dad worked there until he retired."

"Bára, I'd like you to come with me to grill Sigurjóna and we'll look in at Skarfanes on the way."

"Sure," Bára yawned.

"Snorri, my boy. Man the barricades, will you? Won't be long."

Sigurjóna was late. She normally made a point of keeping people waiting for a minute or two, as it reinforced the image she liked to project of being constantly busy. This time traffic had held her up and she was later than usual stepping from the lift and punching in the code to open the office door.

She could hear the hum of voices from her own office and frowned.

"Good morning, can I help you?" asked a girl she didn't recognize from behind the reception desk.

"I'd like to know who's in my office," Sigurjóna snarled back.

"You must be Sigurjóna?" the girl asked sweetly, not waiting for a reply. "Ingólfur Hrafn is here and he's waiting in your office for you."

Sigurjóna's anger deflated. She could hardly bawl out the man who had stepped in to keep her company afloat. "All right. Your name is?"

"Bergdís," the girl replied and Sigurjóna filed the name away for future reference before adjusting her winning smile. She swept into her own office to see Ingólfur Hrafn, Ósk Líndal and a skinny man she knew but couldn't place sitting there.

"Golli," she trilled as the bear-like man in a fashionable suit over a brilliant white T-shirt rose from her chair to meet her. "So sorry I was held up, you know what Friday traffic is like."

They went through the formality of exaggerated air kisses before the big man stepped back.

"Delighted you could make it," he said in a tone devoid of any delight. "I thought we'd better meet straight away to get things on track again, so I've asked Ósk and Reynir Óli to join us."

The thin man with a scrap of beard in the middle of his chin rose to his feet and extended a hand.

"Great to see you again. We met at the PR awards a few days ago," he said with a smile. "I'm looking forward to working alongside you."

"Alongside?" Sigurjóna mouthed soundlessly.

The big man grinned. "You know Reynir Óli? I've brought him across from *Dagurinn* and he'll be reporting to me on progress at Spearpoint," he said.

"But I thought —"

"You know what it's like when you take on a company, Sigurjóna. A new owner always wants to have his own eyes and ears about the place to get the feel of things. Don't worry about it, business as usual, darling. I'm staying in the background."

Sigurjóna caught the despair in Ósk's eyes as she looked about the room.

"Nice office," Reynir Óli said appreciatively, taking in the view. "I'm going to like it here and I'm sure we'll get on just fine."

Sigurjóna pulled herself together with an effort and her steely smile returned.

"I'm sure we will," she purred.

The figure in black overalls and black helmet walked along the quay in the loose-hipped manner of a man carrying a weapon to where a maelstrom of water was being kicked up by the *Juno Provider*'s propeller going half ahead with the rudder hard over. The ship's stern inched away from the quayside and suddenly the roaring of the engine died away.

The man in black walked further along the quay towards where the bow was still anchored to the land by a forespring and a bow rope. A tall deckhand in an orange survival suit and helmet stood looking over at the man in black and beyond him at the track leading down to the little factory from the main road.

The squad car bumped down the track and came to a halt yards from the top of the dock, as another black-suited figure in a helmet stepped in front of it with one hand held up.

"Who are you?" the figure asked gruffly.

"I could ask you the same," Gunna replied. "What's going on here?"

"Who are you? What's your authority?"

"Gunnhildur Gísladóttir, Hvalvík police. And who might you be?"

The man stepped back and moved quickly in front of the police car, muttering into a microphone built into his helmet. Gunna drummed her fingers on the wheel, gradually losing patience as she could see *Juno Provider*'s funnel dribbling smoke at the quayside below.

"I'm sorry. This is a security zone and I have no authority to let you through."

"Don't talk such rubbish. This is a fishmeal factory, not a terrorist cell, now get out of the way, will you?"

Bára's eyes widened as she saw the man swing one shoulder back and push a small machine pistol forward within reach.

"Gunna, he's got a gun. Who are these guys?"

"I don't know and I don't like this. This may well be the fast response team we're supposed to be able to call on, and if this fuckwit doesn't get out of the way, I'm going to run the bugger over."

She put her head out of the window. "Hey! Get out of the way, will you?"

The man made no move to step aside and Gunna put the second-best Volvo into gear to let it roll gently forward. The man put a hand on his weapon and reappeared at the car's window.

"This is a security area and you have no authority," he repeated in the same grim voice.

"Look, mate, some of us have work to do. Bára, ring Vilhjálmur, will you, and tell him to call these cowboys off."

"You don't have clearance," the man repeated, head lowered so close to the car's open window that Gunna caught a whiff of his bad breath. Suddenly he shot a hand inside and made a grab for the keys in the ignition. As he did so, Gunna took her foot off the clutch and the car shot forward.

Hårde stiffened. He was sweating under the plastic helmet in spite of the rain and the chill wind. He saw the squad car come hurtling along the quay. The bow rope had already been taken off and he was furiously hand-over-handing it through the fairlead into a coil on the deck. He glanced over his shoulder to see Terje at the bridge window look down at him impassively. The engine roared again and the spring rope tightened as the angle between the ship and the quay increased. The ship strained against the rope and the squad car rolled to a halt on the quayside. Hårde saw the fat policewoman and a smaller one emerge from the car and stride across the concrete apron of the dock just as the engine noise again died away. The spring rope suddenly fell slack as a second man in black appeared from the shadow of the building that ran the length of the quay.

"Don't let that rope go, you hear me?" Gunna yelled. The man casually raised the machine pistol slung over his shoulder and trained it on the *Juno Provider*'s bridge windows as two more men appeared. Gunna wondered where they were springing from.

The first man waved to the bridge, pointing to indicate that the ship should be brought back alongside, while the other two trained their weapons on the group standing around the mooring lines on its foredeck.

The ship's engines rumbled as the spring tightened again and the ship gently came back to its berth. A gangplank was swung ashore and scraped across the concrete before it came to rest.

On the foredeck, Hårde was trying to understand what had happened. The fat policewoman had obviously been closer on his tail than he had thought, although he had carefully not underestimated the woman's tenacity.

He looked across the narrowing gap at the trio on the quay and looked directly into the fat policewoman's furious eyes as she lifted one hand and pointed a finger at him like a gun. He saw her turn her attention to the black-clad man.

"What's going on here?" Gunna demanded.

"I don't have to say anything. You don't have authority to be on this site. Leave, now, or I'll have you escorted off."

Boiling with fury, Gunna drew herself up to her full height, and wagged a finger at the man. "I've a bloody good mind to have you charged with hindering a police officer in the course of duty. So don't you try lecturing me, sonny. D'you hear me? That man is a wanted criminal and it's my duty to arrest him."

She pointed at Hårde, standing motionless on the *Juno Provider*'s foredeck with the rest of the crew.

"Leave the site immediately," the man repeated.

"Special Unit, my arse. Bunch of tin soldiers wasting taxpayers' money and getting in the bloody way."

The man ignored her and shouted up to the ship. "All of you, come down the gangway one at a time, slowly."

The group from the foredeck trooped down nervously, with Hårde in the middle of the group and Terje bringing up the rear.

"Who are you?" the man demanded of each one. "Which of you is Hårde? And who is the captain?"

Terje stepped forward, and Gunna had to restrain herself from lunging at Hårde as he stepped out of the group. Even with a gun trained on him, the man radiated a quiet menace that made the hair stand up on the back of her neck. The Special Unit officer motioned for two of his men to escort Hårde while he spoke abruptly to Terje in rapid Norwegian.

As they spoke, a black van appeared from the far end of the fishmeal plant. Hårde took off his plastic helmet and smiled coldly at Gunna and Bára where they stood helplessly glaring at the men with machine pistols cradled nonchalantly in their hands.

Terje hurried back up the gangway to the ship, followed by the rest of the crew, not looking at where Hårde stood quietly between his escorts. The black van drew up and one of them opened the rear. The *Juno Provider*'s gangway was quickly swung aboard and the engines rumbled as the ship again strained at its spring rope.

Gunna watched helplessly while the ugly little ship gracefully swung around. The propeller began to bite as the ship moved forward and around out of the bay.

"Keep back," the Special Unit officer warned Gunna and Bára as they watched Hårde taking a seat in the van, still with two guns covering him. As the doors slammed shut, the officer slapped the side twice and it pulled away along the quay before he turned to face Gunna.

"Where the hell are you taking that bastard? Have you any idea who that man is or who he's done?" she raged.

"I'm following orders. I can't comment," the man replied in an expressionless voice.

"What orders?"

"No comment."

"Look here, that man is a known criminal and wanted in connection with three murders. On what authority have you detained him?" she demanded, wagging a finger under the man's nose. Bára held her breath, keenly aware that the man still had a gun in his hand.

"I can't tell you anything. I don't have to answer any questions."

The finger wagging under the man's nose became an open palm and Gunna suddenly gave the man's chest a shove that took him by surprise. He stepped back quickly, trying to keep his balance, but his heel caught the bollard on the quayside and he toppled backwards, spread his arms wide for a moment and was gone.

Gunna peered over the edge at the man treading water far below her.

"Can you swim, mate?" she called down to the man glaring balefully up at her, but he said nothing.

"There's a ladder up there," Gunna said, pointing along the quay to where a set of weed-covered iron rungs emerged from the water.

"Well, Bára, I think it might be best if we were off. Special Unit seems to have everything under control here."

The second-best Volvo juddered along the dock to the end where the first black-clad man was sitting on a pile of pallets, nursing the elbow of the arm that had been inside the car when Gunna put her foot down.

"All right, chum?" Gunna called, leaning out of the window and slowing down as she approached him. The man glowered back at her, but said nothing.

"You might want to go and give your pal a hand," she said, jerking a thumb behind her in the direction of the empty quayside. "He went for a swim."

CHAPTER THIRTY-SIX

Sunday, 5 October

05-10-2008, 1252

Skandalblogger writes:

Ladies and gentlemen, boys, girls and those of you who haven't made up your minds yet . . .

So, what has been happening behind the scenes at Glitnir? For just how long has the Icelandic financial sector been doing the big business equivalent of using its Mastercard to pay its Visa bills?

Children, Skandalblogger has been harping on about the shortcomings of our great leaders for long enough for us to be able to say . . . told you so! But we won't. Let's just say that now things start to look genuinely serious, Geir and his pals in Parliament had better do something right for a change.

Some people just don't get any luckier, do they? Just as Bjarni Jón Environment was about to be hung out to dry for getting caught in the act, Glitnir goes tits-up, the economy's suddenly on its knees and the PM decides government needs to show strength. So BJB's still in a job, his sins swept under the carpet until such time as the present brouhaha blows over, by which time it'll all be loooong forgotten. Still, at least the fragrant Sigurjóna's back in business, even though staff at Spearpoint are taking bets on how long she'll tough it out now she's not the boss any longer and her trademark tantrums are off the menu.

As it happens, word has reached your faithful Skandalblogger that BJB has already been putting it about, passing an old adversary a titbit of advice to oil the wheels of justice. There's nothing like making a real problem into someone else's problem to cheer up a chap who's just been handed a shit sandwich for lunch.

So keep up the good work!

CHAPTER THIRTY-SEVEN

Monday, 6 October

Gunna wondered how she could complete her report honestly and contemplated telling the unvarnished truth of how the men in the black van had spirited Hårde away.

She could still see the man's clear blue eyes gazing directly into hers a second before the doors of the van slammed shut. Gunna frowned and put the computer in front of her to sleep.

"Snorri!"

"Yes, chief?"

"I'm going out. Might be a while. Look after the place, will you?"

"Will do."

Outside the breeze off the sea brought the fresh tang of seaweed with it. It was going to be a windy night, maybe the first proper storm of winter, she decided, settling into the second-best Volvo.

She went home first and scoured Gísli's and Laufey's bedrooms for unwashed clothes before bundling the results into the washing machine. She scouted around the living room, picked up glasses and cups and washed them up, leaving them to drain, thinking hard all the while, wondering how long Gísli and Laufey would want to stay at home.

She took the second-best Volvo for a tour round the village, noticing a few badly parked cars here and there, a broken window at the back of the old fish plant and the station's other car where Haddi had parked outside Palli Jakobsson's workshop.

The InterAlu compound on the far side of the harbour area was closed up. She was astonished at how quickly everything had been wound up. On Saturday all the heavy machinery had been trucked away and on Sunday the shipping containers that housed the site offices and bunkrooms had been collected by the same fleet of trucks. It was already as if the site had been derelict for months. Gunna walked along the chain link fence facing the road and back at the gate she rattled the heavy lock. Although a sign warned that the site was patrolled by fierce dogs, she knew it was deserted, construction halted before it had got beyond concreting the huge foundations.

She contemplated driving out of the village through Sléttudalur to the deserted Lagoon site, but decided against it, and took the other direction instead.

By the "Thank you for driving carefully" sign, Gunna put her foot down as the heavy car enjoyed the upward slope out of the village towards the heath. Rolling into Keflavík, she went straight to the police station.

"Hi, Bjössi."

Bjössi was lounging in the doorway with a cigarette in one hand and a mug in the other. "Ah, Gunna. Congratulations."

"On what?"

"Your bank."

"What do you mean?"

"Don't you listen to the news? Glitnir's been bailed out and nationalized by the government. That makes Glitnir a state-owned bank, hence owned by the taxpayer, so that's you and me."

"When did this happen?" Gunna asked, mystified.

"On the news just now."

"Bloody hell. That'll put the cat among the pigeons."

They stood in silence for a while. Eventually Bjössi ground the stub of his cigarette under his heel and stretched. "Apart from that, Vilhjálmur's not here any more."

"What?"

"That's right. Officially, he's on sick leave."

"But the man's as fit as a flea," Gunna protested.

"I know. That's what's puzzling about it." Bjössi grinned.

"So who's in charge here now?

"Beats me. I suppose Halli Stefáns is the senior man now, or else the top man himself."

"The Sheriff?"

"Yup," Bjössi confirmed, gulping from his mug.

"Is he in?"

"Think so. Why? Got something to discuss, have you?"

"Mind your own business."

Upstairs, Gunna waited until the County Sheriff's secretary smiled and ushered her into his office. This time the Sheriff wore a suit instead of the faded jeans and polo shirt he had been in the last time they met.

"Ah, Gunnhildur. I was going to ask you to come and have a chat," he said with a broad smile.

"That's good, because I need a word with you as well."

His expression instantly became serious. "I can't tell you everything. I'm truly sorry about the incident when our man, er, eluded you."

"I'd have had the bastard if those toy soldiers hadn't got in the bloody way," she said with more anger in her voice than she had intended.

The Sheriff looked embarrassed. "As I said, I'm sorry. What I can tell you is that there was interference at the last moment from much higher up. Special Unit wasn't deployed on my authority. I can't say much more than that, except that the men you encountered were not a regular squad."

"Was this done to make sure Hårde got away? To save some big shots from a lot of embarrassment?"

The Sheriff nodded almost imperceptibly. "This was taken out of my hands, and then handed straight back."

"Was it that National Commissioner's dogsbody?"

"No. Certainly not. This came from . . ." He lifted a hand and pointed upwards.

"From God?" Gunna asked sharply.

The Sheriff laughed humourlessly. "No. But not far off. I don't know the full story either."

"Fair enough. I suppose it'll leak out eventually, around the time I come up for retirement."

"Ah, that's one of the things I wanted to talk to you about." The Sheriff smiled.

"Retirement? Yes, please."

"No, not quite. It's this posting to Egilstadir."

Gunna opened her mouth to speak.

"It's just that Ívar Laxdal was asking after you earlier," the Sheriff continued. "Of course I couldn't say anything, as you hadn't made a decision."

"Go on," Gunna said encouragingly.

"I think you'd better speak to him yourself."

The door opened as he knocked and Kolbeinn the juggler's face broke into a grin as he saw Skúli on the doorstep.

"Come in, there're a few of us here, so you'd better join in," he said happily.

In the flat's large living room, with its big picture window giving a magnificent view over the brooding mountain of Esja and Faxaflói Bay, a group of people lounged on chairs and sofas. Photographs from the march had been blown up and pasted across one wall and Skúli could see one of Kolbeinn in his juggler's outfit in the centre. Music played quietly in the background and a TV on the table had the 24/7 News channel running with the sound turned down. Everyone had a bottle or a glass in hand. Skúli recognized a few familiar faces around the room, including Lára sitting in a wicker chair in the corner, and wondered if the broad grin on her face was directed his way in particular.

"I'm sorry, have I interrupted a party?" Skúli mumbled apologetically.

"It would be a party if things didn't look so grim. It's just a little celebration now that the Hvalvík Lagoon project has been parked."

Skúli felt suddenly uncomfortable. "Look, Kolli, I don't have much time. Could we talk quietly for a minute? Is that OK?"

Kolbeinn still had the grin on his face. "Come in here," he said, stepping out into the hall, crowded with shoes and boots, and into the little kitchen. He lifted himself up and sat on the worktop while Skúli took the only chair and spread his notebook on the table.

"So, what's your take on all this?" Skúli asked.

"A victory for us."

"In what way?"

"In that InterAlu have pulled out and the Hvalvík smelter has been put on hold."

"Surely this was all due to the banking crisis and ESC being insolvent?"

Kolbeinn shrugged. "So? It's had the right result."

A knock at the front door echoed inside the kitchen and Kolbeinn looked up, waiting for someone from the living room to answer it. When nobody made a move, he slid down from the worktop.

"Just a moment. I'll be right back."

"Hi, great you could come," Skúli heard Kolbeinn greeting the person at the door, followed by footsteps in the hall as they made their way to the living room. He caught a glimpse of a sober business suit and sensible shoes as the woman passed the kitchen door with Kolbeinn behind her.

"Here she is!" Kolbeinn announced, and a cheer erupted from the group. Skúli wondered who it was and returned to his notebook.

"Sorry about that. They're making so much noise in there that they can't hear when someone knocks on the door," Kolbeinn apologized, hauling himself back to his seat on the worktop. "Where were we?"

"InterAlu, Spearpoint, ESC."

"Yeah. Well, the smelter was never really our main target. We've focused on the whole issue of these foreign aluminium plants that do nothing for the environment and precious little for the economy, except to keep it at boiling point. In real terms they offer less employment than, say, a shoe factory or something like that."

"All right, you've made the case against aluminium. What was it about this particular site?"

"You know as well as I do."

"But I need to hear it from you."

"Man, where do I begin? There's just so much to be up in arms against. There's the crooked Minister channelling lucrative contracts to his friends and his wife's company, setting up ESC and then making sure it gets a whole heap of public subsidy before being floated on the stock market. That was a great story, actually, and it was your colleague who broke that one."

"But what about the Hvalvík Lagoon power plant?"

"That was the big one. Setting up a privately run power generation plant and taking protected status away from part of a national park to do it was just too much to be ignored. You know, Skúli? There is something you could delve into."

"Which is?"

The smile fell from Kolbeinn's face. "Two of our closest collaborators were murdered in the last year and the perpetrator has never been caught."

"The Norwegian guy?"

"That's him. The policewoman from Hvalvík was right behind him but she was prevented from making an arrest. We have it on very good authority that a unit was deployed on orders direct from the Ministry, and actively prevented the police from arresting this man."

"You're sure?

Kolbeinn nodded again.

"Bjarni Jón? Higher up?"

"Lárus Jóhann."

"But why?"

"God. Can you imagine the uproar if it came to court? There's so much shit that would have come out that it couldn't happen. So he was quietly deported," Kolbeinn said.

"I see," Skúli replied dubiously, wondering if this might be close to the truth or a wild conspiracy story.

"You don't believe me, do you?" Kolbeinn asked, his eyes gleaming maliciously.

"Well . . ."

"I can tell you right now that a slimmed-down Spearpoint will be up and running again tomorrow as if nothing had ever happened."

"You're sure? How can you know?"

Kolbeinn tapped the side of his nose in a theatrical gesture. "Find out what your boss is doing today."

"You mean Rich Golli?" Skúli asked.

"Both of them."

"You reckon Golli's going to be bailing Sigurjóna out?"

"It's a done deal. Sigurjóna didn't have much room to manoeuvre. So she's not a happy lady right now, especially as her husband's also moved out."

"Really? Where to?"

"You need to keep up with the gossip, Skúli," Kolbeinn admonished. "Officially, they're living together, but separated. Unofficially, he's shacked up with a political science doctoral student who probably sees him as a fast-track ticket to somewhere or other."

Suddenly, Skúli felt that he ought to be on his way back to *Dagurinn*'s office, and he stood up, shutting his notebook.

"Check in with me tomorrow," Kolbeinn told him as he showed him to the door. "You'll see."

Walking away from Kolbeinn's flat, he stopped dead in his tracks and almost turned on his heel to go back, remembering that the last time he had seen the woman in the sober suit and sensible shoes she had been sitting at the Minister's side.

CHAPTER THIRTY-EIGHT

Tuesday, 7 October

Steam leaked from the kitchen at the back and hung in a cloud over the serving counter. The atmosphere in Hafnarkaffi was unusually lively and there was only one topic of conversation.

"Good Lord, you'd think these people would have the decency to resign," Stefán Jónsson held forth.

"No shame and no morals," someone else at the same table said.

"Same all over. Same as the bloody government," Stefán added.

"Morning, boys," Gunna offered, joining them at the table with a mug and a sandwich.

"Ah, Gunnhildur. What does the law make of all this?"

"What? The haddock quota? A disgrace, I reckon."

"No. Bloody Glitnir and the government bailing those bastards out with I don't know how many billions of our cash."

Gunna took a long pull at her coffee to wash down the first mouthful of prawn sandwich.

"Well, Stefán. Considering it's your money and mine, I'd be inclined to offer you my congratulations on the bank that you've just become part owner of."

"Well, there is that," Albert Jónasson at the next table turned round to add. "But which one's next? That's what I'd like to know. Landsbanki or Kaupthing?"

"Hi! Stína!" Stefán called out. "Put the wireless on for the news, would you?"

The newsreader's grave voice boomed out and as the first item began Gunna's phone buzzed.

"Haddi. This better be important, disturbing a girl over lunch."

She heard Haddi wheeze before he replied. "Going to be long? There's someone here to see you."

"Who is it?"

"Dunno. Some big shot. He's come from Reykjavík to see you. Though I can't understand why anyone'd come all that way just to see you."

"All right." Gunna sighed. In only a few days since the investigating team had rapidly been disbanded, life had seemed a little empty. "Tell him to come down to Hafnarkaffi if he's hungry, otherwise I'll be back in ten minutes," she decided.

"I'll tell him you'll be back in a minute. I don't reckon people like this go to places like Hafnarkaffi."

"Suit yourself," Gunna replied, reaching for her soup.

"If Haddi had said, I'd have been quicker," Gunna said when she found Ívar Laxdal sitting in the better chair in her office.

"Not a problem, Gunnhildur."

"What about Hårde? I'd love to know what went wrong."

The National Commissioner's deputy looked as awkward as Gunna could expect a man in such an exalted position to look.

"I can't comment. To be completely open with you, I don't know the full story myself, but," he said quickly, indicating that he had no intention of discussing the matter further, "I do need to know whether or not you want to apply for this post in the east. Let me know, will you?"

"I've decided not to apply for it. Family reasons. I'm a single parent and I really don't want to uproot my daughter before she's finished school. Didn't the Sheriff tell you?"

His face brightened. "Well, yes, he did. But I wanted to hear it from you. Interesting."

Gunna was immediately puzzled that he should be pleased. "Why's that?"

"Well, of course in the light of what's happened in the last few days and the uncertain economic future, we have to be prepared for different eventualities . . ."

"You mean Glitnir going bust, all the rumours about Landsbanki going the same way and the whole country going to the dogs?"

"Precisely. However, the National Commissioner and the Minister had already decided that we need to follow the precedent of forces in other countries and set up a dedicated serious crime unit, headquartered in Reykjavík."

"That's nice."

"We decided that if you were to turn down the Egilstadir posting, then you should be invited to apply to join the serious crime unit. You'd stay a sergeant initially, but there'd be a travel allowance and I expect you'd probably be an inspector inside a year."

For a moment Gunna could think of nothing to say. "Why? I mean, why me? Surely the mess that this Hårde case turned out to be isn't much of a recommendation?"

A thin smile ran round Ívar Laxdal's face. "On the contrary. Between ourselves, you resisted interference that came all the way from ministerial level, ran a small team extremely well and simply stuck with it all the way. A fine job, although I couldn't possibly say that officially. You have my number. Let me know in the next few days, would you?" He smiled again, shrugging his way into his overcoat and tucking a briefcase under one arm.

"What did our stuffed shirt want?" Haddi asked, scratching thoughtfully at the side of his nose as Gunna swept past. "Not leaving us, are you?"

At the back of the building, Gunna lit a Camel and tried to take in Ívar Laxdal's offer. She pulled her phone from her jacket pocket, scrolled through the numbers and pressed the green button.

"Steini, hi, it's me. Yup, fine. Just thought you'd like to know I'll be staying after all."

Other titles published by Ulverscroft:

THE WOMAN IN BLUE

Elly Griffiths

Ruth Galloway's friend Cathbad is house-sitting in the Norfolk village of Walsingham, famous as a centre for pilgrimages to the Virgin Mary, when he sees a strange vision of a young woman dressed in blue he thinks may be the Madonna herself. The next morning the woman's body, dressed in a white nightdress and blue dressing gown, is found in a ditch. DCI Nelson and his team are called in and establish that the dead woman was a recovering addict being treated at a nearby hospital. Then Ruth is contacted by an old friend, now a priest, who reveals that she has been receiving vitriolic anonymous letters containing a phrase about a woman "clad in blue, weeping for the world". And when another woman is murdered, Ruth realises she is tangled up in a grisly mystery . . .

THE HOG'S BACK MYSTERY

Freeman Wills Crofts

Dr. James Earle and his wife live in comfortable seclusion near the Hog's Back, a ridge in the North Downs in the beautiful Surrey countryside. When Dr. Earle disappears from his cottage, Inspector French is called in to investigate. At first he suspects a simple domestic intrigue — and begins to uncover a web of romantic entanglements beneath the couple's peaceful rural life. The case soon takes a more complex turn when other people vanish mysteriously, one of Dr. Earle's house guests among them. What is the explanation for the disappearances? If the missing people have been murdered, what can be the motive? This fiendishly complicated puzzle is one that only Inspector French can solve.